W9-AUT-010

"Fire," Sulu told Kostas, and together they loosed the might of their energy weapons.

The creature reeled under the combined firepower and issued a feral cry—whether of pain or confusion, of fear or anger, Sulu couldn't tell.

But then the creature pivoted swiftly and fixed Sulu and Kostas with the gaze of its massive oval eyes. It reared up, its front four legs lifting high into the air, and it roared, the sound from its snout guttural and primitive. On the ground beside the creature, Ensign Young didn't move.

Sulu held up her phaser for Kostas to see, then adjusted it to its highest stun setting. The ensign followed her lead and reset her own weapon. When the creature brought its front legs back down and charged at them, they fired in tandem.

The beams both landed, but the creature dodged to one side. The phaser blasts slowed it, but still it moved with surprising speed for a beast its size and that looked so ungainly. Its long multi-jointed legs ate up the distance to the shuttlecraft in large tracts. The captain judged that she and Kostas had one chance to save themselves.

"Next level," she yelled as she increased the force of her phaser, setting it to kill. She didn't wait to see if Kostas had heard her over the creature's roar, but once more raised her weapon and fired. An instant later, the ensign's beam joined hers.

The creature screamed. It stumbled, one of its legs missing a step and dragging along the ground. Its legs tangled, and it went down hard, its head smashing into the ground face-first, its mammoth body skidding along the earth.

STAR TREK®

THE LOST ERA
ONE CONSTANT STAR

DAVID R. GEORGE III

Based upon *Star Trek*
created by Gene Roddenberry

POCKET BOOKS

New York • London • Toronto • Sydney • New Delhi • Rejarris II

Pocket Books
A Division of Simon & Schuster, Inc.
1230 Avenue of the Americas
New York, NY 10020

This book is a work of fiction. Any references to historical events, real people, or real places are used fictitiously. Other names, characters, places, and events are products of the author's imagination, and any resemblance to actual events or places or persons, living or dead, is entirely coincidental.

First Pocket Books paperback edition June 2014

POCKET and colophon are registered trademarks of Simon & Schuster, Inc.

For information about special discounts for bulk purchases, please contact Simon & Schuster Special Sales at 1-866-506-1949 or business@simonandschuster.com.

The Simon & Schuster Speakers Bureau can bring authors to your live event. For more information or to book an event, contact the Simon & Schuster Speakers Bureau at 1-866-248-3049 or visit our website at www.simonspeakers.com.

Designed by Meryll Rae Preposi
Cover art by Doug Drexler
Cover design by Alan Dingman

Manufactured in the United States of America

10 9 8 7 6 5 4 3 2 1

ISBN 978-1-4767-5021-7
ISBN 978-1-4767-5022-4 (ebook)

To Dana Joseph Robitaille,
the original Dude,
a kind and generous friend
with a raucous sense of humor,
a man of high ideals and bright mind,
a kindred spirit with whom I have shared
many an adventure,
and a true brother to me

But Odysseus, far away hath lost his homeward path to the [. . .] land, and himself is lost.

—Homer
The Odyssey, Book XXIII

2303

Odyssey

Prologue

All at once, a terrible sense of loss overwhelmed her.

Lieutenant Commander Demora Sulu pushed back from the main console of the warp shuttle and turned away from the dizzying tableaux of stars dancing beyond the sloping forward viewport. She dropped her elbows onto her knees and her face into her hands. Nausea roiled her stomach. Though suddenly damp from perspiration, her skin felt cold beneath her touch.

As she huddled in the pilot's chair, the image of her mother rose in her mind, despite that Susan Ling had perished more than twenty-five years earlier. *She's been gone for more than three-quarters of my life,* Sulu realized, *and yet I still think about her so often.* She recalled with great clarity her mother's slender but taut figure, the jet hair that fell in a lustrous spill all the way down to her waist, her delicate features and electric-green eyes. Sulu frequently visualized her in a parade of the stylish, futuristic clothing that Susan Ling once favored.

But she did not imagine her like that as she sat doubled over and alone in the cockpit of the unnamed, unmarked shuttle. At that moment, Sulu remembered the visage of her mother wracked by Sakuro's disease. After her symptoms had manifested, she'd bolted with her daughter from Marris III, but too late. By the time they reached Starbase 189 and its superior medical facilities, Susan Ling had lost so much weight that her body seemed little more than a flesh-covered skeleton. Her musculature had begun to disintegrate and her organs to fail. Fever held her in its grip, sweat matting her tangled ebon tresses. When she coughed, her face—drawn but still beautiful—contorted into a rictus of pain.

Even though Sulu had lived only the first six years of her life with her mother, and though Susan Ling had passed away more than two and a half decades earlier, she still felt her absence. To the child she'd been, the death of the only parent she'd ever known to that point had been devastating. Her mother had not only raised her by herself, but she had never introduced or even mentioned any other family members. When Susan Ling died, she took the young Demora's entire world with her.

And that's what I feel like now, Sulu thought. *Like everything I know in the universe—everyone—has been ripped away from me.* She thought of her father, Hikaru, unknown to her—and she to him—until Susan Ling had, in the provisions of her will, left her to his custody. Demora had resented her mother's erstwhile lover at first, had perhaps even hated him—or at least the idea of him—but over the years, she'd come to accept him as her father, to love and respect him, and to be glad that he'd come into her life.

And now he's lost to me, she thought. *I'll never see him again.* Not him, not her grandmother—whom she had never even gotten to know—and not any of her more than seven hundred crewmates aboard *Enterprise,* many of them friends, some of them very close ones. Not Vanetta Angelis, the engineer she'd been seeing for several months, a woman for whom Sulu's feelings had already begun to deepen. Not Aravesh ch'Vrane, a man who served as one of the ship's xenobiologists, and whom she and Vanetta had recently begun dating. Not even Admiral Sinclair-Alexander, the Starfleet flag officer for *Enterprise*'s operational sector, nor Admiral Aziz, the Intelligence director who'd sent her and Captain Harriman on their current mission.

John, Sulu thought, and she lifted her head from her hands to glance at the doors separating the cockpit of the shuttle from its rear compartment. Back there, she knew, the *Enterprise* captain slept—or he attempted to, anyway. As one day had bled into the next over the previous few weeks, getting rest had become more and more problematic for both of them. Paradoxically, the less they'd been able to do, the more exhausted they'd grown, at least on an emotional level, and yet fatigue had not translated into slumber.

As bad as I feel, John feels even worse. Harriman did not appear to blame himself for the awful predicament in which they found themselves, but he wore the mantle of command heavily. Sulu expected that most, if not all, starship captains did, but she still respected his seriousness of purpose.

Wherever we end up, at least I'll have one friend. She had known the captain for ten years, ever since she'd graduated Starfleet Academy and drawn an assignment as a helm officer aboard the newly launched *Enterprise*-B. The two had enjoyed a cordial working relationship from the beginning, and Sulu had steadily climbed the ship's chain of command. Just eighteen months earlier, Harriman had championed her promotion to the rank of lieutenant commander and her appointment as his executive officer. In that year and a half, the close proximity in which they had to work, along with the level of trust required between any two people in their respective positions, cemented and deepened their already solid bond.

Sulu sat up in her chair, then rose to her feet. Though she had devised nothing more to do, nothing more to try, than she and Harriman already had over the previous twenty-two days, she felt driven to action. She moved to the port bulkhead—just three strides across the breadth of the cabin—and examined the engine readouts. The warp nacelles of the highly modified civilian shuttlecraft remained effectively offline, while the impulse drive idled on operational standby. Thrusters kept the vessel locked in its current position.

Sulu barked out a humorless laugh. *As if our "current position" has any real meaning,* she scoffed to herself. *I never thought I'd yearn to float along the edge of the Neutral Zone—or even to see a couple of Romulan birds-of-prey bearing down on us. If we ever—*

The sound inside the cabin shifted. Sulu distinguished a slight increase in the volume of the thrusters, and felt the familiar but almost imperceptible clutch of the inertial dampers as the shuttle moved. An instant later, the hum of the impulse engines grew to suffuse the compartment, the sublight drive automatically engaged by a navigational routine she'd programmed. Sulu peered through the forward viewport and saw a sight she welcomed: a steady, recognizable pattern of stars, a grouping of seven suns that looked to her like a backward question mark. A surge of profound relief coursed through her.

As Sulu stared at one of the brightest stars in that region of space—Adelphous, she recalled—she heard the doors leading to the rear section of the shuttle whisper open behind her. She wanted to turn toward Captain Harriman, to share with him the development for which they'd been hoping, but she couldn't pull her gaze from the port. As ridiculous as she knew it to be, she had the sense that if she looked away, the array of familiar stars she saw might abruptly vanish.

Harriman walked up beside her. "We're moving," he said. Though the captain spoke quietly, Sulu could hear the flutter of excitement lurking within his words.

"We're back," she said, still focused on Adelphous and the inverted question-mark configuration of stars around it. "We're *home*." Her voice broke on the last word, and her vision swam. Tears pooled in her eyes, a result of the emotion that moments before had fought its way out of her after she'd suppressed it for more than three weeks. The prospect of she and Harriman returning to the Federation transmuted her sorrow into joy, though, her feeling of loss becoming one of salvation.

Not wanting the captain to see her display of feeling, Sulu stepped back across the cockpit and sat down at the pilot's console. Harriman followed, taking a seat beside her. "Verify our location and course," he ordered.

"Checking," Sulu replied. She blinked and a tear slid down her cheek. She quickly swept it away with the back of one hand, then sent her fingers darting over the controls. She read the data aloud as they marched across her monitor. "We're approximately half a billion kilometers from the system's termination shock . . . traveling at full impulse velocity . . . on a vector directly away from Odyssey." The previously unvisited star appeared in the stellar cartography database designated only by a catalogue label, but about a week into their ordeal, they had named it after the ancient epic poem by Homer. Although it fell within the Hertzsprung gap on standard luminosity/spectral-type charts—absolute magnitude +1, class F7—it did not differentiate itself as unusual; the planetless, high-mass star had simply reached the stage in its life cycle when it transitioned from fusing hydrogen in its core to fusing helium.

No, it's not unusual at all, Sulu thought cynically. *Not unless you count what it did to us.* Except that they didn't know with certainty that Odyssey had caused their plight. Circumstances suggested that it somehow had, but the readings of the yellow-white sun that they'd collected and studied had revealed nothing out of the ordinary, let alone any sort of mechanism for what they'd experienced. Eventually, in their attempt to escape and return home, they'd had little choice but to retreat to the outer regions of the star's heliosphere, which necessarily limited the efficacy of the sensors.

"I'm detecting no ships anywhere nearby," Harriman said as he worked beside Sulu. She understood that, although he had no doubt scanned for any vessels, he would have specifically searched for those of the Romulan Imperial Fleet. When she and the captain had first taken their shuttle into the Odyssey system, it had been in an attempt to elude a patrol ship that had pursued them out of the Empire.

But that was twenty-two days ago, Sulu thought. Because of that, it didn't surprise her that they no longer had company in that unexplored region, away from both Romulan territory and the Federation, and far from any established space lanes.

"I'm powering up the nacelles," Harriman continued. Technically, they'd left the warp engines in a state of stasis, significantly reducing the possibility of the shuttle's detection on the long-range sensors of the Romulans—or anybody else—but allowing Sulu and the captain to reinitiate faster-than-light travel without needing an extended startup process. "Sixty seconds to warp capability."

"Course for Foxtrot Three laid in," Sulu said. One of a baker's dozen of subterranean, asteroid-based outposts, the Foxtrot complexes threaded along the Federation side of the Neutral Zone, their crews maintaining a steadfast vigil on the border movements of the Imperial Fleet. The Starfleet base had not been Sulu and Harriman's intended destination once they'd completed their reconnaissance in Romulan space. As their situation had persisted, though, the captain had decided that, should they manage to extricate themselves from their dilemma, they would head not for Starbase 23, but for the Federation facility closest to their location.

Sulu finished reviewing their route on the navigation panel, then risked a glance through the forward viewport. She feared that she would see an arrangement of stars unknown to her—or worse, *numerous* arrangements blinking into and out of existence in rapid succession. Instead, she saw Adelphous tucked in the run of stars that resembled a backward question mark.

"The nacelles have been released from stasis and are fully active," Harriman announced.

Sulu operated the helm controls. "Going to warp." She watched the effect through the port as the shuttle streaked into the starfield. "Warp one," she said after a few seconds, and shortly after that, "Warp two." Although their specially augmented shuttlecraft could achieve a cruising speed of warp three, and in exigent circumstances, could manage a burst at warp four, they sought to avoid drawing attention to themselves. Despite what the sensors promised, the Romulans could be hiding behind their cloaking devices anywhere in the vicinity, and a bird-of-prey could easily overtake the civilian equivalent of a Starfleet *Gagarin*-class warp shuttle, no matter how extensive the modifications.

Sulu looked over at the captain. He wore the same civilian clothing—dark slacks and a long-sleeved navy-blue shirt—he'd had on earlier, which told her that he hadn't even attempted to sleep. Like him, she'd dressed in something other than a Starfleet uniform: black pants and a ruby-colored blouse. They carried nothing in the shuttlecraft that would identify them as Federation officers in the event of their capture. Their masquerade as simple traders would give way, if necessary, to a deeper cover as independent intelligence merchants. The captain had planned the details of their covert mission into Romulan space meticulously.

In the previous five years, Harriman had from time to time left the *Enterprise* for extended periods—usually a few weeks at a clip—under the guise of taking some of his accumulated leave. Perhaps that had occasionally been the case; certainly he'd never returned to the ship without colorful tales of his holiday. But after witnessing the concentration and precision he demonstrated during their current mission, Sulu concluded that Starfleet Intelligence had utilized him on other occasions—although she hadn't asked him any questions on the subject, and he hadn't offered any confirmations.

Exhaustion settled around Sulu like a warm blanket. She closed her eyes, inhaled deeply, then let her breath out slowly. Finally believing that she and the captain had successfully fled the adverse influence of Odyssey, she felt some of the tension in her body ease. "We really *are* home," she said, as though uttering the words aloud again would concretize their validity.

"We really are," Harriman agreed. "But *when* are we?"

The question jolted Sulu. So fixed on their location, she had forgotten about the temporal aspect of what they'd endured. She immediately reached for the controls of the shuttlecraft's internal chronometer, then executed a measurement of sidereal time. The two readings didn't match. She informed the captain as she subtracted one stardate from the other. "We're one hundred seventy-three hours in the future."

"Not the *future*," Harriman said. "Our new *present*."

Sulu nodded her understanding: they'd arrived home close enough to their own time that they needn't risk revisiting Odyssey. "So for us, it's been three weeks since we left Romulan space, but for the rest of the galaxy, four weeks have passed," she said. "Adding in the time we spent in the Empire, that means Starfleet Intelligence thinks we've been gone eight weeks." Their mission to observe and record field tests of the Romulans' latest upgrades to their cloaking technology had been slated for twenty-seven days, including travel time. Instead, nearly two months had passed since they'd disembarked *Enterprise* at Starbase 23. "They probably think we've been either captured or killed," she said. "And who knows what the crew think."

"By now, Captain Rendón will have apprised them of our independent choices to extend our separate leaves," Harriman said. During a major refit of his own vessel, the *Excelsior*-class *Concordia*, Demián Rendón had been temporarily reassigned to command *Enterprise* in Harriman and Sulu's absence. "Or maybe one of us has taken ill, nothing serious, but something contagious and requiring quarantine. Maybe the other of us has been called upon to deal with a family emergency. Whatever their chosen explanations, Starfleet Intelligence will have worked it out."

"But what does S.I. think?" Sulu asked.

"Not that we've been captured, not without proof," Harriman said with confidence. Once more, Sulu perceived that he'd been through similar situations before. "Even if the Romulans suspected Starfleet of espionage, and even if they manufactured evidence to support such a claim, Intelligence would see through it." Sulu remembered the coded phrases and gestures she'd been taught prior to the mission, subtle ways of verifying her identity and disclosing her circumstances in the event she'd been taken prisoner and her likeness transmitted to the Federation. She also knew that Starfleet Intelligence supported a number of undercover operatives, double agents, and informants within the imperial apparat, some of whom occupied positions in which they would be able to substantiate or refute any allegations of Sulu and Harriman's detention. "In the absence of the confirmation of our capture, S.I. likely considers us delayed and possibly missing. It's too early for them to conclude that we've been killed, and far too soon for them to publicly announce . . ." Something appeared to occur to Harriman. He glanced away for a moment, as though in thought.

"Captain?"

He looked back at Sulu. "It's too soon for them to publicly announce our deaths."

The idea of being declared dead troubled Sulu. Not for the first time, she considered the impact of such information, whether erroneous or not, on the people in her life—not least of all her father. Although a Starfleet officer himself and therefore cognizant of the dangers of life aboard a starship, he would still take the news of his daughter's death hard, despite whatever story Intelligence concocted to explain it.

"It's all right, Demora," the captain said, obviously reading the emotions on her face. "Nobody thinks we're dead, and more important, we're *not* dead."

Sulu nodded at the assertion, understanding the power of its simple truth. "You're right, of course." She peered out through the viewport again, saw the reverse question mark formed by seven stars, then leaned back in her chair. "It'll feel good to be back aboard the *Enterprise*," she said, "even if we do have to head to Foxtrot Three first and find our way back to the ship from there."

"I suspect that S.I. will order a vessel to take us from there to Starbase Twenty-Three. They'll want Commander Sasine to debrief us."

At Harriman's mention of Amina Sasine, Sulu actually smiled. After their weeks-long experience at Odyssey, the expression felt foreign on her face. It also felt good. "If they don't send us to Starbase

Twenty-Three, you can always request that they do."

Harriman's brow pinched together. "What does that mean?" he asked. "And what is that smile for?"

"Really?" Sulu replied. "You want me to talk about Commander Sasine?"

"She's the first officer of a crew stationed near the edge of the Neutral Zone and is an expert on Romulan troop deployment," Harriman protested, as if identifying the professional reasons for him meeting with Sasine would mask the personal ones.

"Uh-huh," Sulu said. "And I've never seen you interact with anybody the way you did on Starbase Twenty-Three with Commander Sasine."

Harriman opened his mouth as if to deny her observation, but then he closed it without saying a word. He raised his arms and let them drop onto his thighs in a sign of surrender. "I guess that means I'm not quite as urbane as I'd hoped."

"Well, it's not as though you acted like a schoolboy," Sulu said. "But I've known you a long time, John, and I could tell there was something there." She hadn't though about the captain's behavior around Sasine since prior to their mission, when they'd met her so that she could brief them on recent Romulan activity along the Neutral Zone. Standing a couple of centimeters taller than Harriman, the commander moved with a wispy grace that Sulu had first noticed when Sasine had served a few years previously as *Enterprise*'s second officer. Her tour of duty aboard the ship lasted only ten months before she accepted the position of exec aboard the *Miranda*-class *New York*. From that posting, Starfleet promoted her to commander and transferred her to the role of first officer aboard Starbase 23. "What I find peculiar is that I don't remember any sparks between the two of you when Amina served on the *Enterprise*."

Harriman chuckled. "Good," he said. "At least I know I can be discreet."

Sulu's eyebrows rose. "Really?" she said, surprised. "You two were involved back then?"

"No," the captain said at once. "No, no, no. I was her commanding officer, and given our respective positions, a romance would have been inappropriate." Sulu wondered how Harriman judged her own budding relationship with Vanetta Angelis, not to mention Aravesh ch'Vrane, but neither Vanetta nor Vesh reported directly to her, with significant steps between them in the ship's command hierarchy. "I just meant that I'm glad to hear I was able to conceal my attraction to Commander Sasine when she was posted to the *Enterprise*."

"Well . . . mission accomplished," Sulu said. After all they'd been through at Odyssey, after the continuous drag on her emotions, it seemed incongruous to suddenly be discussing the captain's love life. Sulu embraced the change. "Did you get to spend any time with Amina after the briefing?"

"I did," Harriman said, and it delighted Sulu to see a flush climb up his cheeks. "She stopped by my cabin on the station the night before our departure. She wanted to review the specifications of the upgraded shuttle." Harriman waved his hand to one side, a motion clearly meant to indicate the vessel in which they presently traveled.

"But she knew that the engineer from S.I. had already taken us to the shuttle and shown us its capabilities," Sulu said. "That sounds to me like a pretty thin excuse to see you."

"I thought so too," Harriman said. "So when we were finished going over the specs, I invited her to stay for a glass of wine."

"How urbane," Sulu teased. "I'm taking that it went well?"

"Well enough that we talked about getting to know each other better after the mission," Harriman said. He looked away for a moment, clearly self-conscious.

"You didn't get to know Amina when she was on the *Enterprise*?"

"Not well," the captain said. "I mean, only on a professional level. But I'm hoping to change that now." He paused, and then the right side of his lips curled up in an expression that Sulu found boyish. "I like her a lot," he said quietly, as though confessing a secret.

Sulu leaned forward and touched a hand to Harriman's knee. "That's wonderful, John," she said. "I hope—" A two-toned chirp from the control panel interrupted her. She examined the data that appeared on one of her displays. "Sensors are detecting a rogue planet ahead, seventy-one light-seconds from our path," she reported.

Working at his own station, Harriman operated a series of controls. "I'm still reading no indication of ships in the vicinity," he said. "There could be one or more vessels hiding on the far side of the planet, though, so I'll maintain a sensor lock." The captain didn't mention the possibility of cloaked ships, but Sulu supposed that he didn't need to, since they could do nothing about them. Through the years, Starfleet had developed and installed on many of its starships equipment capable of detecting vessels veiled by the Romulan's stealth technology—equipment with technical requirements that made it impossible to install on a shuttlecraft. None of the Federation's cloak-penetrating matériel worked with one hundred percent effectiveness anyway, not least of all because the Empire continually worked to improve their most significant military advantage—and sometimes to redesign it entirely.

That had been the justification for Sulu and Harriman's covert mission. Intel collected within Romulan space revealed that the latest upgrades to their cloak involved not just incremental enhancements, but a top-to-bottom reinvention. Starfleet Command feared the possibility of Imperial Fleet ships gaining the ability to move undetectably within the Federation. S.I. had therefore tasked Sulu and Harriman with observing field tests of the latest cloak, collecting readings that would aid Starfleet scientists and engineers in penetrating the new technology. They had also been ordered to survey the Empire's military strength and positioning along the Romulan side of the Neutral Zone. Since they had finally escaped the hold of Odyssey and would be able to deliver the data they'd accumulated to Starfleet Intelligence, they could consider their mission a success. They had gathered not just those details they'd been charged with finding, but other information about the Romulans as well. One of those facts suddenly juxtaposed itself in Sulu's head with what had taken place afterward.

"Captain," she asked, "do you think what happened to us at Odyssey could have been caused by an isolytic subspace weapon?" During the course of their mission, they had recorded unusual sensor readings near the Romulan star system of Algeron. Analyzing that data, Sulu concluded that a metaweapon had ripped through that region of space, perhaps as recently as sometime in the prior century.

"I don't know," Harriman said. "What we saw around Algeron was not all that close to Odyssey."

"No," Sulu said, "but when it comes to subspace weapons, 'local effects' can range far in normal space."

"True," the captain said. "And since we're talking about devices that tear through the fabric of subspace, I suppose it's conceivable that such a rent could have been captured in Odyssey's gravitational field, maybe even stabilized."

"Maybe not just stabilized," Sulu proposed, "but expanded."

Harriman nodded slowly. "I'll include all of this in my report," he said. "It's possible Starfleet Command might want to investigate, but I think it more likely that they'll simply designate the area a hazard to navigation and bar Federation vessels from traversing the region."

Sulu considered the idea of a strong gravitational field nabbing a subspace fissure and tried to work out the mathematics in her head. The problem quickly grew too complex, but even if it hadn't, there remained too many unknowns for her to have reached a reasoned solution. "We know so little about the effects of isolytic subspace weapons," she said, "since Starfleet's never even tested them."

Captain Harriman casually returned his attention to his control panel. His nonchalance hinted to Sulu that perhaps she'd made a false assumption, that just because she didn't know an event had taken place didn't mean that it hadn't happened. It troubled her to think that Starfleet had at some point tested a metaweapon of any kind, but she took solace in the sure knowledge that the Federation had eschewed their use on the field of battle.

"We don't know exactly what happened in the Algeron system," Harriman said. "We don't know if the Romulans detonated an isolytic subspace weapon themselves as part of a test, or whether they were attacked with such a weapon, or even if such a weapon was used at all. Our sensor scans suggest that might've happened, but our readings could've resulted from some sort of failed scientific experiment, or from an industrial accident, or maybe even some naturally occurring phenomenon. We just don't know. Frankly, I'm far more concerned about the weapons and military technology that we know the Romulans do use."

Sulu sighed. "I hope the Empire comes back to the negotiating table." Two years earlier, the Federation had invited the Romulans to participate in a summit aimed at entente. Months of long-distance diplomacy ultimately led to a series of meetings scheduled on the neutral world of Drixane IV. After just a few sessions, though, the Romulans had withdrawn from the talks. "I know that the Federation is seeking a durable peace. What I don't understand is why the Empire isn't."

"They trust us even less than we trust them," Harriman said. "And after all, here we are, spying on them."

"For good reasons," Sulu said.

"I'm sure the Romulans justify whatever operatives they send into the Federation in the same way." The captain shook his head. "I know that we need to stay current on the Empire's cloaking technology and their ship deployment along the Neutral Zone, but it all just seems like escalation."

"You're concerned that tensions could erupt into military incidents," Sulu said.

"I'm concerned that we're on a path to war," Harriman said, his expression sober. "There are so few Romulan leaders these days speaking out about the importance of maintaining interstellar peace, and too many drawing an image of the Federation as the great enemy of the Empire. And on our side, there are too many councilors spouting the same sort of thing about the Romulans."

"You sound like you believe war is inevitable," Sulu noted.

"I desperately want peace, but if a genuine rapprochement with the Romulans ever comes, it will be hard won," the captain said. "Thank goodness for the Klingons."

"The Klingons?" Sulu asked, surprised by the statement.

"Yes, thanks to the Khitomer Accords," Harriman said, referring to the historic peace treaty between the UFP and the Klingon Empire ratified a decade earlier. "As long as the Romulans believe that the Klingons might enter any battle on the side of the Federation, they'll be slow to risk war. If that should change . . ." He did not need to finish his sentence to convey his meaning.

"You make it sound liked the Romulans are poised to strike, given the opportunity."

Harriman nodded again. "You and I wouldn't be here if that weren't the case." He hesitated, then added, "Lately, I've been thinking that if we truly want to establish peace with the Romulans, we may have to maneuver them into it."

"'Maneuver' them?" Sulu asked. "How would that work?"

"I'm not sure," Harriman said. "But I think there might just be too many bellicose leaders at the top of the Romulan government right now for negotiation and reason to win the day." His control panel emitted a tone, and he checked one of its displays. "We've passed the rogue planet," he said. "There's still no sign of any vessels in the area."

The news pleased Sulu, as did the fact that they encountered no other ships for the remainder of their journey. When they entered Federation space a day and a half later, they sent a coded burst to Foxtrot III for retransmission to Starfleet Command. Twelve hours after that, they arrived at the outpost, and not long after, *U.S.S. Oglala* carried them to Starbase 23, where, in separate sessions, a Starfleet Intelligence officer and then Commander Sasine debriefed them.

Sulu felt proud in having successfully undertaken her first mission for S.I., believing that the information she and the captain had gathered about the Romulans would contribute to the overall security of the Federation. Their experiences at the star they called Odyssey stayed with her, though, the sense of loss engendered in her during the incident difficult to cast off. She began sending messages to her father on a regular basis, and she made a point to spend as much time as she could with her friends aboard *Enterprise*—especially Vanetta and Vesh—hoping that the increased interaction with her loved ones would fill the emptiness she felt. She wanted nothing more than to put Odyssey and its effects completely behind her, to wall off those few weeks of her life and place them squarely and permanently in her past.

Ultimately, she would not be able to do so.

2319

Enterprise

1

1

As *Enterprise* approached the shrouded world, Captain Demora Sulu leaned forward in the command chair and studied the image on the main viewscreen. The second of seven planets in the unexplored Rejarris system, the dun-colored orb looked lifeless and uninviting, despite that it floated along the inner edge of the star's circumstellar habitable zone. Clouds ensphered the globe, completely obscuring its surface. To Sulu, it resembled the second planet in Earth's own solar system, Venus, and as with that desolate world, the captain expected sensors to describe an arid wasteland, with an atmosphere composed mostly of carbon dioxide, and ground-level temperatures in excess of four hundred degrees Celsius.

"We've achieved standard orbit," reported Ensign Torsten Syndergaard from his position at the helm.

"Initiate planetary scans," ordered the ship's

first officer, Xintal Linojj, who stood to the captain's right. The Boslic woman maintained a workstation on the starboard curve of the circular bridge, but during the course of active operations, she often vacated her panel and took up a position beside the command chair. "Take a set of basic readings," she went on. "Identify anything out of the ordinary that might warrant further study." Sulu and her crew concentrated their survey of previously unvisited solar systems on those that would supply something new to the Federation's body of knowledge. Such contributions typically came when they encountered alien life or discovered something scientifically unusual, but when they found nothing more than common stars and empty planets, they simply collated fundamental data about the astronomical objects and moved on in their journey.

"Aye, sir, scanning," replied Lieutenant Commander Borona Fenn. Sulu glanced to her left, over to where the Frunalian woman crewed the primary sciences station. As Fenn worked her controls, her *eltis*—the flesh-covered sensory appendage that extended upward from her brow, across her hairless head, and down her spine—rippled slowly, like the forward edge of a wheat field beneath the soft breath of an autumnal breeze.

"Continue monitoring for interstellar transmissions and executing long-range scans," Linojj said. She looked aft, past the command chair, toward the freestanding console on the raised, outer ring of the bridge, and Sulu followed her gaze. On one side of the console, Ensign Hawkins Young manned the communications station, while on the other, Commander Tenger kept watch at tactical. "We need to know if anyone enters the neighborhood."

Although Linojj did not specify the Tzenkethi Coalition by name, she didn't need to: on their open-ended exploratory mission, the *Enterprise* crew had taken their ship into an unclaimed, unaligned region of space that, although distant, measured closer to the borders of the Coalition than to those of the Federation or any other known warp-capable power. Aware of the notorious territoriality and belligerence of the Tzenkethi, Starfleet Command had instructed Sulu to avoid not only a confrontation with them, but any contact at all. In the ten months *Enterprise* had traveled the sector, the crew had detected only two Tzenkethi vessels, both of them civilian, and which they'd given a wide berth.

After Young and Tenger acknowledged their orders, Sulu leaned toward her first officer. "Somehow, I doubt we'll be seeing the Tzenkethi around here," she told Linojj. "This star and these planets won't appeal to the Coalition any more than they do to us." With an unexceptional main-sequence sun, five conventional gas giants, and only two terrestrial worlds—both of which appeared unsuited in the extreme for humanoid life—the Rejarris system would offer little in the way of valuable resources, and its remoteness meant that it lacked any sort of strategic worth.

"You're probably right, but it's difficult to know with the Tzenkethi," Linojj said. "They might show up just because we're here."

Sulu nodded her understanding. "They do sometimes seem preoccupied with the Federation, don't they?"

Before Linojj could respond, Lieutenant Commander Fenn spoke up. "Captain," she said, and in just the single word, Sulu could hear surprise in the science officer's voice. "Sensors are reading a nitrogen-oxygen atmosphere."

Sulu looked to Linojj, whose deep-set eyes widened beneath the smooth, protruding ridges of her brow. "Is it breathable?" the first officer asked.

"Yes, but . . ." Fenn started, but then she operated her controls once more. Finally, she turned toward the center of the bridge. While the science officer peered at the captain with one of her eyes, Sulu saw that her other remained trained on her displays—an initially disconcerting sight back when Fenn had first joined the crew, but to which the captain had long ago grown accustomed. The eyes of Frunalians functioned independently of each other, and the organization of their brains allowed the concurrent processing of both sets of visual information. "Surface temperatures are near or below freezing almost all across the planet."

The unanticipated readings gave Sulu pause. Where she had expected a poisonous atmosphere and unrelenting, lethal heat, sensors found non-toxic air and wintry conditions. An explanation began to percolate in her mind, an intuition, but she pushed it away in favor of waiting for concrete information to tell the story. "What about life signs?"

"Indeterminate," Fenn said. "There appears to

be some sort of substrate within the planet's land masses that interferes with biosensors." She turned fully back to her station and worked her controls again. "But I'm reading ports on bodies of water, and ships in those ports. There are buildings . . . what look like towns and cities . . . connected by complex road and transit systems."

"Captain," said Tenger, "there are a number of artificial satellites in low orbit."

Sulu spun her chair to face the security chief. Standing on muscular legs, the stocky Orion had broad shoulders and a barrel-shaped chest. "Has the *Enterprise* been detected?" Sulu asked him.

"Negative," Tenger said. "We have not been scanned. Sensors show that most of the satellites are configured for communications, and possibly for global positioning, but regardless, I'm reading no signal traffic to or from any of the devices."

"And there's no indication of warp travel in or around the system?" Sulu wanted to know.

"No, sir," Tenger said. "At least not recently."

Sulu turned her chair forward again. "So we know that the civilization here has begun to reach out from their world into space. They've sent satellites into orbit, but we've explored most of this solar system and seen no evidence that they've developed interplanetary, much less interstellar, travel." Speaking to her first officer, she asked, "Recommendations?"

"Under normal circumstances, I'd suggest transporting a landing party down to an uninhabited location so that they could gather more detailed readings on both the planet itself and the people who live on it," Linojj said. Starfleet's Prime Directive barred interference with pre-warp cultures, meaning that the *Enterprise* crew could not reveal themselves to the natives of the planet below. "In this instance, when our biosensors aren't able to identify life-forms on the surface, we can launch a high-altitude probe instead. Even if it can't get close enough to the surface to overcome the interference, it can still fly below the overcast and provide visual reconnaissance, which would allow us to definitively pinpoint unpopulated areas."

"Sensors are showing no air traffic and no active monitoring of the skies," Fenn added, "so a probe would likely go unnoticed."

"We can also calibrate the probe's guidance system to use the clouds for cover," Linojj said, "having it emerge only for short periods to ensure the most effective concealment."

"Agreed," Sulu said. "Prepare a class-three probe and launch when ready." As her crew worked to fulfill their orders—Fenn would program the automated device, Tenger would launch it, and Young would validate its telemetry, while Linojj would oversee the entire endeavor—the captain wondered what they would find on Rejarris II. Unbidden, her earlier suspicion about the reason for the conditions on the planet recurred. She hoped that she was wrong.

An indicator on the communications console winked green, and a flood of data poured across the display. "Confirming comlink to the probe," said Ensign Young. "Awaiting visual signal."

"Thank you," the captain said. "Put it on the screen when you have it."

"Yes, sir." Young tapped at his controls to analyze the quality of the incoming transmission. While it maintained its integrity, he saw a slight degradation in the upload rate. Back at the Academy, from which he'd graduated less than a year prior, one or another of his instructors had taught him that such a dip in performance most frequently resulted from a failing component, but his months aboard *Enterprise* told him something different. It seemed more likely to him that the considerable volume of information in the data stream had combined with the high bandwidth of the ship's network processors to cause the generation of noise in the signal. By bringing a few of the backup nodes online and actually narrowing the bandwidth, he could eliminate that noise and thus increase the transmission rate.

Without notifying anybody of his evaluation or seeking anybody's approval, Young made the adjustments to the comm system. He'd learned that as well in his time on *Enterprise*: to have confidence in his abilities, and to recognize the importance of—sometimes even the need for—acting independently. It gratified him to see the upload rate immediately rise, with no corresponding loss of data.

A second indicator on his console flashed from yellow to green, and Young responded at once. "The probe has begun visual surveillance," he said. "Transferring the feed to the main viewer." He operated his controls, marrying the deed to his words.

On the viewscreen, the image of the planet vanished, the dirty arc hanging against the black, star-speckled depths of space replaced by an uneven and rapidly moving field of grayish brown. Young watched in silence, waiting to see what Rejarris II looked like. He wanted to know what the alien world held in store for the *Enterprise* crew in general, and for him in particular. Cities and ports and transportation systems signified an industrial civilization, and no matter how advanced or undeveloped that pre-warp civilization, Captain Sulu would want it studied. She would order a landing party to the surface, where they would study the planet up close and the inhabitants from afar. If the *Enterprise* personnel could learn enough about the alien society— enough so that they could disguise themselves and blend in—they would masquerade as locals and enter a city so that they could surreptitiously observe the culture at close range.

The idea of walking unrecognized through an alien settlement, functioning as a benign observer, thrilled Hawkins Young. At Starfleet Academy, he had studied to become a communications officer, but he'd also pursued a secondary concentration in archaeology. He enjoyed studying the material remains of ancient civilizations, but he also reasoned that possessing such a specialty would help him get off the ship and onto strange new worlds, where he would meet previously unknown life-forms. Since joining the *Enterprise* crew, though, he'd participated in only two landing parties, both of which had involved the study of deserted ruins, offering him no opportunity to encounter a living alien species.

As a result, Young had requested cross-training as a contact specialist. He began receiving his instruction half a year earlier. He took to the discipline at once, enjoying it immensely, and consequently spent many of his off-duty hours studying on his own. It took him only four months to receive his certification as an assistant specialist, but since then, the *Enterprise* crew had worked only a single first-contact mission, on Beta Velara IV, and Commander Linojj hadn't called his name for the landing party. The omission disappointed him, but he understood that, with more shipboard experience and additional training, his chance would come.

On the main screen, the gray brown of the cloud cover suddenly gave way as the probe descended into clear air. Young had expected a burst of color—the greens or crimsons or golds of foliage, perhaps, or some sort of ornamentation on buildings—but the city that hove into view appeared as wan as the overcast sky. The only differentiation in the hues of the pallid landscape came in the form of a dark, almost black body of water that stretched away from the alien metropolis in a torpid expanse.

As Young looked on with the rest of the bridge crew, the probe's optics zoomed in on the city. A legend in the lower right corner enumerated the scale, giving the area visible on the viewer as ten square kilometers. The buildings rose in arcs that fitted into a framework of circular and radial thoroughfares that defined the urban community. With the constant overcast diffusing the light, the sun threw no shadows. The vertical contours of the city dropped as it spread out from the center. Young strained to see some aspect of the design or some detail that distinguished the place from others he'd seen, but the drab setting did not impress him.

As the probe soared directly above the city, Captain Sulu stood up from the command chair and stepped forward, just behind Ensign Syndergaard at the helm and Lieutenant Aldani at navigation. "Do you see it?" she asked without taking her gaze from the viewscreen.

"I don't see anything," said the first officer, who stood beside the command chair. "It's all gray. It looks almost . . . inert."

"It does," Sulu agreed. "Commander Fenn, scan for heat signatures or movement within the buildings."

"Aye, sir." Fenn touched a sequence of control surfaces. A bluish tint washed across the image on the main viewer, blurring the sharp edges of the buildings. Some slight variation occurred in the color mask, but no red points appeared, which would have signified distinct instances of temperature variation or motion.

"There's no movement anywhere," Sulu said. "Not in the city, not along the transit networks, not on the lake. There are no people."

"Sensors are showing no active power sources either," Tenger said.

Sulu paused, then ordered Fenn to return the image to a normal view and magnify it. The tinge of blue faded and the picture sharpened before it shifted, bringing a single square kilometer of the city into focus. Young tried to determine if something specific had caught the captain's attention, but he saw nothing of any note. Sulu asked to see a different section of the landscape, and then another. Finally, she said, "It looks as though everything's been covered by a dull blanket of material. Has it snowed there?"

"No, sir," Fenn said. "The city stands near the planet's equator, in one of the warmer regions. The surface temperature is nine degrees, well above the freezing point of water." Her hands fluttered across her panel. "The ground and buildings are all covered, though, Captain, but not by snow. It's a layer of ash, several centimeters deep."

"Ash," Sulu said, with a disgust that would have been appropriate if she'd had a mouthful of it. For a few seconds, Young did not understand the captain's reaction, but then she asked another, telling question. "How high are the radiation levels?"

Nuclear winter, Young thought, and he understood that everybody else on the bridge would draw the same conclusion. The uninterrupted clouds surrounding the planet, the coating of ash across the city, the lack of movement—it all pointed to the catastrophe of a nuclear war. Young had seen no obvious scars from such an attack, but that did not mean that atomic weapons had not detonated elsewhere on the planet. Indeed, he thought that the city wore its stillness like a cloak of death.

"The amount of ultraviolet radiation reaching the surface is high," Fenn reported. "That corresponds with a lack of ozone I'm reading in the stratosphere, which could have resulted from firestorms across the planet that sent soot up into the mesosphere. But scans are not picking up any indication of fallout. That could be the result of the amplified UV radiation overwhelming the sensors, or because of the interfering substrate in the soil, or simply due to a reduction of those levels over time."

"If it's been long enough for fallout to dissipate, wouldn't the skies have cleared as well?" Sulu asked.

"Probably," Fenn said, "but that would also depend on a number of factors, including the amounts and locations of the nuclear material released, as well as meteorological conditions, both at the time of the release and overall for the planet."

Sulu paced back to the command chair, though she did not sit. "Ensign Young, what do your instruments show?" she asked. He'd been so intent on the planetary conditions and on following the conversation that the mention of his name startled him. "Are you picking up any type of communications signals at all? Even automated ones?"

Young consulted his panel, then performed a quick secondary scan. "No, sir," he said. "I'm not reading any comm traffic at all."

The captain seemed to consider that. "Commander Tenger, adjust the course of the probe. Have it follow one of the transportation routes to another city."

"Aye, Captain."

As Sulu sat back down in the command chair, Young watched the main screen. The city receded from view, until it disappeared when the probe ascended into the clouds. *It's not cloud cover,* he reminded himself. *It's smoke.*

Within just a few minutes, the probe reached a much smaller settlement—less a city than a town. Nevertheless, the same conditions prevailed: a layer of ash covered everything, and the *Enterprise* crew detected no sign of the planet's inhabitants, either inside or outside the buildings. Before the captain ordered the security chief to send the probe onward, though, Fenn espied several distinctive shapes in a field. When she notified Sulu, the captain ordered a close-up view. Half a dozen ash-covered mounds appeared, all with familiar shapes.

"Are those what they look like?" the captain asked.

"They appear to be the skeletal remains of *arivent*-like animals," Fenn said. Young had never heard the word *arivent* before and suspected that it belonged to the science officer's native Frunalian tongue, but then she amended her statement. "Horse-like animals."

"And we still don't see any people," Sulu said. "Not living, not dead." Young thought to point out that perhaps the bodies of the population who had constructed the civilization on Rejarris II lacked any internal structures that would survive decomposition, but the existence of the equine skeletons made such a claim unlikely.

"Maybe this town and the city we saw were abandoned," suggested the first officer. "There's no obvious destruction, so maybe the ash was deposited by some sort of nuclear accident, rather than as a result of a military conflict."

"Maybe," Sulu said. "Commander Tenger, set the probe's course to continue following one of the transportation routes. Let's see what else we can find on this planet."

They found the same conditions prevailing in the next city, although they also discovered a complex on its outskirts clearly designed to launch rockets—a capability consistent with the artificial satellites orbiting the planet. The captain ordered five additional probes deployed, spaced evenly across the surface of Rejarris II. On every continent the probes searched, in every city and town, the *Enterprise* crew encountered the same situation. They also located additional launch facilities, but because they'd already surveyed the five outer worlds and their moons—none of them class M—they knew that the people of the second planet did not evacuate to any of those, and long-range scans of the innermost world in the system showed that it had no atmosphere, resulting in temperature swings from two hundred degrees below zero to five hundred above, all of which ruled it out as a possible haven. Despite being much cooler, neither of Rejarris II's pair of moons held an atmosphere, though Young thought that the captain would likely want to examine the two natural satellites more closely at some point.

Commander Linojj proposed another possibility. "Could the inhabitants have been abducted?" She appeared to hesitate before adding, "This system isn't that far from the Tzenkethi Coalition."

The captain took in a deep breath, then exhaled loudly. "I can't reasonably argue against the aggressiveness of the Tzenkethi," she said, "but could an entire planetary population have been taken against their will? We've seen no signs of destruction anywhere on Rejarris Two."

"Maybe they left voluntarily," Linojj said. "Maybe the Coalition helped them escape whatever caused the pollution in the atmosphere and the ash on the ground."

"Maybe," Sulu said, though she sounded unconvinced. "It would mark the first time I've heard of the Tzenkethi coming to the aid of another species."

"What if it wasn't another species?" asked the navigator, Gaia Aldani. "What if Rejarris Two was the site of a Tzenkethi colony?"

"That would make more sense," Sulu said.

"Or maybe the planet was never populated," offered Syndergaard at the helm. "Could these cities and towns have been built for a colonization that never took place because of a nuclear accident?"

Sulu nodded, then glanced around the bridge. "Well, we have a lot of questions, so let's see if we can find some answers," she said, and then, to the first officer: "Commander, equip a landing party. I want you to transport down to one of the cities and see what you can learn about the people who built it."

"Yes, sir," Linojj said.

"Captain," Fenn spoke up, "because of the interference with the biosensors, the landing party should carry signal enhancers with them."

"Linojj?" Sulu said.

"Understood." The first officer stepped up onto the raised, outer section of the bridge and headed for the starboard-side turbolift. "Tenger, Fenn, Young, you're with me."

For the second time, the sound of his name on an officer's lips surprised Young. He quickly secured his station, then joined Linojj in the lift. As Tenger and Fenn followed them inside, supplementary personnel moved from secondary positions to take over the vacated stations. Young saw the captain rise from her chair and address her exec. "Commander, exercise extreme caution," she said. "Something about all of this—" Sulu glanced over her shoulder at the main viewscreen, which once more showed Rejarris II hanging in the firmament. "—just doesn't feel right."

"Yes, sir," Linojj said.

Young more or less agreed with the captain's assessment, but another feeling overwhelmed whatever trepidation he might have felt: excitement. He didn't know if Commander Linojj wanted him on the landing party as a communications officer or because of his training in archaeology and alien contact, but it didn't really matter to him. He didn't even know if they would find any of the planet's inhabitants, and if not, then what had happened to them, but none of that mattered either. At that moment, all Young wanted was to explore the unknown.

Xintal Linojj resisted the impulse to draw her phaser. As she walked cautiously forward, she slowly moved her head from side to side, casting her gaze upon the round windows that looked out on the landing party from the one- and two-story buildings lining the thoroughfare. She saw no movement anywhere, but the sensation of being watched persisted. Fenn assured her that she read no life signs in the area, and that at such close range, the biosensors of her tricorder readily overcame the interfering substance in the ground. The science officer also confirmed that she detected no power sources or communications signals around them, implying that nobody watched them, even remotely, and no equipment recorded them. Still, it required an act of Linojj's will not to reach for her type-1 phaser where it hung at the back of her black uniform pants, concealed beneath the hem of her brick-red tunic and the cold-weather jacket she wore atop it.

The air felt crisp as she and the five other members of the landing party walked along the center of one of the wide radial avenues that led from the edge of the circular metropolis directly to its center. In addition to pulling Tenger, Borona Fenn, and Hawkins Young from the bridge, she'd added a second security guard, Crewman Darius Permenter, as well as the ship's chief medical officer, Doctor Uta Morell. They had transported from *Enterprise* to the perimeter of the city, where they had chosen to begin their survey. Linojj took point, with Permenter sticking to her side, while Tenger positioned himself as he always did, at the rear of the group, where, as he often said, he could keep all of the people entrusted to his safekeeping within his view.

They had arrived in the city just after midday, and yet the muddy sky lent their surroundings the dim, hazy look and feel of dusk. The high-pitched whines of three tricorders—one operated by Fenn, one by Morell, and one by Young—sounded unnaturally loud as they pierced the silence of the city. The carpet of ash covering the ground muffled the clack of their boot heels against the pavement. Measuring from four to five centimeters deep, the accumulation of the smoky residue kicked up around the landing party as they moved through it, surrounding them at calf level like a miniature, gray snowstorm.

The group reached an intersection, where an avenue that looped around the city crossed the straight thoroughfare they had taken. Linojj stopped and looked around, then called back over her shoulder. "Ensign?"

The communications officer hurried to her, deactivating his tricorder and dropping it to his side. "Yes, Commander?"

"What's your assessment of these buildings?" Linojj asked, waving her hand toward the structures closest to them.

"Sir?" Young said, as though he hadn't understood her question.

"You have archaeological training," Linojj said. "You draw conclusions about historical places and peoples based on what they leave behind. What are your thoughts about this part of the city?"

"I . . . I'm not sure," Young said, his discomfort obvious. He clearly didn't know what she wanted of him, and therefore fretted about providing her bad information.

"Don't worry, Ensign," Linojj said. "This isn't a test." She offered him a thin smile, attempting to put him at ease. "I'm just looking for an opinion as we try to figure out what we've discovered here." As the rest of the landing party congregated about them, Linojj pointed to the nearest building. It rose only a single level and fronted on the arc of the crossing avenue, both its front and back walls shaped to match the curve. Its short side walls ran straight, parallel to the radial thoroughfare. The building featured round windows and a round door, and its roof arched downward, like a flattened dome. Constructed of a seamless, concrete-like material, the entire structure matched the gritty color of the ash all around it.

Young raised his tricorder, but Linojj stopped him. "Forget about sensors," she said. "Tell me what your first impressions are. Is that a home? An office? A lab or commercial establishment?"

Young took a step toward the building. "It's difficult to say just by looking at it, Commander. Archaeologists base their conclusions not only on physical evidence, but what they know about a population and a region historically. In some cultures, citizens tend to aggregate in large numbers, residing not in smaller dwellings like that, but in sizable, multi-unit structures. In other societies, people choose to live by themselves in smaller places. There are also numerous examples of other preferences in other civilizations, but I don't know anything about who lived on this planet, or anything about this city."

"I understand all of that," Linojj said, "but what do you *think* of when you look at that building?"

Young continued to regard the structure without saying anything, and Linojj wondered how badly the situation—or she herself—intimidated him. It hadn't been all that long since he'd left the Academy. She had opted to include him in the landing party so that he could gain experience—and confidence—in the field, but also because she believed that his diverse training could prove useful in such an enigmatic situation.

Finally, Young said, "It's dull."

"What is?" Linojj asked.

"The building," the ensign said. "It's absent anything identifiable as ornamentation. It has the round windows and the round door, but those appear utilitarian, not decorative. The walls and the roof are smooth and drab and featureless." He turned in place and motioned toward the other structures in the immediate vicinity. "All of these buildings aren't identical," he went on, "but they all share a lack of adornment."

"And what does that tell you?" Linojj wanted to know, pleased that she'd gotten the young officer talking.

"Nothing definitive," the ensign said. "I'd need more information even to formulate a working hypothesis. It could simply be that the inhabitants of the city have no artistic sensibilities. It could also be that they prize creativity to such a degree that they mandate its limitation to certain contexts, such as display in a museum. Or it could even be what Ensign Syndergaard speculated: that this place was built for a population who never arrived, and so never had the opportunity to embellish it."

"Thank you," Linojj said. She declined to point out that Young had not actually answered the question she'd asked. They had just begun their investigation, though, and so he might yet contribute to their efforts. Regardless, she would meet with him afterward to discuss whatever shortcomings and strengths he demonstrated on the mission. To Morell and Fenn, she said, "Doctor, Commander, scan that building. I want to be as sure as we can that there's nobody inside."

The two officers held up their tricorders in the direction of the structure. "I'm reading no life signs of any kind," Morell said.

"And there's no movement whatsoever," Fenn added.

"Then let's go find out what's inside," Linojj said. She had taken only a single step when Tenger materialized beside her. She knew that, since she wanted to take the landing party into an unexplored, unsecured interior space, the security chief would insist on entering first and checking it for any potential dangers. She saw that he'd already taken his phaser in hand, although he kept it lowered, almost hidden with the grip of his fingers. With it, he quickly signaled to the other security guard, and Permenter fell back at once to protect the landing party from the rear.

Tenger led the way toward the plain structure, the vibrant green of his Orion skin conspicuous against the grayscale environs of the city. When he reached the door, he turned to face Linojj and the rest of the landing party. "I will enter first," he said, just as the methodical security chief had on so many other missions. "Wait for my signal before you follow." Linojj nodded.

A round handle protruded from the center of

the door. Tenger reached for it with his empty hand. Linojj expected that the door wouldn't open, and that they'd have to force it, but it swung inward at Tenger's touch. The hinges growled out their displeasure, a clear indication that they hadn't been used in quite some time. Tenger called out a greeting. When he received no response, he stepped inside. He did not raise his phaser as he did so, but Linojj knew that he didn't need to: she'd witnessed the swiftness of his reflexes in action.

The security chief stood in the doorway for a moment, his broad shoulders nearly filling the frame, his head swiveling from side to side. Linojj tried to look past him into the building, but she saw only shadows. When Tenger moved inside and away from the door, she waited. After a minute or so, he reappeared, a portable beacon gleaming where he had affixed it to his wrist. "There are four rooms," he said. "They are all empty."

Linojj strode through the doorway and past him. As her eyes adjusted to the dim interior, she saw that Tenger's characterization of the room as empty referred only to people, not to furnishings. The window in the curved front wall provided the only illumination, which marginally brightened a patch of the floor, but did little to reveal the objects filling the space. While the rest of the landing party filed inside behind her, Linojj reached into a pocket of her jacket and pulled out her own beacon. She clapped it onto her wrist and switched it on.

As Linojj shined the light about the surroundings, other beams joined hers. Tenger and Fenn moved deeper into the building through an arched passage, while Morell, Young, and Permenter stayed in the front room. Ash had penetrated inside and coated everything in a fine layer. She saw a number of objects she recognized as furniture, though few she would have wanted to use herself. Two similar pieces that she assumed functioned as the Rejarris II equivalent of chairs featured a compressed, bowl-like bench perched atop a tripodal base. Linojj puzzled over another object with two small vertical boards, one mounted high on a metal pole and the other low, with a crosshatched hoop jutting out halfway up. Something that looked a lot like a desk held a pair of posts atop it, one on either side, with a wide, filmy material suspended between them.

More than the forms of the items, though, the colors surprised Linojj. Where outside the city displayed itself in a neutral, monochromatic palette, the beacons of the landing party picked out a scene dressed in one deep color after another. Linojj pointed her beam down at the floor, which showed red even through the ash covering it. Comprising thousands of small, irregularly shaped tiles, the mosaic reflected both artistry and precision. The first officer squatted down and brushed her fingertips across the floor; they came away coated with particles of ash, leaving behind gleaming red commas where they had swept the floor clean.

"Commander," said Morell. Linojj stood back up and walked over to where the doctor examined a round, open-faced cabinet hanging on an inner wall. Concentric dividers lined its interior, and circular pictures in frames filled most of the spaces between them. "I assume these are—or were—the inhabitants of Rejarris Two."

Linojj studied the images. She couldn't tell with certainty, but based upon their spacing within the cabinet, she thought that a few of them had been removed. In the ones that remained, she saw individuals belonging to a species completely unknown to her. Their bodies looked like one torso on top of another, joined together by a narrower, tubular structure. They stood on a ring of a dozen or more short appendages. They possessed nothing resembling a head or neck, but a number of vine-like limbs hung down from the top of the body. Darker specks stippled their amber-tinted flesh, and a glossy vertical strip stood out on one side of their upper torso. The clothing they wore—also quite colorful, Linojj noticed—mostly wrapped around their lower section. She could not discern any gender traits, but could easily classify the smaller individuals in some of the photographs as children.

"Have you ever seen or heard of beings like this?" Linojj asked the doctor.

"No," Morell said. "They certainly don't look anything like the Tzenkethi, and I've never encountered anything in the medical literature about the Coalition that tells of a member race like that."

"Can you speculate about them?"

"I can't tell much just by looking at pictures of them," the doctor said. "I would guess, though, that the dots of deeper color are cutaneous receptors, probably tactile in function. I'd also bet that the silvery stripe is a sensory organ, perhaps visual."

"What about sex?" Linojj asked.

"No, thank you, Xintal," Morell deadpanned. "I'm married."

Linojj heard a chuckle behind her, but couldn't tell whether it had come from Young or Permenter. The first officer shook her head, an act more of forbearance than vexation. She'd long ago accepted—and even learned to appreciate—Morell's arch sense of humor, which Linojj always thought must have developed as a reaction to the emotional rigors of the CMO's profession and duties. "The aliens, Doctor."

"Of course," Morell said. "Again, it's difficult to draw conclusions based only on pictures, especially since some parts of the body are clothed in every image. The only visible characteristic I see that might be gender specific is the length of the upper limbs."

Linojj smiled, but she elected to choke back the sophomoric rejoinder that occurred to her. Instead, she looked past the doctor as Fenn and Tenger reentered the room, the beams of their beacons dancing along the floor in front of them. "What have you found?" she asked.

"Usage, but not for some time," Fenn said. "The ash that's gotten inside covers every surface and is undisturbed, other than where the landing party has walked. There are furnishings in all the rooms, and we've found clothing, what appear to be household goods and personal items, and many of those items display signs of wear. Sensors also show that the floor has been slightly eroded along some paths, such as the area inside the front door, an area that logically would have seen some of the most use."

"So your conclusion is that this was somebody's home?" Linojj asked.

"Probably so, yes," Fenn said. "At the very least, the physical evidence demonstrates that it was occupied in some capacity, for some reason, over a course of time."

"Did you find any remains?" Doctor Morell asked.

"No, although my tricorder has picked up trace amounts of DNA," Fenn said. "Nothing that we can sequence, though."

"Not only did we find no corpses or skeletons," Tenger said, "we also saw no half-eaten meals, no items out of place, no signs of panic or violence. Whatever happened to empty this place of its inhabitants—to empty this building, and presumably this city, and perhaps even this entire world—it did not come as a surprise to the people who lived here."

"But what *did* happen?" Linojj asked aloud, although she didn't expect an answer, posing the conundrum more to herself than to her crewmates. She paced over to the window and stared out at the flat-hued city beneath the forbidding charcoal sky. "If the unbroken clouds of smoke in the atmosphere and the ash covering the ground are indications of a nuclear war, then where's the damage?" The first officer recalled the case of the cultures on the planets Eminiar and Vendikar, which she had learned about in both the Prime Directive class and the Survey of the Alpha Quadrant seminar she'd been required to attend at the Academy. Until just fifty years earlier, the people on the two worlds had waged a centuries-long war, conducted not with physical weapons, but by computer. Both sides launched attacks mathematically, with the results determined by programmatic simulation. People designated as casualties reported to so-called disintegration chambers, which vaporized them out of existence. In that fashion, the war raged on for hundreds of years, the populations of the two planets at risk, but their societies free from the physical destruction of conventional battle. It was, in Linojj's opinion, both elegant and horrific, a clever means of preserving the material existence of a world, mixed with a callous disregard for the safety of its citizenry.

None of that had any bearing on Rejarris II, Linojj knew. Even if the entire population there had died in a "clean" war conducted on computers, even if every single person willingly marched to their deaths in order to fulfill some fatality toll—a set of improbable circumstances that could justify the *Enterprise* crew finding an intact but unoccupied civilization—that still would not explain the nuclear winter enveloping the planet.

"All right," Linojj said, moving away from the window and toward the front door. "Let's see what else we can find."

The landing party followed the first officer back outside and deeper into the alien city.

Sulu sat at the head of the long conference table in the observation lounge situated aft of the *Enter-*

prise bridge. After the landing party had returned from their journey through the city on Rejarris II, she had summoned its members to brief her on what they'd found—and on what they hadn't. "You saw no signs of life whatsoever?" she asked, baffled by what seemed like the inexplicable disappearance of an entire planetary population.

"To the contrary, Captain," said Linojj, seated directly to Sulu's left, beside Morell and Tenger. Fenn, Young, and Permenter sat across from them. Behind the first officer, through the viewports lining the aft bulkhead of Deck 1, the ship's warp nacelles pulsed with energy. A veiled curve of the planet hung off to port. "We saw signs of life everywhere. In each building we entered, whether one of the smaller structures on the periphery of the city, or one of the twenty-story towers at the center, we found furnishings and personal belongings, equipment and supplies. We identified patterns of wear consistent with everyday use, and recorded numerous instances of trace DNA. We just couldn't find any of the beings who actually lived there."

It sounded to Sulu almost like double-talk. She understood, though, that the crux of the confusion lay not with the language her first officer employed, but with the situation she described. Sulu leaned back in her seat and ran a hand through her hair, a reflex born from years of pushing her long locks away from her eyes. It caught her momentarily off guard when her fingers whisked easily through her cropped coiffure. She'd had her hair cut short only days earlier, something she'd considered doing for a long time, and which the amount of gray strands weaving through the black had finally convinced her to do.

"What about records?" Sulu asked.

"We didn't see anything recognizable as a traditional computer," Linojj said. "Even if we had, the city was without power. We did discover several items that resembled large books, but instead of paper pages, they contained sheets of a film-like substance. Sensors revealed that they had been inscribed chemically. If that's how they stored information, it may take some time to decipher their language."

Sulu reached forward and picked up a personal access display device. She examined the padd's screen, which showed the tawny-skinned form of an alien being, the image copied from a picture—one of many—that the landing party had found down on the planet. "Could it be that the population is there, but we just can't perceive them? Could they be hiding from us?"

"I don't think so," Linojj said. "If they were there but somehow imperceptible to us, they would still interact with the environment, but the undisturbed layers of ash covering everything belies that idea. Nobody's been in that city for some time."

Sulu set the padd back down on the table. "Can we be sure that everything you experienced on the planet was real?" she asked, searching for an explanation.

The first officer looked across the table at Lieutenant Commander Fenn, who held up her tricorder. "We're as sure as we can be, Captain," she said. "Every member of the landing party saw the same things, all of it matched by the data logged on multiple tricorders."

"The readings gathered on the surface are also consistent with what our probes have so far detected," Tenger added. The six class-three devices continued to soar through the skies of Rejarris II, collecting information.

"I imagine it's possible that everything we've seen is some sort of illusion," Linojj said, "or that it was all manufactured complete with trace DNA and signs of wear built in, but to what end? Whether intended for us or for somebody else, what purpose would such a ruse serve?"

Sulu considered her first officer's point. "You're right," she said. "Those possibilities seem even less likely than all the inhabitants of a world vanishing."

"Excuse me, Captain," Young said. He seemed tentative to Sulu.

"You have something to say, Ensign?" she asked. "I called this meeting for discussion."

"Yes, sir," Young said. "I just wanted to point out that the word *vanish* implies something sudden, and in this case, where we're talking about the population of a planet, it also implies some powerful force at work. But while we do know that there doesn't appear to be anybody left on Rejarris Two, we don't know when they left or how long it took them."

Linojj nodded as Young spoke. When he finished, she said, "We uncovered no evidence that the people all died, but I did notice several details that hinted at them simply leaving. It was nothing definite. We found an arrangement of pictures that seemed incomplete, as though somebody had decided to remove a few to take with them. A collection of clothes that looked as though items were missing. Things like that."

"But if the inhabitants of the planet left, where did they go?" Tenger asked. "There are no Class-M worlds in this solar system, and the level of technology we found on the planet tells us that they had yet to develop warp drive. As best we can tell, they only recently visited their moons for the first time." After the landing party had beamed down, the crew had sent a probe to each of the two small natural satellites orbiting Rejarris II. Scans found a pair of automated, uncrewed spacecraft on the larger moon, and a third on the other. Small and liquid-fueled, the trio of landers demonstrated the rudimentary level of space travel that the natives of Rejarris II had achieved.

"Maybe they had help," Linojj said, repeating an idea she'd voiced before transporting down to the planet.

"Where would that help have come from?" Tenger asked. "We surveyed all the other planets and moons in this system, and none are inhabited. That means that assistance would have had to come from outside. The star nearest to Rejarris is almost five light-years distant, which implies that such assistance would have required the use of warp drive, but we've scanned for residual warp signatures and haven't found any."

"Maybe the exodus from the planet took place so long ago," Fenn said, "that the residual signatures have dissipated."

"Or maybe we haven't scanned closely enough

in surrounding space," Sulu said. "Commander Tenger, plot a search pattern for—"

The three-toned boatswain's whistle sounded in the observation lounge. *"Bridge to Captain Sulu,"* came the voice of the ship's navigator, Gaia Aldani, who presently had the conn.

Sulu tapped a control on the intercom set into the conference table. "Go ahead, Lieutenant."

"Captain, one of the probes has found something," Aldani said.

Sulu pushed back in her chair at once and stood up. Everybody else followed suit. "I'm on my way, Lieutenant. Out." She deactivated the intercom with a touch. Addressing the two crew members who did not serve on the bridge, the captain dismissed Morell and Permenter. She then led the others through the nearest exit. Passing doors that opened into her office, a turbolift, and a refresher, she emerged through one of two aft entries onto the bridge.

"Report," Sulu said. She skirted the combined communications-and-tactical console and moved to the command chair, where Lieutenant Aldani had already started to rise.

"One of the probes completed its flyover of the southernmost continent and began mapping the sea floor," she said, pointing toward the main viewer. The blue expanse of a Rejarris II ocean filled most of it, with the edge of an empty brown-and-gray landmass cutting across the bottom left corner of the screen. "The region isn't far from the pole. Ensign Andreas, show the captain what the probe discovered."

"Yes, sir." Fenn took a position at a secondary sciences station as Devonna Andreas operated the primary console. On the viewscreen, a red line appeared and proceeded to trace a rough circle, mostly over the water, but also along an inland mountain range. The blue then faded away, leaving a shaded area of the sea floor showing. The familiar form—a raised rim surrounding a central uplift at the center—told Sulu exactly what the probe had located.

"It's a crater," she said.

"Yes, sir," Aldani confirmed.

"When was it produced?" Sulu asked.

"Based on the minimal amount of erosion and several other factors," Andreas said, "it was probably generated within the last half century."

"So the smoke in the atmosphere and the ash on the ground are not the product of a nuclear winter," Sulu said. "They're the result of an *impact* winter."

"Yes, sir," Aldani said.

"Thank you, Lieutenant, Ensign," Sulu said. "That's good work."

As the captain sat down, Aldani returned to the navigation console, where she relieved Ensign Shahinian. The first officer stepped up beside the command chair. "It seems that an asteroid has solved our mystery," Linojj said. "That's why we didn't see any destroyed cities anywhere on the planet: there was no war."

"It solves one mystery," Sulu said, "but not the other. An asteroid impact didn't vaporize everybody on Rejarris Two."

"No," Linojj said, "but if they studied the skies, then they could have predicted the disaster."

"But you've seen their civilization," Sulu said. "You've seen the satellites that they put into orbit, and their rudimentary launch facilities. Is there any chance that they managed to develop faster-than-light travel?"

Linojj shrugged and shook her head. "Not based on what we've learned so far."

"Then that's our second mystery," Sulu said. "Where did the people of Rejarris Two go, and how did they get there?"

2

Tenger scrutinized the readings on the tactical console for anything that might provide insight, but that the sensor-analysis programs might not flag. A few minutes before, he had noted an unusual concentration of silver-oxide molecules, which he'd then tracked back to a damaged satellite. He scanned the compromised device to find that a micrometeoroid had torn through its casing and embedded itself in a battery pack, which proved to be the source of the leaked particles. Other than that, he'd seen nothing that warranted further attention.

The security chief had arrived an hour early for his shift, displacing Ensign Molina to a secondary bridge station. Tenger typically prided himself on his punctuality, appearing at meetings and for duty at exactly the prescribed times. He had been that way for more than a quarter century, ever since his training at the Academy, when he'd replaced his continual attempts to challenge boundaries with a commitment to formality and discipline.

At the time he'd chosen to apply for entry into Starfleet, he had not yet admitted to himself—and perhaps had not even realized—the role that his sister's fate had played in his decision. Revna had not been a beauty, a rarity among Orion women, but their family had at first counted that fact as a boon. On Lokras IV, where they lived, pirates threatened the colony world on a regular basis, not least of all by seizing beautiful young women they could sell on the interstellar black market.

The Orion Syndicate had also maintained a heavy presence in and around the Lokras region. Their smugglers routinely ran native plants from the planet and peddled them to the manufacturers of illicit drugs, while at the same time trafficking those drugs back to the colony. Their particular brand of avarice instigated a public health crisis on Lokras IV, in turn fomenting terrible social ills. Tenger's parents protected their daughter and son as best they could, even taking the precaution of having tracer chips embedded in their children's sides—chips that would sound an alarm if they moved outside designated safe areas, such as home and school and the routes between.

Tenger, eight years his sister's junior, had still been attending primary school when she'd matriculated at university. Never a tremendously cheerful sort, Revna soon developed a moroseness that everybody in the family attributed to a lack of self-confidence, owing to her short height and broad, almost masculine frame. But nobody—not even Tenger—understood the depth of her pain, and when she didn't return home one evening, it became too late for such understanding to matter.

A police investigation had found Revna's tracking chip at school, which she'd evidently dug out of her own flesh, carrying it with her to places that wouldn't trigger an alert signal, and hiding it in those places when she went elsewhere. She remained missing for five days with no hint at all about where she might have gone or what might have happened to her. Tenger didn't know if his sister had simply run away from home, but something other than a possible threat to her well-being troubled him even more: he hated not knowing.

When the police had at last collected evidence that Revna might have voluntarily or involuntarily left Lokras IV, the failure of everyone in the family to recognize the seriousness of her despair became clear in the shock they all displayed when they learned where she had last been seen: outside the local spaceport, in an alley not far from the freight terminal, in a seedy, disreputable part of town. They learned that she had often visited that alley, and others, in search of an illegal commodity: the Venus drug. According to one of her friends, Revna wanted to change her appearance, to soften her features and round her curves, and she consumed the banned substance daily for months. Long rumored to be a fiction, the Venus drug—or whatever Tenger's sister used—didn't produce the results she so desperately sought.

Maybe that had driven Revna over the edge, or maybe, as Tenger had suspected, some nefarious thug had taken advantage of her hopelessness. However it happened, she stopped taking the Venus drug and instead tried another prohibited substance: blood-gem. The powerful and devastatingly addictive narcotic made her so chemically and psychologically dependent on it that she sold herself into offworld servitude in exchange for a constant supply.

The Lokras IV police had followed Revna's trail to the Erivek system, on the Federation-Klingon border, and from there into the heart of the Empire. On Celos II, weeks of investigation passed without success. Finally, retracting his demand of local officials for an official inquiry into who had brought Tenger's sister there, and waiving any claims that a crime had been committed by a Klingon national or that an interstellar treaty had been violated, the Orion detective settled for discovering Revna's whereabouts. He found her in the morgue, dead from an overdose at the age of twenty.

Tenger had felt as though his world had been torn apart. Too late, his family fled Lokras IV and relocated to the Orion homeworld, where they stayed with Tenger's paternal aunt. Whatever small amount of independence he'd previously enjoyed evaporated. As protective as his parents had been on Lokras IV, they redoubled their efforts to keep their son safe.

Tenger had rebelled. At every opportunity, he fought to escape the constant attention paid to him by the adults in his family—father, mother, aunt, uncle, and an older female cousin. He ignored the restrictions his parents placed on him. He acted out not only as a direct result of the trauma of losing his sister, but also because he knew that, at least in part, he blamed his father and mother for Revna's death. Worse, he blamed himself. He'd only been a boy, but he still believed that he should have grasped the downward spiral of emotion in which his sister had been caught. He didn't know what he could have done—maybe nothing more than telling his parents, but maybe that would have been enough to save Revna.

When a Starfleet officer had visited his secondary school as part of the Federation's cultural outreach, though, Tenger had perceived a means of saving himself. Nonplused by his choice, his family nevertheless did not stand in his way, although they worried that he would defy the structure of the Academy. Instead of railing against the rules, though, he clung to them. In retrospect, it didn't require psychological training to pinpoint his motivation: he did what his sister could not, living within an exacting set of regulations. More than that, he learned to enforce those regulations—on others, but also on himself. In that way, he felt that he honored Revna's memory.

Occasionally, though, Tenger's punctiliousness gave way to his other dominant personality trait, as it had done that morning aboard *Enterprise*. The security chief appreciated all the reasons the captain had given for continuing to investigate what had happened on Rejarris II, from the simple desire to solve a mystery, to the search for scientific and historical knowledge, to the Federation's need to know whether the Tzenkethi had been involved in the disappearance of the planet's inhabitants. In particular, if the Coalition had played a role, it would serve the UFP well to find out whether they had rescued the population or exterminated them. But for Tenger himself, it had been more of a visceral feeling that had driven him to the bridge well before the beginning of his shift: he hated not knowing.

As the security chief studied the sensor readings, a door whispered open. He glanced up from his tactical console to see Captain Sulu and Commander Linojj exiting the portside turbolift. He checked the chronometer on his panel and saw that they had arrived just before the beginning of alpha shift.

"Good morning, Commander," Sulu said, returning his gaze as she approached the command chair. "You've gotten a head start on the day."

"Yes, sir," Tenger said.

"Too many questions, not enough answers?"

"Something like that, Captain, yes." Tenger had begun serving with Demora Sulu eleven years earlier, when he'd transferred from *U.S.S. Comet* to become *Enterprise*'s new chief of security. She knew him well.

As Linojj took her position on the starboard side of the bridge, Sulu addressed Ensign S'Teles, who had taken the conn through gamma shift. He'd risen from the command chair as soon as the captain had entered the bridge. "Good morning, Ensign," Sulu said. "Anything to report, other then the security chief's uncharacteristically early arrival?"

"Other than that, Captain," the Caitian said with a lilt that signaled his amusement, "the *Enterprise* has continued on its orbital search pattern through the night." Tenger heard the soft vibrational sound that often underscored the felinoid's words. "We have so far completed forty-seven percent of our scans. To this point, we have detected no signs whatsoever that any ship with an active warp drive, other than the *Enterprise* itself, has ever visited Rejarris Two."

"Thank you, Ensign," Sulu said. "You're dismissed."

"Yes, sir," S'Teles said. "Thank you, sir."

Over the following few minutes, the rest of the alpha-shift bridge crew arrived to relieve their gamma-shift counterparts. Tenger sent the overnight tactical officer, Cristobal Molina, off-duty, then returned to inspecting the sensor readings as they marched across his display. An hour later, his screen flashed yellow an instant before he registered what the numbers and symbols on his console told him.

"Captain, sensors are picking up what looks like a neutrino trail embedded in subspace," he said. "It could be a residual artifact of a warp signature."

"Where?" Sulu asked.

"In high orbit . . . it's exceedingly faint." He activated a calibration tool on his panel and worked to fine-tune the sensors. "It's difficult to localize."

"I see it too," said Fenn at the sciences station. "My instruments highlighted the reading, but they can't confirm that it's the result of a warp engine."

"If it is," Tenger said, "it could be years old, maybe even decades."

"If the people of Rejarris Two did evacuate their planet," Linojj said from her station, "it could have taken place decades ago. Maybe a warp-capable species did help them."

As the first officer spoke, Tenger saw the sensors highlight something else as unusual and requiring analysis. "Captain, I'm reading a fog of other particles in high orbit, in normal space, in roughly the same location as the potential warp signature."

"I see it as well," Fenn said.

"There's a mix of metallic elements," Tenger said. "Many atoms have been ionized. That could signify the remnants of an explosion."

"Sensors also show a confusing jumble of rocket propellants and vestiges of antimatter," Fenn said. "They could be the residue of spent fuel."

"Is there a satellite in or near that location?" Sulu asked. She got up from her chair and mounted the steps to the outer ring of the bridge.

"Negative," Tenger said. "All the satellites we've seen are in low orbit, but . . . there is a trail."

Sulu stood beside the security chief, peering down at the tactical console. "Where does it lead?"

Tenger examined the trajectory. The result surprised him. "It leads down to the planet," he said. He adjusted the sensors, targeting them to follow the run of particles to their end. "It goes all the way down to the surface."

"What's there?" Sulu asked.

"Scanning," Tenger said. "There is a metal-encased structure. It is intact. It doesn't read like a crash site. In fact . . ." He had focused the sensors narrowly, but the extent of the readings exceeded those limits. He widened the targeted area. "The object is huge. It measures more than a kilometer long . . ." He continued to expand the zone until he could read the entire object. "It is nearly two kilometers long and roughly toroidal in shape. It is lying flat on the ground."

"Is that a building?" Commander Linojj asked, striding over from her first officer's station. "Perhaps a launch facility of some kind?"

"The particle trail tracks directly to the structure, so that is a possibility," Tenger said. He enlarged the region of his scans even further. "There is a series of low buildings eleven kilometers away. The nearest settlement beyond that is several hundred kilometers distant."

The captain looked over to the sciences station. "Are there any life signs?"

"Indeterminate," Fenn said. "The interfering substrate in the crust appears all over the planet."

"Have any of the probes scanned this site?" Sulu asked.

"Checking," Fenn said. It took the science officer thirty seconds to arrive at an answer. "No, sir," she said. "We could route the closest probe to be there in less than four hours, or launch another probe to get there in about half that time."

"Launch another probe," Sulu ordered. "In the meantime, let's send down a landing party to see if we can make sense of any of this."

As Tenger prepared to send another class-three

probe into the atmosphere, Commander Linojj formed another landing party. She selected Ensign Young, Doctor Morell, and Crewman Permenter again, but chose another member of the security team and an assistant science officer rather than Tenger and Fenn, no doubt because of their responsibilities in programming and launching the new probe. Although Tenger would have preferred to transport back down to the planet, it contented him to execute the duties the captain had assigned him. He cared far less about which tasks he performed in the crew's quest for answers than he did about finding those answers. He could only hope that what lay below on the planet surface would help them discover what had happened to the people of Rejarris II.

The brilliant blue-white shimmer of the transporter effect cleared from Linojj's vision, but she immediately squinted at a different sort of brightness. A white-gray spread of snow and ash swathed the ground in all directions. Linojj held up her hand against the glare while she gave her eyes a moment to grow accustomed to it. She didn't think she would need the polarized goggles she'd brought with her, stuffed into one of the pockets in the cold-weather jacket she wore. The smoke that filled the sky dimmed the daytime hours on Rejarris II, and the ash combined with the snow to dull its albedo.

The first officer rounded on her heel to ensure that the entire landing party had successfully transported with her, and that they faced no unforeseen dangers. Doctor Morell stood beside Linojj, with Ensign Young and Assistant Science Officer Sandra

Alderson behind, and security personnel Permenter and Günther Haas at the rear of the group. Linojj could see the water vapor in their breath condensing before each of them in the cold air. The first landing party to Rejarris II had explored a city near the equator, but the second had just beamed down to a location at a more northerly latitude, with commensurately lower temperatures. The snow, at least, indicated that the planet had begun to heal itself after the asteroid strike.

Linojj pulled her communicator from where it hung at the back of her waist, beneath her tunic and jacket, and she flipped open its gold-colored grille. The black gloves she wore, fashioned from a flexibly thin fabric, insulated her hands against the cold weather but did not impede her dexterity. "Linojj to *Enterprise.*"

A moment passed, and then the captain herself responded. "Enterprise, *Sulu here,*" she said. "*Go ahead, Commander.*"

"We've beamed to the planet's surface without incident," the first officer reported.

"*Do you see the structure?*"

Glinveer Ved, the only Tellarite among the *Enterprise* crew and the ship's transporter chief, had followed the run of particles from orbit, setting down the landing party a hundred or so paces outside the structure to which the trail led. "Yes, I see it," Linojj said. "We're on a broad, snow-covered plain, and the structure is lying across our path. It stretches away in either direction until it fades from view."

"*Do you have any initial impressions?*" Sulu asked.

"Like everything else we've seen on this planet, it appears unoccupied," Linojj said. "Other than that, no, sir."

"*All right, Commander,*" the captain said. "*Observe standard procedures. Contact the ship every thirty minutes.*"

"Understood."

"*Enterprise* out."

Linojj returned the communicator to the back of her uniform pants. She heard the sound of first one and then two more tricorders as Morell, Young, and Alderson initiated scans. "Do you read any life signs in the area, Doctor?"

"No," Morell said. Her cheeks had turned rosy on her well-lined face. She wore the same black gloves as Linojj did, as well as a black knit hat pulled down over her curly white hair, but neither seemed to mitigate the effect of the cold on the older woman. "Whatever that structure is, it's not resistant to our sensors. I detect no life-forms inside it or anywhere in the area."

"What about in the set of buildings nearby?"

"I read them," Morell said. "They're eleven-point-one klicks south-southeast of here. At that distance, my tricorder's biosensors can't overcome the interference from the substrate in the soil, so life signs are indeterminate."

"Understood," Linojj said. The news did not concern her. It seemed wildly unlikely to her that the planet would lack life everywhere they searched, but that the natives would populate an isolated building complex. She raised her arm and waved the way forward. "Let's approach."

The first officer started toward the structure. The snow rose ten centimeters and crunched beneath her boots, the footing awkward but not onerous. A light but frosty wind blew steadily toward Linojj and her crewmates, occasionally gusting and carrying granules of snow and ash against the exposed flesh of her face. Although she needed to turn her head and avert her eyes several times as they walked, she counted the wind as an ally, since it likely accounted for the relatively low accumulation on the ground. She imagined tall drifts forming in the distance behind the landing party, swept into existence by the bursts of moving air.

As they neared the structure, its size became apparent. Its dark, blue-gray surface bowed toward them, and she estimated its height at twelve to fifteen meters. Snow and ash dusted its upper half like frosting on a cake—or, considering the structure's shape, like frosting on a doughnut. The curvature of its length took it quickly out of sight to the left and right of the winter landscape. Although smooth along some portions of its visible surface, it also contained numerous seamed areas studded with instrumentation. It looked to Linojj like an enlarged version of a duotronic conduit aboard *Enterprise*.

Ensign Young stepped up between Linojj and Morell. "Its outer surface is composed primarily of titanium, aluminum, and magnesium, although my tricorder is also reading several metal-matrix composites with ceramic and organic polymers. It has a circular cross section of fourteen-point-three meters in diameter, and . . ." Young moved closer to the object and crouched down before it. A narrow, dark brown strip ran tucked beneath the lower arc of the structure, free from snow and ash. "It's also sitting atop a thick metal slab, although it's not connected to it."

"Is that a foundation?" Linojj asked. "Is this a building? Or is it a conduit of some kind?"

"Neither, I think," said Lieutenant Alderson. She stepped forward and walked slowly along the structure, referring to the display on her own tricorder. "It's not hollow, but filled with circuitry. Scans show some recognizable equipment: solar cells, force-field generators, antigravs, thrusters—"

"Thrusters?" Linojj said. "Could this be a spacecraft? Maybe one that didn't originate on this planet?" Solar cells could have been used for energy collection, force-field generators to erect shields for protection during both spaceflight and atmospheric insertion, antigravs for liftoff and landing, thrusters for maneuvering and station-keeping.

"Possibly an automated vessel," Alderson said. "Although I suppose there could be a crew deck or compartment somewhere within the object. It'll take some time to scan the entire ring."

"I'm not sure it's of extraterrestrial origin," Young said, standing back up. "Everything inside falls within the level of technological sophistication we observed in the city. Plus the metal slab it's sitting on could serve as a landing pad."

Linojj considered the object and its remoteness from any cities, but its relative proximity to the nearby buildings. "If this is a spacecraft, or even just a satellite, could the complex eleven kilometers away function as its mission control? A facility utilized to launch and retrieve it, to maintain and monitor it?"

"It's possible," Alderson allowed. "We'd need to investigate the complex to understand its capabilities, and to look for any linkage with the object."

"All right," Linojj said. "Let's learn as much as we can here first. I want to know if this was ever in space, and what its primary function is." The first officer drew her own tricorder out of a jacket pocket as the landing party spread out alongside the object. Permenter took up a position at one end of the group, while Haas stationed himself at the other.

Linojj felt the chill in the air ease as she walked beside the object, which functioned in the middle of the empty plain as a windbreak. Inspecting the display of her tricorder, she saw the profusion of circuitry Alderson had detected. When Linojj had assembled the landing party, she'd considered enlisting the ship's chief engineer, Rafaele Buonarroti, or one of his staff, but at the time, she and the rest of the bridge crew had believed the great ring-shaped structure a building, not some massive technological object. Once she and the others had completed a preliminary examination of it, Linojj would contact *Enterprise* and request the assistance of an engineering team.

The first officer continued along the object, logging everything that her tricorder scanned. A series of narrow tubes in one section read as power-transfer conduits, while those in another section showed as hydraulic hoses. She saw a device mingling solid-state and mechanical components, which she judged an inertial stabilizer. She spotted an external emitter and tracked its connection to an internal gimbal and actuator, clearly one of the thrusters Alderson had mentioned.

"Commander." Up ahead, Ensign Young had turned back to face her. As she walked over to him, he alternately checked his tricorder and gazed up at the object.

"What is it, Ensign?"

"I've found a breach in the object's casing," Young said. "Or its hull. Commander Tenger detected ionized metallic elements in orbit that he thought could have been the result of an explosion, and a stream of those elements led here. If this was out in space, if this *is* a spacecraft or a satellite, this could be what exploded. Maybe that's even why it's here: for repairs."

"Repairs by who?" Linojj asked. She took a few steps back from the object and looked up at it, but she could see no sign of a breached hull. She raised her tricorder and ran her own scan. A gaping wound appeared at once, running from the top of the object and along the upper half of its inner side, out of view of the landing party. "I see it," she said. "I'll call down a shuttlecraft so we can take a look at it firsthand."

Linojj reached for her communicator, but Young stepped to the side and pointed. The first officer followed his gesture and saw two parallel series of evenly spaced notches in the side of the object, leading both up and down as far as she could see. "I think I can scale it," Young said.

Linojj tucked her fingers into one of the indentations. It felt snug, and the first officer imagined that it had been made for a different purpose, or perhaps to fit the tapered ends of the vine-like appendages she'd seen in the pictures of Rejarris II natives. She kicked the toe of her boot into another notch lower down, which also felt tight, but when she lifted up her free foot to test her weight on the makeshift hand- and footholds, they seemed functional enough. "Exercise caution," she told the ensign.

Young pocketed his tricorder in his jacket, then reached up and set his hands in two of the indentations, the right higher than the left. He started climbing, his initial progress slow because of the outward curve of the metal, but when he reached the halfway point, he moved more quickly. Linojj took eight or ten paces backward so that she could better view his ascent. The ensign began stopping at every other notch, letting go with one hand, and brushing away the snow and ash that had collected on the object.

As Young neared the top, he called out. "I see the breach, Commander." He swept away a final patch of snow and ash, then scrabbled up onto his knees. Unlike Doctor Morell, the ensign had not chosen to wear a hat, and Linojj saw his short brown hair whipped into a frenzy, the object no longer running interference between Young and the wind. "There's considerable damage," he yelled down, but the first officer could barely make out his words. She reached for her communicator, held it up for the ensign to see, then opened it with a flick of her wrist.

"Linojj to Young." She saw him take out his own communicator and speak into it.

"*Young here. I was saying that the breach is considerable, Commander. The metal along the edges is mangled and charred. It's also bent inward, not outward. It looks as though it might have been caused by weapons fire. I'm going to scan it.*" Still on his knees, the ensign set down his communicator, then retrieved his tricorder and activated it. Linojj could just hear the shrill plaint of its operation, intermittently carried away by the wind.

After a few moments, Young picked up his communicator again. "*I read charged particles,*" he said. "*The patterns of force do suggest an external explosion.*"

Linojj questioned who would have attacked the people of Rejarris II and why. From what they had so far gleaned, it made little sense to her, since, by all indications, they had barely even left their own planet, and had yet to travel among the stars. The first officer's thoughts led her to consider the Tzenkethi again, not only the nearest spacefaring species, but one with a reputation for an over-aggressive approach to protecting their border regions. At the same time, she wondered about the purpose of the object—was it a spacecraft, or a satellite, or something else entirely? "What can you see inside?" she said into her communicator. "Can you tell anything about it, or about its builders?"

The ensign put down his tricorder and leaned forward on one hand. "*It reminds me of a display at the Museum of Engineering in Rotterdam,*" Young said. Linojj had never heard of either the institution or the place, but she took the ensign's meaning. *"There's a lot of old-fashioned solid-state circuitry organized into—"* Young abruptly stopped talking, and Linojj saw him look to one side, away from her. *"This is odd, Commander,"* he said. *"I'm looking at the ground on the other side of the object. It doesn't seem the same as the ground where you're standing. For one thing, there's no ash or snow."*

"Could it simply be a result of the wind patterns inside the ring?" Linojj asked.

"It's not that," Young said. *"It's that I thought I saw snow when I first climbed up here, but now, as far as I can see, the terrain is dark and strewn with rocks and boulders."*

Boulders? That didn't sound right to Linojj. She examined her own surroundings, and though concealed in sheets of snow and ash, the topography appeared flat. No outcroppings rose up to suggest that any boulders dotted the area. "What do your sensors show?"

Young picked up his tricorder and sat back on his heels. Still holding his communicator, he deftly used one hand to scan the land on the other side of the object. *"This doesn't make any sense,"* he said. *"My tricorder is showing snow on the ground, and high drifts against the inner side of the structure. I'm also getting no readings at all of boulders."* He stood up. *"I can't—"*

A loud hum burst from Linojj's communicator, and she peered down at it, startled. When she looked back up, she saw Young lunge away from her and disappear, as though he had suddenly decided to leap from atop the object and down the other side.

She thought she heard him cry out above the rush of the wind, but then his exclamation unexpectedly ceased. "Ensign!" Linojj called into her communicator, even as she started to run. "Ensign Young!"

When she received no response, she quickly thumbed the reset button on the device before bringing it back up to her mouth. "Linojj to landing party. Emergency. Meet at my location." She reached the object, clapped her communicator onto the back of her waist, and started to climb. She'd reached the halfway point when Permenter and Alderson arrived from one direction, and Haas and Morell from the other.

"Commander," one of the security guards called up to her.

Linojj stopped and called back over her shoulder. "Ensign Young fell from the top of the structure onto the other side, and now he's not responding," she said. "Contact the *Enterprise* and prepare for emergency transport."

"Yes, sir," one of the guards said. Linojj heard the activation chirp of a communicator, followed by words she could not make out over the wind, which had picked up the higher she'd climbed.

As the first officer reached the top of the object, she stopped and carefully let go with one hand. From beneath the back of her tunic and jacket, she drew her phaser. She adjusted it to its highest nonlethal setting, then yanked herself into a kneeling position on top of the object.

The force of the wind struck her first, sending the long strands of her purple hair flying about her head. She ignored it and looked down the other side of the object. She saw the great, dark expanse that Young had described, filled with rocks large and small, but she did not see Young. Thinking he had fallen too close to the structure for her to see, she stood up. She heard a loud hum, and then a bright light flashed just below her. She quickly dropped into a prone position as a cone of golden illumination streaked above her.

Linojj aimed her phaser at the light's point of origin, not much more than a few meters away from her on the surface of the object. An emitter exploded in a shower of sparks. The beam vanished.

"Commander!" yelled one of the security guards.

"I'm all right," Linojj called down. "Stand by." Leading with her phaser, she crept forward, staying low. The surface of the object began to curve downward, and the first officer used the notches—which apparently continued around the entire circumference—to keep from sliding down. She had gone just about as far as she could while facing forward when she at last saw a human foot. Linojj edged forward until she could see Young's entire body. He sat on the ground—on dark earth, amid rocks and boulders. "Ensign," she yelled to him. He cradled one arm in the other, obviously nursing an injury he'd endured in the fall, but he appeared otherwise unhurt. His tricorder lay in pieces beside him. "Ensign!"

Young gave no indication that he heard her. Linojj wondered if he'd struck his head when he'd fallen and damaged his hearing. She tried once more, without success, then reached for her communicator. "Linojj to *Enterprise*."

"Enterprise *here*," said Captain Sulu. "*Commander, sensors are showing power flowing through the structure, and we've detected energy surges at your position.*"

"We're aware that the structure now has power," Linojj said. "Our immediate concern, though, is Ensign Young, who has fallen fifteen meters to the ground from atop the structure. He's conscious, but he hurt his arm and may have suffered other injuries. Doctor Morell can't get to him, so I'm requesting emergency medical transport."

To her credit, the captain did not waste any time asking for additional details. Instead, Linojj heard her say, "*Keep this channel open*," and then, "*Sulu to transporter room. Beam up Ensign Young at once. We have a medical emergency.*" Linojj watched Young, waiting for the bluish-white motes of dematerialization to form around him.

It didn't happen.

"Captain, is something wrong?" the first officer asked.

Linojj heard indistinct conversation over her communicator, and then the captain said, "*Commander, Lieutenant Ved reports that he can establish transporter locks on everybody except Ensign Young.*"

"Maybe the ensign's signal enhancer was damaged in his fall," Linojj conjectured. Because of the substance in the ground that interfered with biosensors, each member of the landing party carried a small tracking device designed to facilitate transport in such conditions; those devices also had the benefit of individually identifying the carriers. Lieutenant Ved understood the transporter and its related systems better than anybody Linojj had ever met, so she knew that if he couldn't establish a lock, then nobody could. "I'll give my enhancer to Ensign Young, which may take a few minutes."

"Understood," Sulu said. *"In the meantime, I'll send down a shuttlecraft just in case that doesn't work."*

"That's a good idea, Captain," Linojj said, "but one of the energy surges your sensors showed was a beam of some kind fired from the structure in my direction."

"Was it an energy weapon?" Sulu asked.

"I don't know," Linojj said. "I didn't have time to analyze it before I destroyed its emitter. I think it might have been a directional beam, though, and that it might have pulled Ensign Young from where he'd climbed up onto the structure."

"It was a tractor beam, then?"

"Or something like it, yes," Linojj said. "Regardless, it could be that the structure is what's interfering with the signal enhancer. It might also explain why I can't reach him by communicator. Ensign Young fell into the interior of its ring shape, while the rest of us are outside it—or in my case, on top of it."

"All right, see if you can move Ensign Young out of there," Sulu said. *"A shuttlecraft will be launching shortly."*

"Thank you, Captain," Linojj said.

"Enterprise *out.*"

The first officer again touched her communicator's reset button. "Linojj to Permenter."

"Permenter here," came the immediate reply. Linojj explained the situation to the security guard,

including her intention to retrieve Young, either by transporter or, if necessary, by physical means. "Have the rest of the landing party stay close. Doctor Morell and Lieutenant Alderson should continue scanning the object, alert for the discharge of any beams. They should learn whatever they can about its power: its source, its distribution, what kind of reserves it might have."

"Yes, sir."

"Linojj out." She peered back down the side of the object at Young, then attempted to contact him again via communicator, to no avail. As she watched him, though, he clambered to his feet and began to study his surroundings. She waved to him, thinking that even if he could not hear her calls or the signal of his communicator, then maybe she could get his attention visually. Even though Young appeared to look all around, and sometimes even in her direction, her efforts didn't work.

The ensign reached to the back of his waist, perhaps for his phaser, but Linojj thought it more likely that he wanted his communicator. His hand came away empty, though, and he began searching the ground about him. After a few moments, he stopped, raised a hand to his mouth, and called out. Linojj heard nothing but the wind.

Exchanging her communicator for her tricorder, she scanned Young—or at least she tried to do so. When sensors did not register the ensign, Linojj directed them at the ground. They didn't reflect what she saw, but instead showed snow and ash covering flat terrain. The disconnect between her own senses and those of the tricorder troubled her. She began to think that when Young had fallen, he'd landed much farther from where he'd started than it appeared.

Trying a different tack, Linojj cautiously rose up onto her knees. She then reached back and, with an underhand motion, tossed her tricorder from atop the object. She watched it fall toward the ground, expecting to see it vanish in midair, to land in the place her sensors read, not in the place Ensign Young stood.

But the tricorder didn't disappear. Instead, it dropped all the way to the ground, landing just a few meters from Young. When it struck, he spun around toward it.

He heard it, Linojj thought. *But he can't hear me, and I can't hear him.* That seemed to buttress her instinct that Young had crossed some threshold and now stood in another place—perhaps in another time or another dimension.

The ensign strode over to the tricorder and bent to examine it. He seemed reluctant at first to touch it, but he eventually did. Linojj wished that she'd recorded a message on it, but at least she knew that, if she needed to make contact with him, she could.

Young glanced upward, as though searching for the source of the tricorder. Linojj wondered if he could see the structure on Rejarris II that the landing party had come to investigate. As though in answer, the ensign looked directly at her, but the first officer saw no recognition in his eyes, no awareness that she was even there.

I have to get him back, Linojj thought. She quickly scrambled around, found the indentations in the metal casing of the object, and began to climb down, toward Young. She descended as fast as she could, but then the toe of her boot struck something hard. Linojj looked down past her body to see that a wide, flat metal surface protruded from the object at the midpoint of its height. She checked left and right and saw that it continued in both directions, like a long shelf.

Linojj tested her weight on it. It held and, more than that, it felt solid. She let go of the handholds and dropped onto it, lowering herself to her knees. She unclasped the signal enhancer from her wrist, then tossed it to the ground.

Young heard the device land, and he immediately went to it. As Linojj had hoped, he strapped it onto his own wrist. He gazed up toward her again, but she could tell that he still couldn't see her.

Linojj contacted *Enterprise* again, informing the captain that the ensign apparently could neither see nor hear her, and that all attempts to communicate with him had failed. The first officer also told Sulu that she'd given her enhancer to Young and requested that he be transported up. Once more, she waited to see him dematerialize. Instead, she heard the captain's voice.

"Lieutenant Ved can't establish transporter locks on either you or Ensign Young," Sulu said.

"Understood, Captain," Linojj said. "I'm going to try to retrieve him myself."

"I sent Commander Tenger down on Amundsen," Sulu said. *"He should arrive before long."*

"Yes, sir. Thank you, sir. Linojj out." She closed her communicator. Below her, Ensign Young faced in her direction. Still on her knees, she quickly bent down to the metal shelf and reached past it. She waved her arm, hoping that Young would see it. When Linojj looked at him, though, she saw his mouth drop open in an expression of surprise, and she reflexively pulled back up.

Pain like she'd never known seared through Linojj's arm. Her eyes slammed shut as her mind shrieked in agony. She thought she cried out too, but she didn't know. She fell forward onto the metal shelf, her shoulder striking it hard, but the impact didn't register at all. Linojj felt only the terrible sensations in her arm, which felt as though it was being torn from her body.

She heard someone breathing hard and realized that it must be her. Wanting to see how badly her arm had been injured, she held it up before her face and opened her eyes. She thought for an instant that she was looking in the wrong place, but then she saw the stub of her arm that remained. Everything below her biceps was gone, as though it had been sheared off. Bright red blood gushed from the wound. Flesh and tendon and muscle fluttered horrifically, and in the center of the mutilated limb, she saw the white nub of her bone.

She screamed until blackness took her.

3

Demora Sulu stood in a place she hated. It made no sense, she knew that, but the emotion persisted—had persisted for decades. It didn't matter that the sickbay aboard *Enterprise* had been the scene of countless recoveries, of wounds healed and illnesses treated, of medical wonders large and small performed by Doctor Morell and her staff. It didn't even matter that, during her twenty-five years aboard the ship, Sulu herself had spent her share of time there.

More than my share, the captain thought. All told, she'd doubtless endured entire days, maybe even weeks, of regular physical and psychological examinations, not to mention innumerable check-ups after participating in landing parties to alien worlds. *And that's not even taking into account the major incidents.* Early in her Starfleet career, she'd marched into a Brevant ambush on Beta Orvis III and nearly paid for her carelessness with her life.

She'd fallen through the surface on an unnamed moon out in Desidera's Loop, where she'd narrowly escaped drowning before facing down death by hypothermia. Even during her first mission as *Enterprise* captain, on the voyage to the Röntgen Wall, she had—

Stop it!

Sulu hated Starfleet medical facilities—sickbays, infirmaries, hospitals, whatever the designation given to them—and she had since the age of six. She understood the reasons she felt that way, conceded the irrationality of her aversion, but recalling the numerous times her health had been preserved or her life saved in such a place wouldn't change her feelings. Even though she knew that the efforts of all the doctors and nurses and technicians in *Enterprise*'s sickbay kept the crew—kept *her* crew—safe, that knowledge didn't loosen the knot that tightened in her gut every time she set foot in there.

As Sulu stood in the doorway of the ship's surgical suite, circumstances compounded her usual discomfort. Her first officer had been horribly wounded on the second away mission to Rejarris II, and another crew member, who'd also been injured, remained alone on the planet and cut off from the ship. The captain waited anxiously as Doctors Morell and Benzon consulted over the unconscious form of Commander Linojj. The Boslic woman had been laid out on the operating table, her long purple hair pulled back and tied behind her head. A series of transparent containers sat on a tall, wheeled cart beside her, the various colored fluids within them flowing through medical equipment and down tubes that connected to her left arm. A green light shined steadily and a yellow one pulsed beside it on a silver metal cuff that had been fitted over the stump of Linojj's right arm.

Sulu swore under her breath. She didn't blame herself for the terrible injury to her first officer or the loss of communication with Ensign Young. Starfleet Command had accorded the *Enterprise* crew with the privilege of exploring the universe, of discovering the undiscovered, of meeting the unknown—an exciting and rewarding duty that did not come without danger. Sulu's people knew their jobs and understood the risks. But even though the captain didn't blame herself for what had taken place, she took responsibility for it. That was part of *her* job.

In addition to that, though, the events on Rejarris II hurt Sulu on an intensely personal level. She had no closer friend than Xintal Linojj. They had served together aboard *Enterprise* for a dozen years, but their friendship stretched back to their Academy days. They had met during Sulu's graduating year, when she'd assisted an instructor in teaching Advanced Astrophysical Navigation. Linojj took the course in only her second year as a cadet, and she outperformed every other student, all of them upperclassmen. When Starfleet transferred her to *Enterprise* just after its refit in 2307, she and Sulu quickly renewed their acquaintance.

And Xintal was there for me when I most needed her. The news that Sulu's father and the crew he commanded aboard *Excelsior* had been declared missing in action and presumed dead had been the hardest time in her life since the death of her mother. While the later incident lacked the fear and confusion and distress of a child trying to cope with such a devastating event, it carried with it the deep pain that came from an adult's understanding. For a while, she had held out hope for her father, which had softened the transition to acceptance, but she didn't know how she would have made it through that difficult time without Linojj's stalwart friendship.

When Sulu had received promotion to *Enterprise* captain, it had been an easy decision to follow the advice of the man she'd replaced, John Harriman, who had recommended the elevation of Linojj from second officer to exec. Since that time, the two women had grown even closer. What Sulu had gone through with Captain Harriman when she'd become his first officer, she experienced with Linojj, albeit from the other perspective. The confidence that they needed to have in each other, and the closeness in which they worked, helped them forge an unshakable bond.

Across the compartment, Doctor Morell finished her conversation with Rentis Benzon, the Betazoid physician second in seniority among the *Enterprise* medical staff. While Benzon moved to speak with a pair of nurses, the chief medical officer headed directly for the captain. Sulu didn't need to ask for a status.

"Commander Linojj's condition is serious but stable," Morell said without preamble. "We're treating her for shock and we have her sedated, but otherwise her vital signs are good. The prognosis is that she'll survive."

But will she live? Sulu thought but didn't say. Not that people with such disabilities couldn't lead fulfilling lives—of course they could, and no doubt did—but permanently losing a limb would require of Linojj enormous adjustments, not just physically, but mentally and especially emotionally. Sulu wanted an easier road for her first officer to travel—for her *friend* to travel.

"As injuries go, hers is better than most of this type," Morell continued. "Her traumatic amputation was remarkably clean, with little damage to her residual limb."

"'Little damage'?" Sulu echoed, skeptical.

"Yes, Captain," the doctor insisted. "When an arm or a leg is lost in the field, there's often a great deal of damage inflicted on the distal end of the residual limb: bones are compressed and sometimes crushed, veins and muscles are mangled and left ragged, the skin is shredded. In the commander's case, none of that happened. Under the circumstances, I'd say that qualifies as good news."

Sulu felt the smallest bit of relief. "I take it that means that you'll be able to fit her with a biosynthetic replacement."

Morell paused before responding, and Sulu read uncertainty in the doctor's hesitation. At last, she said, "Commander Linojj will make an excellent candidate."

"Only a candidate?" the captain said, more sharply than she'd intended. She took a moment herself to rein in her emotions. "I don't understand," she told Morell. "You just talked about how 'clean' the injury was. What's the problem?"

"The only specific issue Doctor Benzon and I can see is that there's some thermal damage to the median and ulnar nerves," Morell said. "As a result, there's a possibility that she won't be able to exercise motor control over artificial muscle tissue."

"When will you know?"

"Not for a while," Morell said. "Not until after the operations."

"Operations," Sulu said. "More than one."

"We need to examine her damaged arm and deal with the thermal damage, debride the burned tissue," Morell explained. "Assuming a successful procedure, we'll then have to surgically attach a new biosynthetic limb, which will take some time to craft. At that point, the commander will have to undergo physical and occupational therapy, as well as counseling."

"Can all of that be done aboard ship?" Sulu asked. *Enterprise* currently traveled outside of Federation space, in unexplored territory, with no specific return scheduled. If Linojj's medical needs could not be met aboard ship, Sulu would need to alter *Enterprise*'s course and, once the crew had recovered Ensign Young, head to the closest Federation facility: Helaspont Station, near the Tzenkethi border.

"Yes," Morell said. "We have the facilities, technologies, and materials to fabricate a biosynthetic limb for Commander Linojj, and Doctor Benzon did his residency at the Loring Institute on Betazed, which specializes in biosynthetics. We have several qualified counselors aboard, including Nurse Veracruz, who has experience with traumatic amputees."

Sulu nodded, satisfied that Linojj's recuperation would not require an added layer of complexity by having to return her to a starbase. She believed that the commander would stand a better chance at a full recovery if she didn't have to be removed from her chosen environment. Sulu also wanted to be there for her friend during her convalescence. "What are Commander Linojj's chances for success?"

"You know I don't like to put a number on such things, Captain," Morell said. "The truth is that even if everything goes medically right, there are no guarantees."

"There are no guarantees in life, Doctor," Sulu said. "How often do these procedures result in a patient receiving a functioning replacement limb?"

"In a case like Commander Linojj's, the success rate is high," Morell said. "Upward of sixty-five percent."

Although the number seemed acceptable—even good—to the doctor, it disappointed Sulu. It meant that out of every three patients in Linojj's condition, one of them would permanently lose their limb. The captain would have preferred better odds.

Returning her attention to the injured crewman still on the surface of Rejarris II, Sulu asked, "Can you tell how this happened?" Crewman Permenter's description of events on the planet shed little light on what had befallen Linojj, as she had been out of everybody's sight at the time.

"We believe that it was caused by some sort of energy discharge," Morell said, "though it's not quite like anything we've seen before."

"Could a weapon have been used against her?"

"It's difficult to say, but she didn't suffer a blast from a phaser or similar weapon."

Before Sulu could ask any more questions, the three tones of the boatswain's whistle sounded in the compartment just outside the surgical suite. *"Bridge to Captain Sulu,"* said Commander Buonarroti, the ship's chief engineer. Fourth in the ship's chain of command, he'd taken over the bridge with *Enterprise*'s top three officers elsewhere.

"Is there anything else, Doctor?" Sulu asked, and when Morell shook her head, the captain headed back out into main sickbay. She moved to the nearest intercom and activated it. "Sulu here."

"Captain, you asked to be informed when Amundsen *was close to returning,"* Buonarroti said. *"The shuttlecraft has just cleared the atmosphere."* He spoke with the elongated tempo of humans brought up in the Alpha Centauri system.

"Acknowledged," Sulu said. "Has there been any contact with Ensign Young?"

"No, sir," Buonarroti said. *"We're continuing our efforts, but so far, we've had no luck."*

"All right," the captain said. "I'm headed to the hangar deck. Have one of your staff meet me there. I need an engineer with medical training."

"Aye, Captain," Buonarroti said.

"Sulu out." She deactivated the intercom and glanced back toward the surgical suite. She thought to tell Doctor Morell to keep her informed about

Linojj's progress, but she knew that she didn't need to do so. While Sulu had enjoyed Captain Harriman's more relaxed command style, she'd gravitated to a more formal atmosphere once she'd taken over *Enterprise* from him. Among other shipboard procedures, she had established protocols for the crew to keep the senior staff apprised of ongoing developments.

Instead, she exited sickbay and headed for the closest turbolift. She didn't know what had happened down on the planet—either to the vanished native population, or to her two injured officers—but it no longer mattered to her. She had made the decision that, once they'd recovered Ensign Young, she would order the ship onward, so that the crew could continue their mission of exploration elsewhere. They had already spilled too much blood on Rejarris II.

The navigational beacon appeared on the shuttlecraft's main display, and Tenger quickly piloted the auxiliary craft onto an intercept course. When he'd maneuvered *Amundsen* into position, he slammed the fleshy side of his fist down on the autopilot control, the sound of his hand hitting the panel loud in the small cabin. For a moment, the security chief's frustration threatened to boil over into anger, but with an effort, he reduced it to a simmer.

Tenger confirmed the autopilot's operation, which included interfacing with *Enterprise*'s automated guidance systems. That would allow the *Excelsior*-class starship to snare the shuttlecraft and bring it in for a landing in the hangar bay. *Amundsen* rocked slightly as an *Enterprise* tractor beam latched onto it.

The security chief turned in his chair and regarded the three members of his staff that he'd assigned to the shuttlecraft with him. The two women and one man avoided his gaze, not out of disrespect or discomfort, he didn't think, but from the surfeit of decorum and discretion their duties often required of them, whether attending Starfleet admirals or Federation dignitaries. Tenger's crew had surely seen his momentary outburst, but in ignoring it, they allowed him the illusion of believing they hadn't, which he appreciated. "We're on approach to the *Enterprise*," he told them before swinging back around to the shuttlecraft's main console.

Through the forward viewport, the gray orb of Rejarris II hung off to port, a dirty speck against the black backdrop of space. Ahead of the shuttlecraft, *Enterprise* awaited, the navigational beacon and the low-power tractor beam streaming from it invisible to the unaided eye, but registering on the helm display. *Amundsen* approached the ship aft, headed toward where the secondary hull curved concavely upward from its bulging forward half. The thick but almost-flat circle of the primary section stretched away at the front of the ship, while the sleek warp nacelles, connected by right-angled pylons to the secondary hull, projected backward in an impressive display of drive power.

With just minutes remaining before *Amundsen* set down in *Enterprise*'s hangar bay, Tenger considered the argument he would make to the captain.

Although Sulu bore the ultimate responsibility for the entire crew, his position as the ship's chief of security made their welfare his number-one priority. He hadn't participated in the second landing party to Rejarris II because the captain had needed him to study the incoming data and assess the threat potential of the large, unexplained structure they'd found on the surface. His absence from the planet didn't mitigate his accountability for what had taken place, though. To his way of thinking, the fact that he'd remained on the ship only pointed out his failure: even though staying on *Enterprise* allowed him to see readings of the entire alien structure, he should have anticipated the danger and insisted on accompanying Commander Linojj to investigate it in person.

Captain Sulu would of course disagree. She would note that Tenger's presence on the planet would not have guaranteed the safety of either the exec or the communications officer. He would contend it didn't matter, that the injuries to Linojj and Young, and the separation of the latter from the ship and crew, provided de facto validation that *Enterprise*'s security chief should've beamed down with the second landing party. He would also petition the captain to assign him to the next one.

In actuality, Sulu *had* ordered Tenger to travel back down to the planet. After Commander Linojj requested emergency medical transport for Ensign Young, and once the attempts to beam him back to the ship failed, the captain ordered the security chief to form a detachment and take a shuttlecraft to the surface of Rejarris II. *Amundsen* had already entered the atmosphere and traveled halfway to its destination before Sulu recalled Tenger and his team back to *Enterprise.*

Apparently, even as the shuttlecraft had headed for the planet, Commander Linojj had been badly injured. According to what the captain told Tenger, one of the ship's transporter operators, Crewman Corvallis, beamed down with a spare signal enhancer for the first officer, who had lost hers. Corvallis and the entire landing party then transported back up to *Enterprise,* with the exception of Ensign Young, who, after sustaining his injury, remained somehow cut off from the crew.

At the time the captain had ordered Tenger to reverse the shuttlecraft's course and return to the ship, he had suggested that he and his team should instead continue on down to the planet. He wanted to directly assess Ensign Young's situation so that he and his security detail could effect an immediate rescue. If that proved impossible, then he would gauge the requirements for a future attempt at recovery.

Captain Sulu had simply said no. She offered no reasons for her decision, but she didn't need to: Tenger had served under her command long enough to know what she intended to do. He respected her for it, even as it motivated him to report her actions to Starfleet Command. He would never do such a thing, though, both because the decisions Sulu made never fell outside the scope of "captain's discretion," and because, in her position, he probably would have elected to do the same thing.

Up ahead of the shuttlecraft, Tenger saw, the

segmented hatches of *Enterprise*'s hangar bay had divided in the center and begun telescoping open. The security chief checked the navigational readouts to validate *Amundsen*'s approach, and to assure himself that he didn't need to resume manual control of the shuttlecraft. As he did so, a message flashed across a display, supplemented by a tonal signal, indicating an incoming transmission. He tapped his panel to permit reception.

"Enterprise *shuttlebay control to* Amundsen," said a male voice.

"Shuttlebay control, this is Commander Tenger aboard *Amundsen*," said the security chief.

"*Commander, our guidance systems are prepared to fully take over landing.*"

"Understood," Tenger said. "I'm shutting down *Amundsen*'s drive." He worked his controls, cutting the shuttlecraft's engine power. The cabin quieted, the hum saturating the compartment— almost unnoticeable because of its constancy— fading completely. On the helm display, Tenger saw the intensity of the tractor beam increase, slowing the vessel for its final approach.

"*We've got you,* Amundsen," said the voice of shuttlebay control. Tenger made it a point to familiarize himself with everybody aboard ship as part of his security protocols, but he didn't always recognize voices. "*Sit back and enjoy the ride.*"

"Acknowledged," Tenger said. "*Amundsen* out."

The hatches leading to the hangar bay had opened fully, revealing the landing pad beyond them. Two columns of green chaser lights raced in parallel lines from the aft end of the deck inward, leading to a circular turntable conspicuously inscribed with a large red X. Past that sat an array of auxiliary craft, including several planetary shuttles like *Amundsen*, as well as a pair each of cargo management units and warp shuttles. Above those vessels, a row of ports stretched across the top of the far bulkhead, and through them, Tenger saw several *Enterprise* crew members moving about the shuttlebay control room.

Amundsen glided through the open hatches, trembling briefly as it passed through the force field that secured the hangar and maintained its atmosphere. Tenger glanced through the forward port at the observation galleries that overlooked the landing party on either side of the bay. Both appeared empty.

The shuttlecraft touched down in the center of the hangar, directly atop the turntable and its red X. Tenger monitored the external hatches until they had fully closed, and then he verified the atmosphere outside *Amundsen*. When the control room opened a channel and announced that the crew could safely disembark, Tenger powered down the shuttlecraft's systems. He then stood up and moved to the port side of the cabin, where he worked a control, still operational via secondary battery power. The hatch whirred open.

"Secure your gear and clear the shuttlecraft," Tenger told his security team. He waited as the three of them gathered up their weapons, tricorders, and cold-weather tackle. He collected his own equipment, then led them through the hatch and into *Enterprise*'s hangar bay.

The quartet marched along a gangway marked on the deck until they reached a wide access portal. Its rounded, rectangular port exposed the door's thickness. It led into an airlock, but with the bay fully pressurized, Tenger and his crew would not require its use. As he reached for the door's control, it opened before him.

On the other side of the airlock, the inner door stood open as well, revealing Captain Sulu and a young officer whose division sleeve identified her as an engineer. Both of them carried cold-weather clothing, and the young woman had both a tricorder and a field kit slung across her shoulder. Tenger didn't know the ensign—Galatea Kostas— but he recognized her from her personnel and security files. She had dark eyes and wavy black hair that had been shaped into a bun behind her head.

As Sulu and the engineer walked through the airlock and into the hangar bay, Tenger and his security team stepped to the side to give them room to pass. He'd anticipated the captain would want to travel to Rejarris II herself, though he hadn't expected to meet her on her way to a shuttlecraft. He wondered if she'd wanted to make sure of his security team's safe return before embarking herself, or if, had *Amundsen* not arrived at that moment, she would have taken a different vessel down to the planet's surface.

Sulu stopped to face Tenger. "Anything to report, Commander?" she asked.

"No, sir," the security chief said. He paused for a moment, then dismissed his crew back to their duty stations. Once they had exited the hangar bay and the airlock doors had closed behind them, he said,

"I'm glad you're here, Captain. I wanted to speak with you about our plan to recover Ensign Young."

"My plan," Sulu said, substituting the word *my* for *our*, "is to take a shuttlecraft to the structure and study the situation. I will contact you and the rest of the senior staff to detail what we find. If possible, I will retrieve Ensign Young, and if not, we will work together to determine a course of action that will allow us to do so."

It did not surprise Tenger at all that Sulu intended to attempt to rescue the ensign herself. It also did not please him. "Begging the captain's pardon, but with Commander Linojj confined to sickbay for some time to come, I am now functionally second in command," he said, striving to keep his voice even so that his words would not sound like a challenge to Sulu's authority. "I would therefore be remiss in my duty if I did not point out that the *Enterprise* crew should not be without its top two officers."

"As you just mentioned, Commander, you are presently my exec," Sulu said. "That means that, even after I depart, one of the ship's top two officers will remain aboard."

"Not the top two officers it left port with," Tenger said, his frustration mounting. "Captain, I can lead a rescue mission down to the planet. As the *Enterprise*'s chief of security, I would argue that it's my duty to do so."

To Tenger's surprise, Sulu did not reply immediately, and instead seemed to consider his argument. After a few seconds, she looked to the young engineer she had brought with her to the hangar bay. "Ensign, board the shuttlecraft and stow our gear," she said, handing over her jacket. "I'll be right there."

"Yes, sir," Kostas said, and she made her way across the deck to *Amundsen*.

Tenger felt deflated. He realized that he'd already lost the battle. Sulu had dismissed Ensign Kostas simply to spare the security chief any embarrassment.

"Commander," the captain said, but then she stopped. She took a step closer to him, moving with evident deliberation into his personal space. Standing several centimeters taller than the security chief, Sulu looked down at him with her dark brown eyes. "Tenger," she said, calling him by name rather than by rank, something she rarely did while on duty. "I understand your concerns, particularly in light of what happened to Xintal. Your job is to preserve the security of this ship, and that necessarily means protecting the life and well-being of its captain. But the crew are my first priority, and after the events on the planet, I'm not prepared to send anybody else down there, into an obviously dangerous situation."

"But I'm volunteering for that duty, Captain," Tenger said, almost pleading with her. It occurred to him that perhaps he should have simply violated Sulu's orders and continued down to the surface of Rejarris II. He thought about calling her by her given name, but he understood that, no matter her sincerity in doing so, she had already mined that rhetorical tactic for whatever value it possessed. "Captain, there is risk in everything we do," he went on. "We travel through the frigid vacuum of space at many times the speed of light. We visit unexplored places and seek out unknown alien life. When necessary, we take up arms to defend the Federation and its allies. *Nothing* we do out here is for the timid."

"No," Sulu said. "You're certainly right about that. But my decision isn't about courage or timidity. It's about my unwillingness to knowingly place my crew in danger, and after the terrible injury to Commander Linojj, we know that there definitely is a danger."

Accepting that he could not change Sulu's mind about undertaking the rescue mission herself, Tenger decided to do what he could to ensure her security. "You're taking Ensign Kostas with you," he said. "Why not choose me instead?"

"I selected Ensign Kostas because she is an engineer cross-trained as a field medic," Sulu said. "She can investigate the structure to learn how it's isolated Ensign Young from us, but if we can figure out a way to recover him, she can treat his injuries at once."

"I understand," Tenger said. "But at least allow me to accompany you."

"I'm taking as few of the crew as I can," Sulu said. "You are also right to argue that the *Enterprise* should not be without both its commanding officer and exec. With Commander Linojj incapacitated, that means that you're the ship's first officer. In my absence, you therefore need to be here."

Tenger surrendered the argument. Knowing the captain as well as he did, he'd never expected any other outcome. Sulu always listened to the judgments and recommendations of her senior staff, and compelling reasons and new perspectives could persuade her to different decisions—but not when it would mean sending members of her crew into known dangers. If she could avoid doing so, she would.

"What are your orders then, Captain?" Tenger asked.

"I've spoken with Crewman Permenter, who told me all he could about what happened on the planet," Sulu said. "I want you to speak with him as well. I'll contact the ship regularly to keep you informed of what we learn, and whether or not we can recover Ensign Young. Under no circumstances is any member of the *Enterprise* crew to go down to Rejarris Two without my explicit order."

"Aye, sir," Tenger said.

The captain offered him a curt nod, then headed for the shuttlecraft. Tenger watched her board *Amundsen* before he withdrew into the airlock. He sealed the entrance to the hangar bay, but he didn't leave. Instead, he stared through the port in the door as the turntable slowly rotated to point the shuttlecraft's bow toward the main hatches, which he saw had already begun to reopen. Moments later, *Amundsen* rose from the deck and started forward. It passed through the force field—blue pinpoints of light flaring around it as it did so—and out into space.

As the shuttlecraft dropped out of sight, carrying the captain down to the structure on the surface of Rejarris II, Tenger wondered if he would ever see Demora Sulu alive again.

✦ ✦ ✦

The shuttlecraft leveled off fifty meters above the snow-covered plain and approached the co-ordinates to which the second landing party had transported. Through the forward viewport, Sulu spotted the mysterious structure where Ensign Young had been hurt and contact with him lost, and where Commander Linojj had suffered her grisly injury. The portion of the structure closest to *Amundsen* did not impress the captain—nothing really distinguished it—but as she followed it with her gaze, first in one direction and then the other, she apprehended its great size. *Enterprise*'s sensors had measured it as a ring more than half a kilometer in diameter and two kilometers in circumference, but the gray weather, along with the snow and ash, concealed its farthest reaches as it curled into the distance.

"Initiating sensor scans," said Ensign Kostas, seated beside Sulu at the shuttlecraft's main console. The captain had tasked the engineer with examining the structure and determining its capabilities, particularly with regard to whatever weapons and defenses it might possess. While Kostas analyzed the readings she gathered, Sulu would transmit the collected data to *Enterprise* for further study. She intended to employ what they ascertained to formulate a plan to recover Ensign Young.

Operating the helm, the captain slowed *Amundsen* as they drew nearer the structure. A beam of some kind had fired at Linojj when she'd stood atop it, and the first officer had hypothesized that the same beam might have toppled Young from there to the ground. Sulu would therefore refrain from flying above the structure, unwilling to risk either an attack on the shuttlecraft, or its capture.

"This close to the surface, biosensors appear to be functioning," Kostas said, "but I'm not finding any life signs in the area."

The captain didn't expect any life-form readings. She reasoned that whatever had prevented the signal enhancers from enabling a transport lock on Young likely interfered with sensors as well. They would have to search for the ensign visually. Sulu hadn't yet resolved whether she would attempt that from the shuttlecraft or on the planet surface, on top of the structure. She would base her decision on what she and Kostas learned.

"No life signs, but I am reading power," the ensign said. "It's flowing throughout the structure." Kostas ran her hands across her console, obviously trying to coax additional detail from her instruments. "The power levels are inconsistent, though . . . they're fluctuating."

"According to Crewman Permenter, the structure's been damaged," Sulu said. "Maybe that's why its power is unstable." She brought *Amundsen* to a stop a hundred meters away, where it hovered above the beam-down location of the second landing party. She studied the structure through the forward port, picking out a section that appeared free of snow and ash. "There," she said, pointing. Even at that distance, she could make out a wide cavity in the inner side of the metal.

"I see it," Kostas said. "Targeting sensors."

Sulu locked in *Amundsen*'s position and secured the helm, then stood and paced through the rows of chairs to the rear of the cabin. At the aft bulkhead, she slid open an equipment drawer and pulled out a set of field glasses. She carried it back to her seat and trained it on the damaged section of the structure. "The metal there has been bent and twisted inward," she said. "It's also been scorched black, suggesting a fire or an explosion or possibly an attack with an energy weapon. If it's—"

Sulu abruptly stopped speaking when she saw something beyond the structure, something visible through the rent in the metal. She rose and stepped to the side, seeking a better vantage. When she narrowed the scale of her view from the structure to the patch of ground past it, the field glasses adjusted automatically, bringing that spot into sharp focus. "I see something carved into the ground," she said. "A letter written in Federation Standard."

Beside the captain, Kostas operated her controls. "Sensors don't detect anything like that in the area."

"Sensors don't, but my eyes do," Sulu said. Though she felt certain of what she saw, she set down the field glasses and worked the helm to move the shuttlecraft closer to the structure. When *Amundsen* had covered half the distance, she brought it to a stop again and peered through the field glasses. Having drawn nearer, she looked down at the letter etched into the ground from a steeper angle, seeing it not through the gap where the structure had been torn apart, but out in the open. She saw not just one letter, but many. "It's a message," she said, shifting the field glasses to find the first letter. She read aloud what she saw.

CAUGHT IN GOLD BEAM, PULLED INTO RING, CAN'T—

Past the last word, a man on his hands and knees used the point of a wedge-shaped stone to inscribe another letter into the ground. "It's Ensign Young," Sulu said. She handed the field glasses to Kostas, who raised them to her eyes.

"I see him," she said.

The captain worked the helm controls to push *Amundsen* closer, halving the distance to the structure once again. She remained vigilant for any beams. "Is there any indication that he sees us?"

"No, sir, not that I can tell."

Sulu reached to the communications panel and opened a channel. "*Amundsen* to Ensign Young," she said. "Captain Sulu to Ensign Young."

She waited, but received no response. She considered simply setting the shuttlecraft down beside him, but she did not want to fly over the structure or into the ring it formed without more information. Given the level of technological sophistication the landing parties had observed on the planet, Sulu suspected that *Amundsen* could withstand any attack waged on it from the surface of Rejarris II, but the loss of contact with Young troubled her.

"Is there a way we can visually signal him?" she asked Kostas.

"I take it you mean other than by flying the shuttlecraft right past him."

"Yes."

"We could dump some of our fuel and ignite it," Kostas said, her tentative tone reflecting the brainstorming nature of her idea.

"I'd prefer not to do that," Sulu said. "We might be alone on this planet, but I'd still prefer not to do anything that could seem antagonistic. What about doing something with the shields?"

Kostas appeared to consider that. Finally, she said, "We could overload the power inputs. That would cause the shields to disburse the extra energy as thermal radiation, which would be accompanied by a bright glow."

"Would that damage the shields or the shuttle-craft?" Sulu wanted to know.

"No, sir, I don't think so," Kostas said. She operated the controls on her console, and the captain saw numbers and equations tripping down the ensign's display. "If we increase the power to the shields in a microburst, they'll dissipate it as a rapid flash of heat and light."

"Do it," the captain ordered.

Kostas made the necessary preparations at her console, then moved to the starboard bulkhead. "In order for the microburst to reach the shields, I'll need to temporarily remove the primary and secondary surge protectors from the generators," she said. She detached an access panel, revealing a maze of duotronic circuitry. Kostas reached in and pulled out a pair of translucent, prism-shaped components and set them on the deck.

When the ensign returned to her seat, she said, "I'm not sure how bright the flash will be, but we should avert our eyes." Sulu turned and faced the aft end of the compartment. "I'm ready on your command, Captain."

"Go."

"It will take a few seconds for the power to build up," Kostas said. "Initiating now." Sulu heard her tap a control surface, and then the ensign turned away from the forward port.

Seconds passed, and Sulu began to think that nothing would happen, but then the cabin began to brighten. She saw her shadow projected onto the deck beside that of Kostas, and then the light flared brilliantly. A loud bang shook the cabin before the lighting returned to normal.

"I'm sorry, Captain," Kostas said. "I should've anticipated that. The heating of the air around the shields caused a rapid expansion of the neighboring atmosphere, which led to a sonic boom."

"It's all right, Ensign," Sulu said, turning back to her console and picking up the field glasses. "As long as the shuttlecraft stayed in one piece." The captain looked out again at Ensign Young. He remained on his hands and knees, chipping away at the ground. Neither the flash of light nor the thunderclap caused by the shields had attracted his attention. "He can't see or hear us," Sulu concluded. "The question we have to answer is: why?"

Kostas moved back over to the open bulkhead, replaced the shield surge protectors, and set the access panel back in place. "What if we tried to land near him?" she asked.

Sulu wondered the same thing, the appeal of such an action strong. But the power coursing through the structure, the beam it had fired toward

Linojj, and the resistance of its interior to transporter locks and sensors concerned her. "For now, continue your scans and try to determine the purpose of that thing out there," she said. "If we wait for Ensign Young to complete his message, maybe he'll provide us with some useful information."

As Kostas worked the sensors, the captain observed Young through the field glasses. He had completed another word—SEE—and begun engraving another. She hoped that once he told them what he couldn't see, it would shed some light on his predicament.

Movement suddenly caught Sulu's eye, a dark shape that had darted behind Young. Only then did she note that the ensign threw a long shadow on the ground, as did the rocks and boulders around him. Outside the structure, the unbroken cloud cover scattered the sunlight, washing everything in a dull cast devoid of shade, but somehow, around Young, Rejarris shined. She noticed then that he had removed his jacket, though she didn't see it anywhere about him.

Sulu slid a fingertip across a control on her field glasses, widening their view. She saw, behind the ensign, an area of rock projecting from the soil, surrounded by boulders and smaller stones. As Sulu inspected the area, one of the boulders moved, shifting upward as though pushed from below, but then falling back into place. Its shadow jumped up and down along with it, which must have been what she'd seen.

The boulder did not remain still, but jerked

upward more violently. It teetered and seemed to balance precariously for an instant, then toppled onto its side. Beneath where it had stood yawned a dark pit. As Sulu watched, a long, tubular black shape rose from within, its tip barbed. What followed looked like something out of a nightmare. Ten multiply articulated legs emerged spiderlike from the hole and lifted the rest of the beast out into the daylight. At the end of a long, twisted neck, a triangular head tapered to a blunt snout. Two large elliptical eyes glistened as though with sinister intent. A pocked, cylindrical body rose up next, spines protruding from it and curving backward, and a flat, spade-shaped tail trailed behind it. Its wrinkled black flesh looked like old leather. It stood almost as tall as Young, but its many limbs made it appear twice his size.

The ensign whirled around when the boulder crashed to the dirt, and when he saw the creature, he reached around to the back of his waist. Sulu could not see the object he took in his hand, but the pose he assumed told her that he had drawn his phaser. The threat made no discernible impact on the creature, which moved toward him with lightning speed. Young fired once, but too late. A red-tinged yellow beam blazed into the creature, but did not appear to even slow it down. With its spiked front appendage, it swatted the weapon from the ensign's hand. The creature struck Young, its head impacting with his chest, sending him flying backward from his feet.

Sulu flung the field glasses to the deck and punched new commands into the helm. "Something's attacking Ensign Young," she told Kostas as the shuttlecraft shot forward. The captain sent *Amundsen* into a dive. Through the port, she could see the creature climbing atop Ensign Young. "Get our phasers," she said, and Kostas immediately raced from her seat.

Sulu brought the shuttlecraft in low over the structure, hoping to startle the creature and scare it away. From somewhere up ahead and somewhere to starboard, two expanding gold beams streaked into *Amundsen*. The shuttlecraft juddered, and Sulu read on her panel the drag placed on its forward momentum. Two more beams appeared and slammed into *Amundsen*, but one quickly sputtered and died.

Kostas returned and leaned in over her console, gripping it in order to keep her balance in the shaking cabin. "They're tractor beams," she said, obviously consulting the sensor display. Sulu ignored the beams, keeping the shuttlecraft at speed. "They seem to be trying to direct us downward," Kostas said.

"That's where we're going anyway," Sulu said, even as the cabin suddenly stilled.

"The tractor beams have stopped," Kostas said.

As *Amundsen* swooped in low over the creature, Sulu saw it turn its oddly shaped head skyward. It stood over Young. The ensign struggled beneath it, fighting against some of its many limbs holding him down.

"Brace yourself," Sulu said. She put the shuttlecraft down hard, and she heard Kostas grunt beside her. The captain reached toward the ensign, steadied her, then held out an open hand. "Phaser," she said, and Kostas slapped a weapon into her palm—not the smaller, concealable type-1, but the type-2 pistol model. Then Sulu raced for the hatch, where she jabbed at the controls set into the bulkhead. The hatch glided open.

Ten meters away, Young scrabbled backward along the ground, away from the creature. It pursued him, the motion of its many limbs like some sort of awkward, frenetic dance. It clapped two of its ten legs down on the ensign's feet, then clambered forward and secured his hands. The creature's front appendage rose and hovered high in the air, its spiked tip aimed downward, as though about to strike and impale the supine form of Ensign Young.

Sulu fired. She didn't even wait to jump to the ground, but raised her phaser and pressed its trigger from inside *Amundsen*. The beam streaked from her weapon and caught the creature square in its cylindrical body. It lurched to one side, several of its legs coming off the ground, but it did not let go of Young.

The captain leaped from the shuttlecraft, past the port engine nacelle, and onto the ground. As she aimed her phaser again, Kostas alighted beside her. The creature struck at Young, bringing the point of its front appendage straight down at him.

"Fire," Sulu told Kostas, and together they loosed the might of their energy weapons. The creature reeled under the combined firepower and issued a feral cry—whether of pain or confusion, of fear or anger, Sulu couldn't tell.

But then the creature pivoted swiftly and fixed Sulu and Kostas with the gaze of its massive oval eyes. It reared up, its front four legs lifting high into the air, and it roared, the sound from its snout guttural and primitive. On the ground beside the creature, Ensign Young didn't move.

Sulu held up her phaser for Kostas to see, then adjusted it to its highest stun setting. The ensign followed her lead and reset her own weapon. When the creature brought its front legs back down and charged at them, they fired in tandem.

The beams both landed, but the creature dodged to one side. The phaser blasts slowed it, but still it moved with surprising speed for a beast its size and that looked so ungainly. Its long multi-jointed legs ate up the distance to the shuttlecraft in large tracts. The captain judged that she and Kostas had one chance to save themselves.

"Next level," she yelled as she increased the force of her phaser, setting it to kill. She didn't wait to see if Kostas had heard her over the creature's roar, but once more raised her weapon and fired. An instant later, the ensign's beam joined hers.

The creature screamed. It stumbled, one of its legs missing a step and dragging along the ground. Its legs tangled and it went down hard, its head smashing into the ground face-first, its body skidding along the earth.

The captain reached out and shoved Kostas in the arm. The ensign staggered to the side and her phaser beam ceased, but Sulu continued to fire, wanting to ensure the creature's incapacitation. She tried to time her escape, but waited a second too long. As she stopped firing and threw herself to the side, the creature crashed into the shuttle-craft. The end of one of its legs lashed across Sulu's hip and rammed her against *Amundsen*'s hull. Her elbow struck and her entire lower arm went numb, while pain flashed hot in her right side.

Sulu collapsed to her knees, her body doubled over the creature's thick, muscular leg that had pinned her against the shuttlecraft. She didn't know the creature's status—dazed, unconscious, or dead—but she felt no movement where its leg touched her. She could feel the heat of its leathery hide, though, could smell its sweat. She gagged, but managed not to vomit.

"Captain," a voice called as though from far away, and Sulu realized that she felt light-headed. She didn't know if she had struck her skull against *Amundsen*, but she guessed that she must have. She didn't want to lose consciousness, not outside with a predatory creature that might still be alive.

Even if it's dead, Sulu thought, *where there was one, there will be others.*

"Captain," a voice said again, and that time, Sulu recognized it as belonging to Ensign Kostas. Sulu looked up to see the engineer coming around the unmoving body of the creature. "Captain, are you hurt?"

"I'm banged up, but I think I'll be all right," Sulu said. "Help get me out of here." She pushed at the creature's heavy leg, and Kostas reached her arms around it, dug her heels into the ground, and pulled. It moved a few centimeters at a time at first, before finally dropping from Sulu's waist and onto the ground. "Thanks," she said around deep breaths of air. She gazed about and realized that she could not see the officer they had come to rescue. "How's Ensign Young?"

"I don't know," Kostas said. "He wasn't moving, but I came to check on you first."

"I'll be all right," Sulu said again. "Get a medkit and tend to Mister Young."

"Yes, sir." The ensign hesitated, though, and then said, "Captain, I don't think you should stay here beside this thing."

"Believe me, I won't," Sulu said. "None of us will. Now, go."

Kostas looked past the captain toward the open hatch of *Amundsen*. The creature blocked the way, and the ensign had to climb over one of its legs to board the shuttlecraft. Sulu stepped away, leaning heavily against the hull. She eyed the creature warily, then called to the ensign to bring her a tricorder.

Kostas reappeared quickly. She handed the captain the tricorder she'd requested, then jumped down past the creature and made her way around it, toward Ensign Young. Sulu took a couple of slow, deep breaths in an attempt to regain her bearings. Finally, she activated her tricorder and scanned the creature. She recognized only some of what she saw inside it, but it appeared to have both circulatory and respiratory systems, neither of which showed any movement: the creature was dead.

Sulu expanded the range of the sensors and scanned the area, both above- and belowground. She read life-forms—from microorganisms, to worms, to bugs, to several small animals—but nothing remotely resembling the one that had attacked them. Satisfied about the immediate safety of the landing party, she padded slowly around the carcass of the creature.

As the captain stepped past its flat, stationary tail, the two ensigns came into view. Young lay on his back, while Kostas kneeled beside him, ministering to whatever injuries he'd suffered. Sulu saw his chest rising and falling steadily, which pleased her, though she saw no other movement. When she drew closer, she saw Young's eyes closed. She also saw a great deal of blood.

"What's his condition?" she asked.

"He's been hurt badly," Kostas said without looking up. She had set her own tricorder down on the ground, as well as the medkit, from which she extracted a small pair of scissors. She used them to cut off Young's uniform shirt around the front of his right shoulder, revealing a fifteen-centimeter gash. "I think that thing did this," Kostas said. "It's deep, but fortunately it didn't reach his lung. His hand has also been slashed, and he's got some damage in his other shoulder; it appears that he dislocated it at some point, but pushed it back into place himself."

"That might have happened when he fell," Sulu said, and she gazed up at the structure.

Except that there was no structure.

Sulu thought that she must have become disoriented after striking her head, and so she turned and looked all around her. She saw only a vast, rocky landscape beneath a setting orange-red sun. No structure. No snow or ash.

"Can Ensign Young be moved?" Sulu asked.

"Once I stabilize his shoulder," Kostas said. "I have to clean and dress both his wounds, but the key will be to keep his shoulder from tearing open further. That's about all I can do. He's going to need surgery."

"Do the best you can, Ensign, and do it as quickly as you can," Sulu said. She peered out over the empty plain, at the clouds scudding across a cerulean sky, and she wondered precisely where and when they were. "I think we might be in trouble."

4

"**C**ommander, sensors are showing two energy surges at the structure," said Lieutenant Rainbow Sky.

Tenger—*Enterprise*'s chief of security and, in the absence of Demora Sulu and Xintal Linojj, the ship's acting captain—rotated the command chair to face the Native American officer crewing the tactical station. "Can you tell the nature of the surges?" he asked. Captain Sulu had arrived at the planet's surface aboard *Amundsen* only a few minutes earlier, and already Tenger's concerns for her welfare grew.

Rainbow Sky's hands gamboled across the tactical console with speed and grace, eliciting a series of chirps and tones in response. "The surges originated at different points on the structure," he said. "Energy beams of some kind are firing on the shuttlecraft, and . . . I'm reading a third beam now . . . and a fourth."

Tenger looked to Lieutenant Commander Kanchumurthi at the communications station. "Open a channel to *Amundsen*." As the comm officer worked his panel, Tenger stabbed at the controls on the arm of the command chair. "Bridge to transporter room."

"*Transporter room,*" came the coarse voice of Lieutenant Ved. "*Go ahead, Commander.*"

"Establish transporter locks on Captain Sulu and Ensign Kostas aboard *Amundsen*," Tenger said. "Prepare for emergency beam-out."

"*Yes, sir. Right away.*"

"Channel open to *Amundsen*," Kanchumurthi said.

Tenger tapped a second control. "*Enterprise* to Captain Sulu."

"Commander," said Rainbow Sky, urgency in his voice. "*Amundsen* just fell off sensors."

Tenger didn't hesitate. "Transporter room, energize." He waited, knowing that it was already too late. A few seconds later, Lieutenant Ved confirmed it.

"*Bridge, this is the transporter room,*" he said. "*Emergency beam-out failed. I established transporter locks, but lost them just before the order to energize. Subsequent attempts to reacquire the locks have been unsuccessful.*"

"Acknowledged," Tenger said. "Keep trying, Lieutenant."

"*Yes, sir.*"

"Bridge out." Tenger rose from the command chair and climbed the steps beside the tactical console. He could feel the tension mounting among his crewmates, so he asked loudly enough for all of them to hear the question to which they all needed an answer. "Was the shuttlecraft destroyed?"

"No, sir, not that I can tell," Rainbow Sky said. "Sensors did not pick up any indications of an explosion or a crash."

"What about the beams?" Tenger wanted to know. "Could they be masking the shuttlecraft?"

"I don't think so," Rainbow Sky said. "For one thing, they've stopped. For another, I could read the shuttlecraft even after the beams started, and their intensity didn't increase while they lasted. In fact, one of the beams, the last one, failed almost immediately."

Tenger tried to consider all of the possibilities. "Could they have been transporter beams? Could they have beamed *Amundsen* away?"

"They didn't read like that," Rainbow Sky said. "Plus the infrastructure on the planet and the level of technology suggest that the native population hadn't yet developed transporters."

"That's not categorical, though," Tenger said. "And we're not that sure of our facts. The structure is isolated from every settlement on the planet, so it's possible that it might not even be of indigenous origin."

"Still, they didn't read like a transporter," Rainbow Sky said. "If anything, they resembled tractor beams, although I saw fluctuations in them, which you wouldn't expect from a directional force."

Tenger glanced at the tactical display, where a readout showed a line rendering of the structure and *Amundsen* above it. "Where did the sensors lose contact with the shuttlecraft?"

"Here," Rainbow Sky said, pointing to an area inside the ring. "Very close to where Ensign Young fell from the structure."

"What was *Amundsen*'s altitude when it dropped from our scans?" Tenger asked.

Rainbow Sky touched several controls in a short sequence. The image on the display changed, rotating from a vertical view to a horizontal one. Seen through the linear representation of the structure, the shuttlecraft flew not very far above the ground. "Between seven and eight meters."

"They were landing," Tenger said, more to himself than to Rainbow Sky. "They were landing, and they were going to come down inside the structure. When Ensign Young fell into the structure, we lost contact with him, even though Commander Linojj could still see him."

"Do you think the shuttlecraft is still down there, and that we simply can't communicate with the captain?" Rainbow Sky asked.

"Perhaps," Tenger said. "Captain Sulu might have landed *Amundsen* in an attempt to retrieve the ensign."

"Meaning that the shuttlecraft could reappear at any time," Rainbow Sky said, "once the captain recovers Ensign Young and starts back to the ship."

"Perhaps," Tenger said again, though he suspected that a resolution would not prove quite so simple. "Monitor that area on sensors for any sign of *Amundsen*."

"Aye, sir."

Tenger considered how best to proceed. One thing seemed abundantly clear to him: with three crew members—including Captain Sulu—out of touch on Rejarris II, and a fourth in sickbay with a missing limb, the security chief would refuse to send anybody else down to the structure, either by transporter or shuttlecraft. "How long before the probe reaches the structure?" The captain had ordered the probe to the site when the crew had first discovered the unexplained object.

Rainbow Sky checked his console. "Twenty-five minutes, sir."

"All right," Tenger said, stepping back down from the outer ring of the bridge. "I want to see images the moment the probe is in position." He sat in the command chair, wondering what those images would show. He expected to see *Amundsen* intact on the surface of the planet, inside the structure, and to verify that Captain Sulu and the others had survived. If so, he and the crew would need to figure out how to get them back to *Enterprise*, and before that, how to communicate with them.

About the latter, Tenger already had an idea.

From where she sat at *Amundsen*'s main console, Sulu looked over her shoulder to the starboard aft corner of the cabin, where she and Kostas had moved away the chairs in favor of an antigrav stretcher. As she watched, the engineer-cum-medic finished securing the portable cot to the bulkhead. After the ensign had treated Young's injuries as best she could, Sulu had returned to the shuttlecraft so that she could position it closer to the wounded man. Before moving *Amundsen*, though, the captain had attempted to contact *Enterprise*, without result.

Once Sulu had relocated the shuttlecraft, she and Kostas had deployed the stretcher. They carefully shifted Young onto it, then carried him aboard. He remained unconscious by virtue of a sedative.

Kostas walked back to the front of the cabin and sat beside Sulu. "We're all set, sir."

"Good. I've programmed a course that follows in reverse the shuttlecraft's precise movements, not just once we reached the planet's surface, but all the way from orbit," Sulu explained. "I'm not sure if the structure is still out there and we just can't see it or scan it, if it's disguised somehow, or if our perceptions are somehow being altered or manipulated, but I want to retrace our route to see if we can get back to the *Enterprise* that way."

In truth, Sulu suspected something entirely different. While Kostas had been tending to Young outside the shuttlecraft, the captain had turned toward the section of the structure closest to them—toward where she remembered that section to be—and she'd begun walking. She moved carefully, with one hand held up, palm out, in front of her chest. She estimated the distance of their location from the structure at between ten and twenty meters. She turned back once she'd gone fifty.

"While we're close to the surface, scan for the structure," Sulu told Kostas. "Once we're in orbit, look for the *Enterprise*."

"Yes, sir."

The captain executed a standard safety checklist, then lifted off. *Amundsen* rose only a short distance, then glided back to where it had first touched down. It landed beside the dead creature, then launched again. As the shuttlecraft reached the point where the gold beams had shot toward it, Sulu saw Kostas brace herself with a hand to the edge of her console. The captain didn't bother, and the moment passed without incident.

Sulu kept her attention on the view through the forward port. She hoped to see the structure suddenly reappear, to see a broad plain mantled in the off-white mixture of snow and ash, but as *Amundsen* traveled outward to twenty-five meters, and then to fifty, and finally to a hundred, she thought that less and less likely. Instead, she glimpsed a nearby mountain range she hadn't seen on the journey down from *Enterprise*, covered in what looked like old-growth trees, something completely missing from the impact-winter landscape they'd to that point observed on Rejarris II.

As the shuttlecraft gained altitude, the captain hailed *Enterprise*. She made multiple attempts. She received no reply. When Sulu at last stopped, Ensign Kostas spoke into the ensuing silence.

"Captain, there's no continuous cloud cover," she said quietly. "The continent below us has mature vegetation and a different coastline than our probes mapped. Gravity—" Her voice dropped to a whisper when she uttered the word, as though she wanted to hide what she intended to say—perhaps not from Sulu so much as from herself. "The planet's gravity is ten-point-two-nine meters per second squared. The *Enterprise*'s sensors recorded it as nine-point-six."

"Ensign," Sulu said, "I don't think that's Rejarris Two below us anymore."

"No, sir," Kostas replied, the resignation in her voice not quite masking a hint of fear. "But how? And where are we?"

"I don't know where we are," Sulu said, "but I think that the structure acted as a gateway. When we descended into it to rescue Ensign Young, we passed into another place."

"But then why didn't we return to Rejarris Two when we flew back up?" Kostas asked.

"I don't know, Ensign," Sulu said. "The best theory I can formulate is that the gateway physically displaces items that pass through it into another location, to wherever we are now. But the gateway doesn't exist here, only on Rejarris Two, so we have no means of returning there."

"Then how are we going to get back to the *Enterprise*?"

"Ensign, what I just told you is only a theory, so the first thing we're going to do is test it," Sulu said. "That means achieving orbit and searching for the *Enterprise*. It might be that our initial readings of Rejarris Two were inaccurate, that our senses and sensors were somehow deceived. If that's the case, then the *Enterprise* might still be circling the planet."

"Yes, sir," Kostas said. She sounded unconvinced.

They continued their journey in *Amundsen*, mostly in silence. Kostas regularly checked on the status of Ensign Young, whose condition she continued to report as unchanged. The captain periodically attempted to raise *Enterprise*, never successfully.

Once the shuttlecraft achieved orbit, Kostas scanned for the starship. Sensors could not find *Enterprise*, although they did detect the same neutrino trail embedded in subspace that Tenger and Fenn had earlier. Sulu didn't know what to make of that, but it seemed to her too significant a reading to discount as coincidence. It probably meant that the same starship had visited both Rejarris II and the planet below—and they did seem to be two different worlds, considering that two moons circled the former, and Sulu and Kostas could find none revolving around the latter. Neither could they locate any of the artificial satellites that had been orbiting Rejarris II.

"Why?" Kostas asked.

"Why what, Ensign?" Sulu asked.

"Why would anybody construct a gateway that operated only in one direction?" she asked. She sounded frustrated, but the captain also suspected that the young officer worried about being stranded in an unknown place, with no means of getting home.

"Perhaps they didn't have the time or the knowledge to build a two-way gateway," Sulu suggested. "Or perhaps they only needed to travel in one direction."

The ensign's eyes widened in sudden understanding. "The asteroid," she said.

"Yes," Sulu agreed. "Maybe the people of Rejarris Two knew that an asteroid was headed for the world and that the collision would have a devastating effect, not only on the people it killed directly, but on all those left behind to endure an impact winter. They didn't have warp capability, but maybe they discovered another way to escape the pending disaster."

"But then where are they?" Kostas asked.

"I don't know," the captain said, "but on our way back down to the surface, scan for life signs."

"We're heading back down to the planet?"

"At the moment," Sulu said, "we have nowhere else to go."

Amid the tension pervading the bridge, Rafaele Buonarroti felt out of place at the first officer's station, even though he'd reconfigured half of it as an engineering panel. He'd certainly crewed the exec's console before—had done so on numerous occasions—but never as the result of such disastrous circumstances, with Captain Sulu missing and Commander Linojj so terribly wounded. Consequently, when he peered at the image on the main viewscreen, he couldn't contain his reaction. *"Cosa nell'universo è?"* he said: *What in the universe is that?*

"The probe's sensors are unable to read anything on the ground inside the ring of the structure other than ash and snow," said Borona Fenn from her position at the sciences station.

"Not to point out the obvious," said Gaia Aldani at navigation, "but there's no snow or ash visible anywhere that I can see except *outside* of the structure."

Buonarroti studied the scene on the viewer, transmitted to *Enterprise* from a probe dispatched to observe Rejarris II inside its cloud cover. The chief engineer realized that he hadn't even noticed the lack of the mixed accumulation within the structure, so focused had he been on the black beast in the center of the screen. He did note, however, that he saw neither the shuttlecraft nor any members of the landing parties—including Demora Sulu. "Is that a projection we're seeing, then?" he wondered aloud. "Are we looking at an image created by the structure, maybe to hide what's actually there?"

Fenn operated the probe's sensors. "Nothing I see substantiates that," she said.

"I agree," said Rainbow Sky at tactical. "The structure is under power, but I do not detect anything like a visual projection. Even if an attempt were being made to hide something from view, though, our sensors are reading what is actually there."

"Unless that too is a deception," Buonarroti said, although he immediately saw the illogic of such a scheme, which Fenn quickly spelled out.

"If that were the case, why wouldn't the two false images—the one presented to our eyes and the one presented to our scans—why wouldn't they match?" she said. "It wouldn't make sense to hide something by presenting two illusory images, when the very inconsistency of them would demonstrate that at least one of them must be false."

"There is no deception," Tenger said, his tone certain. He stood from the command chair and moved to the center of the bridge. "Commander

Fenn, magnify the area that includes the many-legged animal, out to a distance of ten meters all around it."

"Aye, sir."

On the viewer, light-blue lines drew a rectangle about the designated area, which then expanded to fill the screen. The beast looked to Buonarroti as though some mad scientist had grafted spider and porcupine DNA onto that of a rhinoceros, then covered the result in black paint. He found it hideous. Since the probe had maneuvered into position above the structure and transmitted a live feed of it to *Enterprise*, nobody on the bridge had seen the beast move, and yet its still form unsettled Buonarroti.

Tenger circled the helm, climbed to the outer part of the bridge, and strode to the main viewer. He stood for a moment with his muscular arms folded across his burly chest and examined the image on the screen, then pointed to a section of the ground beside the beast. "What do you make of this?" he asked, apparently addressing everybody present.

Buonarroti rose and walked past the outer stations until he reached Tenger. He inspected the screen until he saw what the tactical officer had indicated: a long, straight-edged depression in the soil, slightly rounded at its extremities, with a perpendicular series of narrow V-shaped grooves toward one end. Up close, Buonarroti recognized it at once. "That's the imprint of a shuttlecraft engine nacelle."

"I believe it is," Tenger said, and he gestured

to a second depression parallel to the first, just visible near the bottom of the screen and not quite as easily discerned. Seen together, the markings could hardly be mistaken for anything but the artifacts of a Starfleet planetary shuttlecraft.

"Can you provide a scale for these?" the chief engineer asked Fenn.

"Because sensors are reading something different than what we see at that location, I can only establish an approximate scale," Fenn said. "I can base it on the assumption that the altitude of the probe is the same above both the ground that the sensors detect and the ground that we see." A distance gauge appeared at the bottom left-hand corner of the screen, and blue lines traced the linear measurements of the two indentations.

"Those are the right dimensions," Buonarroti said. "The shuttlecraft did land there."

"But why isn't it still there?" asked Torsten Syndergaard at the helm.

"Because Captain Sulu and Ensign Kostas presumably recovered Ensign Young," Tenger said, "after which they attempted to return to the *Enterprise.*"

"'*Attempted* to return'?" Buonarroti said.

"Clearly they have not returned to the ship," Tenger said, "nor have we detected them in orbit or received any messages from them. Considering everything that the crew have seen, scanned, and experienced, I have concluded that the structure is a portal of some kind."

"Yes," Fenn agreed. "A *unidirectional* portal."

"Yes," Tenger said.

"So you're saying that Ensign Young fell from atop the structure, or was pulled from it, and passed into another place?" Buonarroti asked.

"Into another place or another time," Tenger said. "Or perhaps both."

Buonarroti considered whether the captain and the other members of the crew might have been displaced to another part of the planet, but then discounted the possibility. If they had ended up elsewhere on Rejarris II, they surely would have contacted *Enterprise*. Also, although the substrate in the planet's soil interfered with biosensors, the probes had still made a visual record of every area over which they flew, and none of them had observed any large animal life, and especially nothing like the beast currently visible on the main screen, all of which bolstered the argument that the landscape they could see within the structure did not exist on the world they orbited. Tenger's theory also made something else clear. "The one-way nature of the portal explains why none of our three missing crew have returned."

"It might also explain Commander Linojj's injury," Fenn said. "If she reached her arm through the portal, past the threshold that marks the transition between one place and another, and then she tried to pull it back . . ." The science officer did not finish expressing the gruesome thought.

"What are we going to do?" Ramesh Kanchumurthi asked at communications. In response, Tenger turned toward Buonarroti, and the chief engineer understood why.

"If the portal functions in one direction, then

we may be able to make it function in two," Buonarroti said. "Or we might be able to reverse its flow."

"Once you begun studying the device, choose the course that seems most quickly achievable," Tenger said.

"Right," Buonarroti said. "Can we transport an engineering team down, or should we use another shuttlecraft?"

"Neither," Tenger said. "Until we have a solution, I will not risk losing any other members of the crew."

"Meaning we'll have to use ship's sensors and those of the probes to analyze the guts of that thing," Buonarroti said. "I'll probably need Commander Fenn and some of her people. This is likely to be as much a scientific problem as it will be an engineering one."

"All the resources of the *Enterprise* are at your disposal," Tenger said.

Buonarroti thought about the enormous size of the device—essentially a tube fourteen meters in diameter stretched into a ring more than two kilometers long. He took some solace in the idea that the inhabitants of Rejarris II had reached a level of technological sophistication far short of the Federation. Still, if the portal possessed more than even a small fraction of unique components, it could take more than a few days or weeks, and more than the complement of a single starship, for the *Enterprise* crew to achieve their goal. Buonarroti didn't bother to mention that to Tenger, who surely understood the complexity of the situation and would undoubtedly point out that the sooner their efforts began, the closer they would be to retrieving the captain and the two ensigns. In his position as the ship's security chief, Tenger often acted with a dedication to poise and logic almost Vulcan-like in its consistency.

"Sir, until we have a means of altering the portal," Aldani asked, "what about the captain and the others?"

Though he said nothing, Buonarroti wondered if the missing crew members were all still alive. The second landing party had not mentioned seeing the beast, meaning that it had entered the area around the time that Captain Sulu had taken *Amundsen* down to the surface. Its motionless body suggested a battle that the shuttlecraft crew and Ensign Young had won, but at what cost?

"Since circumstances have brought us to this conclusion, I assume that they will bring Captain Sulu and Ensigns Young and Kostas to the same conclusion," Tenger said. "Since they have actually passed through the portal, though, they may possess additional information about it that would be of use to us in devising their return to the *Enterprise*."

"But . . . what difference does that make if the portal functions in only one direction?" Syndergaard asked. Buonarroti wondered the same thing.

"It does not function *entirely* in one direction, a fact we have all witnessed," Tenger said. "Because of that, I intend to have a conversation with Captain Sulu."

✦ ✦ ✦

Amundsen glided in over the mountains and across the rocky plain, all of it awash in the pink glow of a gathering dusk. As on the shuttlecraft's journey into orbit, Sulu had programmed their course to match its previous movements between earth and sky. She had no specific reason for doing so, other than the uncertainty of the situation.

"Scans are showing the carcass of the creature just ahead," Kostas said. "It does not appear to have moved."

"Thank you, Ensign," Sulu said. She felt relieved at the information, not because the creature hadn't somehow come back from the dead and scrambled away, but because she'd feared that they wouldn't be able to locate the area to which the gateway had sent them, that somehow their setting had changed again. "I'm going to land in the area," she told Kostas, "but beside the message Ensign Young etched, rather than next to the creature." She worked the helm to alter the end of their flight plan. As she did, a warning klaxon blared to life in the cabin.

"Proximity alert," announced Kostas. The ensign quickly quieted the alarm. "There's something moving up ahead of us." Once they had returned to *Amundsen* after battling the creature, Sulu had ordered Kostas to set the sensors to notify them of any significant motion within three kilometers of the shuttlecraft. "Scanning," the ensign said. "It's near our landing site. Near the body of the creature."

As Sulu waited for more information, an indicator brightened on her console, accompanied by an alert tone. "We're receiving an incoming transmission," she said.

"From who?" Kostas asked, perplexity blended with excitement in her voice. Sulu shared her confusion; they hadn't been able to communicate with Young through the gateway, nor had they been able to raise the ship once they'd followed the ensign, and so they'd inferred such contact impossible.

Sulu checked the provenance of the message before accepting it. "It's on a Starfleet emergency channel," she said. "It's carrying a starship identification marker on it: it's from the *Enterprise*."

"They must have modified the gateway," Kostas said, her bewilderment apparently dying away. "Maybe we can travel back through it now."

"I don't think we can leap to that conclusion," Sulu said as she continued to evaluate the message. She checked its transmission source, which confirmed her suspicions. "This is being sent by a log buoy."

"Do you think something happened to the *Enterprise*?" Kostas asked, clearly concerned. The crews of Starfleet vessels employed log buoys when circumstances prevented them from using their ship's communications system while facing the impending capture or destruction of their starship.

"No, I think the ship is fine," Sulu said. "I think that the crew have made the same determination that we have, that the structure is a gateway, and they sent the buoy through as a means of contacting us."

Kostas worked the sensor panel. "Scans confirm that the movement up ahead was a log buoy setting down."

Sulu accepted the transmission and turned to her left, to a display set into the port bulkhead. The skewed chevron of the Starfleet emblem appeared briefly, replaced by the olive-green face of Tenger. He sat at the desk in her office. Behind him, visible through a large port, the taupe form of Rejarris II spun slowly on its axis.

"*Captain, I am recording this message for transfer to a log buoy, which I intend to send down to the planet and into the interior of the structure there,*" the security chief said. "*I am hopeful that you, Ensign Kostas, and Ensign Young are in good health. During your approach to the structure, sensor scans showed multiple energy surges, and we detected beams fired at* Amundsen. *We immediately attempted to establish transporter locks on you and Ensign Kostas, but were unable to do so. The shuttlecraft then vanished from sensors.*"

Tenger exhibited the same professional demeanor he always did, but the captain thought she could perceive anxiety in him. Although the ship's second officer, he'd rarely commanded the ship in times of crisis, since Sulu and Linojj seldom left *Enterprise* simultaneously. The captain didn't think his unease the result of the sudden demands placed upon him, though, but of his concern for his four colleagues, two of whom she counted as close friends; Sulu and Linojj had been Tenger's crewmates for more than a decade.

"*When we could not reach you,*" Tenger went on, "*we continued with our plan to send a probe to the structure in order to study it visually. We can presently see the imprints of* Amundsen's *en-*

gine nacelles in the ground, though we cannot see the shuttlecraft. We have formed the opinion that the structure is actually a spatial or temporal portal that has conveyed Ensign Young, Ensign Kostas, and you to another space or time." Sulu hadn't considered the possibility that the gateway might have sent her and the others into the past or the future. *"We also believe that the portal functions in only one direction, though this is in part based upon our assumption that you tried unsuccessfully to return through it aboard the shuttlecraft, a fact we need you to confirm or refute."*

Sulu wondered just how Tenger thought she could do that, considering the one-direction nature of the gateway and their inability to establish a communications channel between *Amundsen* and *Enterprise*. *Does he want me to use semaphores?* she thought caustically. She then realized that she actually could do that—or at least something like it.

"Commander Buonarroti is currently leading an engineering team in evaluating the sensor readings and images of the portal, with the intention of learning how to modify it to allow us to safely retrieve you. Commander Fenn is likewise guiding a scientific team to find those answers. If there is any information you can provide from your perspective, it could aid us in our efforts."

The captain would inform the *Enterprise* crew that the gateway—or the portal, as Tenger called it—did not exist in the place and time to which she and the ensigns had been delivered, thus confirming its one-way operation. Other than that, she didn't know what she and Kostas could tell them that would assist with their rescue attempt. *But maybe*, it suddenly occurred to her, *they could find a means of procuring such information.*

Tenger's message continued. "*We have appended to this transmission a program that will allow you to record a message on a padd that will then be translated into text and continuously scrolled across the display. It will also transcribe sensor readings. If you return the shuttlecraft to its previous location and place the padd atop it in scrolling mode, the probe above the portal will allow us to read your message.*"

Sulu thought the proposed method an inelegant yet likely effective solution to resolve their inability to communicate normally through the portal. She also noted that Tenger referred to the shuttlecraft's previous location, singular, but she had landed *Amundsen* in two separate places: in the area beside which the creature lay dead, and the area beside where Ensign Young had begun to carve out his own message. She thought that meant that the *Enterprise* crew probably hadn't seen the ensign's improvised communiqué, perhaps because it had been swallowed by late-afternoon shadows. Sulu would therefore inform them of the words Young had so painstakingly engraved.

"Excuse me, Captain," Kostas said, and Sulu reached forward to pause the security chief's message. "We've almost reached the landing point."

Sulu confirmed their location and course on the helm panel, then glanced through the forward viewport. Up ahead, the unmoving form of the creature sprawled across the landscape. Since last they had seen it, its legs had splayed out across the ground about it, like a visual representation of its life force slipping away. Beside it sat the *Enterprise* log buoy, a cylinder sitting on a three-legged base, with a bright green light blinking atop it.

The captain pulled the shuttlecraft from the flight plan she'd laid in and engaged manual control. She spotted the message Young had chiseled into the ground and landed beside it. *Amundsen* settled with a reassuringly solid thud.

"Any other movement out there, Ensign?" Sulu asked.

"No, sir," Kostas said.

The captain resumed the playback of Tenger's message. *"It is possible that the portal has sent you to a present-day location in a neighboring star system, or within starship range of the Federation—or even to a world within the Federation itself. If such is the case, then we will abandon our rescue efforts and transmit a message to Starfleet Command so that the* Enterprise *or another vessel can be sent to retrieve you. You may be able to ascertain your position by analyzing the star patterns where you are."*

Sulu had already performed such an analysis when she and Kostas had taken the shuttlecraft into orbit in search of *Enterprise*. The computer had been unable to match any location within the Milky Way that had the starfield surrounding the planet. Wherever the portal had sent them, it had not been close to home.

"At the present time, Captain, I am not permitting anybody else to travel down to the surface of

Rejarris Two, either by transporter or shuttlecraft. I may have to revisit that decision should a solution require a hands-on modification to the portal. Until then, we will work aboard the Enterprise *to figure out a means of bringing you and the other crew members back to the ship. If you require any supplies, please let us know and we will send them through the portal to you."*

"At least we won't die of thirst or starve to death," Kostas said wryly. The ensign's half-smile pleased Sulu, who'd seen earlier that the reality of being marooned far from *Enterprise* and the Federation filled Kostas with dread.

"I will provide a status report to you every two hours," Tenger said. *"The* Enterprise *carries only two more log buoys, after which time we will have to modify probes to carry our messages to you. It will take some time to exhaust those, but if necessary, we can begin transporting down encoded padds to a point just above the portal, with the expectation that gravity will then conduct them to you. We will maintain a continuous vigil on the shuttlecraft once it comes into view of the probe, so that you can relay a message to the ship at any time."* The security chief paused, as though searching for more to say. Finally, he ended the transmission with a simple, *"Tenger out."*

When the Starfleet logo appeared, Sulu thumbed off the display. She checked the incoming feed and saw a file appended to it. Sulu saved it to the shuttlecraft's internal memory. "I'll get a padd," she told Kostas. "Make sure that our proximity alert remains set."

"Yes, sir."

Sulu headed toward the equipment drawers in the aft bulkhead. She would load the program Tenger had sent onto a padd, then record a message to the security chief. She agreed with his decision not to allow any more of the crew down to Rejarris II, and she endorsed having the crew study the sensor readings of the portal. She would inform him of her own plans to take the shuttlecraft and—

As the captain pulled a padd out of an equipment drawer, she heard a hiss, like air escaping through a hole in an environmental suit. She imagined damage to the shuttlecraft, and even envisioned another creature outside tearing through the hull. When she followed the sound, though, it led her to Ensign Young, and the hiss turned into a gasp. "Ensign Kostas!" Sulu called, dropping the padd and moving to her ailing crewmate. "We have a problem."

As Kostas hurried from the front of the cabin, Young began to cough, and pink spittle appeared on his lips. Sulu threw her hand beneath his back and hauled him to a sitting position. Kostas pulled her medical tricorder from where she'd set it on a chair and scanned Young.

"There's fluid buildup in his lungs," she said, her voice rising. "I need to . . . to administer a drug to dilate his veins." She sounded as though on the verge of panic, though not uncertain about what she'd said. She spun around and looked all about the cabin, clearly searching for her medkit.

Sulu quickly wrapped an arm around Young's chest and moved him backward, propping him up against the aft bulkhead. Then she turned to Kostas and took her by the shoulders. "Ensign, you can do this," she said firmly. "I know you haven't had much experience out in the field as a medic, but you trained for this. Let that take over."

Kostas nodded mutely once, then said, "Yes, sir." She took a deep breath, let it out. "Thank you, sir." She looked back over at Young, then found her medkit where she'd left it, in a recess beneath the antigrav stretcher. As she armed herself with a hypospray and began preparing its contents, she said, "He's going to need oxygen, Captain. There should be an emergency supply aboard."

"I'll get it," Sulu said. She marched through the opening in the aft bulkhead and into the equipment storage area. She found several canisters of oxygen and masks by the environmental suits. *If necessary,* she thought, *we can have the crew send down more oxygen from the ship.*

The captain brought the canister and mask back out to the main cabin. Kostas kneeled beside Young, wiping away the blood-tinged spittle from his lips with a cloth. Sulu could see him already breathing easier. She held out the oxygen to Kostas.

"Thank you, Captain," she said. She attached the mask around Young's face and activated the canister. A digital display indicated its function. Kostas exchanged her medkit for her tricorder and monitored her patient. Sulu stayed with her. After a few minutes, the ensign said, "Hawk's doing better."

"Do you know Ensign Young?" Sulu asked, recognizing the familiarity in Kostas using an obvious nickname for Hawkins Young, though the captain herself had never heard it used aboard the ship. Then again, he'd only been a member of the crew for a relatively short time. "Do you know him well, I mean?"

"Not well," Kostas said. "He was a year behind me at the Academy. We think we once had a class together, but we could never figure out if that was true. We both enjoy swimming, though, so we've seen each other a few times down at the ship's natatorium."

"What's his condition?" Sulu asked. "Will he be all right?"

"For now," Kostas said. "He's suffering from pulmonary edema. I've administered a preload reducer to lower the pressure in his lungs, and the oxygen will help. I'll need to keep an eye on him, and at some point, he might need assistance breathing. We can adapt an environmental suit, if necessary. Even though his condition is stable right now, the underlying cause has to be treated."

"What is the underlying cause?"

"I can't be sure, Captain, but I think the creature injected him with venom," Kostas said. "I can treat Ensign Young, but I don't have the training to develop an antivenin."

"No, of course not, and nobody would expect you to be able to do that," Sulu said. "But Doctor Morell leads an impressive medical staff aboard the *Enterprise*, and we now have a means of communicating with her, so she'll be able to help."

"Yes, sir," Kostas said. "Thank you, sir."

"I'm going to record a message for Commander

Tenger," the captain said. "I'll append Ensign Young's medical readings and any observations about his condition you want to add."

"Yes, sir."

Sulu found the padd where she'd dropped it to the deck, then made her way back to the forward console. Before she sat down, she put her hands on her hips and stared out at the barren alien landscape. She attempted to gather her thoughts, to consider all that she needed to tell Tenger. As she worked through the content she would include in her message, she noticed a shape outside, maybe eight or ten meters from the bow of the shuttlecraft. She thought it might be another life-form, and she leaned forward on the main console as she tried to make out any details.

She suddenly stood up straight and slammed her eyes closed. It didn't matter. She knew what she'd seen, and she doubted that even time could ever cleanse her mind of the image: Xintal Linojj's severed arm.

5

Doctor Uta Morell circled out from behind the desk in her office and accepted the padd from Malthus Dey, one of the medical technicians on her staff. "The results look promising," Dey said with a smile. Morell appreciated the statement and the positive attitude—both especially meaningful coming from the crewman. An expert in toxicological preparation and testing, Dey offering his imprimatur on any prospective treatment usually heralded a high probability of success. For that reason, *Enterprise*'s chief medical officer had five years earlier lured Dey away from his position at the Central Hospital of Altair IV's prestigious Toxin Assessment Wing. Her promise to him of an opportunity to encounter exotic and previously unknown poisons had not gone unfulfilled.

"That's good to hear," Morell said, gazing down at Dey. Though not particularly tall herself at one and five-eighths meters, she still towered over the Pygorian, who barely reached a meter in height. Average in size and coloring for his people, he had exceedingly fair skin, which lacked pigment, as did his eyes, though a small disk of dark hair crowned his head. "How close are we, do you think?" Morell asked.

"Very close, I believe," Dey said. "The parameters you provided for the antivenin allowed me to use a formulation partially harvested from *zabathu* antibodies in response to the venom of a stinging centipede."

"A zabathu?" Morell said, concerned. "That's an Andorian animal, isn't it?"

"Yes, and so is the stinging centipede," Dey said. "And thanks to our three Andorian crew members, that's why we have the zabathu antibodies in sickbay's stores. Even though Ensign Young is human, the fraction of the antivenin that's Andorian in origin is just enough to elicit an autonomic response in humans, but not enough to alter their biochemical balance." He pointed to the padd he had handed to the doctor. "You'll see."

"My concern is that we're trying to produce antivenin without having an actual sample of the venom it's designed to counteract," Morell said.

"I know," Dey said. "It's an unusual set of circumstances, but we do have the biosensor readings that Ensign Kostas provided to us, both of Ensign Young and of the animal that attacked him. We're just fortunate that the human reaction to the venom mimicked that of the Andorian reaction to the stinging centipede."

"If this works, Malthus, you're going to make the medical literature again."

"The preservation of Ensign Young's life will be reward enough," Dey said. "That wouldn't even have been possible without the quick intervention of Ensign Kostas."

"Galatea has done a noteworthy job," Morell said, "not just in her initial reaction to Hawk's distress, but in keeping him alive for the three days since." The young engineer had taken some rudimentary medical classes at Starfleet Academy, and in her two years aboard *Enterprise*, she'd supplemented that education with regular training sessions in sickbay. That she had enough knowledge and skills to follow instructions well enough to manage Young's pulmonary edema for seventy-two hours without being able to treat the underlying cause bespoke her abilities as a field medic. Among other difficult tasks, Kostas had been required at one point to perform a tracheotomy on the ailing ensign. "Thank you for this," Morell said, holding up the padd. "I'll take—" The doctor clipped her sentence short when she saw Nurse Veracruz appear in the open doorway. "Yes, Rosalinda?"

"Commander Linojj is asking to speak with you, Doctor," the nurse said.

"All right, thank you," Morell said. "Please tell her I'll be right there."

"Yes, Doctor." The nurse withdrew.

"Malthus, would you please take this to Doctor Benzon," Morell said, handing the padd back to Dey. "Ask him to begin reviewing the results and tell him that I'll join him shortly."

"Of course." Dey took the padd, and Morell followed him out of her office. While the med tech headed left down the short corridor that connected to sickbay's main ward, Morell went right, toward the surgical suite. She passed intensive care—mercifully empty at the moment—and entered recovery, where they'd kept Commander Linojj since operating on her residual arm.

"Good afternoon, Xintal," Morell said, keeping her tone light and upbeat. The first officer had been understandably devastated to lose a limb, and indeed, the entire crew had reacted to the terrible incident with a collective sense of shock. But Doctor Benzon had begun counseling Linojj, which had already helped stabilize and improve her emotional state. The news that morning that preliminary tests graded the viability of fitting her with a biosynthetic arm as high had only advanced her progress.

In fact, the report of Linojj's prospective limb replacement had bolstered the disposition of the whole crew. Three days earlier, when the first officer had suffered her injury and the captain and the two ensigns had vanished, the mood aboard *Enterprise* had sunk dramatically. Even though Sulu, Young, and Kostas remained separated from the ship, the reestablishment of contact with them had sown hopeful expectations for their eventual recovery.

"Thank you for coming so quickly, Doctor," Linojj said. She sat propped up on a bio-bed, pillows behind her back and an active padd in her lap. She wore the powder-blue jumpsuit provided to patients, its right arm ending just past the shoulder, where the silver metal cuff protected Linojj's compromised flesh and bone. "I wanted to talk to you about my progress."

"All right," Morell said, though she hesitated to say anything more than she'd already told the first officer. The doctor looked up at the diagnostic display above the head of the bio-bed and examined the readings shown there. "Your overall physical condition is good," she said. "Your wound remains stable, and you know what this morning's test showed: when we've finished preparing your biosynthetic arm, you should be able to undergo replacement surgery in short order. If successful, your recovery should take—"

"Doctor," Linojj said, interrupting. "Excuse me, but we've gone over all of that. I wanted to talk to you about when I can be released from sickbay."

"I see," Morell said. "Xintal, I know you'd be more comfortable back in your own quarters, but since you won't be doing much of anything anyway, it's best to keep you here for the time being so that we can monitor your physical condition continuously." The doctor did not reveal that she wanted Linojj under psychological observation as well.

"I'm not talking about going back to my cabin," the first officer said. "I'm talking about returning to duty."

"Oh," Morell said, surprised. "Honestly, I hadn't really anticipated you going back to active duty for some time."

"Until after the replacement surgery," Linojj said.

"Yes."

"But there's no guarantee that the operation will succeed, is there?"

"No," admitted Morell. "But as we learned this morning, the chances are very good."

"And I'm happy about that," Linojj said. "But what happens if I can't have a biosynthetic replacement arm? What happens if my body rejects it, or I can't make it work?"

"There are other types of prosthetics," Morell said. "Not as sophisticated, but still useful."

"Right," Linojj said. "But my point is that why should I wait to see if I'll be able to keep a biosynthetic arm, when I might not be able to. Fit me with something else for right now and let me go back on duty." The first officer delivered her words with a commanding tone, as though issuing an order.

"I'm afraid it's not that simple, Commander," Morell said, resorting to a more formal demeanor to match Linojj's own. "We have surgically repaired your residual limb in preparation of attaching a biosynthetic replacement. Providing you with a different arm in the interim would likely undermine that preparation. Additionally, even a less sophisticated prosthetic would require counseling and occupational therapy."

"Then forget about a substitute limb," Linojj said. She picked up the padd from her lap and tossed it onto a shelf by her bio-bed. "The captain has been away from the ship for three days now, and in her absence, my place is on the bridge." She spoke quickly, her manner becoming agitated.

"When you're injured, Commander, your place

is in sickbay," Morell said, "and right now, it's my job to keep you here."

"I don't think so, Doctor." Linojj swept the bedclothes away and swung her legs over the other side of the diagnostic pallet. When she did, she overbalanced and started to fall to her right; her shoulder moved, but with no arm on that side, she could not brace herself. Morell lunged awkwardly across the bio-bed and caught the first officer at the sides of her torso, keeping her upright.

Linojj yelled, not in pain, but in obvious frustration, pounding the pallet with her remaining fist.

"It's all right," Morell said gently. She came around to the other side of the bio-bed to face the first officer. The trident-shaped hollow in Linojj's forehead flushed lavender, and tears spilled from her eyes. The doctor reached forward and took hold of her patient by the sides of her upper arms. "Everything's going to be all right, Xintal," she said quietly, her words barely more than a whisper.

Linojj let herself slip from the side of the bio-bed and into the doctor's embrace. Morell stood a head shorter than the first officer, and yet Linojj felt small, almost insubstantial, in her arms. The doctor held her tightly as her body convulsed with her weeping.

Morell thought about the report she had yet to read on the antivenin Dey had prepared and tested. She knew that Benzon could ably handle the medical appraisal, though, and so she put it out of her mind. Instead, she would stay with Xintal Linojj for as long as the first officer needed her.

✦   ✦   ✦

The rocky plain stretched in one direction toward foothills that eventually escalated into mountains, but in another, it gave way to a dense forest. Sulu flew the shuttlecraft at a height of just fifty meters, alternately inspecting her scans of the surface and gazing through the forward port at the verdant expanse of tall leafy trees. By herself aboard *Pytheas*, she traveled with the autopilot engaged.

The captain had begun exploring the planet not long after reestablishing contact with *Enterprise*. While her crew studied the portal on Rejarris II, she sought to locate those who had created the device—who had done so presumably for the purpose of fleeing the asteroid that would ultimately drive their planet into an impact winter. The evidence of a ruined but empty world suggested that they had been successful in their escape. Even if they could not reverse the flow of travel through the portal, they might still provide enough information about the device to assist the *Enterprise* crew in doing so. Through two and a half days of searching, though, Sulu had yet to find any of those who had abandoned Rejarris II.

It's not just that I haven't seen any people, she thought. She also hadn't seen any sign of their continued existence—or even of their *past* existence. She saw no settlements of any kind, and no indications that anybody had ever even traveled in the area.

That's consistent with what we saw from orbit, Sulu thought. *Or what we didn't see.* Although the captain had kept a keen eye on the planet surface during their search for *Enterprise* aboard *Amund-*

sen, she had seen no lights that could have corresponded to cities. As far as she could tell, the planet that she, Young, and Kostas had accidentally come to was as devoid of a population as Rejarris II.

Except that this place is alive. Where Rejarris II had been strangled by unbroken clouds and smothered in fields of ash, the world below sported open skies and clear ground, painted not in the grays of epic destruction, but in the greens of thriving flora. Sulu had also spotted fauna: birds flying above the trees, along with an occasional larger animal lumbering below breaks in the canopy, though she had seen nothing like the creature that had attacked Ensign Young.

The captain glanced at the chronometer and realized that she would need to turn back soon. She also saw her scheduled contact with Kostas about forty minutes away. Once they had regained contact with the *Enterprise* crew and Sulu had decided to scout the surrounding areas, she'd chosen not to remove Ensign Young from the destination point of the portal. Although Kostas had performed admirably in keeping him alive, he remained unconscious and in serious condition. It seemed obvious—and Doctor Morell had verified—that the instant the *Enterprise* medical staff completed production of an antivenin, it should be delivered through the portal and administered to Young.

Because Kostas needed to stay with her patient, the captain had ordered Tenger to dispatch a second shuttlecraft. On Sulu's authority, Lieutenant Verant piloted *Pytheas* down to the surface of Rejarris II, but only to within five kilometers of the portal. After she programmed the autopilot to finish the shuttlecraft's journey, Lieutenant Ved transported her back to *Enterprise*. Sulu and Kostas watched as *Pytheas* seemed to appear out of nowhere, at a distance from them of thirty meters, providing a margin of safety. Not very high above the ground, the shuttlecraft quickly descended and alit.

When Sulu took her excursions across the local region, she left Kostas aboard *Amundsen* to look after Young, but leaving the ensign behind served a second purpose. Not wanting to deplete *Enterprise*'s supply of log buoys and probes, the captain had ordered communications carried through the portal on padds, which did not have the capability of broadcasting over long distances. Remaining in place aboard *Amundsen*, the ensign could therefore transmit any messages from the ship directly to Sulu. Likewise, because she stayed in the line of sight of a probe hovering above the portal, Kostas could relay the captain's responses back to *Enterprise*. Sulu had also implemented a policy that she would contact the ensign every two hours for a status report.

Down below, an orange glow bathed the wide span of the forest. Evening approached as the sun set. Sulu released the helm from autopilot and prepared to turn *Pytheas* around. As she did, though, she saw a wide break in the trees stretching across the path of her shuttlecraft. She checked the sensors, which revealed a river winding its way through the forest. Knowing that most populations that evolved on Class-M planets required fresh water for their survival, the captain decided to begin her eventual loop back to Kostas and Young aboard *Amundsen* by following the river, at least for a short while.

After Sulu settled the shuttlecraft onto its new heading and reinitiated the autopilot, she looked out at the water. It flowed placidly along, averaging seventy-five meters in width as it wended a path through the trees. Scans showed a diverse fishery, with at least a dozen different varieties. Animal life teemed in the forest along the banks. She saw something resembling a small bear ambling along in the shallows, as well as several four-legged creatures that resembled deer, but for their burgundy coloring.

Burgundy, Sulu thought with a grin. *I would love a glass right about now.* The last few days had been stressful, but her desire for red wine originated not from the need to calm herself, but from her connoisseurship of the grape. Her father had long ago introduced her to the world of fine wines, an appreciation she had subsequently cultivated. Serving aboard a starship that took her throughout the Federation and beyond—throughout the *quadrant* and beyond—offered her innumerable opportunities for new tastings, and the privileges of rank meant that she could keep a small stock of wines in her quarters aboard ship. Sulu did not collect wines, but acquired them to enjoy and share with friends. Her father might not have convinced her of the joy in most of his leisure pursuits, but he had certainly helped make her an oenophile.

Dad, she thought, wistful. She still missed him,

and she knew she always would, but she felt grateful that she had spent so much time with him. Sulu had known her mother for only six years, but her father for three decades. She'd really gotten to know him, first from a child's perspective, but then as an adult.

Although Dad always had the enthusiasm of a child, Sulu thought. She frequently teased him about the sheer volume of his interests, insisting to him that he changed avocations as often as most people changed clothes. He usually just smiled and quoted the writer Robert Heinlein: *Specialization is for insects.* She loved him for that, and for the fact that he didn't so much take pride in his numerous and varied hobbies, but that he honestly and fully enjoyed them. He was, she supposed, a Renaissance man, given his interest and knowledge in so many diverse fields: botany, fencing, antique firearms, xenophilately, genealogy, archery, bibliophily—

In her peripheral vision, Sulu saw something that snapped her from her reverie. She looked off to port and saw a long, narrow break in the forest. She had flown over clearings during her recon, but the shape and size of the hole in the canopy seemed peculiar to her.

Once more, the captain took control of the shuttlecraft and altered course. She flew toward the area maintaining altitude and saw an area almost completely devoid of vegetation, though dead leaves covered some of it. On her second pass, she dropped to just above the treetops, which allowed her to distinguish a slope in the ground. Finally, after employing sensors to ensure that no large animals roamed near the area—and none of the spiderlike leviathans tunneled beneath it—she maneuvered *Pytheas* into the odd clearing and set down at one end.

Sulu checked the temperature, and though it had dropped a few degrees during her journey, she didn't feel the need to don any outerwear. She did, however, arm herself with a phaser pistol, a tricorder, and a communicator. The chronometer told her that she still had twenty minutes before she would check in with Ensign Kostas, although the deepening shadows outside the shuttlecraft reminded her that she should already be heading back to her crew.

The captain exited *Pytheas*, making sure to close the hatch behind her. The slope she had seen from above started at the floor of the forest and angled downward. It had rounded sides and looked almost like a crater. Sulu walked beside it, measuring its length at fifty-six meters, and the depth at its farthest end at eight. Fallen leaves littered the bottom of the grade, but the soil along the sides appeared blackened. The trees that had once stood there lay toppled in the surrounding forest, some of them in fragments, and all of them similarly charred and aiming away from what must have been the point of impact.

When she gazed back toward the shuttlecraft, the view solidified her intuition that something had crashed to the ground there. Activating her tricorder, she scanned the depression that had been gouged out of the forest floor. The details that appeared on her display did not contradict her conclusion: the ground and trees had been burned, the soil along the bottom compacted by the high pressure of something that had collided with it at speed.

Sensors also showed a small piece of metal buried at the end of the trench. It too had been subjected to intense heat, but Sulu read refined duranium and tritanium among its components—advanced materials commonly used in the construction of starship hulls. Clearly a large vessel had not crashed there, but she thought it likely that something smaller had.

Something like a shuttlecraft, she thought. The idea sent chills through her. Something about the situation seemed wrong to her. *No, not wrong,* she thought. *Oddly familiar.*

Sulu walked back toward the shuttlecraft and the shallow end of the trench. She wanted to walk down into it and dig out the piece of metal that she had scanned, but the sun had eased lower in the sky, dimming visibility as dusk took firm hold of the land. She could no longer see the far end of the cavity that had been carved into the ground. She would have to return the next day.

Back aboard *Pytheas,* the captain recorded the planetary coordinates so that she could readily find the location again. She didn't know if the crash site marked the path of those who had fled Rejarris II, but she would scour the surrounding area in the hopes of finding additional clues, or possibly even the people themselves.

Sulu set a course back to Ensign Kostas and Ensign Young aboard *Amundsen.* The shuttlecraft rose from the forest into a brilliant sky filled with the pinks and oranges of a dazzling sunset. Sulu took a moment to appreciate the beauty of the scene before heading back to the place that had become a temporary and unwelcome home.

The doors whispered open before Tenger, and he strode through them into the engineering laboratory. The noise within struck him first; it filled the large compartment: the commingled voices of two dozen or more crew members, joined together with the chirps and tones of console feedback, the whine of tricorders, the hum of the transporter. Not quite a cacophony, it fell short, perhaps, in the organization of its individual sounds.

Platforms fronted by control stations lined each of the bulkheads, all of them utilized to design, analyze, and test components. Tenger saw pieces of equipment on almost all of them, with engineers laboring over various devices and a number of the ship's scientists assisting. The commander recognized some of what he saw, but most of the components seemed outsized and, if not primitive, at least archaic.

Four square holographic stages sat in the middle of the lab, with operating panels on either side of the grouping. Tenger noted that the stages had been networked together, creating one large platform, which clearly had been done so that the combined unit could accommodate the huge structure currently projected atop it. The security chief studied the great cylindrical slice of equipment, clearly a cross section of the portal. Commander Buonarroti and one of his engineers, Lieutenant Warren Roscoe, stood before the impressive hologram, their heads together and their hands buried inside the glut of circuitry.

Tenger climbed the steps to the stage, then waited for an opportune moment to approach *Enterprise*'s chief engineer. He did not want to interrupt the analytical process. While Captain Sulu and Ensigns Kostas and Young appeared to face no immediate dangers—inside the shuttlecraft, they could readily escape the clutches of any other hostile beasts that attacked—Tenger did not wish to test the situation for long. He hoped to return them to the ship as quickly as possible.

When Buonarroti and Roscoe finally stepped back from the reproduced segment of the portal, the silver-haired lieutenant espied Tenger first. "Commander," he said.

"Lieutenant," Tenger said, and then, as Buonarroti turned to face him, "Commander. I wanted to check on your progress."

"I'm not really sure we can call it *progress* just yet," Buonarroti said.

Tenger felt his brow knit together. "Are you finding equipment that you don't understand?" he asked.

"No, it's not that," Buonarroti said. "Everything we've seen so far corresponds to the level of technology that the landing parties encountered on Rejarris Two, and so it all falls well within our understanding. The difficulty is that we still haven't discovered how all of this—" He gestured toward the holographic cross section of the portal.

"—accomplishes what it does. The answer must be in there somewhere, but the structure is just so big, and there's no one component or set of components that stands out from the rest."

"We've scanned the entire length of the torus-shaped structure that forms the framework of the portal, and we've found virtually no empty space," Roscoe added. "That means we're researching more than two hundred fifty thousand cubic meters of equipment."

"Can it be done?" Tenger wanted to know.

"I'm confident that it can be done, and I'm confident that we can do it," Buonarroti said. "I just haven't developed a feeling yet for how long it's going to take us to understand how the portal functions, or how long it will take us to reverse its flow—if that's even possible."

"And what if it's not?" Tenger asked.

"Once we know how the portal works," Buonarroti said, "we may be able to construct a smaller version of it and deliver it to Captain Sulu."

"Calibrating it could be problematic, though," Roscoe said. "In addition to needing to figure out how the structure creates a pathway from origin to destination, it's also unclear how it's set for that destination. We're not even sure if it's creating a passage through space or time or both. It might even be linking a point in our universe to a point in another."

The chief engineer nodded as if in agreement, but then said, "All of that's true, but no matter how the portal functions and where it sends people, if it's been done once, it can be done again."

"But you can't estimate the length of time it will take to do it?" Tenger asked.

"We might find the answer in an hour, or in a week, or in a month," Buonarroti said. "But the more work we do, the more we study the portal, the better able we'll be to evaluate how long it will take us to understand it and retrieve the landing party."

The chief engineer's response, while understandable, did not satisfy Tenger. To Roscoe, he said, "Carry on, Lieutenant." The engineer started, evidently not expecting to be dismissed at that moment. He recovered quickly, though, and moved back to the holographic copy of the portal segment.

Tenger descended from the platform, with Buonarroti following behind him. When they had moved far enough away from everybody else in the lab to afford them some degree of privacy, the security chief and acting captain stopped. "Commander," he said quietly, "I know that this is a difficult task, not only to achieve the return of the captain and the others, but to approximate how long it will take to do that. What I need to know from you right now is whether I should contact Starfleet Command. Do we need the assistance of other starship crews? Do we need to bring in the Starfleet Corps of Engineers?"

"This is taking longer than any of us want it to, and it's frustrating that we can't know just yet the amount of time we'll need to get this done," Buonarroti said. "I could guess, but that wouldn't serve any of us." He leaned in closer and spoke even more quietly. "Tenger," he said, clearly intending to emphasize his words by using the security chief's name, "if you're asking my opinion, it seems like a very bad idea to call out the cavalry so close to Tzenkethi space. We're far enough away that the *Enterprise* went unnoticed, or if not unnoticed, then it didn't raise enough of an alarm within the Coalition for them to send one of their ships after us. But if other Starfleet vessels descend on the same solar system so near their borders, you can believe that they'd take an interest—not just in us, but in whatever it is that's brought us here."

"Meaning the portal."

"You know how belligerent the Tzenkethi can be," Buonarroti said. "They might well view the portal as a dangerous technology, one that Starfleet is attempting to exploit and weaponize."

"Yes," Tenger said, recognizing the truth of the chief engineer's words. The territorial and distrustful Tzenkethi might imagine the Federation creating a portal that opened directly into Coalition space, and then sending a squadron of Starfleet vessels through to attack. If positioned out in space, even an *Excelsior*-class starship like *Enterprise* could easily fit through the portal. "Yes, you're right, of course," Tenger said. "I'm just concerned about Captain Sulu, Ensign Kostas, and Ensign Young."

"We all are," Buonarroti said. He glanced back over his shoulder in the direction of the holographic stage, then back at Tenger. "We're all working as diligently as possible to accomplish this, and I know that you know that. I promise you that if we get to a point where the process is taking too long and I can't tell you how much more time we're going to need, or if I determine that our efforts will be measured in months or years rather than in days or weeks, I'll let you know at once."

"Thank you, Rafe," Tenger said, using Buonarroti's nickname among his friends, pronouncing it *Rah-fee*. "When you have—"

"Commander Tenger," a voice suddenly called out. The security chief looked around to see Lieutenant Commander Fenn staring over at him with both eyes. The intensity of her gaze and the tension in her body language conveyed a sense of exigency. Tenger quickly headed in her direction, with Buonarroti at his side.

"What is it, Commander?" Tenger asked when he reached Fenn. The science officer stood before a testing platform, upon which sat a metal plate filled with a patchwork of rudimentary solid-state circuits. The console before it contained four displays, three of the screens stacked beside a larger one. They each presented a distinct view of a section of the portal. The trio of smaller displays showed, from top to bottom, a panel that looked to Tenger like a solar cell, an emitter node, and the area of the structure that had been compromised, possibly by weapons fire. The fourth screen held an image of an entire arc of the portal that included the two *Enterprise* shuttlecraft beside it. As Tenger watched the larger display, it jumped.

"Did you see that, sir?" Fenn asked, her agitation plain. She peered at Tenger with only one of her eyes, while the other observed the console.

"Do you mean the flicker?" Tenger asked. "I'm sure Commander Buonarroti can have one of his engineers replace a faulty display."

"Commander, the display isn't failing," Fenn said. "I've run two diagnostics on it."

Tenger glanced at the other displays just as the larger one blinked again. "I think there might be something wrong with your diagnostics, Commander."

"Sir, these—" Fenn pointed to the three smaller screens. "—are exhibiting still images of the portal recorded by our probe, but this—" She indicated the large monitor. "—is a live feed."

Tenger watched the display again. Nothing happened for a full minute, and then another, but finally the image once more jumped, and he saw something he hadn't before: the structure of the portal remained precisely the same, but the two shuttlecraft vanished. So too did the rocky plain inside the framework, replaced by the same grayish white expanse that stretched away outside the framework. After just an instant, though, the image reverted to its previous state.

"What's going on?" Tenger asked. "If it's not an error in the display, could it be a problem with the probe or the transmission signal?"

"Lieutenant Rainbow Sky ran a diagnostic on the probe, and Commander Kanchumurthi verified that its transmission signal is strong and shows no signs of interference," Fenn said.

"Then what is the explanation?" Tenger asked.

"The portal is failing."

The impact on Tenger would not have been greater if the science officer had drawn a phaser and stunned him with it. "What?"

"When the portal is functioning as designed,

we can see within it the destination to which things can travel through it," Fenn explained, "but when it's not, we see the surface of Rejarris Two."

"It's the power," Buonarroti said, speaking as though coming out of a daze himself.

"Yes," Fenn agreed. "I think so."

"The portal uses solar cells as its primary power source," Buonarroti said. "With the extreme cloud cover surrounding the planet, though, those cells run at a significantly reduced rate. In passing objects through it and generating tractor beams, it might have overextended the current capacity of its solar energy collection."

"What will happen if it loses power completely?" Tenger asked, already knowing the answer.

"We'll lose the ability to see the two shuttle-craft and Captain Sulu and the others," Buonarroti said, "and to communicate with them."

"We won't be able to send anything through the portal to them," Fenn said. Tenger understood the terrible repercussions of such a situation.

"Can we do something about it?" he asked. "Can we provide it a different power source?"

"Maybe, but it would likely require several days," Buonarroti said.

"We probably wouldn't be able to replace the power source before the portal shuts down completely," Fenn said.

Even though the recovery of the *Enterprise* landing party remained the top priority and ultimate goal of the present operation, another situation required more immediate attention. The security chief found the intercom on Fenn's console and activated it. "Tenger to sickbay."

"*Sickbay here*," came the response. "*This is Doctor Morell.*"

"Doctor, what is the status of the medication you're preparing for Ensign Young?"

"*We've tested several different antivenins and have seen good results,*" Morell said. "*We're confident of one particular formulation, but because of the circumstances, where the medication will be administered away from sickbay, with no provisions for anybody other than a medic to treat the ensign should he respond badly, we're continuing to refine it. We should have it within the next twelve to twenty-four hours.*"

"It might not be possible to deliver the medicine to Ensign Young at that time," Tenger said. "Which would be medically more advisable, to give him what you've prepared right now, or to give him nothing more for several days?"

Morell did not reply right away. As the silence extended, Tenger fought his inclination to urge her for an answer. She knew her job, and he allowed her the time she needed—though he had no way of knowing exactly how much time they had left before such a decision would be rendered meaningless. Finally, she said, "*I cannot fully warrant the effectiveness or even the safety of the antivenin at this point, but failing to treat Ensign Young for several days will probably result in his death.*"

"Prepare the medication for delivery through the portal at once," Tenger ordered. "Report to the transporter room with it as soon as you're ready."

"Understood," Morell said. *"I'll be there in five minutes."*

Tenger tapped the channel closed. "Keep me informed," he said to Buonarroti and Fenn. "Both of you." Then he exited the engineering lab, on his way to meet the chief medical officer in the transporter room in an attempt to save Hawkins Young before it was too late.

Sulu stood at the front of *Amundsen*'s cabin, staring through the viewport, waiting. Behind her, Ensign Kostas cared for Ensign Young, whose condition had worsened. His breathing had grown more labored, the already rough sound of his respiration through the tracheostomy tube becoming shallower and more erratic.

The captain glanced at the padd in her hand and set it down on the main console. A patch of brown dirt clung to one corner, doubtless where it had fallen to the ground. Just moments earlier, an alert had told them that sensors detected a padd dropped through the portal by the *Enterprise* crew. The captain had retrieved it and brought it back aboard the shuttlecraft, where she'd listened to the single message recorded onto it.

"Captain, this is Tenger," the security chief had said, and Sulu could tell that the normal tension with which he conducted his duties had increased dramatically. *"Our view of the two shuttlecraft through the portal has become intermittent. Scans show that the portal is losing power, likely because it employs solar cells, which have been adversely effected by the continuous cloud cover. As a re-*

sult, it is possible that the portal will lose power completely, meaning that we will lose our ability to communicate with the landing party."

And also making our return a virtual impossibility, Sulu had thought.

"Commander Buonarroti believes that he and his engineers will be able to restore power to the portal," Tenger had continued, *"though because we are still studying how it functions, he isn't sure how long that will take. Because we might be out of touch with the landing party for several days, we are immediately loading a log buoy with the antivenin for Ensign Young. Doctor Morell wanted to do more testing, but she would prefer that the medication be administered to the ensign sooner rather than later."*

Via messages scrolling across a padd on top of *Amundsen*, Sulu and Kostas had kept the chief medical officer apprised of Young's condition. The captain understood that, because neither Morell nor any of the doctors on her staff would be able to monitor in person the ensign's reaction to the antivenin, she would want to test the treatment as thoroughly as possible beforehand. It seemed the right choice, though, not to risk waiting days to deliver the medicine.

"It is unclear how soon the portal will lose all power," Tenger had said. *"For that reason, we will not launch the log buoy, but will transport it to a point above you, as we've done with the padds. The buoy will be under power, though, and will descend through the portal and land beside you. We will continue to deliver our regular status re-*

ports to you every two hours for as long as we can. If the portal does shut down, we will contact you immediately once it is functioning again." The security chief paused, and Sulu thought that he might include a personal note—*Good luck*, or something of that nature—but he simply said, "*Tenger out.*"

As Sulu watched the sky through the forward port, she wondered how the chief engineer intended to restore power to the portal. She'd had her own ideas about that, and so she'd recorded a message back to the ship, which she'd delivered by way of a scrolling padd. She feared that modifying the portal to utilize a different power source could alter its function, thus permanently separating the landing party from the *Enterprise* crew—and home.

Thirty meters ahead of *Amundsen*, three dark points suddenly appeared in midair. They descended and lengthened, as though growing out of nothing. Sulu recognized them as the landing legs of a log buoy. The drumlike main body appeared next, but then suddenly the device plummeted, clearly no longer under power. It canted as it fell. One leg struck the side of a boulder and collapsed inward. The buoy crashed against the hard stone, then tumbled to the ground and onto its side.

Sulu understood at once what had happened. The portal had obviously lost power just as the buoy moved through the transitional plain between Rejarris II and the unnamed world on which the captain and her two crew members found themselves. With the portal no longer functioning, the rest of the buoy could not complete the journey. No longer whole, the part of the device that had come through failed; unable to fly, it plunged to the ground.

The captain reached to the sensor panel and scanned the wreckage. Depending on how the buoy had been compromised, it could pose a danger, either through the release of radiation or the explosion of its power system—if, for example, the coolant system remained on Rejarris II. Fortunately, Sulu read no such issues, nor did she detect any life-forms nearby, above or below the surface.

Moving to the hatch, the captain told Ensign Kostas, "The buoy is here. I'm going to retrieve the antivenin." She could only hope that the medication had not only made it through the portal, but that it had survived the crash intact. Carrying a phaser and a communicator with her, she exited *Amundsen*.

Sulu studied the buoy as she approached it. The device looked to her like a wounded animal: its leg bent, its metal casing dented in numerous places, the fractional portion of its main drum looking as though its upper section had been sliced off cleanly by an impossibly sharp blade. It made her think of the terrible ordeal that Linojj had endured.

Sulu looked in the direction of the spot where Ensign Young had first fallen. Linojj's arm no longer lay there on the ground, a grotesque, lifeless monument to the first officer's traumatic injury. The captain had collected the severed limb and placed it in a secure specimen container, which she'd then stowed in the equipment storage area aboard *Amundsen*. Although the arm would be of no use to Linojj, it seemed wrong to Sulu to leave a part of her friend to rot on the soil of some distant, unknown world.

At the buoy, the captain examined the two small panels that allowed access to a pair of storage compartments. Located at the bottom of the main body, the hinged doors—and presumably the spaces beyond—had passed in their entirety through the portal. Sulu tapped at the control padd beside one of the panels, but nothing happened. The buoy had lost power.

The captain lowered herself to the ground, flipped over onto her back, and slid in among the legs of the buoy. She located the manual release for one of the doors and pulled the inset handle. The panel popped open with an audible *click*. When she extricated herself from the buoy's legs and checked the storage compartment, though, she found it empty.

The manual release for the second access panel proved more difficult. Sulu didn't know if its mechanism had been damaged in the crash, or the door wedged shut, but she ended up having to force the handle with a well-chosen rock. When she opened the compartment, a clear, yellow-tinted liquid spilled out.

Bitter disappointment clutched at Sulu, who understood the implications for Ensign Young. When she looked inside the storage compartment, though, she saw not only the pieces of a broken container, but a second, intact ampoule, as well as another padd. She reached in and grabbed both items, then read the small label affixed to the vial: ENSIGN HAWKINS YOUNG; ANTIVENIN FOR VENOM OF

UNKNOWN ANIMAL. A list followed of the chemicals utilized in creating the serum. When Sulu checked the padd, she saw a single entry recorded on it.

Back in the shuttlecraft, the captain handed the vial of antivenin to Kostas, and then the padd. "It contains a message to you from Doctor Morell," she said. Sulu assumed her chief medical officer had instructions for Kostas about treating Young.

While the ensign listened to the message and then apparently read through some written material appended to it, Sulu waited, pondering what she should do next. For the moment, she would assume that Buonarroti and *Enterprise*'s engineers would be able to reactivate the portal. That might not come to pass, but she could deal with that if and when the time came. In the meanwhile, she needed to be prepared once Tenger reestablished contact with her.

"I'm ready, Captain," Kostas said. Sulu watched as the ensign pulled her medkit from beneath the antigrav stretcher. She extracted a hypospray, inserted the ampoule into it, then—after hesitating for just a moment—injected the antivenin into the front of Young's shoulder.

Sulu didn't notice any immediate difference in the wounded ensign's respiration, but Kostas picked up a tricorder and scanned her patient. "There's already a small improvement in his lungs," she said. "Since the edema has lasted as long as it has, it may take some time to clear up."

"Well done, Ensign," Sulu said.

"Thank you, sir, but I'll need to keep Ensign Young under observation," Kostas said. "It's important to ensure that the venom is completely counteracted, and that he suffers no side effects from the medication. Doctor Morell issued instructions about what to watch for, as well as about prospective treatments."

"Good," the captain said. "The portal has lost power, and so for the time being, we're out of touch with the *Enterprise*."

Kostas nodded and glanced nervously at Young, but then she recovered enough to conceal her obvious anxiety. "So then what do we do now?" she asked.

"That's a good question, Ensign," Sulu said. At the moment, the captain could think of only one thing to do next, which troubled her. As a starship captain, as a leader of more than seven hundred crew members, often in dangerous situations, she liked to have options. Facing circumstances that allowed for just a single reasonable course of action could be liberating in a way—it removed the responsibility of having to weigh various possibilities and make a choice among them—but Sulu thought that it more often than not meant that she had failed to consider every aspect of a situation. "For now, I'm going to continue what I've been doing: searching for the people who constructed the portal. When Ensign Young recovers, you and he can join me."

"What if we can't find them?"

"From all we can tell, the inhabitants of Rejarris Two successfully escaped a catastrophic asteroid strike on their world," Sulu said. "They did not have warp capability, but they had to have gone somewhere. The portal seems their likeliest salvation. And remember, I did find evidence today of somebody having visited this planet."

"But that was just one small crash site," Kostas said. "What if that's not evidence of the people who built the portal? Or even it if is, what if we can't find them? What if those who escaped through the portal intentionally changed its destination after passing through it? Or what if its settings changed over time?"

"Those are all possibilities, Ensign," Sulu admitted. "But while it's important to be prepared for different eventualities, it's a mistake to concentrate on the pessimistic view. We have to figure out what will provide us the best chance of returning to the *Enterprise*, and then work to make that happen."

"Yes, sir," Kostas said, lowering her head.

Sulu offered the engineer a tight-lipped smile. "It's all right, Ensign," she said. "Look after your patient. I'm going to chart search routes for us."

As Kostas took additional tricorder readings of Young, the captain walked back to *Amundsen*'s main console. She downloaded the navigational logs of *Pytheas* to *Amundsen* before beginning to plan the route they would take across the planet. She would first revisit the site of the apparent crash, then continue in that general direction.

In the back of her mind, though, she asked herself all of the questions that Kostas had, and more.

Rafaele Buonarroti wanted to throw something. More than that, he felt the urge to race from the engineering lab to the transporter room, beam down to Rejarris II, and level a phaser at the portal. The device should not have been so complicated.

Except it's not that complicated, is it? he asked himself. *And that's part of the problem.* A device constructed with a greater degree of technological sophistication would have been easier to understand, and easier to modify. The sciences team still hadn't determined just how the portal managed to create a link between two noncontiguous points, or even whether those two points were separated by space, time, or both—or whether they even existed within the same universe.

For his part, Buonarroti had surrendered the task of figuring out how to reverse the flow of the portal, in favor of working to reenergize it. It had taken more than a day to realize that the singular integration of the solar cells might point to the lack of a backup power source, and it had required another day to examine the massive structure and confirm that. Forty-eight hours after losing contact with Captain Sulu and the landing party, they had made no progress.

Having found no external interfaces, Buonarroti and his staff had spent two more days searching for a place they could adapt to a secondary power supply. They identified half a dozen such points, but every model they ran resulted in energy streaming unevenly through the portal, leading to overloaded circuitry and damaged components. Eventually, they realized they had to abandon the approach.

The chief engineer had then conceived of finding a solution by introducing secondary power at multiple points, rather than at just one, thereby balancing the flow. The *Enterprise* engineers spent another day programming and executing such simulations. They all finished with the device actually exploding.

Five days, Buonarroti thought. *Five days and we're nowhere.* He understood, of course, that every step they took, even *false* steps, helped bring them closer to their ultimate goal. But he also understood that, with each day that passed, Captain Sulu, Ensign Kostas, and Ensign Young faced potential dangers on an unexplored world.

"Commander?"

Buonarroti looked up from his console, on which the outcome of his latest simulation had just completed unsuccessfully. Science Officer Fenn stood beside him. "What can I do for you, Borona?"

Fenn's head jerked back a couple of centimeters, as though she'd been slapped. Buonarroti realized his mistake, addressing her by her given name while on duty. Though he never minded such familiarity, even in a professional setting, and he didn't think Fenn did either, the captain's formal demeanor had, of necessity, influenced the entire crew.

"Sorry, I'm just tired," he said. "How can I help you, Commander?"

"I'm hoping that I can actually help you," Fenn said. "We haven't quite figured out the physics of it yet, but we've at least determined how the portal creates a link between two points."

"Without the underlying physics, I'm not sure how much that helps," Buonarroti said.

"Allow me to show you," Fenn said. She held

out her hand and opened it, revealing a data card. Buonarroti took it and reached to insert it in an input slot on his console.

"What is it?" he asked, even as a schematic of the portal appeared on his display.

"These are readings the probe gathered while the structure was in operation," Fenn said. She leaned in and, at the four compass points, touched the circle representing the portal. Five-pointed stars blinked onto the screen, each of them colored yellow. "These are field generators," she said.

"What type of field?" Buonarroti asked.

"That's the surprise: the generators produce subspace fields," Fenn said.

"Subspace?" Buonarroti asked. "I thought the population on Rejarris Two wasn't that advanced."

"We didn't think they were," Fenn said. "The generators are very rudimentary, though, and it might be that they developed them while working to produce the portal." Fenn double-tapped at the screen with all of her fingers, then made a twisting motion. The four stars representing field generators duplicated and moved into new positions around the circle of the portal. Fenn did it a second time, copying the eight stars and making them into sixteen. "These are all the generators in the structure," she said. "Together, they somehow create the extra-dimensional path away from Rejarris Two. What's particularly important is that the number, intensity, and relative positioning appear to be critical to forming the pathway, but there are no variables controlling the point in space and time to which the portal links."

"That sounds like it might not be possible to reverse the flow," Buonarroti noted, the information more than a little disappointing.

"It means that the people who built it couldn't do it, or at least didn't do it," Fenn said. "It doesn't mean that we can't do it. But it does mean that maybe Captain Sulu's solution to reenergize the portal might be the right one."

Just before contact had been lost with the landing party, the captain's last message had been to suggest a means of powering the portal again: by reestablishing it in orbit about Rejarris II. The structure contained both antigravs and thrusters, indications that it had been designed for space. Additionally, the trail of particles they had detected in orbit had led them directly to the portal in the first place.

"I'm sure we could maneuver the structure back into orbit," Buonarroti said, "but I was reluctant to do that because, without knowing how it works, it could alter its settings and therefore its destination."

"But now we know that the pathway, at least with how the portal is presently configured, is static," Fenn said. "If we haul it back into space, the destination will move into space above the planet on the other side."

"Captain Sulu's reasoning was sound," Buonarroti said. "By taking the portal back into orbit, above the cloud cover, we provide it with its original power source: the sun. We wouldn't have to alter the device, and therefore wouldn't risk disrupting the way it functions."

"It might seem like an audacious plan," Fenn said, "but I think it's the one with the best chance of succeeding."

"I think you might be right," Buonarroti said, but something else troubled him. "But all we're talking about is restoring power to the portal so that we can reestablish contact with Captain Sulu's landing party. We're still not addressing how to bring the captain and the others back."

"No," Fenn agreed, "but the captain's last message also told us that she intended to keep searching for those who actually constructed the portal. If she can find them, and if they can help us modify the device, then being in contact with the landing party could be critical."

"I heard too many *ifs* in that sentence for my liking," Buonarroti said. He pressed a control and Fenn's data card slid out of the input slot. He took it and stood up. "Come on," he told the science officer.

"Where are we going?" Fenn asked.

"To make our case to Commander Tenger."

Sulu lay on the deck of *Amundsen* in a bedroll, trying to rest but failing miserably. She had trouble shutting her mind down. Bad enough that she had been involuntarily flung through the universe to a place she didn't know, and from which she might never return, but the responsibility of having two of her crew marooned with her exacerbated the situation. She felt sad and lost, and she knew from experience that hopelessness lurked somewhere close.

Five days, she thought. *It's been five days.* She knew that the *Enterprise* crew hadn't abandoned their attempts to power up the portal, to reinstitute communications with the landing party, and ultimately to rescue them. Still, even though the captain knew such efforts would require time, she had to admit to herself that she'd expected to hear something from Tenger by that point.

Sulu raised her head to glance over at Ensign Young. He sat with his feet dangling over the edge of the antigrav stretcher, a padd in his lap. His attention had wandered from whatever he'd been reading, though, and he stared over at the captain. He reached up and covered the end of the tracheostomy tube protruding from his neck. "Are you all right, sir?" he asked. His voice sounded rough and weak.

Sulu pushed herself up to her knees. "I'm fine, Ensign," she said. "How are you feeling?" Young's recovery had initially been slow, his edema easing but not abating during the first three days after Kostas had administered the antivenin. At last, though, on the fourth day, his condition had shown significant improvement, his breathing finally returning close to normal. *And today he was actually able to rise and move about the cabin,* Sulu thought. *And his color's back.* Until that day, his skin had displayed a sickly pallor.

"I'm improving," Young said. "And I'll be happy when I can remove this thing." He pointed to the tracheostomy tube, a smaller version than the one Kostas had initially inserted into his neck. The young engineer had so far demonstrated proficient skills as a medic, but still preferred to wait until they got back to *Enterprise* so that Doctor Morell could do the final removal.

"It'll come out soon enough," Sulu told him. "In the meantime, don't strain yourself. Save your voice."

Young nodded as Sulu stood up and moved to the front of the cabin, where she took a seat beside Kostas. "Couldn't sleep, sir?" the ensign asked.

"No," Sulu said. "I guess I'm not used to having so much time off."

Kostas chuckled. Since losing contact with the *Enterprise* crew, the captain and her two crew members had spent the intervening five days searching the surface of the planet on which they found themselves. They first stopped at the break in the forest Sulu had found, where they'd managed to excavate the small piece of metal her tricorder had found. Not even as large as a human fingertip, the nodule looked like nothing of any particular note. Scored black, with a rough patch where it might once have attached to another piece of metal, it could have come from the hull of a spacecraft, as the tritanium and duranium within it suggested, but it might also have been a part of an aircraft fuselage or even something else entirely.

Since then, Sulu and Kostas had been taking shifts at the helm, tracing the search pattern that the captain had devised. At first, they had followed grids in a spiral centered at the portal's destination point, where they had left *Pytheas*. In that way, they stayed close enough to the area that they could return there in relatively short order should they receive a transmission from *Enterprise*. After three days, though, the captain had chosen to fly farther afield, concerning herself more with finding those who had created the portal than reestablishing contact with her crew.

Sulu gazed through the viewport. A rolling grassland passed beneath the shuttlecraft, its gentle rises and mild falls putting the captain in mind of a rolling green ocean. A small herd of four-legged animals roamed atop the next hill, but Sulu saw no signs of civilization—no cities, no towns, no primitive settlements.

And then she heard the sensor panel emit a three-toned signal. She and Kostas had programmed alerts to sound if scans detected signs of intelligent life: controlled power, road systems, manufactured structures, and the like. The ensign read from her display. "Sensors are showing refined metal," she said.

"Are there any life signs?" Sulu asked.

"No," Kostas said, skillfully working her panel. "But I'm seeing tritanium . . . duranium . . . rodinium—"

"All materials commonly used in constructing starship hulls," Sulu said. "Where is it?"

"Bearing three hundred thirty-five degrees," Kostas said. Sulu operated the helm and brought *Amundsen* to port. When she had straightened the shuttlecraft's course, she looked out, eager to see what they had found. One hill drifted below, and then another. Eventually, Kostas said, "Range: one hundred thirty meters." She pointed ahead of them. "It's just over the second rise."

The land flowed and ebbed and then flowed again. Sulu watched as the land fell away once more after that to reveal not merely a valley beyond it, but a midsize crater, several dozen meters across. In the middle of the sinuous prairie, among tall grasses waving gracefully in the wind, a circular hole had been gouged from the earth, the soil within it charred and left devoid of life.

There could be no doubt of the cause. Wreckage littered the crater. Whatever had crashed there had been reduced to fragments. No one could have survived.

"Was it a ship?" Kostas asked.

"I don't know," Sulu said. "Maybe a small one." And she thought: *Like a shuttlecraft.*

"Did it belong to the inhabitants of Rejarris Two?" Kostas asked. "The ones who built the portal?"

"I don't know," Sulu said again. "Maybe." The idea filled the captain with melancholy, but at the same time, if it had been a vessel manned by Rejarris II natives, then it could mean that Sulu and Kostas and Young had a good chance of finding others. After all, an entire planetary population had gone missing, and not just the complement of a single small ship. "We need to find out."

Sulu changed course and started *Amundsen* on a descent into the crater. As the shuttlecraft slipped down past the rim, the nature of what had taken place there became even clearer. The ground appeared blackened and sterile, and no part of the vessel had survived intact.

As Sulu set *Amundsen* down, Kostas moved to

the aft bulkhead. She returned with two phasers, tricorders, and communicators. The captain instructed her to leave a communicator with Ensign Young as well, so that he wouldn't have to cross to the front of the cabin if he needed to contact Sulu and Kostas. "We'll check in every fifteen minutes," Sulu told Young. She didn't bother to give him instructions on what to do if they failed to keep in communication with him, because what could he do?

Outside, Sulu closed the hatch and paced slowly to the center of the crater. Fragments of metal lay all around, most no larger than a fingernail. She scanned the area with her tricorder and saw that some of the debris had been driven deep into the ground.

"There are a few larger pieces," Kostas said, consulting her own tricorder. The ensign walked a short distance away while Sulu dropped onto her haunches. The captain picked up a small piece of metal and held it in her palm. She did not want to imagine the incredible force required to tear the vessel apart so thoroughly, nor what such a force would have done to anybody inside it.

Sulu scanned several bits of metal, confirming the readings Ensign Kostas had taken aboard the shuttlecraft. She stowed several of the fragments in a small compartment in her tricorder, then stood back up. She looked over at Kostas and saw her agape. The ensign stood motionless, her gaze glued to a larger section of metal that she held in one hand. It had ragged edges and was as large as her forearm.

"Ensign, what is it?" Sulu asked, walking over to her. "Have you found something?" By way of explanation, Kostas handed the metal piece to the captain. Sulu looked at it and saw its scorched gray-white surface adorned with a single word in Federation Standard, the name of a Starfleet vessel she recognized.

It was *Excelsior*.

2308

Excelsior

6

Captain Hikaru Sulu exited the starboard turbolift and walked onto the bridge of *Excelsior*. That late at night, at the beginning of gamma shift, the lighting had dimmed as part of the simulated circadian cycle aboard ship. The dusky setting matched Sulu's mood: his fatigue left him bleary-eyed. He found great satisfaction in the crew's current exploratory mission out on the frontier, but it had been months—*Nearly a year,* he thought—since the ship had visited a starbase. No matter the activities and amenities aboard *Excelsior*, no matter the participation in an occasional landing party, it sometimes became emotionally imperative for the crew to get off the ship specifically for rest and recreation.

As Sulu crossed the bridge to the command chair, he glanced over at the main viewscreen. He expected to see some particularly beautiful M-class world composed of blue skies, green continents, and white clouds, or a spectacularly ringed planet, or maybe even something completely new to him; although still in his first year aboard ship, Gallin Ressix had served on *Excelsior* long enough to know what qualified as unusual when viewed through the prism of the captain's long experience in Starfleet. Instead of some marvelous or strange astronomical sight, though, the curve of a beclouded, nondescript planet filled the bottom half of the viewer. "Lieutenant," Sulu said as he reached the command chair, "this better be interesting enough to keep your captain from a good night's sleep." Sulu had been in his quarters, about to climb into bed, when Ressix had contacted him; he'd had to put his uniform back on before going up to the bridge.

The young Bolian officer stood up from the command chair. "Begging the captain's pardon," Ressix said, "but what would a virile man like you need with sleep?"

Sulu maintained a steady expression, but he felt like both smiling and wincing at the jest. He felt good, both physically and mentally, but, more than a year removed from his seventieth birthday, he had to admit that he had slowed down some. "Bucking for promotion again already, Mister Ressix?" he said. "You just made lieutenant last month."

"Somebody has to be ready to step in when the captain's asleep."

Sulu offered Ressix a curt nod and a smile that touched only half his mouth. "Do you know what else happens when the captain sleeps?" he asked.

"All over the ship, refreshers are cleaned." Ressix responded with a knowing smile that suggested he enjoyed the byplay, even when it turned at his own expense. Sulu appreciated the young man's sense of humor, with which he walked the line between acerbic insouciance and outright insubordination— a delicate balance, even for seasoned veterans.

The captain also saw a great deal of potential in the junior-grade lieutenant, who, like Sulu, had chosen in his nascent starship career the position of helm officer; also like Sulu, he'd elected to do so as a member of the command division. Ressix typically piloted *Excelsior* during gamma shift, but when Crajjik had devised that month's duty roster, he'd approached the captain about giving the young officer a taste of the center seat. Sulu had agreed with his first officer. He supposed he would soon learn the wisdom of that decision.

"So what's interesting enough for you to call the captain to the bridge after twenty-four hundred hours?"

Ressix gestured toward the main viewer. "This is Rejarris Two," he said. At the end of alpha shift, when Sulu had left the bridge, the crew had been studying the third planet in the system, a task they had been near to completing when he'd asked for a status report during beta shift. "We finished surveying the last of the five gas giants orbiting this star, and we arrived here at twenty-one fifty." Rejarris numbered just one among many of the charted but unexplored suns *Excelsior* had visited since the ship had departed Helaspont Station ten months earlier. With no set agenda, no predefined course, and a mandate from Starfleet Command to explore simply in the pursuit of knowledge, the crew had added several scientific discoveries to its list of achievements.

Rejarris II, though, did not impress. "It looks rather dull to me," Sulu noted.

"It might look that way, sir, but I don't think it is," Ressix said. "Or at least I don't think it *was*."

"'Was'?"

"The clouds appear to be the byproduct of a massive event," Ressix explained. "Possibly an asteroid strike, an offworld attack, or a nuclear conflict. Scans of the surface show intact cities all across the globe, though, so Ensign Millán favors the strike theory." An assistant science officer, Felicia Millán crewed a station on the port side of the bridge.

"I take it this is a pre-warp civilization," Sulu said. If there had been any indication of a spacefaring society on Rejarris II, the *Excelsior* crew would have bypassed the outer planets upon entering the system. If such indications had come later, during beta or gamma shift, the captain would have been notified immediately. Since Ressix had not led with the discovery of a warp-capable culture, Sulu assumed the reverse.

"It appears that way," Ressix said. "Sensors show very basic, automated spacecraft on the planet's two moons."

"What's the planetary population?"

"That's where things get interesting, sir," Ressix said. "Something on the planet is interfering with our bio-scans. There's a string of artificial satellites in orbit, though, and so I thought to monitor their activity in the hopes of extrapolating the size of the populace based on communications traffic."

"Resourceful," Sulu said, eliciting a smile from the lieutenant. "What did you find?"

"None of the satellites show any activity," Ressix said, "and several have deteriorating orbits and are on the verge of falling back to the planet."

"So what do you think that tells us?" the captain asked. "That this civilization wiped itself out? Or that an asteroid did? Or that after whatever calamity befell this world, the survivors either lost the capability or the interest in using the satellites they'd put in orbit?"

"I'm not sure, sir," Ressix said, "but in the course of examining the satellites, we discovered something else." The lieutenant turned toward the long console situated above and behind the command chair, on the outer ring of the bridge. On one end, Ensign Tobias Benton crewed the tactical station, and on the other, Crewwoman Page Aaron worked communications. "Ensign," Ressix said, addressing the security officer, "please show the captain what we found."

"Aye, sir," said Benton. "Magnifying." He worked his controls, and the image on the main viewer shifted. Rejarris II and its opaque atmosphere disappeared, replaced by a flurry of stars strewn across the darkness of space. A great curved object hung in the void.

Sulu took a step toward the viewscreen. "What . . . what is that? A space station?"

"Negative," Ressix said. "There are no life signs."

From the sciences station, Millán added, "If the object had a crew, there'd be no place to put them. It's filled with circuitry, with no room for personnel."

"Even for personnel who are only centimeters tall, Ensign?" Sulu asked, his question a response to what he considered a teaching moment for the young officer—for all the young gamma-shift bridge crew. "Or for energy beings?"

"Well . . . maybe in those cases there would be room," Millán said, her manner sheepish. "But sensors aren't detecting life signs of any kind."

Sulu nodded, curious. He moved around the small hexagonal table he'd had installed in front of the command chair and sat down. "So what can you tell me about the object?" he asked Ressix.

"It occupies a high orbit, and it's the only one of its kind about the planet," said the lieutenant. "It's big and circular." On the viewscreen, the object appeared elliptical, but only, Sulu realized, because it floated with its edge oriented at an angle with respect to Excelsior. "It measures more than five hundred meters across, and its frame is fourteen-point-three meters through. Solar panels are mounted on the ring, undoubtedly for energy collection."

"What about shields? Weapons? Drive systems?"

Benton spoke up from tactical. "My scans show no phaser or disruptor banks, no directed-energy reserves, no weapons of any kind," he said. "I do read low-power force fields protecting the solar panels."

"There's no drive," Millán said. "Thrusters are keeping it in position, and it also has antigravs."

"What about communications?" Sulu asked. "Are any signals being transmitted to or from the object?"

"No, sir," said Aaron. "Not since we've been monitoring it."

Sulu folded his arms across his chest. "So what is it?" he asked. Crewman Khaled Rehan and Ensign T'Jen glanced back at the captain from the helm and navigation stations, but they offered no answers. "Do we have any idea whether it even originated here? Could it have been brought to this planet from somewhere else, for some unknown purpose, by a more advanced species?"

"It's possible, though we've found no trace of warp travel within the system," Millán said. "We've also scanned the orbiting satellites and the spacecraft on the two moons, as well as some of the cities. It's difficult to know with complete confidence, but all of the technology seems consistent with what we see in the object."

"Could it just be a solar collector?" Ressix asked. "Maybe gathering energy and beaming it down to the surface?"

"Maybe," Sulu said, but the idea didn't sound plausible to him. "But why would there be just one of them?"

"It might be a failed experiment," Ressix suggested. "Or an incomplete one."

"But it's such an inefficient design," Sulu said. "It encompasses so much area, and yet the solar panels are only on the periphery." The object puzzled the captain. He felt as though he was missing something, some observation or perspective or piece of information that would answer all his questions. "Have you viewed the object from the other side?"

"No, sir," Ressix said. "We came upon it while in orbit, and when it showed up on sensors, I stopped the ship."

"All right, then, let's take a look," Sulu said. "Mister Rehan, take us around slowly. Ensign T'Jen, pass it on the spaceward side." Although his crew had identified no interaction between the object and the surface of the planet, the captain did not want to risk traveling between the two. "Mister Benton, keep the viewscreen focused on the object."

"Aye, Captain."

As *Excelsior* climbed away from Rejarris II, Sulu watched the ship's progress on the main viewer, its alignment with the object changing by degrees. He leaned forward in his chair, unfolding his arms and leaning on the small table, trying to discern whatever details he could. As the ship passed in front of the object, it looked less and less elliptical, until the captain could at last make out its circular shape.

Suddenly, the viewscreen erupted in a flood of golden light. From points all around the object, beams burst forth, widening as they laced toward *Excelsior*. The ship lurched hard, throwing Sulu from the command chair onto the deck. Both of his legs struck the table as he fell, and jolts of pain flared in his knees. Lieutenant Ressix flew backward through the air, struck the railing dividing the outer ring of the bridge from the inner section, and went down hard.

The inertial dampers took a moment to compensate as *Excelsior* reeled again, the ship heaving to port. Even as Sulu grabbed for the command chair to prevent himself from rolling across the deck, he anticipated the voices of the bridge crew, who would deliver a situation report, a damage assessment, and recommendations for action. He waited as the ship shook, but no announcements came.

Sulu steadied himself with his grip on the command chair and looked around. He saw Ressix sprawled on the deck, facedown, not moving. At the navigator's station, T'Jen righted her seat as she fought her way back to her panel. The helm sat uncrewed, and the captain saw Rehan scuffling to stand, shaking his head as though to clear it. Around the perimeter of the bridge, supplemental personnel had also been knocked from their feet. From Sulu's vantage, he could not see past the long aft console to the communications and tactical positions. "Red alert!" the captain called out, hoping that Benton still stood at his post. "Shields!" Though only seconds had passed, Sulu lamented the slower reaction time of his gamma-shift crew. *They're only children,* he thought as he pulled himself up by the arm of his chair. They were more than that, of course: they were trained Starfleet personnel—but they were also inexperienced.

"Shields up!" the captain heard Benton cry out, but *Excelsior* continued to tremble beneath the attack. The alert klaxon shrieked its call to battle stations as the emergency lighting bathed the bridge in a red glow.

"Ready main phasers," Sulu yelled. As much as

he didn't want to fire on a less-advanced civilization, and even though doing so could be considered a violation of the Prime Directive, he would do what he needed to do to protect his crew. He looked to the main viewer and saw it imbued with a golden aura. At least a dozen beams—*More,* he thought—radiated out from around the circular construct, all of them aimed at *Excelsior.* Sulu noticed with dismay that the object had grown in size to fill the entire screen, and as he watched, the top and bottom arcs disappeared from view. *Whatever that thing is, it's drawing the ship toward it.* Benton confirmed that a second later.

"Those aren't weapons," the crewman called out above the shrill insistence of the red-alert klaxon. "They're tractor beams."

"Silence the bridge," Sulu ordered, and the klaxon quieted. Just two arcs of the object showed on either side of the main viewer, like a pair of enormous space-bound parentheses. Sulu could still see half a dozen beams ensnaring the ship. "Helm, can you break us free?"

Back at his console, Rehan stabbed at his controls. "Trying, Captain," he said. "Thrusters are making no appreciable difference."

Thrusters! Sulu thought, judging the conservative and ineffective choice as further evidence of his gamma-shift crew's lack of experience. "Impulse power now," he ordered. "Navigator, plot a course directly away from the object."

"Impulse power, aye," Rehan replied.

"Course laid in," T'Jen said.

The low-pitched hum of the ship's sublight

drive rose in the bridge, a familiar cushion of sound and vibration that provided Sulu with hope. He had no idea who sought to capture his ship and crew or why, but he would do everything he could to prevent it. Almost at once, though, the drone of the impulse drive increased in pitch, beginning to wail as it struggled to counteract the pull of the tractor beams. Sulu didn't need a status report to know that the ship was failing to break free.

"Helm, go to one hundred twenty-five percent of impulse," he said. He wouldn't risk engaging the warp engines this deep in a planetary gravity well, or that close to another object, but he would burn out the impulse drive if necessary—and then, if pushed to it, open fire.

"One hundred twenty-five percent of impulse, aye," Rehan said, working his console.

As the thrum of the sublight engines grew louder and deeper—an encouraging sound to the captain—the starboard turbolift doors whisked open. Beskle Crajjik, Sulu's first officer, dashed onto the bridge. He headed toward the captain, who pointed at the inert form of Lieutenant Ressix lying on the deck. Without a word, Crajjik dropped to his knees beside the young man and began examining him.

Once more, the impulse drive started to whine, but not as much as it had previously. "The tractor beams are showing signs of strain," Benton said. "Our movement toward the object has stopped."

"Impulse engines are threatening to overload, Captain," Rehan said.

"Let them," Sulu said. "We need to break free."

He heard one of the aft doors open, and then, from the tactical station, came a familiar voice, calm and steady. "I'm here, Captain," said the ship's laconic, stone-faced chief of security, Ryan Leslie.

"Target—" Sulu began, but he never finished the order. *Excelsior* pitched violently, the strong, abrupt motion hurling him to the deck.

"Several tractor beams have failed," Benton yelled, not from the tactical console, but clearly from some secondary station.

Sulu got up and looked at the main viewer. He saw a single section of the object, much larger than before. Something else suddenly appeared, circling in from the edge of the screen. Although the captain recognized it at once, the context at first confused him. He then realized that when the struggles of the impulse engines to overcome *Excelsior*'s seizure caused some of the tractor beams to fail, the ship's drive had carried the newly unencumbered section of the ship in one direction and the rest of it in the other. As Sulu watched, *Excelsior* yawed to port, sending the warp nacelle on that side of the ship hurtling toward the object.

The captain opened his mouth to give an order, but the words never made it to his lips. *Excelsior*'s port nacelle slammed into the inner side of the object. Sulu toppled back to the deck, the thunderous sound of the collision painfully loud. He lifted his head as the ship quaked. On the viewscreen, a gash exposed the inside of the object to space, and pieces of wreckage glinted in the sunlight as they floated away from the point of impact. The remaining tractor beams continued to pull *Excelsior* into the object.

"Targeting tractor beams," Leslie said, but before he could fire, the pylon supporting the port nacelle snapped. The warp engine struck the engineering section of the ship and shattered, raining down destruction upon the hull. An explosion sent fiery wreckage hurtling into space, and the emergency lighting went out without even flickering first, leaving the bridge bathed in the glow of control consoles.

"Leslie, separate the saucer section!" Sulu yelled, not trusting the complicated maneuver to the green Crewman Rehan in such dangerous conditions. The captain floundered back to his feet as the rock-solid form of his security chief bounded from the outer ring of the bridge and over to the helm, where Rehan barely had time to get out of his way. "Aaron," Sulu said, "contact all transporter rooms and have them beam the crew over from the secondary hull." During a call to battle stations, operators staffed all of the ship's transporters.

"The saucer's locking mechanisms aren't responding," called Leslie. "We can't separate."

Sulu threw himself toward the command chair. He groped for the panel on its arm and found the controls he needed, but before activating them, he took one more look at the viewscreen, just in time to see a chunk of compromised hull tear into the second nacelle. The captain brought his fingers down on two separate control surfaces. A booming alarm even louder and more insistent than the red-alert klaxon went up through the ship.

"*Abandon ship*," ordered a male voice distinctly different from the usual female identity of *Excel-*

sior's library-computer interface. "*All personnel report to escape pods. This is not a drill.*"

Sulu peered in Crajjik's direction, though he could barely see him in the darkened bridge. He spied two silhouettes, though, as the first officer helped Lieutenant Ressix to his feet. At the navigator's station, T'Jen had risen, and she and Rehan looked to the captain, as though for additional guidance. "Go!" he yelled at them, pointing toward the hull panel beside one of the turbolifts, which had already swung open to allow access to the passage leading to the escape pods. A dim but much-needed emergency light shined from within. Fortunately, Starfleet equipped those systems in every section of every starship with their own independent power supply. The announcement to abandon ship, the automatic opening of hull panels, the lighting in the passages beyond them, and the escape pod launchers would be the last functioning equipment aboard *Excelsior*.

As the bridge crew hurried toward the open hull panel, a hand grabbed the captain strongly by his biceps and pulled him from the command chair. Standing five or so centimeters taller than Sulu, the security chief gazed down at him, the reflected illumination of a control panel revealing urgency in his eyes, but a demeanor otherwise remarkably composed. "You have to go," Leslie told him. "Now."

Sulu looked all around the bridge and saw nobody left at any of the stations. He nodded to the security chief, and together they headed for the passage leading to the escape pods. Once there,

Leslie stepped aside to allow the captain to enter first, but Sulu stopped and pushed his hand into the small of the commander's back. The security chief hesitated, but then went first. Sulu followed.

The ship's hatch allowing access to the first escape pod hung open. Leslie moved past it. Sulu stepped up, peered inside the pod, and counted out the crew in his head: Millán from sciences, Benton from tactical, First Officer Crajjik with the injured Ressix, and Boyle, De Luco, Luckman, and Ybarra, the four supplementary personnel who'd been working at secondary consoles.

Eight of the crew for eight seats, Sulu thought. Crajjik moved toward the hatch, plainly intending to exit after having loaded Ressix aboard, but the captain held up his hand. When the first officer stopped, Sulu reached in and pulled the pod's inner hatch shut, then backed up and swung *Excelsior*'s hatch closed atop it. The crew could have launched themselves, but Sulu didn't wait. He opened a panel in the bulkhead, verified the pod's readiness, and then shot the handle that would allow eight of his seven hundred thirty-two crew to make their escape from their doomed vessel. He heard a hydraulic sound, and then the round port in the hatch showed nothing but empty space.

Leslie had moved on to the next escape pod, the second of the three that served the bridge. Sulu joined him, and when he looked through the hatch there, he saw Rehan from the helm, T'Jen from navigation, and Aaron from communications, leaving only the security chief and the captain behind. "It's time to go, sir," Leslie said.

"Yes, go," Sulu said.

"Captain—"

"No arguments, Ryan," Sulu said. "I'll be the last one off the ship." He had first met Leslie decades ago, when they'd both served under Captain Kirk aboard *Enterprise*. When *Excelsior*'s former chief of security, L. J. Akaar, had left the ship a few years earlier to become second officer aboard the *Larson*-class *Kuala Lumpur*, Leslie had applied for the vacated position, and Sulu had accepted his transfer from space station KR-1.

"There's nothing more you can do here," said the security chief. "The ship is dead. There's no reason for you to join it."

"I have no intention of doing so," Sulu told him. "But I *will* be the last one off the ship."

Leslie stared at the captain for almost too long a time, and Sulu wondered if *Excelsior*'s security chief was considering throwing a punch in an attempt to incapacitate his commanding officer and abduct him from his own ship. But then the commander relented. He ducked through the hatch and into the escape pod. Sulu reached in after him to pull the hatch closed, but Leslie turned to face him before he could do so. "Don't wait too long, Hikaru," he said. "Now more than ever, this crew needs its captain."

Sulu nodded, then shut both hatches. After he dispatched the second pod, he gazed out through the port. Past the bulkheads in which the escape pod had nestled, he saw the long shape of an *Excelsior* warp nacelle—or part of a nacelle, anyway—tumbling end over end through space, blue gas jetting from a breach in its side. He looked for the rest of the ship, but couldn't find it. Neither could he see the alien object that had been the cause of the disaster. He did see sunlight gleaming off fragments of debris floating through space, as well as a dozen escape pods. The ship carried fifty of the emergency vehicles, all but five of which could carry twenty-four individuals.

How did this happen so fast? Sulu knew that only a combination of training, experience, and adrenaline prevented him from falling into shock.

The ship shook again, and the captain guessed that something else had exploded somewhere. He raced back along the passage until he found the dedicated control panel that recorded the present status of *Excelsior*'s escape pods. A chill ran through him as he saw a line of red indicators in one section. ENGINEERING, AFT DORSAL, he read. Five pods had been damaged or couldn't be launched, but that still left more than enough to evacuate the entire crew. Sulu counted seventeen green indicators, then watched as others changed from yellow to green.

Excelsior shuddered, throwing Sulu against the outer bulkhead. He pushed himself off and went back to the status board. Twenty-five escape pods had launched, he saw. Twenty-six. Twenty-seven. He wanted to wait for thirty of the large pods, which, in addition to the two smaller ones that had already left, could, if filled to capacity, evacuate the entire crew.

The ship jolted again, and Sulu crashed once more into a bulkhead. He looked through the port and saw not the blackness of space, but the blues and browns and whites of a planet. *But not Rejarris Two*, he thought, recalling that world's complete cloud cover.

At the moment, though, none of that mattered. The ship—or what was left of it—would go down soon. Sulu looked again at the status board and saw that only one more indicator had turned green. He wanted to wait longer, but knew that any more time might be too much time.

The captain rushed down the passage, *Excelsior* rumbling and shaking about him. He staggered along, thrown left and right. He tripped at one point and went down to one knee—it twisted and exploded in pain—but he shoved himself back up and hobbled on.

When Sulu reached the third escape pod, he stumbled into it, pulling the shipside hatch closed behind him. Once inside, he closed up the pod, then opened the control panel in the bulkhead. He reached in and worked the handle to launch the escape vehicle away from *Excelsior*.

Nothing happened.

Sulu retracted the handle and then pushed it a second time, and still the pod remained in place. He peered at the control panel and saw a red indicator, signaling that the launch mechanism had failed. With the tremendous damage done to the ship and the amount of wreckage floating around, it didn't surprise him. The door on the outside of the compartment enclosing the escape pod could have become wedged shut, or if something had penetrated the hull there, the walls around the pod or the tracks on which it accelerated out into space could have become impaired.

Sulu moved to the other side of the hatch and found the panel securing the emergency release. He flipped it open and took hold of the lever inside, but he hesitated. The emergency release would fire explosive bolts on the outside of the pod to propel it out of the ship. If the outer door wouldn't open, though, or if the compartment wall or the tracks would not allow the escape pod to pass, Sulu could set off explosions that, instead of sending him away from *Excelsior* to safety, could destroy his only avenue of escape—and him along with it.

Ryan said, "Don't wait too long," the captain thought. *And I won't.*

Sulu detonated the explosive bolts.

Commander Ryan Leslie stood outside the escape pod that had delivered him and three other crew members safely to the surface of Rejarris II.

Except that this planet isn't Rejarris Two, is it? Leslie thought. According to the gamma-shift bridge crew, the ship had arrived at the planet not long before they'd come on duty. A terrestrial world, Rejarris II revealed itself to be in the aftermath of some cataclysmic event that had left it completely blanketed in thick clouds of particulates. As he peered upward, though, he saw only a few wisps of cirrus clouds interrupting an otherwise-clear expanse of blue sky.

Leslie trusted the *Excelsior* crew, even the relatively inexperienced officers on gamma shift. Still, he'd taken the time to verify their reports with the beta-shift bridge officers who'd been on duty when the ship had arrived at the second planet in the Rejarris system. It seemed as though the place they'd landed bore only a passing resemblance to the world *Excelsior* had been orbiting.

Or maybe that's only what we've been led to believe. Leslie had served long enough in Starfleet— more than half a century—to know that the complexities of the universe, not to mention those of the myriad beings who populated it, often made it difficult to draw accurate conclusions about a situation. Aboard *Enterprise*, *Lexington*, *Ingersol*, and *Excelsior*, he'd visited enough alien worlds to fill a galactic atlas. He'd witnessed shape-shifting creatures perfectly mimicking historical figures, his crewmates, and in one memorable instance, Captain Kirk's command chair. He'd seen energy beings who could take on any form, a civilization that transformed the thoughts of its visitors into a simulacrum of reality, and even a planet that chased a starship through space. The Talosians could impose an illusion of their choosing on others, the Aegis could hide an entire solar system, and the Tracon could send large populations into long periods of hallucinatory sleep. In any puzzling situation he encountered while out exploring the universe, Leslie rarely considered the deductions that he or anybody else made as conclusive.

Maybe we're on Rejarris Two or maybe we're not, the security chief thought, *but right now, it has no bearing on what I need to do.*

Leslie leaned in to the hatch of the eight-passenger escape pod. Inside, alone, Crewwoman Aaron worked at the small communications panel. "Anything?" the security chief asked.

Aaron looked up, and Leslie saw weariness written in her features. He knew that her exhaustion came not from physical or mental exertions, but from the emotional toll exacted by their abandonment of *Excelsior* and the ship's subsequent destruction. Still a young member of the crew, less than a year out of Starfleet Academy, Aaron had likely never endured such a harrowing experience. Despite that, she had maintained her composure during the long journey down to the planet's surface, and her professionalism shined through as she continued to monitor communications on Leslie's order.

"Yes, sir," Aaron said. "Commander Azleya just reported in from escape pod number forty-seven." That emergency vehicle, Leslie knew, launched from the starboard aft section of engineering. "She reports a full complement of twenty-four personnel in her pod."

"Injuries?" Leslie asked.

"A crewman suffered burns on one leg, and another broke his arm," Aaron said, "but otherwise, the commander described the rest as superficial wounds. She also states that hers was the last pod to depart the secondary hull." Leslie would have expected nothing less of Terim Azleya, *Excelsior*'s chief engineer.

"Where are they now?"

"I'm having problems picking them up on biosensors," Aaron said, "but the communications range finder puts them one hundred seventy-one kilometers northeast of us. According to Commander Azleya, their homing equipment failed immediately after they launched. She attempted to follow the other escape vehicles visually and correct course manually, but there was only so much she could do after atmospheric insertion. Once she sees to her people's basic needs, she plans to reset the guidance system and make her way to us."

"Understood," Leslie said. Without the ability of Azleya's pod to automatically track the rest of the escape vehicles, it frankly amazed the security chief that she'd been able to set down within two hundred klicks of them. He tried to let the feat bolster his confidence in the situation, but it did little to allay his immediate concerns. Including Azleya's, thirty-one escape pods had so far been accounted for on the surface of the planet, carrying a total of six hundred eighty-seven personnel. Reports of the survivors identified a dozen of the crew who had perished aboard *Excelsior*, leaving thirty-three missing—most notably, First Officer Crajjik and Captain Sulu.

I should never have left without Hikaru, Leslie thought, just as he had numerous times over the last several hours. In his mind, he relived that moment outside the second bridge escape pod, when for a few seconds he had actually considered physically hauling the captain through the hatch and forcibly removing him from *Excelsior*. But he also knew that he couldn't fixate on who might not have safely evacuated the ship. Without Sulu and Crajjik around, command fell on Leslie's shoulders.

"Sir?" With no small amount of discomfort,

the security chief realized that Aaron had been speaking to him while he'd been mired in his own thoughts.

"I'm sorry," Leslie said. "What is it?

"I'm detecting what could be a communications signal from another pod, but it's very weak," Aaron said. "So far, I haven't been able to establish a link."

"Keep trying," Leslie said. "I'll check with Lieutenant Carville about it." Lieutenant J. S. Carville served *Excelsior* as its lead comm officer. While Aaron worked in one of the eight-passenger pods, Carville manned communications in one of the larger escape vehicles.

"Yes, sir," said Aaron, and she reached over and handed him a padd. "Here are the details."

Leslie took the padd. Before he left, he told the young crewwoman, "You're doing good work." The statement provoked a tired but seemingly genuine smile.

"Thank you, sir."

Leslie turned away from the hatch. All around, at unequal distances and in nearly every direction, twenty-nine of the larger pods sat arrayed on an arid plain. With roughly square footprints and about the size of shuttlecraft, the escape vehicles together looked like a collection of rudimentary dwellings scattered haphazardly across the landscape, as though an ad hoc village had sprung up overnight.

Except that our humble lodgings also appear as though they've been sitting on the leading edge of a war, Leslie thought. The lower portions of all the hulls had been charred black during their plunge through the atmosphere, and a number of the pods showed scars from where they had collided with debris from *Excelsior*. And while most of the escape vehicles had landed on level ground, two of them rested unevenly atop some of the boulders littering the area.

Most of the ship's complement had disembarked, but they largely stayed close to whatever pod had carried them to the planet's surface. For the most part, they tended to the injured among them, arranged for the dispersal of rations, and aggregated reports from their various shipboard duty sections about what had taken place on the lost *Excelsior*. Under direct orders from Leslie, some personnel had begun setting up emergency shelters, while others monitored sensors and communications. Automatic distress beacons already broadcast calls for help toward the Federation.

The security chief headed toward the pod emblazoned with a large number *13*, which had alit off to the left, at a distance of about seventy-five meters. The dry ground crunched beneath Leslie's boots as he walked. He hadn't yet checked, but he thought that the pull of gravity on the planet seemed slightly higher than the artificial field maintained aboard *Excelsior*.

As Leslie made his way to the pod where Lieutenant Carville monitored communications, some of the crew gazed toward him. He consciously kept his stride sure and unhurried, wanting to sow confidence in his shipmates. After all that they'd endured to that point, and with Captain Sulu and Commander Crajjik still among the missing, doubts and fears could understandably rise in even the most seasoned of Starfleet veterans.

As Leslie reached Carville's escape pod, Lieutenant Sevol emerged through the open hatch. The ship's alpha-shift helmsman flipped open a communicator, but then stopped when he saw the security chief. "Commander, I was just stepping outside to contact you," Sevol said. He closed his communicator and affixed it to the back of his belt. Despite his Vulcan reserve, even he showed visible signs of the strain that the previous few hours had wrought. "Commander Ajax wishes to speak with you." Josefina Ajax headed *Excelsior*'s sciences division.

Leslie nodded his acknowledgment, and when Sevol stepped aside, the security chief ducked through the hatch. Inside the pod, several of the ship's senior staff worked over padds, while Carville crewed the escape vehicle's communications panel, and Ajax operated the sensors. Everybody glanced up when Leslie entered, and he didn't need to be a counselor to read the concern on their faces. He knew at once that something else—something bad—had happened.

"Lieutenant," the security chief said, gazing past the escape vehicle's built-in seats—arranged in five rows of four—toward the bulkhead opposite. There, to the left of the two pod-control positions, Carville sat before the comm console. Leslie sidled through the twenty clustered seats to the other four. "Aaron has heard from Commander Azleya. She's landed about two hundred kilometers from here with a full escape pod."

"That's excellent news, sir," Carville said.

"Aaron has also detected what she thinks is a weak comm signal." Leslie handed the padd to the lieutenant. "She's recorded the details for you."

"Very good, sir. I'll see what I can find."

Leslie watched Carville study the padd for a moment. Bracing himself, the security chief then turned toward Lieutenant Commander Ajax, who sat on the other side of the pod-control consoles. He paced over to her. "Lieutenant Sevol said you wanted to see me."

"Yes, sir," she said, peering up at him from the sensor panel. "As you know, I've been scanning for any more of our escape pods. I just found something four hundred ninety-three kilometers south-southeast of our position. I'm reading duranium, rodinium, and titanium."

"Hull materials," Leslie noted.

"Aye," Ajax said quietly. "But if what the sensors are detecting was one of our escape vehicles, it's no longer intact."

Ever since leaving *Excelsior* without Captain Sulu, Leslie had tried to convince himself that he hadn't made a mistake, that his commanding officer had abandoned ship before the vessel had been completely destroyed. *And maybe he did succeed in getting away from* Excelsior *in time*, he thought, *but what difference does that make if his pod crashed?*

"Life signs?" Leslie asked, his voice falling almost to a whisper. He dreaded the answer he would receive.

"None, sir."

Equal measures of grief and guilt inundated the security chief. He had known Hikaru Sulu for such a long time, he considered him more than a commanding officer; they had become friends. *And I failed him on both counts.*

Leslie struggled not to show any outward response to those members of the crew present. Instead, he announced that he would reconfigure one of the pods and send a team to investigate the apparent crash site. He waited while Ajax transferred the details to a data card, which she then handed to him. "Keep searching," Leslie said, and then he headed back toward the hatch.

Outside, the security chief saw that Lieutenant Sevol had moved away from the escape pod. He stood thirty or so paces away, where he spoke with Ensign Frisch, one of the ship's transporter operators. Neither of the two men seemed to notice Leslie, for which he felt grateful. The security chief stepped to the side of the hatch and took a moment to collect himself. He might've failed Captain Sulu, but he would not fail the *Excelsior* crew. More responsibility had fallen to him at that instant than he'd ever had before, and he recommitted himself to living up to it.

Leslie took a deep breath, then let it out slowly. He started toward Sevol, whom he would task with modifying one of the pods and checking the readings that Ajax had found. He had only taken a few steps when a small boulder not far from the helmsman thrust upward and toppled onto its side. With stunning speed, a black, many-legged creature climbed from the hole that had been revealed.

Even as Leslie reached for his phaser, the grotesque beast charged toward Sevol and Frisch. The security chief raised his weapon and fired, his instincts and training working flawlessly, but still too late. The creature slammed into the two officers, sending Frisch sprawling onto the dirt. It then took hold of Sevol with several of its many limbs, lifting the helmsman from the ground.

As Leslie raced toward the two officers, red-tinged golden fire streaking from his phaser, more movement captured his attention. He looked away once, quickly, even as he continued forward. "Phasers!" he called out to any *Excelsior* personnel within earshot, and then, "Close the hatches!" It horrified him as he realized how many of the crew remained outside the escape pods.

All about the area, boulders began to topple.

2319

Enterprise

7

The turbolift doors glided open, and even before she stepped out of the cab and onto the bridge, Xintal Linojj felt all eyes turn toward her. *You're imagining it,* she told herself—but of course she wasn't. Some of the crew looked up and saw her, then quickly cast their attention back to their consoles. Others kept right on looking, while still others glanced up furtively.

Linojj left the turbolift without hesitating. She'd learned a long time ago not to delay even a single step when you knew the course you needed to travel, no matter how long that course, no matter how difficult or frightening, no matter the obstacles that stood in your way. The Romulans had invaded her homeworld of Cort during her youth, and they'd stayed for nearly a decade before the Boslic had finally been able to drive them out for good. As a girl, she saw less than most, protected by her family as much as possible from the effects of the attempted Romulan conquest, but as time passed, Linojj discovered for herself the awful truth. Once she had, she rebelled however she could against the intruders, most often in subtle, personal ways that some might refuse to label rebellion at all. At the height of hostilities, when the Empire occupied her hometown, she abstained from eating all of the rations provided her, so that she and her family could subsist on what she saved should the Romulans later deny them sustenance. She refused to learn any words in the Romulan language, and thus never understood when one overseer or another ordered her to do something. She never slept at lights-out, but stayed awake into the night, planning her life free of the Empire. It had been then that she had first contemplated leaving Cort, not to abandon her people, but to find a means of protecting them, and those like them.

Linojj had been thinking about eventually joining the Boslic Interstellar Force on the day that she'd come home from school to find her mother bound in the kitchen, her arms and legs tied to a chair. Only twelve, Xintal Linojj stood and stared while the loud, clumsy sounds of an unfamiliar man emerged from the refresher. Her mother told her to run out, quickly, to meet Bornya, her older sister, on the way home from school and go with her to a friend's house.

But Linojj hadn't moved. She froze, knowing that the man in the 'fresher wasn't her father, who at that time of day would be in the mines, unearthing the cormaline the Empire so desperately sought. More than that, she knew that the stranger must be a Romulan, that no Boslic would commit such an act. In hushed, hurried tones, her mother begged Xintal to find Bornya, and for the two of them to stay away from the house.

And still Linojj hadn't moved, not until the man had come out of the 'fresher and seen her. She bolted then, dropping her textbooks and racing for the front door. She never made it.

The rest of that day had been a blur. The man—a Romulan who reeked of alcohol—locked her in the cellar. She yelled for a long time to be let out, and wept uncontrollably when she heard her sister's voice—and screams—through the door. Her father found Xintal that night at the base of the cellar stairs, hugging herself tightly and whimpering.

Her mother and sister had survived their ordeal, and once the Boslic had finally repelled the Romulan forces for good, the two had even found a measure of peace in their lives. As far as Linojj knew, her sister never spoke of that day, and her mother did only once, years after the fact, when Xintal, as an adult, attempted to apologize for her failure to immediately do as she'd been told. "You only reacted to the situation the way that any twelve-year-old might." Her mother, she knew, intended to exonerate her of her guilt, but the word *might* haunted Linojj, for she *might* have run away at once, saving at least her sister from a terrible wrong.

Never hesitate when you know what you need to do, she told herself as she made her way toward the command chair. She'd absorbed that lesson many times over, thanks to the Romulans, but never more so than on that day when she hadn't prevented her sister from coming home. Linojj had suffered far worse indignities than parading wounded and incomplete before people she had known and worked with for years—and in some instances, for more than a decade. *These are my crewmates,* she thought as Tenger stood up to face her. In many cases, they were also her friends. It didn't matter whether they looked at her and her missing right arm with sorrow or even pity; she knew that, no matter what they felt, they supported her.

"Commander Linojj, returning to duty," she said as she stopped before Tenger. The security chief's gaze held no judgment, even though he had gone on record advocating that, given her condition, she not resume active duty so soon, especially in the middle of a crisis. It had been seven days since the portal had ceased to function, and ten since Linojj had lost her arm. It would require another couple of weeks before sickbay and the medical labs finished fabricating a biosynthetic replacement for her. After surgery to attach the new limb, she would need a recovery period, as well as physical, occupational, and emotional therapy—the last of which she had already begun. Tenger had stated in his log that he believed the best course of action, for both Linojj and the crew, would be for her to wait until after all of that had been completed before she resumed her position as the ship's acting captain.

But the security chief appeared to carry none

of those opinions with him as he regarded her in her first moments back on the bridge. Ever serious in the conduct of his duties—like so many of the Starfleet security personnel she'd met throughout her career—he showed no resistance to her decision to resume her station on *Enterprise*. It didn't surprise her. He had never brought their friendship onto the bridge, nor even the closeness they'd once shared when, years ago, they had briefly been lovers.

"You have the conn, Commander," Tenger said. "I stand relieved."

"Return to your post, Commander."

"Aye, sir.

Linojj watched Tenger as he moved to the tactical console and relieved Lieutenant Rainbow Sky, who shifted to a secondary station. When the first officer sat down in the command chair, she ran her hands along its arms, grateful to be back where she belonged—except that, no matter how much it felt as though she used both her hands, she didn't, and couldn't. It still seemed impossible that her right arm ended not at her hand, but at a metal cuff affixed just below her shoulder.

No hesitation, Linojj reminded herself. She knew what she had to do. She had already grieved for her traumatic loss, and she would doubtless continue to do so—though the fact of a replacement limb virtually indistinguishable from the original would mitigate her loss—but at that moment, she had responsibilities to discharge. "Status report."

"Portable tractor beams have been installed on

all of the shuttlecraft, including both warp shuttles, and all but one have been dispatched to the surface," Tenger said. "All CMUs have likewise been deployed." *Enterprise* had begun its current mission with a complement of a dozen class-H shuttlecraft, though only nine remained: *Amundsen* and *Pytheas* had traveled through the portal, and *Eriksson* had been destroyed eight months earlier, during the crew's exploration of the massive construct they'd discovered in the Jalidor Lambda system. The ship also carried a pair of *Gagarin*-class warp shuttles, along with a half dozen cargo management units, the latter of which came equipped with tractor beams. "All auxiliary craft are in position," Tenger went on, "and we are awaiting final placement of the antigravs."

The first officer looked at the main viewscreen, where an engineering technician stood on the plain of snow and ash to which Linojj and her landing party had transported ten days earlier, just before she'd lost her arm. On the outside of the portal, the technician lifted a two-handled panel and set it squarely on a smooth patch of hull. "How long before we'll be ready?" Linojj asked. Over the prior days, she'd requested that Tenger brief her on everything that had happened during her time in sickbay, as well as on the continuing efforts to recover the captain and the others.

"Commander Buonarroti estimates that preparations will be completed within fifteen minutes," said the security chief.

"Acknowledged," Linojj said. "Show me the entire portal."

"Aye, sir," Tenger said, and the first officer heard his fingers dancing across the tactical console. The image on the viewer, provided by an *Enterprise* probe, pulled back to reveal the entire structure of the portal, spreading out with a diameter of more than half a kilometer. Unidentifiable at such a remove, the ship's auxiliary craft appeared only as specks evenly spaced around the outside of the circular construct. A moment later, though, insets appeared on the screen, picturing and naming the sixteen vessels.

Linojj quickly picked out the missing registry: NCC-1701-B/7, *Galileo*. She knew that one shuttlecraft had been left behind on the hangar deck because the security chief had not wanted to leave *Enterprise* completely without support vessels. Linojj wondered if he had specifically chosen to keep *Galileo* aboard, since it happened to be her favorite.

The next step in the plan to recover the captain and her landing party was simple: employing the ship's auxiliary vessels and the tractor beams temporarily installed on them, the crew would lift the portal from the surface of Rejarris II and settle it in orbit, where its solar cells could renew its power, and therefore its function. Antigravs installed along the circumference of the structure would provide added stability. Though a delicate operation requiring pinpoint synchronization, it also seemed a straightforward effort and the most likely to work in a relatively short amount of time.

One of the other possibilities Tenger and Buonarroti had considered had been to utilize the facilities located eleven kilometers from the site of the portal. After contact with Captain Sulu and the other two crew members had been lost, and after efforts to determine how to reenergize the portal had gone on too long, Tenger had rescinded his previous order not to permit any of the crew on the surface of Rejarris II—both because of the exigency of recovering Sulu, Kostas, and Young, and because the danger the portal posed had disappeared with its loss of power. Lieutenant Commander Fenn led a landing party to the run of one-story buildings. As with every other place the crew had visited on the planet, they found it empty, but by virtue of the equipment there, they confirmed that it had been used to control the launch and reentry of the portal.

To exploit the capabilities of the facility, though, the crew would have had to overcome two impediments: they would have had to restore power to the buildings, and they would have had to learn how to operate the alien equipment. Even if they could quickly overcome the power requirements, the second problem stopped them cold. In the days since Linojj and the first landing party to Rejarris II had found books comprising chemically inscribed pages, Lieutenant Commander Kanchumurthi and his communications staff had tried to decipher that language. They believed that the inhabitants of Rejarris II "read" those chemical markers with a specialized sensory organ, but without knowledge of that organ, it made it extremely difficult to comprehend the process. As a result, even if the crew reestablished power to the launch complex, any attempt to raise the portal into orbit would have to be done blindly, with *Enterprise*'s engineers unable to read the labels and gauges on the equipment. With so much at stake—damage to the portal could result in the elimination of any chance to retrieve the captain and the others—Tenger and Buonarroti did not want to take the risk, except as a last resort—a position with which Linojj agreed.

"Commander Buonarroti reports that preparations are now complete," Tenger said. "All antigravs have been put in place, all engineering personnel have returned to their assigned auxiliary craft, and all pilots have signaled their readiness." Tenger had reached deep into the ship's roster to identify the sixteen crew members best suited to helming the shuttlecraft and CMUs. Fortunately, while only a dozen personnel had been rated for posting to *Enterprise*'s helm position, Starfleet required all personnel to qualify to take the position in an emergency, and virtually everybody had spent time in simulators during their tenure as cadets. For the most part, the ship's computer would handle flight operations anyway, because of the need for exacting coordination.

"Commence the operation," Linojj ordered.

"Signaling all auxiliary craft to lift off," Kanchumurthi said from the communications station. On the main viewer, nothing seemed to happen.

"Isolate one of the shuttlecraft on-screen," Linojj ordered.

"Aye, sir," Tenger said, and the image shifted to show *Enterprise*'s number 9 class-H vessel, *de Laroche*, rising beside the portal. It continued up for a short time before stopping and hovering. "All auxiliary craft have reached a height of thirty-five meters," said the security chief.

"All vessels are reporting that they are in position to activate their tractor beams," Kanchumurthi said.

"We are ready to switch control of the operation over to the computer," Tenger said. Commander Buonarroti and his engineering team had calculated the forces that would put the least amount of strain on the portal during its move back into orbit, including the distance of the shuttlecraft and CMUs from the structure, the strength and number of the tractor beams, and the rate of ascent. In addition to placing antigravs at regular intervals around the portal for stability, they had also affixed remote sensors to the structure in order to actively and efficiently monitor the stresses during the lift.

"Engage computer control," Linojj said.

"Aye, aye, sir," Tenger said. On the main viewer, a bluish white cone of light emanated from below the bow of *de Laroche*, where the engineers had attached the portable tractor beam. It swept out to the portal and took hold of the massive structure.

"All remote sensors are reporting," Fenn said at her sciences console. "Stresses are evenly distributed throughout the portal and within expected tolerances."

"The auxiliary craft are beginning to rise," Tenger said. The vessels would accelerate steadily to a safe, predetermined velocity until they had passed through the thermosphere and had reached the exobase. Once in the exosphere, they would increase speed again, at a considerably greater rate, until they could establish the portal in medium or high orbit. The operation would take hours to complete.

"Let's see the whole structure again," Linojj said. On the viewer, the image changed once more to display the entire portal. Although *Enterprise*'s auxiliary craft again became impossible to distinguish, Linojj could see the blue-white radiance of the sixteen tractor beams, which looked almost like glowing quills on the outside of the portal. The strategy called for the shuttlecraft and CMUs never to cross above the structure.

The assemblage took less than two hours to achieve its initial static atmospheric velocity. Linojj watched the procedure unfold, both in wider and narrower aspects. Over the course of the two hours, she ordered Tenger to cycle through close-up views of the six numbered cargo management units, the two warp shuttles—*Armstrong* and *Tereshkova*—and the eight class-H shuttlecraft—*April*, *Shintral*, *Baré*, *Mitrios*, *McAuliffe*, *Archer*, and *Winter*, in addition to *de Laroche*.

Almost three hours into the operation, Linojj heard the tactical console emit an alert tone. On the viewscreen, one of the tractor beams veered wildly, losing contact with the portal. "*Shintral* has a problem," Tenger said.

Linojj pushed herself up, careful to remind herself that she had only one arm with which to do so. "Open a channel."

"Open, sir," Kanchumurthi said.

"*Enterprise* to *Shintral*."

"*Shintral, this is Verant,*" came the immediate reply. The identity of *Shintral*'s pilot pleased Linojj. Although she had since moved into engineering, Verant had begun her tour of duty aboard *Enterprise* as a helm officer, and so she had experience in both disciplines. "*We're maintaining our course, but we've lost our hold on the portal.*"

"What happened?" Linojj asked.

"*We don't know,*" Verant said. "*Ensign Michaels is investigating.*"

"Commander," Fenn said, "sensors are showing increased stresses in the portal's hull where *Shintral* lost contact."

"How bad?" Linojj wanted to know.

"Within tolerances," Fenn said, "but increasing."

Linojj quickly reached for the controls on the arm of the command chair and activated the intercom. "Bridge to Buonarroti," she said. "Do you see what's happening out there?"

"*Buonarroti,*" the chief engineer said. "*Aye, I see it.*"

"Do we stop the shuttlecraft until we can fix whatever's happened?"

"*No, I don't think so,*" Buonarroti said. "*Decelerating will cause additional stresses.*"

"Understood. Out," Linojj said. Then, "Lieutenant Verant, have you located the problem?"

"*Michaels here, Commander,*" came the voice of the ensign. "*It appears that one side of the mount for the portable tractor beam has failed and come loose.*"

"Can you repair it?" Linojj asked, but Tenger spoke up before Michaels could answer.

"The direction of the tractor beam is beginning to fluctuate," he reported. "If it should contact the portal at a different point—" Linojj didn't need him to finish to understand the danger of altering the exactingly calculated stresses on the structure.

"*Shintral*, shut down your tractor beam now," she said. On the viewscreen, the shuttlecraft's beam winked off at once, but Linojj waited a beat until Tenger confirmed the deactivation. "Ensign Michaels, can you effect repairs?"

"*If we return to the ship or to the planet's surface, I can take a laser welder to it,*" Michaels said.

"How much time?" Linojj asked, but she already knew the answer would be insufficient to stave off a catastrophe. She imagined transporting an environmental-suited engineer onto the roof of one of the other shuttlecraft in flight and having Verant maneuver *Shintral* over to it so that the mount for the portable tractor beam could be fixed, but she dismissed the scheme as too risky. Not waiting for Michaels to reply, Linojj said, "Lieutenant Verant, move your shuttlecraft away from the portal. Ten kilometers. Then wait for *Enterprise* to contact you."

"*Aye, Commander,*" Verant said, without hesitation. Linojj made note to commend the lieutenant for her responsiveness.

"*Enterprise* out," Linojj said.

"*Shintral* is moving away," Tenger said.

"Captain, the stresses—" Fenn began, but Linojj talked over her.

"Syndergaard, take us in, fastest possible speed," she said, striding over to stand beside the helm officer. In response, the ensign sent his hands dashing across his console. The sound of the ship changed as power increased and the ship moved. "Tenger, prepare the *Enterprise*'s tractor beam to substitute for *Shintral*'s. Can you tie the ship in to the computer's coordination program?"

"We'll have to," Tenger said. "The *Enterprise*'s tractor beam is far more powerful than the portable models we attached to the shuttlecraft. We'll need to make adjustments with respect to our distance from the portal and the intensity of our beam. We'll also need to tie in to the helm to match velocities with the shuttlecraft."

"Have engineering get on it *now*," Linojj said. She rested her hand on Syndergaard's shoulder. "Get the necessary distance information from Commander Buonarroti. Bring us into position and match speeds as best and as quickly as you can."

"Yes, sir," Syndergaard said.

Linojj looked at the main screen and saw that *Shintral* had already departed the operation, its missing tractor beam noticeably absent, giving the scene an unbalanced quality. "Viewer ahead." The image jumped almost at once to show what lay before *Enterprise*: the murky form of Rejarris II, cloaked in its impact winter, filled the screen.

For Linojj, time seemed to pass too slowly. She turned aft and peered at the communications station. "Open a channel to all auxiliary craft," she said.

Kanchumurthi worked his controls. "All vessels are receiving you, sir."

"Linojj to all shuttlecraft and CMUs," she said. "The portable tractor beam on *Shintral* has failed. The *Enterprise* is moving in to take its place, and the synch program will be adjusted accordingly. Maintain your positions. *Enterprise* out."

"Commander, the portal's hull is at risk of fracturing," Fenn said.

"How long?" Linojj asked Syndergaard.

"Less than a minute."

"Tenger?" Linojj asked.

"Commander Buonarroti has modified the synchronization routine to adapt the *Enterprise*'s tractor beam to match the intensity and sweep of the portable versions," said the security chief. "But there isn't enough time to couple the ship's helm with those of the shuttlecraft and CMUs."

Linojj wanted to pull Syndergaard from his console and take over the task herself. The first officer had spent four years at the helm of *Enterprise* and had more experience there than anybody aboard the ship. With only one arm, though, she could not outperform Syndergaard. *And I don't have to outperform Torsten,* she thought. *He's as good as they get.*

"Ensign Syndergaard, you'll have to fill in for the computer," Linojj said. "Do you think you can match speeds precisely with the shuttlecraft?"

"Yes, sir. Absolutely, sir." Linojj appreciated hearing the confidence in the helm officer's voice, which thankfully fell short of arrogance.

"Take us into position as soon as we arrive at

the portal," Linojj said. "Tenger, ready to engage the tractor beam program."

"Aye."

Seconds passed, and then Linojj heard the sound of the engines change even before she saw the portal become visible on the viewer against the backdrop of clouds. The first officer wished that *Enterprise* could have towed the structure into orbit by itself, but it could only have made such an attempt by employing its tractor beam over just a section of the enormous structure, and therefore unevenly. The ship's emitter had neither the power nor the range to distribute a beam effectively around a circular object more than half a kilometer in diameter, and then to haul it into space from deep within the gravity well of a planet.

"We have arrived at the portal and are moving into position now," Syndergaard said. Linojj watched the lieutenant's fingers move nimbly across his panel. "Matching velocity with the shuttlecraft . . . and we are a go for tractor beam."

"Tenger," Linojj said at once. *Never hesitate.*

"Engaging computer control of our tractor beam."

On the main screen, although she hadn't requested it, the image changed from a view ahead to one of the portal section directly below *Enterprise*. A hazy blue-white beam appeared and unfurled toward the structure. Almost at once, Fenn announced, "Sensors are showing dramatically reduced stresses in *Shintral*'s arc of the portal."

Linojj wanted to clap her hands together, something she wouldn't have done even if she hadn't lost one of her arms. The thought amused her, though, which she thought probably a good sign. "Well done, everybody," she said. "Tenger, have Lieutenant Verant take *Shintral* back down to the surface and repair its tractor-beam mount as quickly as possible." Under normal circumstances, she would have brought the shuttlecraft back aboard, but she didn't want to risk impacting the current operation with a rendezvous inside the atmosphere.

"Aye, sir," Tenger said.

"And prepare *Galileo* with a portable tractor beam as well, just in case we need it."

Tenger relayed the order to Buonarroti, who confirmed that his engineers would set to modifying *Galileo* at once. As it turned out, the *Enterprise* crew didn't need the services of the last shuttlecraft for the operation. By the end of alpha shift, the portal had been placed in high orbit.

Demora Sulu sat at the main console on *Amundsen*, staring out at the terrain passing below without really seeing it. Instead, the face of her father rose in her mind, a frequent occurrence in the three days since the shuttlecraft crew had found the remnants of the *Excelsior* escape pod. As she had for the last few years, she tried to remember the last time that she'd actually seen him in person. For a long time, she thought it had been when *Enterprise* and *Excelsior* had overlapped their crews' shore leaves at Starbase 11 a year or so before Command had lost all contact with her father's vessel. Sulu retained a strong memory of sitting with him at the Black Hole Saloon, sharing a bottle of Aldebaran sparkling wine she'd saved for the occasion.

At some point, though, Sulu recalled that she'd broken out that particular vintage for Captain Harriman, on the day in 2307 when *Enterprise*'s refit had been completed and the ship returned to active status. Had she sipped a different wine with her father, or had it been another time when the two had last been together? During the long months of the modifications to *Enterprise*, Sulu had split her time between the engineering labs at Utopia Planitia, familiarizing herself with the forthcoming upgrades to the ship; Starfleet Academy on Earth, where she both taught and took classes; and, toward the end, in the shipyard, where she assisted Harriman in overseeing and reviewing the changes to their vessel. At the beginning of that period, though, she took three weeks' leave, traveling to Riviera to enjoy her time off, and on the way back, she diverted to Starbase 71, where *Excelsior* had docked for repairs to its deflectors after an explosive encounter with a Revot destroyer. She spent half a day with her father aboard his ship.

But I know *we had a drink together at the Black Hole,* she thought. *When was that?* At any time through the years, she could have gone back through her logs and figured it all out, and perhaps one day she would, but she had so far chosen not to do so. She tried not to think about her confusion too much; she supposed that she preferred to cling to the memory of her time with her father at Starbase 11 as their last meeting, if only because it happened—or she thought it happened—closer to when he and his starship had gone missing.

"Captain?" Sulu realized that she had been addressed more than once. Ensign Young stood beside her, a concerned expression on his face.

"Yes, Ensign?" she said. "I'm sorry. I was just thinking."

Young sat down next to her at the main console. His condition had improved considerably in the past couple of days. Kostas had capped his tracheostomy tube, making speech easier for him, and he had begun moving about the cabin. "Were you thinking about your father?"

Sulu blinked in surprise. "You certainly don't lack for nerve, Ensign." Rarely did young officers approach her with personal questions about her life. *Not rarely,* she corrected herself. *Never.*

"I'm sorry, sir," Young said. He gazed down into his lap, obviously abashed. Sulu immediately regretted her response. Not only had Hawkins Young been through a great deal already in the past couple of weeks, but like herself and Kostas, he remained cut off not only from *Enterprise,* but from the entirety of what had been his life.

"No, Ensign, I'm sorry," she said. "Yes, I was thinking about my father."

Young raised his head, and Sulu recognized the genuine interest in his eyes. "I learned about him at the Academy," he said. "Both in class and out. A few of my instructors had served with him, and they sometimes told the cadets stories. I also read about him on my own. I've always been interested in the histories of the great starship captains."

Sulu felt her eyebrows rise. "I think my father would be surprised, and more than a little uncomfortable, being categorized as a 'great starship captain.'"

"I'd have to argue with him, then," Young said with a smile. "He had an amazing career, even going back to his days before he made captain. He was the third officer on the *Enterprise* when he had to take the conn and face down the Klingons at Organia. And when he served on the *Courageous* as second officer, he saved the Bajoran colony of Pillagra. There was also the part he played in retrieving Captain Spock, and then in saving Earth from the whale probe. And those are only a few of his exploits before he took over as the captain of the *Excelsior*."

Exploits, Sulu thought, and she couldn't prevent herself from smiling. She felt a sense of contented reflection, mixed with melancholy. Over the course of many years, she had heard about those incidents, and so many others, firsthand from her father. She imagined that she could provide Young with quite a few details that hadn't made it into the official record. "He was a man with many talents, and with more interests than some entire crews. He could really tell a story, and as you've apparently learned, he had a lot of them to tell. He had a big laugh and was quick to use it, and he was fiercely loyal to his crewmates and friends. I think, in his own quiet way, he was a great man." She paused for a moment, a bit apprehensive about speaking on such a personal level with the ensign, but also gratified to be remembering her father and talking about him. "He saved my life," she concluded.

"I know," Young replied. "At Askalon Five."

Sulu hadn't been thinking about that confusing and difficult time, which had ended with an army of rampaging clones pursuing her and her father, and the two Sulus nearly leaping together to their deaths. "I wasn't actually referring to the incident at Askalon Five," she told Young. "I was talking about when my mother died."

"Oh," Young said. Sulu could see that the prospect of learning more about his commanding officer intrigued him, but also that she'd shaken him by mentioning the death of her mother. "I . . . I'm sorry . . . I didn't—"

"It's all right, Ensign, you couldn't know what I meant," she said. Sulu became aware that Kostas, who had been sitting at the rear of the cabin and working on a padd, had turned her attention to the conversation. The captain, who scrupulously maintained her privacy around her crew, considered putting an end to the exchange, but she discovered that she didn't want to; she wanted to talk about her father. *What difference is it going to make, anyway?* she thought. *If we can't get back to our own place and time—*

But she didn't want to contemplate that possibility just then. "I was six years old when my mother died," she said. "She wasn't with my father at the time, and so I didn't even know him." She surprised herself with her candor, but she didn't feel the need for discretion. "I was devastated when I lost my mother; I was just a girl, and she was my whole world. I don't really know what I would have done, where I would've gone or how I would've turned out, if not for my father welcoming me into his life when he found out about me."

Young stayed silent for a moment, and then he finally managed again to say, "I'm sorry." He could have intended his words about the death of her mother, or even about their own situation, separated from *Enterprise* and with their futures becoming more uncertain by the day, but she thought he referred to the crashed escape pod they'd found.

"It's fine, Ensign," Sulu said. "I suppose it's good to finally know for sure what happened to my father." *Except that I don't really know what happened to Dad, do I?* Sulu asked herself. A destroyed *Excelsior* escape pod likely meant the destruction of the ship, but that didn't tell her how or why that had taken place. *Or how a pod ended up on this planet,* she thought. Had her father and his crew abandoned ship near Rejarris II, and one or more of the escape craft passed through the portal? Or had *Excelsior* itself traveled through the looking glass, only to meet its demise on the other side—wherever and whenever that other side happened to be. *Not only don't I truly know the fate of my father,* she thought, *I now have more questions than ever—including the one I don't really want to ask.*

She asked it anyway. *Could any of the* Excelsior *crew—including Dad—still be alive?* If the survivors had passed through the portal, either on *Excelsior* or in escape pods, that could explain Starfleet losing contact with the crew, but that didn't necessarily mean that they had all died.

Sulu didn't like the question because it lacked

a ready answer. Eleven years earlier, she had raised similarly unanswerable questions, over and over again, across months. Against all odds, she had held on to the hope that, despite his ship's disappearance, her father had not perished. Coming to accept his death over time had perhaps made the process easier for her than it might otherwise have been, but she had no wish to do so all over again.

"It's possible that he and the *Excelsior* crew could still be out there somewhere," Young said.

"I suppose we'll find out," Sulu responded without much enthusiasm. After tricorder scans of the wreckage had confirmed its material consistency with that of Starfleet escape pods, she and Kostas had eventually located two more hull fragments that contained identifying information—in each case, a partial registry number. The first read *C-200*, and the second, *CC-2*, both consistent with *Excelsior*'s NCC-2000 designation. They had also detected genetic material, but it had been too badly damaged to classify, and in insufficient quantity to determine whether or not anybody had died there. Still, she could do little other than conclude that the pod had been launched by *Excelsior*.

On that basis, and allowing for the theoretical chance that one or more of the ship's crew could have survived whatever calamity had befallen their ship, Sulu had initiated the continuous transmission of a message out across the planet. So far, they had received no response—neither from *Excelsior* survivors nor anybody else. She didn't think that they would. *Or at least that's what I keep telling myself.*

It actually troubled Sulu a great deal more that they had yet to receive word from *Enterprise*. It had been more than a week since the portal had lost power, severing her landing party's contact with the ship. It clearly could require more time than that for the *Enterprise* crew to reenergize the structure, but she also wondered if something else had happened. Efforts to restore power to the portal could have inadvertently damaged it, or altered its settings, or even destroyed it. Even the most benign of those possibilities could add months or even years to a rescue attempt.

Because Sulu, Kostas, and Young had spent their time exploring the planet on which they found themselves, they'd traveled farther and farther afield from the area where they'd all first arrived. To ensure the continuity of communications with that location, from where the *Enterprise* crew would seek to contact them, the captain had seeded two comm relays along their exploratory path. Several times each day, they sent a transmission via the relays to *Pytheas*, the shuttlecraft that remained at the portal's destination point, triggering it to transmit a return message. To that point, they had sent and received each message successfully. Sulu could only hope that they would hear from the *Enterprise* crew soon.

If we ever hear from them again, she thought, though the captain chastised herself for her negativity. Still, in addition to her responsibility for her own life, she had to consider Hawkins Young and Galatea Kostas. At some point, she would need to begin thinking about their next course of action. Even if they didn't hear from the *Enterprise* crew in the near term, Sulu expected that she and the others would continue to search the planet in the hopes of locating those who had constructed the portal. If that effort ultimately failed, if she, Kostas, and Young could find no means of helping themselves return home, and if they did not hear again from the *Enterprise* crew, then Sulu would have to figure out a way to reach beyond the world and the planetary system where they'd been marooned— although she did not relish the prospect of facing an entirely unknown universe.

Except it's not entirely unknown, is it? she thought. That much, at least, she believed she had verified. After sunset each day, she used the shuttlecraft's sensors to record details of the night sky, and although virtually nothing looked familiar either to her or *Amundsen*'s computer, she still thought she'd found what she'd been searching for. With only a pair of planetary shuttlecraft on which to travel, though, it could prove impossible to cross the interstellar void to get her landing party where she wanted to take them. If she—

"Look," Young said. Sulu saw him pointing through the forward port. Her heart raced for a moment, but when she gazed ahead of the shuttlecraft, she saw only more of the same unremarkable, undeveloped, unpopulated lowlands. "It's a body of water."

Sulu looked again, and that time, she did indeed see a band of blue just below the horizon. Kostas walked up from the rear of the cabin and peered through the port as Young operated the sensor panel. Eventually, he declared, "It's an ocean."

"An ocean?" Kostas echoed. "What should we do, Captain? Should we cross it so that we can search the next continent?"

"We haven't finished exploring this one yet," Sulu said. She didn't add that she thought it far more likely that, if some of the *Excelsior* crew had survived, the shuttlecraft crew would find them not on the ocean, but on land.

Since leaving *Pytheas* behind, Sulu had flown *Amundsen* in the direction of the rising sun. As the shuttlecraft neared the shore, Sulu took control from the autopilot and banked to starboard. "We'll follow the coastline for a while," she said, "and then we'll head back across the continent."

In her mind, though, Sulu thought again about how she, Kostas, and Young could make it through interstellar space. With the resources on hand, it seemed impossible. But Sulu vowed to herself that, if she had to, she would find a way.

Rafaele Buonarroti stood in the middle of the *Enterprise* bridge beside Commander Linojj, trying to keep his eyes on the image on the main viewscreen. He had difficulty concentrating. The chief engineer felt extremely uncomfortable, though he admonished himself for indulging such a selfish emotion.

Buonarroti had spent the previous two days down in the hangar deck and main engineering, first preparing to lift the portal from the surface of Rejarris II and return it to orbit, and then in the actual execution of that plan. Commander Linojj had returned to duty during that time, and he had spoken with her several times, but only via intercom. When he had walked onto the bridge a few moments earlier, it marked the first time that he had seen the results of her injury. Although he knew that she would be fitted with a biosynthetic replacement—he was actually assisting Doctor Morell and the medical staff with some of the synthetic components—seeing her with only one arm shocked him in a visceral way. He could only hope that he had succeeded in hiding his distress—or if he hadn't, that she would forgive him.

I also need to be forgiven for not visiting her in sickbay, Buonarroti thought. They had been crewmates for a dozen years, and friends for almost as long. He could plead that he had been entrenched in the efforts to restore power to the portal, which would not be a lie, but he also knew that he could have—*should* have—stopped by sickbay to see her, which was a more important truth.

"What's your assessment?" Linojj asked him.

"Um . . . well . . ." he stammered, but he had nothing to say. He felt foolish, like the boy in school who did everything at his desk but pay attention, and then, when asked a question by the teacher, had to hem and haw his way through a non-answer.

"Let's take a closer look," Linojj said quietly, and she headed around the navigation console toward the forward section of the bridge. Buonarroti dutifully followed, wondering if the first officer—and current acting captain—was taking him out to the woodshed. He trailed her up the steps to the bridge's outer ring, then over to stand beside her in front of the viewer. So close to the large screen, he could not make any sense of what he saw.

Before he could say anything—and he really didn't want to complain, not after the way he'd behaved—Linojj leaned in toward him. She moved in so close that, without thinking about it, he expected to feel her arm against his. When that didn't happen, the incredibly serious nature of her injury struck him again.

"It's okay," Linojj said, so softly that the chief engineer doubted anybody else on the bridge could hear her. "I know how squeamish you can be."

His initial reaction, no doubt born out of masculine pride, was to dissemble, but he quickly rejected that approach. He'd already let down his friend—and himself—and he would not compound his transgression with an affront to Linojj's intelligence. "I'm sorry," he said, keeping his voice low. "I should've come to see you in sickbay, I should've—"

"Rafe," Linojj interrupted. "I said it's okay, and it really is. I know how hard these things can be for you, and I also know how busy you've been in helping to figure out how to recover the captain and the others."

"Even so," Buonarroti said, "I feel badly that I didn't visit you."

"Well, we're still friends," she said.

"Thanks," he said. A rush of affection for Linojj filled him up. He didn't think that even a Betazoid could have demonstrated more empathy than she just had. *And after what she's been through*—

"We're still friends," Linojj said, "but right now, I need the *Enterprise*'s chief engineer." She turned and made her way back down to the center of the bridge, circling around the helm. Once again, Buonarroti followed.

When he looked up at the viewer, he saw the surface of Rejarris II. There, a great circular structure lay on its side. It looked like the portal, back in the same place from which virtually *Enterprise*'s entire fleet of auxiliary craft had lifted it a day earlier. "What . . . what happened?" He could barely ask the question, considering the implications it had for the captain's rescue.

"That's not the portal, Commander," Linojj said. "But that is where it was."

"I don't understand," Buonarroti said.

To Tenger, she said, "Magnify."

"Aye, sir."

The image skipped to a much tighter view, showing only a portion of the great circle. That close, Buonarroti could see that the portal no longer stood there, but had been replaced by a dark, flat surface set into the ground. A single silver stripe ran along its center. "What is that?" he asked.

"It's a metal slab that rested beneath the portal," Linojj said. "Ensign Young noticed it when we first transported down to the structure."

"But it wasn't attached to it?"

"No," Linojj said. "But it measures precisely the same linear dimensions as the portal. So my question to you is the same as yours was to me: what is that?"

Buonarroti stared at the viewscreen, then raised his hand and wrapped it around the bottom of his face. He felt stubble and realized that he hadn't shaved that morning. "Does the slab contain any circuitry?" he asked.

Linojj looked toward the tactical station. "Not that the landing party's tricorders or the probe's sensors can detect," Tenger said. "It's thick—twenty-five centimeters through—and as best we can tell, solid steel, with a band of platinum running through it."

Buonarroti considered what little they knew about the portal, including what they'd actually witnessed. "I think it could be a landing pad," he said.

"That's what Ensign Young suggested as well," Linojj said.

"Would a landing pad be made of such an unforgiving surface?" Tenger asked. "It has no antigravs, no tractor beams, no guidance systems."

"It needs to bear the weight of the portal," Buonarroti pointed out. "The portal itself has antigravs and tractor beams, and the complex eleven kilometers away—what we believe is a launching-and-landing control facility—has equipment we recognize as a guidance system." He paused, then asked, "How did we find the portal in the first place?"

"We followed a trail of particles from high orbit down to the surface," Tenger said.

Buonarroti nodded, thinking about how various civilizations maintained their satellites. "The portal was damaged in space," he said. "Maybe a meteor strike, or something else in orbit colliding with it, or even some internal piece of equipment failing catastrophically."

"We believe it might have been fired upon with an energy weapon," Linojj said. "At least, the evidence seems consistent with that possibility."

"Whatever happened to it, the technicians at the launch-and-recall facility must have brought it back down to the surface so they could repair it," Buonarroti reasoned. "Or if the damage occurred after the inhabitants of Rejarris Two had already departed, then the facility could have been preprogrammed to recall the portal."

"So you think the metal slab is just a landing pad, just a target?" Linojj asked. "You don't think that it's vital to the operation of the portal, that the platinum ring plays some part in establishing the transition from Rejarris Two to wherever it leads?"

"No, I don't think so," Buonarroti said. "The portal has thrusters and antigravs, it has a facility designed to launch it. It was meant to function in orbit, not down on the planet."

"But why?" Linojj wanted to know. "If you're going to transplant people from one planet to another, why not do so on the ground, if that's possible—and we've seen that it is."

Buonarroti shook his head. "I don't know. Maybe to increase the efficiency of the solar cells. Maybe the portal caused ecological problems inside an atmosphere. Or maybe it once functioned in both directions, and the inhabitants of Rejarris Two feared something coming over from the other side."

Linojj seemed to take in the chief engineer's opinions. As she did so, Science Officer Fenn said, "Commander, sensors indicate that the portal has reached full power."

"Put it on-screen," Linojj said as she walked to the command chair and sat down. Buonarroti moved to the periphery of the bridge, to one of the engineering consoles. On the main viewer, the metal band on the surface of Rejarris II vanished, replaced by the circular form of the portal, hanging in space, its dark form gleaming where the system's star reflected off it. Around it, four shuttlecraft held it in place with tractor beams.

"It looks no different," Tenger noted, and Buonarroti agreed. Nothing on it moved, no lights shined, no thrusters functioned. The chief engineer worked his panel and tapped into Fenn's sensor scan. He confirmed her readings. *Enterprise* sat a hundred kilometers away from the device, and in a higher orbit—plainly a safe distance.

"One thing that's different is that I don't see any tractor beams other than our own," Linojj said.

"The portal's tractor beams have power," Fenn reported. "But as you noted yourself, Commander, its beams engaged and pulled Ensign Young through it only once he stood on the device itself. The tractor beam that reached out for you did so only after you had climbed atop it as well. And the beams that attacked Captain Sulu's shuttlecraft did so when it crossed over the portal's perimeter."

"So it has a threshold that, if crossed by an object, activates the tractor beams, which then pull the object through the portal," Buonarroti said. "Imagine a cylinder at right angles to the circle. Anything that enters that cylinder triggers the beams."

"It must have a range," Tenger said.

"I'm sure it does, and we're about to find out what it is," Linojj said. "Commander Tenger, you have probes ready to launch?"

"Aye, sir," Tenger said. "We prepared some for testing purposes, and we programmed one to travel to the location Captain Sulu and the ensigns traveled to when they passed through the portal; it will then transmit your message to the captain."

"Acknowledged," Linojj said. "Commander Kanchumurthi, contact the shuttlecraft and have them return to the *Enterprise*. Remind the pilots to keep their vessels well outside the activation perimeter of the portal's tractor beams."

"Right away, sir," said Kanchumurthi. As the communications officer relayed Linojj's orders, the shuttlecraft's tractor beams shut down, leaving the portal in orbit under its own power. The auxiliary vessels quickly departed the area.

"The portal's thrusters are firing," Fenn said. On the viewer, Buonarroti could just make out small bursts at various points around the circular hull. "It appears to be aligning itself perpendicular to the surface of the planet. It is not moving far."

"Commander Tenger, you said that you initially found the portal by following a trail of particles that originated in orbit?" Buonarroti asked.

"Aye."

"Did the shuttlecraft bring the portal to the beginning of that trail?" Buonarroti asked.

"They did," Linojj answered. "We believe that's where the portal orbited, so that's where we placed it."

"Then that's why it's realigning itself, but not moving very far," Buonarroti said. "You've placed it where it belongs."

"That was the plan," Linojj said.

Ten minutes later, Tenger reported that all four shuttlecraft had returned without incident to the ship. "The first probe has been programmed to travel directly toward the center point of the portal. Once it has passed through, it will travel one kilometer in a straight line, reverse course, and attempt to return to the *Enterprise* in the opposite direction."

"Deploy the probe and keep it on-screen," Linojj ordered. Buonarroti watched with the rest of the bridge crew as Tenger launched the probe. The missile-shaped device had a hooded tip containing a sensor cluster, as well as an outboard sensory ring that circled its midsection. Nobody spoke but Tenger, who provided a countdown of the probe's range from the portal every twenty kilometers. At ten, he began announcing the distance in increments of one.

Buonarroti kept expecting tractor beams to streak out into space and take hold of the probe, but even as it drew closer to the portal, nothing happened. The closer it got, the more the chief engineer feared that, in hauling the structure from the surface of Rejarris II and into orbit, the *Enterprise* crew had somehow damaged it, preventing its function. If that had happened, then they might have destroyed any chance to rescue the captain and the two ensigns.

"Three kilometers," Tenger intoned. "Two kilometers . . . one kilometer . . ."

And still nothing happened.

Buonarroti felt defeated as the probe soared through the portal. Almost at once, though, tractor beams lashed out. Snared by the gold beams, the probe slowed. After it came to a full stop, it was dragged backward along its course. When it passed through the portal a second time, it vanished. "We're on the wrong side," Buonarroti said.

"Ensign Syndergaard, take us around to face the portal from the other direction," Linojj said. "Lieutenant Aldani, maintain a minimum one hundred kilometer distance at all times, and keep us outside its cylindrical threshold, no matter how far from it we are." After the two officers acknowledged their orders, Linojj said, "Commander Tenger, as soon as we're in position, prepare to launch the message to Captain Sulu."

In her dream, Demora Sulu fell.

At first, she had been striding down a corridor on *Enterprise*, the ship bustling with activity. Her crew moved about, their familiar faces a comfort to her. She saw Xintal Linojj and Tenger, Rafaele Buonarroti and Uta Morell. Hawkins Young and Galatea Kostas. John Harriman passed by, but even though that should have seemed wrong, it didn't.

From around the curve of the corridor, Borona Fenn had approached—but not Fenn as Sulu presently knew her. A younger, pre-Shift version of the Frunalian. The science officer's chitinous exomembrane still covered her youthful gray-green flesh, which had yet to darken and harden to its eventual leathery consistency. Her four mammary glands had not developed, nor had her eltis, the sensory organ that stretched like a fleshy mane from the top of her nose, across the center of her skull, and down the back.

As Fenn had neared, small fragments of her exomembrane had fallen away, dropping like dead leaves at her feet. The closer she got to Sulu, the larger the pieces that sloughed from her body, the pieces of chitin crashing to the deck and shattering with a ringing, insistent clatter. When Fenn walked by, Sulu watched as the ridges on the backs of the Frunalian's shoulders fractured and plunged to the floor, where they splintered into uncounted bits and added to the clamor.

Up ahead, Demora's father had strolled through an open door. He had no arms. She passed him without saying a word, continued along the corridor, through the entryway, and into a desert waste. An empty, arid plain reached in every direction, and when Demora turned, *Enterprise* had gone, leaving her alone on the open plateau.

And then the ground collapsed beneath her and she fell, sliding down a hard incline.

Sulu woke with a start. Her arms flew to her sides, her movements limited by the bedroll in which she slept. Somebody screamed and kept on screaming.

Sulu opened her eyes in dim light. Awareness snapped back to her at once, a manifestation of her many years high up in a starship's chain of command. As second officer of *Enterprise*, as first officer, and as captain, she had often been awakened in circumstances urgently requiring her attention. She immediately recalled the situation: unable even to contact her ship, she was stranded with two of her young officers in a shuttlecraft on an unknown world, in an uncertain place and time.

Something felt wrong, though—something more than the screams Sulu heard, which her waking mind distinguished not as somebody's voice, but as the proximity alert the *Amundsen* crew had set before retiring for the night. She pushed herself up, but too easily: the deck beneath her had canted, lowering her feet beneath the level of her head. She quickly pulled her arms from her bedroll and reached up along the bulkhead, searching for the control panel there.

When Sulu at last found it and switched on the overhead lighting panels, a confused jumble of shapes greeted her in the cabin. The rear section of the compartment had dropped a meter or so below the bow, and she had slid down the deck feet-first into the aft bulkhead. Opposite her, Ensign Young had slid down the length of his antigrav stretcher, his head and shoulders pressed into a rear corner as he scrambled out from beneath his bunched bedclothes. Sulu did not at first see Ensign Kostas, who had also slept in a bedroll on the deck, but then the engineer's hand appeared from the equipment storage area, where she had clearly been thrown. Kostas pushed aside a tangle of the three freestanding chairs they had not removed from the cabin, which had piled up together in front of the entry to the storage compartment.

"What happened?" Young called out over the blaring alarm. He sounded dazed.

"Proximity alert," Sulu yelled back, though she knew that didn't answer the question. She crawled out of her bedroll and pulled herself up the deck, improvising handholds along the bulkhead. When she reached the main console, she perched on the front edge of one of the two seats there, both of which had been fixed in place.

Sulu deactivated the alert, bringing welcome silence down around them—except that, as she searched for both the cause of the alarm and whatever had thrown the shuttlecraft about, she heard other, gentler sounds. A patter almost like a light rain trickled down on the hull of *Amundsen* at various points. Stressed metal occasionally offered a low groan. Another sound, a scraping sort of a noise, but deeper, seemed to translate through the hull as though from far away.

The captain looked through the front viewport and made out broken walls of earth all around. She pushed herself forward so that she could peer straight up, where she saw a scrap of dawn sky just visible perhaps ten or so meters above the shuttlecraft. "The ground collapsed beneath us," she told Kostas and Young. When they had halted their explorations of the planet the previous night, they had set down on the edge of a desert. "*Amundsen* fell into a sinkhole, or maybe a cave system." As she gazed upward through the port, a drift of dirt sprinkled down against it, explaining the rainlike noise she heard.

Something moved up above, blotting out the small patch of sky, and an instant later, a great, dark form landed on the ground before the viewport. Sulu recoiled, and she heard one of the ensigns cry out in surprise behind her. Two large oval eyes stared into the shuttlecraft from a triangular head that swayed from side to side at the end of a long, serpentine neck. The many-legged bulk of the creature filled the port.

For a strangely quiet moment, the fearsome beast did nothing but look into the cabin. Sulu remained still, but in her mind, she visualized the console before her, marking the locations of the controls she needed. The shuttlecraft carried no armaments and possessed no real defenses beyond a navigational deflector and a force field for the hull. She hoped the latter would be enough for her purposes.

When the creature jerked its head back and raised its spiked front appendage high, Sulu knew what would come next. She looked down at the main console, thrust her hands across the control surfaces to activate and intensify the force field around the hull, then threw her arms up to protect her head. The creature's appendage slammed into the viewport with staggering power. The creature uttered a short, low howl, but it didn't move away.

Instead, it reared its front appendage back and drove it once more into the port. Sulu reached for the helm controls, but then the shuttlecraft moved, the aft end slipping backward and the bow crashing down. The captain fell forward. Her head struck the console. She wiped her hand across her hairline, and her fingers came away streaked with blood.

Ignoring her injury, Sulu glanced up through the port. The shuttlecraft had leveled off, but she could no longer see the sky. She didn't know if she could maneuver *Amundsen* up and out of the pit into which it had been dropped, but she would try.

Her head throbbed as she worked the helm controls. The drive rumbled to life, its steady thrum undoubtedly magnified and quavered by the surrounding earth and stone. She directed the shuttlecraft to rise, and it did, but not even a meter at best.

Beside her, Kostas threw herself down into the cockpit's second seat. "I'm on sensors," she said, her voice strong, if not completely steady.

Sulu pushed the shuttlecraft, trying to force it upward. It didn't move. The drive moaned in response.

"We're eleven-point-two meters beneath the surface," Kostas said. "We're in what looks like a chamber that's been hollowed out. It's barely larger than the shuttlecraft. There's almost no room to maneuver, and virtually no space at all above the bow. It also looks like several boulders have fallen into the hole after us."

Blocking our escape route, Sulu thought but didn't say.

Amundsen rocked again. Sulu peered through the port. The dark hulk of the creature that had already assaulted the shuttlecraft moved in the shadows up ahead, but it had not attacked again. That meant that a second had joined the first.

As though to confirm her inference, something thumped above the rear of the shuttlecraft, which shook once more. "How many?" she asked Kostas. "How many of those things are out there?"

"I'm having trouble isolating life signs," the ensign said. "Actinides in the rocks are interfering with biosensors."

"Check for movement," Sulu said, raising her

voice as another blow rained down on the roof at the aft end of the shuttlecraft. The force field around the hull appeared to prove no impediment whatsoever to the creatures.

Kostas jabbed at her controls. "One in front, one behind . . . there may be two on top of the shuttlecraft . . . and I'm reading more movement coming down the hole."

Five of the creatures! Sulu thought, recalling well how it had required two phasers set to kill to bring even one of them down.

The creature in front of the shuttle charged. It rammed into the viewport at speed, turning to the side at the last instant and sending the mass of its cylindrical body against the transparent pane. To Sulu's horror, a jagged crack formed.

"The force fields aren't stopping them," Kostas said, even as another thunderous noise resounded atop *Amundsen*.

Up ahead, the creature scuttled backward, and Sulu knew that it would storm the shuttlecraft again. *Amundsen* shuddered before it did, attacked that time from the rear. "They're pounding the shuttle on three sides: fore, aft, and overhead," Kostas said.

"Brace yourselves," Sulu called out. She operated the helm again, and the shuttlecraft surged forward. The bow struck the creature in front of them and smashed it against boulders at the side of the hole. *Amundsen* crashed to a halt, throwing Sulu and Kostas up against the console. The creature issued a piercing wail, and when Sulu pushed herself back into her chair, she saw trails of a syrupy violet ichor running down the cracked viewport. Several of the creature's mangled limbs twitched, but its head lolled on its long neck at a sickening angle.

Sulu worked the helm, trying again to fly *Amundsen* up and out of where it had fallen. The drive yowled as it attempted to translate power into velocity, but the shuttlecraft didn't move. Sulu changed tactics, reversing course. *Amundsen* surged backward, until it could move no more, slamming to a stop. She heard the rasping cry of another creature as a string of indicator lights on her panel flashed red. The drive sounded in one moment as though it might explode, but in the next, it cycled down with a whine.

That's two of them down, Sulu thought. "Movement?" she asked.

"Checking," Kostas said. Sulu saw the ensign's hands trembling as she tried to cull information from the sensors. "The creature in front of the shuttlecraft isn't moving, and neither is the one behind. There's motion partway down the hole—"

Two massive blows struck *Amundsen* from above. Sulu looked back and saw dents in the overhead. She also saw that Ensign Young had gathered phaser pistols. "Two per person," Sulu told him, and he turned and picked up three more weapons. He darted to the front of the cabin and handed two each to the captain and Kostas.

Another set of blows beat down on the shuttlecraft. Small cracks appeared in the overhead. The creatures continued pounding the hull. "Set phasers to kill," Sulu said, adjusting both of her weapons.

Amundsen quaked again and again. In one aft corner of the cabin, just above Sulu's bedroll, a flap of the overhead peeled away from the bulkheads and bent downward. A rank odor spilled into the shuttlecraft.

More blows struck the roof, and the flap of the overhead bent down farther, opening up a larger whole. Sulu saw the black tip of a creature's leg for an instant as it worked to give itself access to its prospective next meal. Sulu raised both her weapons. "Ready," she quietly told her crew.

Suddenly, the pounding on the roof of the shuttlecraft stopped. Kostas cocked her head to one side, listening intently. "What—"

The creature moved with amazing swiftness. It folded its legs through the hole it had opened in the shuttlecraft, pulling its body through until it stood there, facing them, a malevolent force bent on killing. It moved like a swarm, its many limbs and joints a sea of motion. Its triangular head swayed on its long, twisting neck, its outsize eyes cold and menacing. It was larger than the one that had attacked Ensign Young.

"Fire!" the captain yelled as she depressed the activation pads on the grips of her phasers.

Six reddish yellow beams streaked into the creature, the high-pitched keens of the weapons loud in the enclosed space, the heat produced by them immediately noticeable. The creature charged through the phaser fire. One of its legs jammed into Sulu's chest, pushing her backward into the main console. The beams of her phasers veered wildly, and she saw one strike the aft bulkhead. She stopped firing.

The creature's spiked front appendage swung through the air, missing her face by mere centimeters, but then she heard Kostas cry out next to her. The creature's body loomed over her. Sulu brought her hands up and pushed the emitter ends of her phasers against it. She fired.

The creature bellowed, its cry a mixture of shock and pain. It fell back. Sulu glanced to her side and saw Kostas down on the deck, blood spilling from a deep cut in the right side of her face, from ear to mouth.

"Keep firing!" she told Young, who had dropped his phasers to his sides. He raised them again and sent directed energy into the creature.

Sulu kneeled down beside Kostas, who moaned in agony. She had lifted her hand up to her face. Blood flowed between her fingers. Sulu desperately looked about for anything she could use to stem the bleeding. One of the bedrolls lay just a meter away, and she scurried forward on her hands and knees to grab it, aware of the phaser beams shooting not that far above her.

The captain grabbed the bedroll and pulled it over to Kostas. Sulu set down her phasers and bunched the fabric in one hand. With the other, she lifted the ensign's hand away from her face, pushed the bedroll against her wound, then let Kostas hold the makeshift bandage in place.

Sulu quickly retrieved her weapons, crawled away, and stood back up. Even as the beams of Young's phasers blasted the creature, it lurched forward. Two of its legs suddenly stabbed toward the ensign, knocking the phasers from his hands as he was thrown against the bulkhead. He fell to the floor, unmoving. With no phasers firing, a momentary, deathly silence enveloped the shuttlecraft.

The creature swung its neck down, bringing it face-to-face with Sulu. The captain couldn't tell what she saw in its eyes. Anger and pain, certainly, but did she see some level of understanding as well? Or was that simple hunger? She didn't know, and at that moment, she didn't care.

Sulu brought both arms up and fired point blank into the creature's head. It shrieked and tottered backward, seeming to try to stay on its feet. Sulu continued firing. The smell of singed flesh filled *Amundsen* like a noxious fog.

At last, the creature collapsed. Another stood behind it.

Sulu redirected her aim, but too late. The second creature—*The fourth,* Sulu told herself, *with another coming down the hole*—raced across the crumpled body of the first and thrust its front appendage at her. Sulu felt the impact, but she was surprised when she wasn't thrown backward by the blow. She looked down and saw the creature's appendage sticking into her abdomen. She knew that in the next moment, it would pull the barbed tip back out of her body, eviscerating her. With almost no thoughts and no hope, Sulu placed her phaser against the appendage and squeezed the activator pad. The limb exploded in a hail of burned flesh and blood.

Sulu tried to fire again, even as she heard the welcome whine of more phasers. *Kostas!* she thought, realizing that the ensign must have found the determination and strength to find her weapon and shoot, though all of that seemed very far away, at the end of some hazy tunnel. Sulu could no longer stand, and she dropped to her knees, then fell down onto her side.

Her breathing grew shallow, and she felt cold sweat streaming down her face. Pain like nothing she had ever felt radiated up from her midsection, but like her conscious mind, it seemed to fade with each passing second. With her head against the deck and her eyes focused on the space just before her, she could not see the battle, but she still heard it. Phasers firing, roars from the creature. It seemed to go on for a long time, but she knew that she could no longer trust her perceptions. Still, even in extremis, it pleased her to hear the sounds of her crew's weapons. It meant that they yet survived, and even if Sulu herself wouldn't, it gave her hope. She held on to her certainty that the *Enterprise* crew would find a way to reenergize the portal and reestablish contact with Kostas and Young. And even if Linojj and the crew couldn't figure out a means of bringing the two ensigns back, Sulu thought she knew how it could be done.

And it needs to be done, Sulu thought. *I don't want Kostas and Young just to survive; I want them to* live. For that, she knew, they would have to return home.

Time seemed to take on a malleable quality. Sulu didn't know if seconds or minutes or even hours passed. Her consciousness brightened and darkened, something that felt no longer anchored to reality. She tried to refocus, and she saw Ensign Young across the cabin from her, propped up against the bulkhead. A phaser lay on the deck beside his open hand, which was covered in blood. Beside him, a tangle of legs and viscera and violet ichor brought bile into Sulu's throat. She closed her eyes against the image.

Sounds of movement drifted to her in the self-imposed darkness. She remembered that Kostas had counted five creatures: one in front of the shuttlecraft, one in back, and two atop it, with one descending down into the hole. Sulu opened her eyes and looked for her phaser. Though she could not move her head, she hoped she could find the strength to take her weapon in hand one final time. If she could do anything to prevent it, she would not die as some nightmarish creature's meal, even if that meant finishing her life by her own hand. She had faced similar choices before, and had made similar decisions.

"Captain," she heard a voice call, though it sounded like neither Kostas nor Young. Across the cabin, the creature she'd believed dead began to move, which sent a chill through her failing body, but then she saw legs—humanoid legs in a Starfleet uniform—pushing past the remains. "Here, Captain."

Yes, I'm here, she thought, *but not for long.* But she rejoiced. The *Enterprise* crew must have restored power to the portal and then found a way to make it function in both directions. They had come to bring Sulu and her crewmates back home—too late for Sulu, but that no longer mattered to her. What mattered was that Kostas and Young would be saved.

A face suddenly filled Sulu's vision. She didn't recognize it. *Am I wrong?* she asked herself. *Is this not my crew? Is this some other lost crew—maybe that of* Excelsior?

"Captain, it's all right," the man said. "Help is on the way." He looked away, then pointed somewhere. "There," he said, though not to Sulu. When he peered back at her, he said, "Hang on, Captain."

She didn't think she could. She closed her eyes again, waiting for death. Then somebody else said something to her in a voice she hadn't heard in a long time, but she knew it at once. She opened her eyes again.

Her father looked back at her, his eyes filled with tears. "I'm here, honey," he said. "Stay with me."

"Lost," Demora said—or tried to say. The word came out in a spray of blood. "You're still lost." Barely a whisper, but she saw that her father had heard her.

"Yes, I'm still lost," he said. "I'll tell you all about that, but first we need to get you better." He turned away from her and raised his voice. "Get the doctor down here *now!*"

Now *won't be soon enough*, Sulu thought as she felt herself fading. But she had one final duty. With the last bit of strength she could muster, she lifted her hand and reached out to her father. Even if she could not save herself, maybe she could still save him . . . save Kostas and Young . . . save whoever else there was. "Tell Linojj," she started, but then her voice sputtered into a cough. The movement sent fresh spasms of pain coursing through the middle of her body.

"It's all right, honey," her father said. "Don't try to speak."

"No . . . no . . . listen to . . ." she said, then stopped to refocus. "Tell Linojj on . . . *Ent'prise* . . . contact Ad . . . Ja Harr'man . . ." Her vision began to blur at the edges, and she knew she didn't have much time. "Tell him . . . I confirm . . . Odyssey solution."

That was all she had. She hoped it would be enough. Demora Sulu closed her eyes, and that time, she kept them closed.

2319

Helaspont Station

8

Captain Amina Sasine tilted her champagne flute and sipped the 2306 vintage Dom Pérignon. The effervescent, pale golden liquid gave off a crisp, fresh bouquet, and its complex taste blended more flavors than she could possibly identify, though she felt certain that Demora Sulu could provide a lengthy discourse on the sparkling wine's notes and accents, on its hints and undertones, on its structure and finish. Sasine could only declare for sure that she heartily enjoyed the prestige champagne. "I know we say it every year," she told her husband, Admiral John Harriman, "but that woman really knows her wines."

Across the small, square table, John took a sip from his own glass. His eyes twinkled, reflecting the two candles that the restaurant's waitstaff had placed on the white tablecloth. John had recently shaven the goatee he'd worn for the previous couple of years, and the result softened his face. *Not just softened,* Sasine thought. *He looks younger.* Seven years older than John—six and a half, really—Sasine had occasionally felt self-conscious about their age difference, not because she'd ever perceived any disparity between them, but because, when they'd first begun seeing each other, he'd looked not seven years her junior, but seven*teen*—or more. Fortunately, his graying hair had gone some way into narrowing that superficial gap.

John offered a hum of appreciation as he put down his champagne flute. "We always say Demora knows her wine because it's true."

A friend to Sasine since the two had served together aboard *Enterprise* around the turn of the century, and a friend to John for even longer, Sulu had first given them a bottle of wine fifteen years before, when the couple had celebrated the one-year anniversary of their becoming romantically involved. That tradition continued annually until the two married. For their wedding, Sulu presented them with a magnum of Elestor sparkling wine from Alpha Centauri, and she had sent a double bottle of bubbly every year since. That year's anniversary gift arrived several weeks earlier on a shipment from Earth, which they found especially thoughtful, considering how far in advance the starship captain must have had to plan it: *Enterprise* hadn't been inside the Federation for eleven months.

Sasine settled her glass down beside her appetizer, a savory mushroom and leek galette, one of her favorites among Georges' dishes. The proprietor and chef at Sur Le Mer Coucher, Georges Rochambeau prided himself not only on his gourmet cuisine, but on the elegant, romantic atmosphere he provided his patrons. Weeks prior, Sasine had reserved the table tucked into the far end of the dimly lighted dining room, where a beautifully patterned and textured wall met the outer, transparent bulkhead, which provided a breathtaking view of the spectacular Helaspont Nebula, a sprawl of blues and indigoes and violets. In truth, as commander of the space station, Sasine realized that she enjoyed a certain prestige and privilege, and that she needn't have made a reservation so far in advance—or even made one at all—but she preferred to conduct herself like any member of the community, eschewing the power of her position.

She gazed across the table at her husband, so handsome in his dark, sophisticated suit. Sasine smiled as she realized that he'd chosen a tie that matched the vibrant colors of the nebula. "I can't believe it's been eight years already," Sasine said.

"Eight years married, and eight years together before that," John said. He shook his head in his own apparent disbelief. "And yet, in some ways, it seems like we just met."

"In some ways," Sasine agreed. "But it also seems like we've been with each other forever. I can't really remember what it's like not to have you in my life." Sometimes, when Sasine recollected something she'd done or someplace she'd traveled before she'd even met John, she recalled him being with her, she could picture him at her side, even though she knew that hadn't been the case.

"I guess we both married the right person," John said.

"I guess so." Sasine took another bite of her galette, then eyed her husband's appetizer. "How's yours?"

"Delicious," John said. "The dressing is amazing." He had a frisée salad with a white truffle vinaigrette.

"May I?" Sasine asked, even as she reached across the table and speared a sprig of the curly endive. After popping it into her mouth and cooing over the flavors, she said, "Would you like to try mine?"

"No, thanks," John said. "Hey, do you have any word yet on when we might get away?" For the better part of the prior two months, they had been attempting to schedule leave together around their anniversary, with little success. John had just returned a few days earlier from Denobula, where he'd conducted an inspection tour of Starfleet vessels in the sector, and the day after next, Sasine would host a trade summit on the station, although she'd at one point thought she might be able to sneak away during the meetings.

"No, but it won't be soon," Sasine said. "The trade summit begins the day after tomorrow, and it turns out that the Gorn will be sending representatives after all, so Starfleet Command really wants me here. After that, you've got the Exploration Committee on Tellar, and Admiral Mentir just moved up the test-bed schedule, so by the time you get back, we'll already be into the *Ambassador*-class trials." Sasine didn't know about the prudence of Starfleet conducting assessments of its next-generation starship prototype on the brink of

Tzenkethi space, but she imagined that Command considered it a viable means of preemptively facing down the confrontational Coalition.

John puffed out his cheeks in an exaggerated sigh. "No rest for the weary," he said. "Well, at least we've got tonight and tomorrow."

"I'll drink to that," Sasine said, and she raised her glass once more. She really did find it remarkable that she and John had been together for so long. When it had begun, it seemed a relationship unlikely to last for any length of time. They initially had to conduct it across a great many light-years, with Sasine assigned as the first officer of a space station and John the captain of a starship. Fortunately, *Enterprise* put into Starbase 23 a fair number of times during those years, and later, after she took command of Foxtrot XIII, to that outpost. They also experienced good fortune in arranging for simultaneous leaves, which they used to visit quite a few memorable destinations. They dove at Suraya Bay on Risa; danced the night away in Jennita on Pacifica; swam in Devil's Pool, at the edge of Victoria Falls, on Earth; toured Lingasha, the unusual land-based city built by the aquatic Alonis; hiked the Azure Peaks on Betazed; explored—and got lost in—the Cleary Labyrinth on Onelia IV; and viewed the rings of Saturn from the Space Needle on Titan. They invariably returned exhausted from their shared vacations, but also energized by the time spent with each other on, as John put it, "another Sasine-Harriman adventure."

But then after the Tomed *Incident* . . .

John had never spoken much about what had

taken place in Foxtrot Sector when a Romulan admiral had attacked the Federation, wiping out thirteen populated outposts along the Neutral Zone, as well as *U.S.S. Agamemnon.* The *Enterprise* crew barely escaped the devastation, but more than four thousand Starfleet officers did not. Already at the brink of war with the Romulan Star Empire, the Federation avoided open hostilities only when the heinous act convinced the Klingons to side with the UFP.

Not long after the destruction of virtually the entire Foxtrot Sector, John had chosen to resign his position as a starship captain—and he'd even considered going further than that and leaving Starfleet completely. Instead, he ended up with a promotion in rank and the posting of his choice. He naturally selected Helaspont Station, where he and Sasine could finally enjoy their relationship on a predominantly day-in, day-out basis. They'd wed, and had lived together happily since then.

It didn't take a great deal of insight to understand John's motivation, Sasine thought. Just prior to her assignment to Helaspont Station, she had commanded Foxtrot XIII. The outpost had been the first wiped out by the Romulan vessel *Tomed,* the *Ivarix*-class starship turned into a devastatingly effective weapon when containment about the singularity that drove it was lowered while the ship traveled at warp.

Had all of that happened just weeks earlier, I would have been killed. Although John had never explicitly tied the events in the Foxtrot Sector to his choice to leave *Enterprise* and relocate to

Helaspont, she nevertheless understood that such a connection existed. He could no longer abide the possibility that the dangers of their careers would one day steal them from each other. By renouncing his starship command, he foresaw a life that they could live mostly together.

John lifted his flute of champagne and tapped it against Sasine's, producing a light, musical ring. "Here's to life on the edge of the nebula," he said.

"To the nebula."

"Which, it strikes me, is a lot like you," John said. Sasine saw another twinkle in his eye, something distinct from the reflection of the candles flickering on the table. "Luminous, vibrant, and beautiful," he whispered to her through a smile. "Enhancing every day and brightening every night." Even sixteen years after he first pressed his lips gently to hers, he could still make her heart race.

"I bet you say that to all the space station commanders," Sasine teased.

"Just you," John said. "Only you. Always you."

Sasine reached her free hand across the table, and John did the same. They interlaced their fingers, and a memory rose in her mind so swiftly that she nearly reeled from it. It had been a moment on the very first night she and John had seen each other personally, not at the small theater on Starbase 23 where they'd taken in a film, but at the bistro afterward, where they'd shared a late supper. They had been speaking about relationships, and she'd described what she hoped one day to experience by raising her arms and entwining the fingers of her right hand with those of her left.

And we have that, Sasine thought, marveling at what they'd found in each other. Prior to John, she'd had several serious romantic relationships, a couple of them lasting a few years. *But none of them came close to what John and I have.* Before they met, Sasine could not have imagined spending her life with the man of her dreams, but after sixteen years, she could not imagine living without him.

"So what shall we do with our one night and one day before the trade summit?" John asked. They set their glasses down and disentangled their fingers so they could continue with their meal.

"It's not like we can get anywhere and back in that time," Sasine said. On the frontier of Federation space, the nearest inhabited system floated light-years distant, too far for a day-plus round trip on one of the station's standard shuttlecraft.

"What if we used one of the new warp shuttles?" John asked, as though reading her thoughts— a not uncommon occurrence between them. Starfleet Operations had recently posted two high-warp shuttlecraft to Helaspont Station, primarily for the purposes of ferrying dignitaries and carrying small but important shipments to and from the starbase.

"I think Operations and Command would take a dim view of us expropriating one of their *Mercury*-class shuttles for our own private use," Sasine said— although the notion actually did appeal to her.

"We could say we're field-testing them," John suggested with a wry grin.

"Uh-huh," Sasine said. "Those shuttlecraft are my responsibility, but if you want to use your superior rank to order me . . ."

"Right," John said. "Any man who claims higher rank in a marriage will lie about other things too."

Sasine scoffed at her husband's joke. "Perhaps a long walk in the arboretum, then."

"That sounds nice," John said. "We could watch a movie too. We just received a few twentieth- and twenty-first-century films from Earth, plus there's *Dreams Together Fall*, the Tholian work that somehow leaked out of the Assembly."

"I hear it's impenetrable," Sasine said, "but I'd be fascinated to see what a Tholian movie even looks like."

"So would I."

They planned the rest of their day as they continued eating their appetizers. The moment they finished, their server, Javier, appeared to clear away the plates, and a moment later, Chef Rochambeau emerged from the kitchen and stepped up to the table. "*Bonsoir*, Captain, Admiral," he said, bowing his head to both officers. Rochambeau cut a hale and hearty figure, dressed in chef's whites and wearing a *toque blanche* atop his graying hair. He had a wide, doughy face and a pencil-thin mustache. "I trust that your appetizers were satisfactory." His words veritably dripped with his thick Gallic accent, almost a caricature of Sasine's own light French pronunciation.

She and John both greeted the chef warmly. "The galette was *splendide*," Sasine said. "As always."

"Ah, *bon, bon*," Rochambeau said. "Your entrées will be out shortly. I wanted to wish the two of you *joyeux anniversaire de mariage*, and to thank you for allowing me to honor you with a special meal." After Sasine had made the reservation to celebrate their anniversary, Rochambeau had contacted her to ask if he could have the privilege of creating their menu for them. She had agreed at once, thanking him and noting only the particular bottle of champagne that she and John would be bringing with them.

"The honor is ours," John said. "We've been looking forward to this for weeks."

"It is my hope that the memory of my food will remain with you for years," Rochambeau said. He could not have displayed a greater sense of confidence, though Sasine could attest that his abilities in the kitchen justified his self-assurance. "For madame, I have prepared eggplant gratin with saffron—"

"*Pardon*," said Javier, returning to the table. "I am sorry to interrupt, but Ensign Bartels from the operations center would like to speak with you, Admiral." Though the space station's comm system functioned inside the restaurant, Rochambeau had received special dispensation to allow its use only in emergencies. Bartels crewed the communications station during beta shift, so Sasine imagined that John had received an incoming transmission from Starfleet.

While Rochambeau looked dismayed by the disruption of the meal he had specially prepared, John stood from his chair. "Thank you, Javier, and excuse me, Chef," he said. He gazed across the table at Sasine with an expression she had both seen before and offered to him, a look that acknowledged the choices they had made in their lives and the responsibilities of their positions, as well as the love they shared, ultimately untouched by any of it except in the most surface of ways. John reached across the table, took her hand in his, and squeezed it. "I'll let you know what's going on, and I'll be back as soon as I can. I love you."

"I love you."

John left the table, crossing the dining room and disappearing from view near the host stand. Sasine returned her attention to Rochambeau. "You were saying, Chef?"

"Yes," Rochambeau said, recovering his poise. "For madame, I have prepared . . ."

Sasine smiled appropriately as the chef described the entrées he had created for the anniversary meal, but she paid little attention to the details. Instead, she wondered what had called her husband away. She feared that the night and a day they intended to spend together before the trade summit had just been stolen from them.

Admiral John Harriman slipped into his office atop the main cylinder of Helaspont Station. The overhead lighting panels automatically activated as he entered, illuminating the room to match the soft glow of the starbase's simulated evening. He reached for the control panel to the right of the door, intending to bring up the lights fully, but then he decided to leave them as set; perhaps, depending on the message he'd been sent, he could salvage his state of mind, and therefore the rest of the night with his wife. Given the conditions of the incoming transmission, though—priority one, eyes only—

he doubted that he would be able to get back to Amina anytime soon.

Another anniversary interrupted, he thought. He and his wife seemed to have a knack for it. During one of their celebrations, the risk of a reactor breach had developed, causing the evacuation of the station for more than a week. On another of their special occasions, a trident-shaped Tzenkethi frigate unexpectedly came calling at the starbase. *And then there was the time that my negotiations with the Pyrithians threatened to devolve into a shooting war before lunchtime.*

Harriman smiled. He knew that it didn't help matters that he and Amina found so many reasons to observe various dates: their first meeting, back when she'd come aboard *Enterprise* as his second officer; their reentry into each other's lives—for good, it would turn out—when she briefed him at Starbase 23 on the specifics of a secret mission into the Romulan Empire; their first social outing, which they liked to call *The Night of the Perfect Kiss;* and, of course, their wedding day. That list didn't even include their birthdays. They both enjoyed having so many different events to commemorate, but Harriman recognized that it also increased the chances of something disrupting their festivities, especially given the nature of their postings. As the commanding officer of Helaspont Station, Captain Amina Sasine had more responsibilities than any three starship commanders, and Harriman's own assignment as admiral-at-large kept him more than a little busy.

Which is just Starfleet Command's way of teach-

ing me a lesson, he thought. Although the commander-in-chief, Admiral Margaret Sinclair-Alexander, had maintained that she completely understood Harriman's decision to step away from starship command after the *Tomed* Incident, several other admirals had objected, citing the service's investment in him and the relative rarity of wholly qualified and capable captains. Pushed to accept command of another starship, Harriman instead submitted his letter of resignation directly to the c-in-c. He didn't intend his departure from Starfleet as a threat, but the next time he spoke with Sinclair-Alexander, she claimed never to have received the document. She did, however, offer him a promotion in rank and the position of admiral-at-large. Though such a posting would require occasional travel—*Sometimes more than occasional,* he lamented—it also came with the privilege of selecting his own base of operations, which in turn allowed him to make a home with his wife. He had accepted the commander-in-chief's offer, and he'd lived on Helaspont Station with Amina ever since.

Harriman crossed his relatively spartan office—the antithesis of his wife's, which she filled not only with work-related materials, but also artwork, photographs, and other personal memorabilia. He kept only a hologram of Amina on his desk and a few images on the walls. He had handsome renderings of the starships on which he'd served—*Laikan, Hunley, Sojourner,* and *Enterprise*—as well as the one on which he'd been born, *Sea of Tranquility.*

The admiral passed between the sofa to his left and his desk on the right. He stood at the transparent outer wall and gazed at the impressive view. The beautiful indigo form of the Helaspont Nebula provided a spectacular backdrop. Below him, a crossover bridge reached out from the center of the starbase's large, central section to one of its two smaller, adjunct cylinders. The station's crew utilized the pair of outlying structures as docking facilities, as well as centers for civilian establishments and services. At the moment, two starships—*U.S.S. Kazanga*, a science vessel, and *U.S.S. Marvick*, an engineering support craft—were docked at the Sea of Marmara arm of the base, in addition to an Andorian cargo transport. He knew that several other civilian ships had docked on the opposite side of the station, at the Aegean Sea arm.

Harriman longingly regarded the Sea of Marmara, where Amina still sat in the restaurant, finishing their commemorative dinner without him. He really hoped that he could get back to her before too long. When the operations center had contacted him about the message, he hadn't asked his aide to come into the office, but as the minutes dragged on, he wondered if he should have brought Lieutenant San Luis in; somehow, Juan always managed to speed things up and get things done. *Without him,* Harriman thought, *I don't know if I could've held on to this position for so long.*

A few minutes later, just as he considered contacting operations to ask about the delay, the communications panel on his desk chirped. "*Ops to Admiral Harriman.*"

He quickly moved behind his desk and sat down, where he tapped at the communications-

and-computer interface. The Helaspont Station emblem—a stylized epsilon over a silhouette of the starbase—disappeared from the screen, replaced by the image of Ensign Bartels. "Harriman here," he said. "Go ahead."

"*I'm sorry for the wait, Admiral,*" Bartels said. "*The transmission required a heavy level of decryption. The message is now available, keyed to your biometrics.*"

"Thank you, Ensign. Harriman out." The admiral closed the channel, then called up the incoming transmission. After voice-print and retina scans, he read the source of the message: *Enterprise.* Wondering what his former first officer wanted, he started playback. The image of Demora Sulu did not appear on the screen, though, but that of her own first officer, Xintal Linojj. As she identified herself—though she needn't have, since she had served as Harriman's second officer for four years—he noticed that she sat in the captain's office. He also saw, to his horror, that she had been dismembered, that her right arm ended in a silver cuff just below her shoulder. He felt immediate concern for both Demora and Xintal, former crewmates whom he still counted as his friends.

"*Admiral, I'm contacting you for Captain Sulu,*" Linojj said. She then related a tale about the *Enterprise* crew finding a world that had experienced an asteroid strike and the impact winter that ensued—a world with an industrial but pre-warp society that appeared to have somehow escaped their planet. In the course of studying the absent civilization, three officers, including Demora Sulu, passed through what they later determined to be a one-way portal to another location, possibly to another time, possibly to another universe.

Another universe, Harriman thought, pausing the message. He remembered his own experience with Demora—*What? Twenty years ago?* After a covert mission into Romulan space, the two of them had been inadvertently thrown into another universe. He recalled those days in the warp shuttle with her, the terrible sense of isolation they shared, despite having each other to lean on, their sorrow and feeling of tremendous loss. They had eventually escaped what could have been a lonely fate, but Harriman had thought at the time that their return home had mostly been the product of mere good fortune. He still thought that.

Harriman resumed the message. Linojj detailed the way the *Enterprise* crew communicated with Demora through the portal. The first officer talked about how the device had lost power, temporarily cutting them off from their captain. *"Once we restored the portal's function by carrying it from the planet's surface up into space, we sent another probe through it, carrying a message to the captain and the other stranded officers. We provided the orbital coordinates for the device. When one of the shuttlecraft arrived on the other side of the portal and we looked through its forward viewport, though, we did not see Captain Sulu—not Demora Sulu, anyway; we saw her father."*

Hikaru is alive? Harriman thought. He had difficulty believing it. Starfleet had lost contact with the elder Sulu's ship, *Excelsior,* more than a decade earlier. After enough time had passed, it had been assumed destroyed with all hands. Harriman had attended the memorial, and he'd comforted Demora about the loss of her father. That he had been found alive must have astounded her and made her so happy.

"*Demora's father held up a padd against the port, and we read its scrolling message; it told us the story of the* Excelsior," Linojj went on. "*Long before the* Enterprise *arrived at Rejarris Two, the* Excelsior *crew had a catastrophic encounter with the portal. The ship ended up passing through it, but was crippled beyond repair. The crew had abandoned* Excelsior *before it was ultimately destroyed, and they ended up on an uninhabited world, with no means of getting home—or even of knowing where they were. They survived as best they could.*"

Poor bastards, Harriman thought. He knew how terrible it had been simply to be faced with the possibility of such an existence. *How much worse to actually live it.*

"*Then, after eleven years, the* Excelsior *crew received a message in their only remaining escape pod that still had any power,*" Linojj said. "*It was from Captain Sulu—Demora—as she searched the planet for the people who had constructed the portal and presumably escaped through it. The* Excelsior *crew attempted to reply to her message, but couldn't, so they used their escape pod to track her down. When they found her, though, she and her two crewmates had just been attacked by native wildlife. One officer was killed, and Demora suffered life-threatening injuries; according to what the* Excelsior *crew told us, she is currently in critical condition. The* Excelsior's *chief medical officer doesn't know how long she can keep her alive without access to a sickbay to treat her."*

The irony did not escape Harriman. *For Hikaru to be missing all these years, but still alive, and then for Demora to end up finding him, but to be so badly injured . . .*

"Demora is unconscious, and there's no guarantee that she'll survive her injuries," Linojj said. *"Before she lost consciousness, she told her father to have me contact you. She wanted me to tell you that she confirmed an 'Odyssey solution.'"* Linojj stopped and looked away for a moment, as though gathering her thoughts. *"The* Enterprise *crew have been working on trying to figure out how the portal functions so that we can find a means of bringing all those lost Starfleet personnel home. So far, we've made no progress. We would request that Starfleet Command send us help from the Corps of Engineers, but we're on the cusp of Tzenkethi space; we can't just move in a massive research team."* Linojj shrugged, an awkward gesture with her missing arm. *"Admiral . . . John . . . I don't have any idea what Demora meant, or even if her words can be taken seriously, considering her condition at the time she said them. I researched* Odyssey *in the library-computer and found nothing but a reference to an ancient human literary work."*

Linojj could find nothing on the star that he and Demora had dubbed *Odyssey* because Starfleet did not know it by that name. Regardless, Federation charts marked the entire region around it as hazardous to navigation. The star's effects—like his and Demora's covert mission into the Romulan Empire—remained classified at the highest levels of Starfleet Intelligence.

"John, there are five hundred and sixty-five members of the Excelsior *crew still alive on a desolate world, and they've been marooned there for eleven years. Even if we can find a way to get them back, it's going to take time . . . maybe a long time . . . and definitely more time than Demora has left. If there's anything you can do . . . or if you even just know something that could help us . . ."*

It seemed to Harriman that Linojj wanted to say more, but he didn't know what else she could say. She had a terrible problem, impossible for her to solve, and so she desperately searched for any possible answer, no matter how unlikely. He couldn't blame her. He couldn't blame her at all—even though he wanted to.

"Please let me know, John," Linojj finished. *"I hope you and Amina are well.* Enterprise *out."*

The message ended, Linojj's visage replaced by the Helaspont Station insignia. Harriman thought about playing it again, but he really had no need to do so. He had no way of knowing if he could save Demora Sulu and her father and the surviving members of the *Excelsior* crew, but he could try. More than that, he knew that he *had* to try.

"Damn," he said in a whisper. He deactivated the interface. Beside it sat a framed hologram of Amina. A candid shot, it had been recorded at the wedding of two of their friends—a wedding at which he had officiated and she had performed a reading. In it, Amina wore a flattering black gown, and at the moment the image had been captured, she had her head thrown back, laughing through her beautiful smile. It was his favorite holo of her, since it so perfectly depicted who she was. He loved her more than he ever thought he could love anybody, and yet, from one day to the next, his love for her only grew. It seemed impossible, but then, wasn't that what love was supposed to do?

Harriman stood up and glanced through the outer wall of his office, toward the Sea of Marmara arm of the station. He wanted to go back to the restaurant, back to Amina, so that they could enjoy their anniversary celebration. It hurt him that he couldn't do that. And it hurt him even more that the life that he knew, the life that he had built together with Amina, might have just ended.

Harriman picked up the framed hologram of his wife and marched out of his office.

Sasine stood in the doorway that led from the living area of their quarters into the bedroom. She watched for a moment as her husband extracted clothes from his closet and stowed them in a duffel. It saddened her that not only wouldn't they have time to take leave anywhere near their anniversary, but it appeared that the one night and one day they'd counted upon being able to spend together might not materialize either.

"What's happened?" she asked. John jumped, startled. He evidently hadn't heard Sasine enter their cabin. *That's never a good sign,* she thought. *John is usually so observant.* "I'm sorry."

"It's all right," John said. He walked over to Sasine and kissed her, then wrapped his arms around her body. "I'm sorry about dinner." After he had left the restaurant, she'd continued with her meal. As a matter of course, she didn't mind dining alone, but she would have preferred to share their anniversary dinner with her husband. Still, she understood the dictates of their positions and accepted the reality that their duties sometimes interfered with their personal lives. She had certainly been required to leave John by himself on any number of occasions.

"It's fine," Sasine said, waving away the apology. "We should both be accustomed to it by now." Not long after John had left the restaurant, he'd contacted Javier and asked him to inform Sasine that he would likely be unable to return there that night. Not wanting all of Georges' kind efforts to go to waste, she finished her meal—a deliciously tender eggplant, layered with a Gruyère cognate, spiced with basil, and topped with a saffron custard, followed by strawberries drizzled in dark chocolate and Grand Marnier Cordon Rouge. "I really think it's Chef you need to ask to forgive you," Sasine said lightly. Though Rochambeau hid his emotions well, Sasine knew that Georges had to be disappointed that his specially prepared dinner had not been enjoyed in the way he'd envisioned. Sasine departed Sur Le Mer Coucher with a promise to Chef that she and John would dine there again very soon.

"He may never let me back in the place."

Sasine shrugged. "Georges might not mind shunning a Starfleet admiral, but I think he'll be careful not to take issue with the commanding officer of the space station that hosts his restaurant."

"Perhaps you're right," John said. "Sometimes I forget how formidable you can be."

"Does that mean I need to find a way to remind you?" Sasine taunted.

"Oh, no, believe me, I remember." John took her by the hand and led her out of their bedroom and into the living area. They sat down on a sofa beneath a wide port that looked out onto open space, the stars glistering like jewels in the night. "I need to tell you what's going on."

"I already know about the *Cassiopeia*," she said. "Ops contacted me after I left the restaurant." The beta-shift duty officer, Lieutenant Esther Freemantle, had notified her that Admiral Harriman had rerouted a nearby starship to Helaspont Station. The *Constellation*-class *Cassiopeia*, designated NCC-2531, would arrive at the starbase within eighteen hours. "Is there anything you need from me, other than one of my docking bays?"

"Actually, there is," John said. "I need to disembark almost all personnel from the *Cassiopeia*, except for a skeleton crew."

The request surprised Sasine. "Assuming that means you'll keep twenty or thirty officers aboard, you're still talking about Helaspont providing accommodations for more than five hundred personnel."

"I know you've got the trade summit beginning in two days, so it won't be a simple matter," John acknowledged.

"No," Sasine said, already trying to work out the logistics in her head. "I don't know why you need a starship with a skeleton crew, but wouldn't it be possible to utilize either the *Kazanga* or the *Marvick*?" As soon she asked the question, she realized that John would already have asked it himself.

"The *Kazanga* is a science vessel, and the *Marvick* is a support craft," John said. "I need a ship that's larger and faster." He paused, then added, "I also need one with more firepower."

Sasine didn't like hearing that. Rather than respond as a wife concerned about her husband's safety, she continued to speak as the commanding officer of Helaspont Station. "How long will the *Cassiopeia*'s crew be here?" she asked.

John shook his head. "I don't know." The reply seemed out of character for him, since he normally took a detail-oriented approach to his duties.

"Can you at least give me an idea?" Sasine asked. "A week? A month?"

"Perhaps longer," John told her quietly. "Potentially much longer."

"'*Much* longer'?" Sasine blurted, her reaction more that of a wife than of an officer.

"All I can tell you is . . . maybe," John said. "I honestly don't know."

John's answers had begun to alarm Sasine, and so she took refuge in her role as a Starfleet captain. She stood up from the sofa and paced across the room. "Admiral," she said carefully when she turned around, "removing most of a starship's crew and relegating them to an indefinite period of shore leave is an act that typically requires the involvement of Starfleet Operations."

"I'm aware of that, Captain," John said, without rancor. They had long ago learned how to conduct their professional relationship in a manner divorced from their marriage. "But on the edge of Tzenkethi space, contacting Starfleet Command about this situation, enduring the inevitable debate, and then waiting for a decision would take far too long. As an admiral-at-large posted to Helaspont Station, the needs of Starfleet in this region dictate my movements and missions. I have a great deal of autonomy."

"I know," Sasine said. "I know, but . . . with all due respect, sir, the imprecise reassignment of a *Constellation*-class starship and most of its crew is an action at the very limits of your authority."

John looked at her for a long time, his face a mask. She could almost always tell what he was thinking, but that time, she couldn't. She hoped that he didn't think that she'd overstepped her bounds as a captain . . . or as his wife. Finally, he said, "What I'm doing may be *beyond* the limits of my authority." He stood up. "It doesn't matter. I have to do this."

Do what? she wanted to know, but she couldn't ask. She trusted that John would tell her all that he could. She waited.

"Amina, please come here," he said gently, motioning toward the sofa. "Let me tell you what's happened." Sasine crossed the room and they sat down together again. He took her hands in his. "I received a message from the *Enterprise*."

"From the *Enterprise*?" Sasine said. "I thought Demora was out in unexplored territory."

"She is, but not all that far from Tzenkethi space, just a few days from here at high warp," John said. "Except that I didn't hear from Demora; I heard from her first officer, Commander Linojj."

Sasine experienced a sinking feeling. "Has something happened to Demora?"

"Yes," John said, and Sasine could see the pain in his eyes. She felt the same emotion. "She's been badly injured. She's received medical attention, but she needs the support of a sickbay to have any chance of survival."

"And obviously the *Enterprise* can't provide that for some reason," Sasine concluded. "That's why you're commandeering the *Cassiopeia*." She offered her words as observations, not as questions.

"In part, yes," John said. "Demora and two of her crew were unintentionally thrown onto an unpopulated, undeveloped planet in another universe. They arrived there after traveling through a portal that functions in only one direction."

"Do you intend to abandon the *Cassiopeia* and send it through the portal, then?" Sasine asked. "So that Demora's crewmates can somehow get her aboard in order to get her to the ship's sickbay."

"I do plan to get Demora into the *Cassiopeia*'s sickbay," John said. "But there's more to it than that. There's something else that's happened. It turns out that eleven years ago, the *Excelsior* also passed through the portal."

"Demora's father?" Sasine asked, feeling her eyes go wide.

"Hikaru Sulu," John said. "He and almost six hundred of his crew have been stranded on that empty planet for all of that time. They've lived a rugged existence, and they need to be rescued."

"Which is why you require a larger starship," Sasine said. "You want to provide a place for them to live."

"Yes," John said. He glanced down for a moment, and he squeezed her hands when he did. When he looked back up, Sasine saw that his face had hardened—not in anger, but in an attempt to hold his tears at bay. She had been with John for sixteen years; she knew when something affected him. "I'm bringing the *Cassiopeia* to provide medical care for Demora and a home for the *Excelsior* crew. But I also mean to bring them back home."

"But if the portal operates in only one direction . . ." Sasine let the question fade on her lips. John's use of the word *bring* brought her up short. *He's going to take the ship through the portal himself.*

"The *Enterprise* crew believe that there may be a way to reverse the direction of the portal's flow," he said. "Regardless, another solution exists."

"I'm not sure what you mean," Sasine said.

"I'm afraid that I can't say more. It's classified, but once I take the *Cassiopeia* through the portal, I may be able to bring Demora and her father and everybody else home safely."

"John, you said you *may* be able to bring them home." Sasine deserted her position as a Starfleet captain and stepped fully into her role as a wife. "That doesn't sound hopeful."

"I *am* hopeful," John told her. "It's true, though, that nothing is certain."

"What happens if the prospective solution fails?" Sasine asked, clearly following what John told her, but unwilling to accept the implications. "Does that mean you'll be trapped in another universe?"

John could only nod his head.

"Can't somebody else take on this mission?" Sasine asked meekly, already knowing the answer, but having to ask anyway. "Somebody without a spouse?"

John threw up one shoulder in a half-hearted shrug. "I don't know if any such person exists who has possession of the classified information needed for this mission. But even if there is, how could I ask another person to take a risk I'm unwilling to take myself?"

It was Sasine's turn to look down. She gazed at their hands, at the marvelous contrast between his flesh and hers, pale and dark, yin and yang, two halves of a whole. She didn't even realize she'd begun crying until a tear dropped onto her husband's hand. "What about me, John?" she asked in a whisper. She raised her head and peered at him. "What about *us*?"

"Amina, you know I love you," he said. "I think I loved you even before we ever met. In my heart, I knew who you were, the fullness of your heart, the depth of your mind, the music of your laughter. I knew all that about you and more, and I had only to find you. And I did."

"We found each other," Sasine agreed, smiling through her tears.

"We found each other, and I don't want to lose you," John said, almost pleading with her, as though she planned to take on the mission and he wanted to stop her. "You mean more to me than anything else."

She squeezed his hands. "If that's so, then how can you do this? How can you take this chance?"

"Because I have to do this," John said. "As far as I know, nobody else can. Even if somebody could, they might not be able to reach Demora in time to save her." He reached up and wiped away Sasine's tears. "Demora and I have been friends for more than a quarter of a century. Hell, I served with her aboard the *Enterprise* for eighteen years. That's even longer than you and I have been together."

"Demora is my friend too, but she doesn't mean to me what you do."

"I'm not saying that Demora is more important to me than you are," John said. "But she was a fine officer in my crew, she served with distinction and loyalty, and she literally saved my life on more than one occasion. I *have* to do this because it's the right thing to do."

"I know," Sasine admitted, both to John and to herself. "But how can it be the right thing if it takes us away from each other?"

"I don't know," John said. "I just know that we don't do the right thing because it's easy or convenient or what we want. We do the right thing *because* it's the right thing. If I don't do this, then I'm not the man you fell in love with anyway."

Sasine examined her husband's face, searching for a solution she knew she wouldn't find. After a moment, he leaned forward and took her in his arms. They held each other like that for a long while.

Then John finished packing.

Harriman sat at the desk in his office, studying his after-action report of the first mission he had ever undertaken with Demora Sulu for Starfleet Intelligence. He also pored over SI's response initiative. It had taken sixteen hours for them to reply to his request and transmit the encrypted files to Helaspont Station from their nearest black site.

The admiral had hoped to find something of value to assist him with his upcoming mission aboard *Cassiopeia*. As he reviewed the material, though, he found no detail that he didn't already recall from his and Demora's encounter with the star they had called Odyssey. Starfleet Command had designated the region off-limits to space travel. Presumably because of the star's proximity to Romulan space, or perhaps because of the tremendous risk, no attempts had been made to study the phenomenon.

At least, there have been no attempts that I'm authorized to know about, Harriman thought. Regardless, so far as he could tell, no other known contacts had ever been made with the mysterious star. *Of course, anybody who did experience the effects of Odyssey might never have returned to our universe so that they could report it.*

Commander Linojj had said that Demora wanted the admiral to know that she had "confirmed an Odyssey solution." *But what does that mean?* From what Linojj had told him, Demora and two of her crew had been marooned with a pair of planetary shuttlecraft on an empty world. If that world actually orbited Odyssey, then Demora would have been able to attempt a return herself. That seemed unlikely to Harriman, both because Demora hadn't made such an attempt, and because in none of the universes to which they had traveled did the star possess any planets.

Harriman therefore wondered how Demora could have confirmed anything about Odyssey, other than the simple fact of its existence. *She couldn't,* he realized. She could only look to the right part of the sky and verify the color and magnitude of the star there. She would have no way of knowing whether or not the conditions that she and Harriman had encountered still existed—or if they had ever existed at all in that universe.

The admiral checked the time, then closed the files and deactivated the communications-and-computer interface on his desk. *Cassiopeia* would arrive at Helaspont Station shortly, and he would have to have a difficult conversation with the ship's captain. After that, he would depart the station, prepared to find out if Odyssey really did exist in Demora's universe, and whether it could send them all back home.

2319

Enterprise

9

Seated at the main console on *Pytheas*, Captain Hikaru Sulu checked the proximity alert, as well as the sensors that, in the right circumstances, should trigger that alert. He also ran his own scans. He'd done all of that periodically since he'd landed the shuttlecraft. Such examinations had become a habit over the years, though up until the last four days, he'd had to utilize a tricorder to check for indications of the arachnoids. As he knew too well, deposits of various elements all around the planet often masked the subterranean bio-signs—and sometimes even the movements—of the deadly creatures. He defended against that by frequently verifying the integrity of the ground in the immediate area.

For eleven years, the arachnoids, as *Excelsior*'s crew had come to call them, had been a bane. The ship's complement had numbered seven hundred thirty-two. As best they could tell, twelve died in the collision with the portal, and another eight perished when their escape pod failed during its descent and crashed. That meant that seven hundred twelve of Sulu's crew made it safely to the surface of the unknown planet. Since then, one hundred forty-seven had succumbed to various maladies and dangers—the majority of them killed by the arachnoids, either as the direct result of injuries suffered in an attack, or from venom injected into their bodies. Most of those casualties had occurred early on during their time on the planet, but Janet Whistler, one of the crew's medical technicians, had died just eight months prior, when she'd gotten too close to what she'd thought had been a freshly killed creature. Ironically, she'd been attacked by the nearly dead arachnoid while attempting to harvest its venom for use in producing antivenin, a necessity since their remaining stock would soon lose stability and potency.

Satisfied with the state of terrain around and below the shuttlecraft, Sulu turned in his chair so that he could see his daughter—even though seeing her in her present condition broke his heart. In her crew's battle aboard *Amundsen* with four of the grotesque arachnoids, one of the creatures had driven its envenomed front appendage into her abdomen. Christine Chapel, *Excelsior*'s chief medical officer, had been able to remove the section of the barbed limb from Demora's body and treat her wounds, thanks in part to medical equipment— and antivenin—that the *Enterprise* crew had sent through the portal, but the doctor could only do so much. Demora's condition had stabilized for the time being, but she required surgery and support that would be better, safer, and more effectively carried out in a Starfleet sickbay.

Sulu regarded the unconscious form of his daughter, laid out on an antigrav stretcher in an aft corner of the shuttlecraft. Chapel and one of her nurses, Vigo Eklund, tended to her. On a chair behind them, on the other side of the cabin, Demora's torn and bloodied uniform tunic lay in a bunch. He noted the captain's insignia, and despite his concerns for his daughter's health, he took great satisfaction in her rank. With everything else that had taken place over the previous four days, he hadn't had much of a chance to think about her promotion. The last time he'd spoken with Demora before his disappearance, she'd been serving aboard *Enterprise* as Captain Harriman's executive officer. It didn't surprise him at all that, in the time since, she'd made captain and taken over command of the ship. He felt abundantly proud, which just made the situation all the more difficult.

Sulu almost couldn't bear what had happened to his daughter, not when they had, against all odds, ended up in the same place years after he had forsaken any chance of ever seeing her again. After *Excelsior* had collided with the portal and passed through it, he had been the last member of the crew to leave the dying vessel. Blasting away from the mortally wounded ship by firing the explosive bolts on his escape pod, he successfully fled *Excelsior*, but discovered on his trip down to the planet that his emergency vehicle had been badly damaged. As the pod plummeted wildly through the atmosphere, Sulu worked feverishly to gain flight control. He managed to do so only at the last possible moment, leveling off just above a forest. His pod plowed through trees that slowed it enough to avert his death. When it finally struck the ground, it dug out a long trench, leaving him buried in the escape vehicle eight meters beneath the forest floor, battered and unconscious. Since he came down nearly a thousand kilometers from the rest of his crew, it took them days to find him.

After *Excelsior* had been destroyed, Sulu had championed all attempts to escape the planet and return home, although he privately concluded that they had involuntarily traveled to another universe. The patterns of stars in the night sky told the crew that they'd ended up incalculably far from the Federation. It had taken months, and in some cases years, but they had all ultimately accepted their aggregate fate to one degree or another. They still took what few actions they could to foment their rescue, although, as time wore on, their expectations diminished to almost nothing.

When Sulu had come to realize that he might never again see his daughter, it had for a time beaten him down. He missed her terribly, but worse than that, he understood that his disappearance—and the eventual presumption of his death—would cause her great pain. He hated to think of Demora mourning him, of her hurting and sad, with the endless ache of uncertainty preventing her from ever achieving closure.

And then when I heard her voice . . .

Sulu still had difficulty believing that he wasn't

experiencing some sort of hallucination or dream—or nightmare, considering Demora's condition. Four days prior, Ryan Leslie had visited the last of their escape pods still under power. *Excelsior*'s emergency craft had been designed to keep a full load of passengers alive while adrift in space, or, if necessary and possible, to safely land them on a nearby world. Each pod carried a month of provisions, along with enough supplies and battery power to maintain life support, communications, and rudimentary helm control for the same amount of time.

Once the *Excelsior* crew had landed on the planet, they'd rationed everything they had. After eleven years, only a single escape pod retained a functioning battery. Where they had initially transmitted distress calls on a daily basis, they had, over time and in the interest of conserving power, reduced that to once a week, and finally to once a month.

Sulu had promoted Leslie to first officer just after the destruction of *Excelsior*, when Beskle Crajjik's escape pod had failed during its descent, crashing and killing all eight crew members aboard. Still the security chief, Leslie took on the task of regularly sending out a distress call. He had just finished doing so when he unexpectedly *received* a message—one delivered in Federation Standard. He listened as a woman issued a call to any *Excelsior* survivors. Leslie replied at once, but he received no response. The message, clearly on a loop, then repeated, and the speaker identified herself as Captain Demora Sulu of *U.S.S. Enterprise*.

According to Leslie, he had almost knocked himself cold bolting from the escape pod to find Hikaru.

When Sulu had returned to the pod with his first officer, the two men had listened to the message together. The captain recognized his daughter's voice immediately, and it filled him with an odd mixture of potent elation and a peculiar sense of dislocation. He then realized that Demora's presence on the planet could mean that she had traveled through the portal and become stranded as well—a disheartening thought he hoped would turn out not to be the case.

Sulu had repeatedly tried to contact his daughter, unsuccessfully. He didn't know if environmental or meteorological conditions caused the problem, or if the transmitter in the escape pod had failed, or even if Demora might have equipment issues of her own. Since the pod could still fly, though, Sulu formed a team—essentially a planetary version of a landing party—and set out to locate her.

At dawn the next day, they'd found *Amundsen*. But as Sulu and his team flew toward the shuttlecraft, the ground swallowed it whole—an occurrence that, through the years, had stolen a number of the *Excelsior* crew's escape pods. The arachnoids would sometimes carve out large cavities in the earth, essentially creating sinkholes that would trap their prey and allow them to attack.

Sulu had set down the escape pod a safe distance from the opening in the ground. Armed with phasers set to kill, he led his team to the edge of the hole—and then down into it. By the time they had scaled the earthen walls, *Amundsen*'s hull had been wrecked, its bow staved in, its roof perforated and mangled. One arachnoid had been crushed dead in front of the shuttlecraft, and the legs of a second hung motionless where it had been trapped between the stern and a rock wall. Inside the cabin, two more of the creatures lay lifeless, as did a young female ensign. Another ensign, a young man, had been badly injured, but still breathed. Demora had collapsed to the deck, a disembodied alien limb protruding from her abdomen, her respiration shallow, her color ashen.

Removing the injured personnel from beneath the ground had not been easy. While Doctor Chapel treated Demora and the ensign at the scene, Sulu and the rest of his team excavated parts of the hole, blasting boulders into dust with their phasers and ensuring a clear path for their escape pod. They then flew down into the hole, where they used antigrav stretchers to carry out Demora and the ensign through the compromised roof of the shuttlecraft. They also retrieved the body of the female ensign.

Sulu had then returned to the camp that the *Excelsior* survivors called home, a collection of dwellings constructed primarily of native materials. They kept the powerless escape pods in various nearby locations, mostly for use as emergency shelters in the case of extreme weather or an attack by the arachnoids. Limited by their lack of medical facilities and supplies, Chapel and her medical staff did what they could for Demora and the ensign.

Later that day, the surviving ensign—Hawkins Young—had regained consciousness. He explained what had happened—to him, to Demora and Ensign Kostas aboard *Amundsen*, and to the portal, which the *Enterprise* crew had found not in space, but on the surface of Rejarris II. Sulu wondered if *Excelsior*'s collision with the alien device had activated some sort of retrieval protocol that had brought it back to the planet for repairs. Young also revealed the plan of the *Enterprise* crew to restore power to the portal by hauling it back into orbit.

In anticipation of that taking place, Sulu had ordered Leslie to monitor for messages. The next day, he intercepted one sent to Demora by Commander Xintal Linojj, one of the names that Sulu's daughter had uttered before losing consciousness, and whom Ensign Young identified as *Enterprise*'s first officer. Transmitted by a probe that had been directed through the reenergized portal and down to the planet, the message provided instructions on how to respond: by recording a reply onto a scrolling padd and then taking it into orbit, to a specific set of coordinates, and holding it up against the forward viewport.

Sulu and several of his crew had flown their escape pod to the second *Enterprise* shuttlecraft on the planet, where they'd found the scene Young had described to them: *Pytheas*, surrounded by a probe, two log buoys, and the decaying body of an arachnoid. Sulu found the scrolling-enabled padds aboard the shuttlecraft, and he recorded his own message onto one of them. He identified himself and told an abbreviated account of the events that had resulted in him and his crew being stranded.

Sulu had then taken *Pytheas* into orbit, to the coordinates specified by Linojj. He and his team saw nothing there, but they held the padd up to the viewport, as instructed. They allowed it to play through once, and then a second time.

Just after they'd begun a third playback, a probe had appeared before them, as though it had just emerged from behind some hidden fold in space. It sent a transmission to the shuttlecraft, and specifically to Captain Hikaru Sulu, informing him that Linojj had read his message. In her response, she expressed surprise and satisfaction at the news of his crew's survival, as well as concern for *Enterprise*'s own missing officers. She also asked what she could send through the portal to the *Excelsior* crew, most especially to aid in the medical care of her captain.

From there, Sulu had begun a dialogue with Linojj, starting with all of Chapel's requests for medical equipment and supplies. He then told the *Enterprise* first officer about his daughter's final words to him. He suspected that Demora's reference to "Ad Ja Harr'man" had been to her former captain, John Harriman. Linojj agreed, and said that she would pass along the message to him, despite its inscrutable—and possibly nonsensical—content.

That had taken place three days earlier. Within twelve hours of informing the *Enterprise* first officer of Demora's message, Linojj had received a response from Admiral Harriman's posting, Helaspont Station. His reply was brief: "Maintain position and initiate subspace radio silence. Continue to support all Starfleet personnel lost on the other side of the portal. Help is on the way."

As Sulu regarded the unconscious and badly wounded form of Demora from across the shuttle-craft cabin, he could only hope that the help Harriman spoke of would arrive in time to save his daughter.

Acting Captain Xintal Linojj had wanted the ship's entire senior staff—other than Commander Buonarroti, who remained otherwise occupied—to attend the meeting, but she sat at the conference table in *Enterprise*'s observation lounge with just one other person: Admiral John Harriman. She hadn't seen her former commanding officer in several years. He looked well: both his lean body and long face had filled out some, replacing the boyish quality he'd previously retained with a more mature appearance. His brown hair had gone gray, and though it had receded a bit, she thought that, together with his blue-gray eyes, it gave him a flinty countenance.

"Your chief engineer reports that preparations are nearly complete," Harriman said. He had arrived at Rejarris II ten hours before, aboard *U.S.S. Cassiopeia*. Rather than its regular complement of five hundred thirty-five, it carried a skeleton crew of twenty-three, including the admiral as its commanding officer—a fact Linojj almost found suspicious, since she knew the *Constellation*-class vessel's current captain, Gabe Márquez. The commander had known John Harriman a long time, though, and she trusted him. More than that, he had responded to the message she'd sent to him with greater haste than she'd expected, and she knew that he'd come to rescue Demora Sulu and Hawkins Young and the surviving crew of *Excelsior*.

At least, she thought she knew that. Captain Demora Sulu's cryptic message to the admiral—that she had confirmed an "Odyssey solution"—sounded positive to her, if also slightly mysterious. And Linojj certainly couldn't argue that those words hadn't brought Harriman racing to Rejarris II. When she had spoken to the admiral after he'd first arrived, she'd asked about the phrase. He deftly moved the conversation in another direction without actually answering her question, and, coupled with her inability to find any Starfleet references to Odyssey in the library computer, she concluded that the term actually carried significant—although perhaps classified—meaning.

"Once my engineers and computer technicians have transported back to the ship," Linojj asked, "what are your orders, sir?" Upon *Cassiopeia*'s arrival, Harriman had enlisted a team of *Enterprise* personnel to assist him aboard his vessel. He had initially declined to discuss his intentions, causing Linojj to harbor paranoid delusions about Starfleet Intelligence sending him on a covert mission to destroy the portal, consequently stranding Captain Sulu, her father, and all the others on the other side permanently. Harriman's occasional participation in SI operations had long been rumored. The admiral must have perceived her concerns, though, because he'd then volunteered that he aimed to do everything he possibly could to bring all the marooned Starfleet personnel home.

"When Commander Buonarroti and his teams return to the *Enterprise*," Harriman said, "the twenty-two crew members I brought with me will transport over with them."

Linojj felt her eyes involuntarily narrow. It sounded as though the admiral would leave *Cassiopeia* empty of any personnel, but a starship could not safely pilot itself, at least not for long. Even if Harriman planned to send the vessel uncrewed through the portal, and even if he had devised a ready method for Hikaru Sulu to get aboard, Linojj didn't understand how that would allow the starship to bring its passengers home. She feared that the admiral's "solution" to the plight of Demora Sulu, Ensign Young, and the *Excelsior* crew would be to provide them a vessel on which to travel, leaving them on their own to find their way home—or simply to find a comfortable place to make a new home.

Odyssey, Linojj thought. She had believed the lone reference to the word that she could find irrelevant to the current situation, but she'd read that the ancient human literary work told the story of an epic journey. *Could that be what Captain Sulu intended?* Linojj asked herself. *Did she discover where the portal had sent her and conclude that a long starship journey could eventually get her back to the Federation?*

"Once your crew and the *Cassiopeia* crew are aboard the *Enterprise*," Harriman continued, "you are to maintain subspace silence and travel to Helaspont Station. Once you've offloaded the *Cassiopeia* crew, I want you to contact Starfleet Command and provide them with a detailed account of everything that's happened at Rejarris Two."

"Sir?" Linojj said. "You haven't informed Starfleet Command already?"

"Further," Harriman said, completely ignoring the question, "you are to deliver to Command my recommendation that the Rejarris star system should be designated a hazard to navigation and rendered off-limits to Federation traffic."

"Yes, sir," Linojj said, "but . . . you're not coming with us?"

In response, Harriman looked away and shook his head, then took a deep breath. His reaction seemed completely divorced from what Linojj had just asked him. When finally he gazed back at her, he said, "Commander, I will not be returning to Helaspont Station aboard the *Enterprise*. I am taking the *Cassiopeia* through the portal in order to recover Captain Sulu—*both* Captains Sulu—Ensign Young, and the remaining crew of the *Excelsior*."

"By yourself, Admiral?" Linojj asked, incredulous. It pleased her that Harriman obviously must have the means of reversing the direction of the portal, but the notion of one man piloting a *Constellation*-class starship sounded like madness. "I know it will only be a short journey through the portal, but there's no guarantee of the conditions on the other side, or how long it will take to get the *Excelsior* crew aboard—or if one person can even do all of that."

"That's the effort that Commander Buonarroti has been leading," Harriman said. "Once complete,

I will be able to control helm, navigation, the impulse engines, and the transporter from a single station."

"Even if you centralize control," Linojj argued, "that's a lot for one person to take on."

"As you mentioned, it will only be a short journey through the portal," Harriman said. "After I'm through and established in orbit, I will begin beaming people up to the ship, specifically bringing aboard crew who can take over all those functions from me."

"Begging the admiral's pardon, but it's been more than a decade since the *Excelsior* crew have operated a starship."

Harriman actually smiled, although Linojj didn't know what she'd said that could have been considered even remotely amusing. "Xintal," he said, "I'm not sure how long it's been since I've sat at the helm of a starship, but I'm confident that my training, abilities, and experience haven't deserted me."

"But you brought a minimal crew with you on the *Cassiopeia*," Linojj noted. "Why can't you bring them with you, simply in the interests of prudence? Or even some additional *Enterprise* personnel, just to ensure you don't encounter any problems that you can't overcome?"

Harriman did not answer immediately, and he appeared to consider what he would tell her. "Because," he finally said, "the portal operates only in one direction."

"Admiral, I assumed that if you chose to travel through the portal, you had a means of returning through it," Linojj said. She glanced through the ports in the outer wall of the observation lounge, where *Cassiopeia* kept station nearby. At the aft end of its thick saucer section, two pair of warp nacelles connected to it, one above and one below. "Otherwise, why would you do this?"

"Because there may be another way to bring everybody home."

Linojj thought about that. "The 'Odyssey solution' Captain Sulu spoke of."

"I can neither confirm nor deny that," Harriman said. "Please consider Sulu's position in Starfleet and her security clearance. There is classified information that she is in possession of, that I am in possession of, that you are not, and I'm afraid it has to stay that way."

Linojj thought about that, but one detail of the admiral's unspecified plan troubled her more than any other. "Sir, you've implied that you won't take anybody else with you aboard the *Cassiopeia* because there's only a possibility that you can return. Aren't you risking the sacrifice of your life? Your career? Your colleagues? Your friends?" She deliberately did not mention family, as she knew that he had no living blood relations; his parents had both died, all four of his grandparents, and even his lone sibling, his older sister, Lynn. "And what about Amina?"

The last question seemed to strike a nerve. "The discussion is closed," the admiral said. He pushed back from the conference table and stood up. "Everything I've told you is classified."

"You haven't told me *anything*," Linojj pointed

out, frustrated. She desperately wanted to recover Demora Sulu and Hawkins Young and the *Excelsior* crew, but not at the risk of permanently stranding even one more person. She stood up and faced the admiral, deciding to take a chance at being charged with insubordination, relying on their personal relationship to convince him of her good intentions. She reached out to him across the corner of the conference table and placed her hand on his shoulder. "John," she said, "please reconsider your—"

The up-and-down notes of the boatswain's whistle interrupted her. *"Bridge to Commander Linojj,"* said Kanchumurthi.

She took her hand from the admiral's shoulder and activated the intercom set into the table. "This is Linojj," she said. "What is it, Commander?"

"Sir, there's a Starfleet warp shuttle approaching at high speed," Kanchumurthi said. *"It's just relayed a priority-one message from Starfleet Command."*

"Transfer it here," Linojj said.

"There are no audio or visual components to the message," Kanchumurthi said. *"It's text only."*

Linojj eyed Harriman, but the admiral appeared as uncomfortable with the situation as she felt. "Read it to me, then," she said.

"'Enterprise and Cassiopeia are ordered to maintain their positions until a courier arrives aboard Antilochus with new orders,'" Kanchumurthi read. *"'Signed, Admiral Los Tirasol Mentir, Chief of Starfleet Operations.' I have verified the authenticity of the message."*

Harriman placed both hands on the table and leaned heavily on them. He looked frustrated, perhaps even angry. "Commander Kanchumurthi," he said, "what's the registry of the shuttle?"

After a beat, the communications officer said, *"NCC-Twenty-Two-Twenty-Three, assigned to Helaspont Station."*

"One of the new shuttles," Harriman said, more to himself than to Linojj. Then, to Tenger, "How long before it arrives?"

"At its current speed, fifty-three minutes."

Harriman nodded. "Before the *Cassiopeia* will be ready to go," he said. Again, he did not seem to be speaking to anybody but himself. "Commander Kanchumurthi, I want to be informed as soon as the shuttle is on its final approach to the *Enterprise.*"

"Yes, Admiral."

"Keep me informed as well, Commander. Linojj out." She deactivated the intercom, then looked to Harriman. "Do you know what that's about, Admiral?"

"Maybe," he said reluctantly, then amended his response: "I think I do."

After everything that Harriman had told her—and all of the things he had not—the arrival of orders from Starfleet Operations carried by a courier raised her suspicions even higher. "Admiral," she said, "are you conducting this mission without proper authority from Starfleet Command?" Linojj had no desire to arrest Harriman and place him in the brig, but she also could not allow a rogue operation by a lone admiral—even one she considered a friend.

"I am a part of Starfleet Command," he said.

Stretching the purview of your admiral-at-large position just a bit, Linojj thought.

"I am acting on recognized and defensible authority."

"Then why is a warp shuttle heading this way with new orders?" Linojj demanded, challenging him.

Harriman seemed to deflate. "I have an idea why," he said, "but it's not what you think it is."

"Do you intend to follow the orders we've just been given, to maintain our positions?" Linojj asked. "Do you intend to follow the new orders when they arrive?"

"I'll keep the *Cassiopeia* here and wait for the orders," Harriman said. "I don't want to hang any of this on you, Xintal."

"That's not what this is about," Linojj snapped back, her voice rising. She took a moment to calm herself. "I'm sorry, Admiral, but this isn't about me. It's about you running a rogue mission and putting lives in danger."

"One life," Harriman admitted. "*My* life."

"It doesn't matter that it's your life," Linojj contended. "You are a Starfleet asset. We need you."

"Right now, Demora needs me," Harriman said quietly. "And Hikaru."

"John, don't you think I want to bring them back, too?" Linojj asked him.

"Of course you do," he said. "Listen, right now, my orders to you still stand. We'll also obey Admiral Mentir and wait for our new orders. Then we'll go from there."

"I don't need to lock you up in the brig, do I, Admiral?" Linojj asked him.

"Not yet," Harriman said, and the quick smile he offered returned a boyishness to his face. "But I'll let you know when you do."

Linojj left the admiral in the observation lounge so that he could contact the crews aboard *Cassiopeia*. The *Enterprise*'s first officer headed for the bridge. Despite Harriman's assurances, she realized that she could not possibly predict what actions he would take in the next couple of hours.

Harriman waited outside the airlock door, tapping one hand anxiously against the side of his leg. He had trouble sorting out all of the emotions he felt: disappointment, anger, frustration . . . and, of course, love. He knew that when *Antilochus*'s hatch opened in *Enterprise*'s hangar deck, a Starfleet officer would disembark carrying orders from the chief of Starfleet Operations—orders that Amina had made happen, and that would unquestionably seek to prevent him from attempting to recover Demora Sulu and the other Starfleet personnel trapped on the other side of the portal. He understood *why* Amina needed to stop him—she loved him and he loved her, and they had built a strong, happy life together—but he couldn't believe that she had acted on that need.

Beside the airlock door, an indicator light switched from red to green, signifying that he could safely enter the hangar bay. He tapped a control, and the door opened before him. He stepped past it and waited for it to close. Through the rounded, rectangular port in the second door, he saw the warp shuttle sitting in the middle of the landing deck, its hatch folding down to form an access ramp. He worked a control and the airlock door glided open with a mechanical thunk.

Harriman strode quickly along the marked gangway that led to the shuttle. He had made it halfway to *Antilochus* when the officer conveying new orders to him from Admiral Mentir appeared at the top of the access ramp. It was Amina.

"John," she said when she saw him, her eyebrows lifting in obvious surprise.

Harriman marched the rest of the way to the shuttle as Amina descended the ramp. They met just as she stepped onto the deck. She held a padd in one hand. "What have you done?" he demanded, taken aback by the ire he heard in his own voice. He also identified something else that he felt: betrayed.

Amina regarded him coolly. She stood just a couple of centimeters taller than he, and she stared levelly at him, her dark eyes deep and alive, but also wary. "Permission to come aboard, Admiral," she finally said, her tone flat despite the archness of her words.

"There's nothing funny about this," Harriman told her.

"No, John, there isn't," Amina said. "These are our lives. This is our life *together*."

"And so you went to Mentir to stop me?" he said. "How could you?" He turned and walked several steps away, his frustrations mounting. He spun back around to face her, raising his arms beseechingly. "You know that I have no choice but to do what I'm doing."

"We *always* have choices, John," Amina said.

"And no, I don't completely know what it is that you're doing because you can't or won't tell me. But if I'm supposed to know that you *have* to do this, then how can you accuse me of trying to thwart you? You've known me for as long as I've known you—almost twenty years now. If I'm supposed to know you, then shouldn't you know me, too?"

Harriman took a couple of steps toward her. "What does that mean?" he asked. "That if I feel justified in doing what I have to do, then you should feel justified in what you have to do—namely, stop me?"

"John," Amina said, shaking her head. "John, how have I stopped you?"

"Isn't that why you're here?" he asked. "You convinced Admiral Mentir to keep the *Cassiopeia* and the *Enterprise* in place long enough for you to bring me new orders."

"Because I knew that, in this particular rare case, you wouldn't listen to me," Amina said. "I don't mean that you wouldn't do as I suggested; I mean that you wouldn't even *listen* to what I had to say." She strode forward, her movements strong and supple, her carriage an exercise in grace. When she reached him, Amina tucked her padd beneath her arm, then took one of his hands in both of hers. "I knew you wouldn't listen to me because, even if I don't know the exact nature of the mission you're going on, I know the reason you're going. I understand the importance of the bonds you share with certain people." She shrugged, and the corner of her mouth lifted, causing a dimple to form in her cheek. "They say you can't pick your family, John, but in the entire time I've known you, that's precisely what you've done. Everybody in your life who you were related to by blood is gone—and frankly, some of them weren't worth having in your life anyway. But you've chosen your own family. I know because I'm in it. So is Demora. She's the sister you never really got to have."

The reference to Lynn squeezed Harriman's heart, as it almost always did. He'd loved his sister, older than he by two years. At the age of eighteen, during a break from university, she'd tagged along with friends on a trip to a border outpost. There, local law enforcement believed, she'd unintentionally witnessed a crime, a chance occurrence that had resulted in her murder.

"My sister," Harriman said, and he thought about how Demora really had fulfilled that role in his adult life. "My friend. She's in trouble, Amina, and I'm the only one who can possibly save her— her, and more than five hundred other Starfleet personnel."

"I don't quite understand how it is that only *you* can save Demora, because you won't tell me," Amina said, though with no hint of reproof. "But I believe you. I believe you because I love you, and because I *do* know who you are. You would tell me if you could."

"I really would." He considered telling her at that moment, regulations and security clearances be damned. But the classified nature of the information wasn't the only reason he hadn't told Amina. He also feared that, if she knew what he intended to do, she would never be able to let him go.

Amina patted his hand. "As a Starfleet officer,

I appreciate your dedication to duty," she said. "As your wife, not so much. But you are who you are, John, and I happen to love that man."

"You don't know how much that means to me," Harriman told her. "Especially now."

"I love you," she said. "For now and ever." They had used the phrase with each other almost since the very beginning of their relationship. It had been the title of a sonnet that Harriman had written for her.

"I love you, for now and ever." He moved forward and kissed her, his hand coming up to cradle her head. Staff in the shuttlebay control room could see them if they looked, as well as anybody who happened to be in either of the observation galleries, but he didn't care.

When they ended the kiss—warm and gentle and soft, filled with all they felt for each other— Harriman asked the question to which he had to have an answer. "If you're not here to stop me, then what are Admiral Mentir's new orders?"

"You're not taking the *Cassiopeia* on its mission by yourself," she said.

"What—?" he began, but he really didn't know what to ask.

"The chief of Starfleet Operations has temporarily reassigned me to the *Cassiopeia*," Amina said. She handed him the padd. "Length of tour to be determined."

Harriman took the padd and reviewed the order. His mouth fell open. He didn't know how to react. He felt elated and terrified at the same time— elated that he would not have to leave Amina, and terrified what it would mean for her life. "But . . . the station . . ."

"I've left my exec in command," Amina said. "I think Farish has been waiting for an opportunity like this for a long time. When I informed him, he practically ushered me to the warp shuttle."

Harriman chuckled, and the lightness of the moment felt good. "You may never get your command back."

"No, I guess I might not." The simple statement contained several levels of meaning, the most serious of which Harriman felt he needed to address.

"Amina, this mission—"

"I don't want to hear anything about the dangers involved," she said. "I'm a Starfleet officer . . . a captain, not some deskbound admiral. I've served on starships, and I've spent more time on the edge of the Romulan Neutral Zone than almost anybody in Starfleet, including you. And I also don't want to hear about us maybe never being able to come home. That's the whole point. *This*—" She tapped a finger to where her heart beat beneath her chest. "—is my home . . . and *this*." She touched the left side of his chest.

"I love you," Harriman said, and he wrapped his arms around his wife.

"Let this be a lesson to you, John Jason Harriman the Second," she whispered into his ear. "If you ever leave me, I'm going with you."

10

Tenger didn't like it, but then, nobody had asked his opinion. Sending a virtually empty starship to collect a stranded crew made sense, and transporting injured personnel up to a vessel with a functioning sickbay also had a certain logic to it. But if you considered that none of those recovered individuals would actually stop being marooned, or that the cost of taking on that action would be to leave two more people cut off from the Federation, it simply ceased to add up.

The security chief knew that Linojj thought it foolish to allow one or two officers to pilot a starship on their own, even for a brief journey, but Tenger disagreed with that as well. If Buonarroti and the engineering staff could centralize the controls so that Harriman—or Harriman and Sasine, as it turned out—could command the ship, then why not automate it totally? They could send *Cassiopeia* through the portal with the shuttlebay doors left open but its force field in place. Captain

Hikaru Sulu could then land *Pytheas* in the hangar deck, make his way to a transporter room, and begin beaming his crew up from the surface. The result would be the same as with Harriman's plan, except that neither the admiral nor his wife would have to be placed in the same plight as the people they were attempting to save.

Something else is going on, Tenger concluded. Maybe Harriman did have a means of reversing the portal's flow—although if he did, why would he keep that from the *Enterprise* crew? Again, something didn't seem right to him, and he figured that some vital piece of information must be missing from his understanding of the situation.

Beside him, on the other end of the combined communications-and-tactical console, an indicator signaled an incoming transmission. Kanchumurthi acknowledged the alert with a touch, then brought up a window of the sender's identifying information. "Incoming message from the *Cassiopeia*," he said.

"Put it on-screen," said Linojj from where she sat in the command chair.

Kanchumurthi did as ordered, and the main viewer blinked, the image of the *Cassiopeia* bridge replacing that of the ship itself. "*Commander Linojj,*" said Harriman, "*the* Cassiopeia *is ready to commence its journey. We've sent a probe with a message notifying Captain Sulu that we'll be coming through the portal shortly.*" The admiral did not sit in the center of the bridge, but at a peripheral station on the port side. Captain Sasine crewed the communications panel.

"Acknowledged," Linojj said. "We wish you—"

"Admiral!" Sasine said, just as Tenger saw what she must have seen appear on *Cassiopeia*'s tactical display. *"I have three bogeys incoming."*

"Confirmed," Tenger said as he worked his controls to accumulate profiles on the approaching vessels. "They're Tzenkethi. Three frigates, coming fast."

"Profile?" Linojj asked.

"Trident-shaped," Tenger said. "Highly maneuverable, armed with disruptors and plasma cannon. Firepower and deflectors almost as strong as an *Excelsior*-class vessel, stronger than a *Constellation*-class vessel. Faster than both."

"Admiral," Linojj said, standing and moving to the center of the bridge. "If you're going, I'd say that now is the time."

"Agreed," Harriman said. *"Engaging thrusters and bringing us about."*

"We'll wait until you've cleared the portal," Linojj said.

Tenger expected the admiral to countermand Linojj, to order *Enterprise* out of the system and back to Helaspont Station, but instead, he said nothing. Then the security chief recalled that, to ensure safe passage through the portal, Harriman intended to use only thrusters, employing the impulse drive only once he'd cleared the alien device. If the notably belligerent Tzenkethi arrived before Harriman and Sasine had made good their escape, *Cassiopeia* would be no match for even one frigate—even if *Cassiopeia* had a full crew.

"Time until the Tzenkethi arrive?" Linojj asked.

Tenger calculated the frigates' velocity and distance. "Less than five minutes."

"Admiral," Linojj said, "can you make it through the portal by then?"

"*We can if we punch it,*" Harriman said. "*Increasing speed.*"

As the seconds passed, Linojj walked over to stand between the helm and navigation stations. "Lieutenant Aldani, set a course directly away from the Tzenkethi Coalition. Let's not give them any reason to think we're interested in their territory."

"Yes, sir."

"Ensign Syndergaard," Linojj continued, "on my order, I want you to break out of the system as quickly as you can. At the earliest possible moment where we have a safety margin, accelerate to warp nine."

"Understood, sir."

Linojj walked back toward the command chair, but she didn't sit. Instead, she looked up at Tenger. "Time until the *Cassiopeia* makes it to the portal?"

"One minute," Tenger told her. "The Tzenkethi have just dropped out of warp. They will arrive in less than ninety seconds." Suddenly, a new reading appeared on the tactical console, which emitted a series of alert tones.

"What is it?" Linojj asked.

Tenger checked the sensors. He couldn't believe what he saw. "There are three more Tzenkethi vessels headed this way—two frigates and one of their next-generation warships. They are no more than twenty minutes out."

"Raise shields and charge weapons," Linojj said.

"No," Harriman said. He wanted to rescue all of the Starfleet personnel stranded on the other side of the portal, he had come to the Rejarris system specifically to do that, but he could not risk a war to do so—or even short of that, he could not leave the *Enterprise* crew outgunned by an antagonistic force, six starships to one. *Not that a second Starfleet vessel will make a difference,* he thought. But he was the ranking officer on scene, and he would live up to that responsibility. "Stand down, Commander Linojj," he said as he worked his controls to turn *Cassiopeia* away from the portal. "Let's not give the Tzenkethi any reason to fight."

"*With all due respect, Admiral,*" Linojj said, "*the only reason the Tzenkethi need to fight is that we're from the Federation.*"

"*Captain,*" Tenger said, "*we're being hailed.*"

"Captain Sasine, open a channel with the *Enterprise* and the Tzenkethi ship," Harriman said. He set a course to return to *Enterprise*'s flank.

"Yes, Admiral," Amina said. She worked the communications console. "The Tzenkethi message is audio only." Harriman knew that the Tzenkethi typically eschewed visual communications with other species, although their reasoning remained a source of speculation within Starfleet.

"Let's hear it."

"*Tzenkethi squadron to Federation starships,*" said a voice interpreted by the universal translator into Federation Standard. The software lent the speaker's voice a soft lilt, a fair approximation of the Tzenkethi, whose verbal communication, when heard firsthand, sounded more like a carillon than speech. "*This is Gedlin Siv Vel-B.*"

"Gedlin Siv," Harriman said, using the Tzenkethi's

given name, followed by his title, "this is Admiral John Harriman of the *U.S.S. Cassiopeia*."

"*Admiral Harriman, I demand to know why two Federation starships have made incursions into Tzenkethi space.*"

At the communications console, Amina pointed toward the main viewscreen. On it, the image of the portal had been replaced by that of three Tzenkethi vessels, arrayed in a triangular formation. Each had the form of a trident, with the tine-like hulls forward and a wide, single base behind. The two outer hulls curved outward from where the third hull met the base. The ships had no angles, only a collection of smooth, flowing surfaces, all a lustrous metallic green. The forward tips of the tines, Harriman knew, hid a collection of disruptors and plasma cannon.

"Gedlin Siv, the Federation knows of no claims to this star system, or to any system in this sector, by the Coalition," Harriman said.

"*The Tzenkethi Coalition is not required to inform the Federation of its territorial imperatives,*" said Gedlin, the gentle rendering of his voice by the translator no mask for the vexation in his words.

"Certainly not," Harriman said, trying to strike an appropriate tone and find the right approach to extract the two Starfleet vessels from the situation without any shots being fired. "I did not mean to imply that the Coalition has any obligation to the Federation. I simply wanted to point out that we are not willfully violating Tzenkethi territory."

"*And yet you are nevertheless in violation,*" Gedlin said, apparently unwilling to try to find any common ground.

"As you say, we are in violation," Harriman told the squadron leader. "We will therefore withdraw at once, if that will satisfy your grievance." He checked to ensure the active status of the impulse engines as he waited for a response, but he received only silence. *It's no wonder I've never heard anybody ever utter the phrase "Tzenkethi hospitality."* "Commander Linojj, you've heard the request of Gedlin Siv that we vacate this star system, as well as my agreement to do so."

"*I have, Admiral,*" Linojj replied. "*What are your orders?*"

"We will withdraw," Harriman said. He wanted to make a run for the portal, but for so many reasons, he couldn't. Not only would that leave the *Enterprise* at the mercy of three Tzenkethi frigates—all faster and, in aggregate, far more powerful than the single *Excelsior*-class vessel—but three more Coalition vessels would arrive shortly, including one of their brand-new marauders, which Starfleet believed could match up against any Federation starship. But even if the *Enterprise* crew could manage to get their vessel away and clear, Harriman couldn't take *Cassiopeia* through the portal for fear that the Tzenkethi would follow. It had been difficult enough to prepare the ship to be controlled for a brief period of time, over a short distance, by one man; he and Amina could not hope to survive taking *Cassiopeia* into battle, nor would they be able to lower the shields in order to transport up members of the *Excelsior* crew.

But if we withdraw, Harriman thought, *the Tzenkethi will likely find the portal anyway.* It seemed to him that if one of the Coalition vessels vanished through the structure, or was even caught by its tractor beams, the other Tzenkethi ships would probably destroy it. *Either that, tow it home, or set up a research project at Rejarris II.* None of those cases would allow for the continued safety of the stranded Starfleet personnel.

"Admiral Harriman?" Gedlin asked. *"I am waiting for your ships to withdraw."*

"We need a few moments to prepare for warp speed," Harriman said, trying to buy some time—except that, in just minutes, the other three Tzenkethi starships would arrive. "This is an old vessel, but I'm sure you can see from your own sensor scans that you have nothing to fear from us. We are running with our shields down and our weapons offline." He hoped that Linojj had hewn to his orders.

"You have no more time," Gedlin Siv said. *"Withdraw at once, or pay the price for your trespass."*

"Understood," Harriman said, and he immediately looked to Amina and made a slashing motion across his neck.

"Channel to the Tzenkethi muted," she said. "You're still on with the *Enterprise.*"

"We're here, Admiral," Linojj said.

"Perhaps now would be a good time to fake our own deaths," Harriman told her, only partially joking. *And it's not like I haven't done something like that before.* "Commander Linojj, leave your shields down and your weapons offline. I'm setting a course out of the system that will take us directly toward the portal. Follow half a kilometer behind. When the *Cassiopeia* is exactly one kilometer from the portal, transport Captain Sasine and me directly to the *Enterprise* bridge."

"*Admiral?*" Linojj asked, skepticism evident in her voice.

"That's an order, Captain," Harriman said, not harshly. "But Xintal, you need to trust me. I'm taking a chance, but it's the *only* chance we have to save the crews of both the *Enterprise* and the *Excelsior*." Harriman waited only a beat, but Linojj's silence seemed to go on far longer than that. *If she won't —*

"*The* Enterprise *is ready to follow the* Cassiopeia, *Admiral,*" Linojj said.

"Excellent," he said. "Harriman out." As Amina closed the channel to *Enterprise*, he set about turning his starship slowly and unthreateningly away from the three Tzenkethi frigates. "Put Gedlin on," he told Amina. She did so, then nodded. "Gedlin Siv, as you can see, we are withdrawing. We will depart the system, go to warp, and head directly for Federation space." He very carefully laid in *Cassiopeia*'s course.

"*See that you do,*" Gedlin said. "*We will be watching for Federation treachery.*"

You'd better be watching closely, Harriman thought, *or you're going to miss it.* "Harriman out," he said, and Amina nodded once she'd closed the channel. He checked the navigational sensors and saw that *Enterprise* followed *Cassiopeia* at a distance of half a kilometer, just as he'd ordered. *Well done, Xintal.*

"What are we going to do?" Amina asked.

"A little sleight of hand, I hope," Harriman said. "Otherwise, if we ever do make it home, we might find the Federation at war with the Tzenkethi." He offered the words as though delivering a punch line, but he knew they contained more than a little bit of truth.

"Maybe I should have stayed on Helaspont Station after all," Amina said.

Harriman shrugged. "Too late now." He kept his gaze glued to the navigational sensors. "The *Enterprise* is keeping pace," he said. "But so are the Tzenkethi frigates."

"I don't think they trust you," Amina said.

He shrugged again. "Go figure." He watched *Cassiopeia*'s distance to the portal diminish. "We're getting close to transport," he told Amina.

"Not close enough," she said. "The Tzenkethi are hailing us."

"Put him on."

"*Tzenkethi squadron to Federation starships,*" Gedlin said. "*Admiral Harriman, what is the large circular object for which your ships are heading?*"

"Yes, what is it?" Harriman asked, raising his voice. "What *Tzenkethi* treachery have you been hiding?"

"*That is* not *Tzenkethi technology,*" Gedlin said. "*Clearly the Federation—*"

"Clearly the Federation has much to distrust about the Coalition," Harriman said, lacing his words with anger. He waved Amina over, and she circled the bridge to the station where he sat. "Here is physical evidence that the Tzenkethi are developing a metaweapon to use against us. No wonder you wanted our ships out of this system." He engaged the impulse engines, and the ship hummed to life around them. Then he stood up and took Amina's hand.

Gedlin Siv Vel-B began to rage, but his words drifted away from Harriman as the familiar whine of a transporter beam started to form.

Linojj watched from the command chair as Admiral Harriman and Captain Sasine materialized at the forward end of the bridge, directly in front of the main viewer. Behind them, the screen showed two distinct images: on the left, *Cassiopeia* charged toward the portal, its velocity suddenly increasing just before Lieutenant Ved had beamed the two officers aboard, and on the right, the three Tzenkethi frigates following closely behind *Enterprise*. As soon as the transport process completed, the admiral sprang into action. Giving him the trust for which he'd asked—*And which he earned from me in my time as his second officer,* Linojj thought— she'd prepared her crew for that moment by instructing them to act on his orders without first seeking her approval.

"Tenger, shields up," he said. "Navigation, head us directly through the center of the portal. Helm, full impulse, now!"

Linojj saw the admiral's plan unfolding and understood where it would take them. Considering the circumstances, she agreed with his assessment that, if they wanted to attempt to save both crews— that of *Enterprise* and that of *Excelsior*—they had no other alternative. The immediate responses of the *Enterprise* bridge crew to Harriman's orders inspired and impressed her.

"The Tzenkethi are firing on us," Tenger said an instant before *Enterprise* trembled.

"Ignore them," Harriman said.

Linojj opened her mouth to object—*Why not fire on an adversary who's fired first?*—but then she grasped the admiral's reasoning. If they did manage to escape the Tzenkethi, why leave them with any physical evidence that a Starfleet vessel had attacked them? The last thing the Coalition needed was any more motivation to declare war on the Federation; they seemed to mine that from their own psyches quite well.

"They are firing again," Tenger said, and again, the ship rocked beneath a Tzenkethi disruptor blast.

Harriman quickly sat on the railing at the front of the bridge, threw his legs over it, and jumped down in front of the navigation console. "Keep us on target," the admiral told Aldani. "The portal will probably emit tractor beams." He glanced over at Linojj. "Right?"

"Yes, to guide us through," Linojj confirmed.

"Don't fight them," Harriman said. Another disruptor blast slammed into *Enterprise*, that time without the virtue of Tenger announcing it ahead of time. "Keep the ship aimed directly for the center of the portal."

"Yes, sir," Aldani said.

Harriman looked toward the main viewer. On the right side of the screen, a green bolt of energy emerged from the tip of the first ship's central tine and streaked toward them. On the left side of the screen, the *Enterprise* closed rapidly on the portal, overtaking *Cassiopeia*. As it did so, it confirmed for Linojj what she'd thought: that the admiral had set the *Constellation*-class vessel on a collision course with the alien device. Once destroyed, the Tzenkethi would not be able to follow *Enterprise*. *Of course, there will also no longer be any possibility of anybody modifying the portal in order to get us back home.*

"Viewer ahead," Linojj said, and the image of the Tzenkethi frigates disappeared, leaving the portal in the center of the screen. Streaks of golden light shot from points all around the circular structure, all aimed directly at *Enterprise*. The ship bucked momentarily, but then continued on its course. The portal grew on the viewscreen as they neared it, until all that remained was an unfamiliar starscape.

11

Admiral John Harriman stepped from the starboard turbolift onto the *Enterprise* bridge. As much as he loved his wife, as much as he appreciated her professionalism and valued her considerable abilities, he still preferred a busy, fully occupied bridge to one crewed by just the two of them. As he moved toward the command chair among a number of people with whom he had once served—Xintal Linojj, Tenger, Borona Fenn, Ramesh Kanchumurthi—he realized that he felt comfortable. He didn't experience a sense of homecoming, despite having commanded *Enterprise* for nearly two decades—he had moved on in his life, and believed himself better for it—but he did feel that he belonged.

Some of his self-assurance, Harriman knew, stemmed from all that he had helped to accomplish over the past couple of days. Once *Enterprise* had traveled through the portal, he had ordered the ship hard to port, then brought it about to wait for any Tzenkethi vessels to follow. None did, nor did any probes arrive to perform recon. That likely meant that the admiral's plan to destroy the portal by crashing *Cassiopeia* into it had succeeded. If the timing worked as he'd intended, then Gedlin Siv Vel-B and the rest of the Tzenkethi squadron witnessed the explosion an instant after *Enterprise* had passed through the alien device, concluding that both Starfleet vessels had been destroyed.

What the Tzenkethi believed mattered only in terms of political fallout. If they thought that the *Enterprise* crew had somehow escaped the area by employing some new technology, which they had then intentionally eradicated by crashing *Cassiopeia* into it, then they likely would take issue with the Federation. But if Gedlin believed that nobody from either Starfleet vessel had survived their encounter with his squadron, the Coalition would probably never address what had taken place—not when doing so would necessarily point to the deaths of hundreds of Federation citizens.

Harriman paced toward the command chair, where Linojj stood up to greet him. He still hadn't grown accustomed to seeing her with only one arm, but according to Doctor Morell, she and her staff had almost completed crafting her biosynthetic replacement. "Good morning, Admiral," Linojj said. "I trust you slept well."

"Not as well as I'd expected," Harriman admitted. "Maybe because the last couple of days have been so intense."

Linojj nodded. "I know what you mean, sir."

After it had become clear that the Tzenkethi would not or could not pursue *Enterprise* through the portal, Linojj had left a probe in space at that location. It would function as a gatekeeper that would monitor the area, notifying the crew if a ship or probe appeared anywhere in the vicinity. Efforts then began in earnest to recover all of the Starfleet personnel down on the planet.

"Has there been any additional word on Captain Sulu?" Harriman asked. Demora had been the first person transported up to the ship. The *Enterprise* captain had been taken directly to sickbay and straight into the surgical suite. Doctor Chapel, already familiar with Demora's physical condition, performed the surgery, an involved set of procedures that lasted several hours. *Enterprise*'s chief medical officer characterized the operation as a success, but also noted it as only the first of several the captain would require. Chapel and Morell considered Captain Sulu's prognosis good. They also expected Ensign Young, who had been treated for his injuries as well, to make a complete recovery. The entire medical staff had also begun to examine all five hundred sixty-five surviving members of the *Excelsior* crew, a process that would take days to finish.

"I actually visited Captain Sulu this morning before my shift," Linojj said, making no effort to hold back the smile that blossomed on her face. "She's looking better."

"Is she awake?" Harriman asked. "I thought they were going to keep her sedated for another day or two." The admiral had yet to visit sickbay, believing it wiser to allow the doctors and nurses to perform their duties without the distraction of his presence.

"They actually brought her out of it for a little while not long after surgery," Linojj said. "But yes, Doctor Morell wants to leave her unconscious for a little while longer as she starts healing. I only got to see the captain, not to talk with her, but it's good just to see her back aboard the ship."

"I'm sure it is," Harriman said. "So now that we've retrieved everybody from the planet, are you prepared to try to get back to the Federation?" Once they had escaped the clutches of the Tzen-kethi, Harriman had ceded command of the ship back to Linojj, although, as the highest-ranking officer aboard *Enterprise*, he could have remained in charge for the duration of their journey. Similarly, because of their positions as starship and starbase captains, he could have assigned the center seat to either Hikaru Sulu or Amina. He'd spoken with both of them, and they'd agreed with him that, after everything the *Enterprise* crew had endured, including having to deal with the potential loss of their captain, it would benefit morale to leave Linojj in the big chair on the bridge.

"I think we're all ready to get back home, sir," Linojj said. Harriman had briefed the commander, as well as Hikaru and Amina, on what Demora had viewed as a means of returning back to their place and time: the effect of a single star that apparently existed across many universes and somehow provided a gateway between them. Both the existence of the strange star and its location remained classified by Starfleet Intelligence, its general area designated on all Federation charts as an extreme hazard, and therefore off-limits, but because the admiral intended to utilize it as a means of returning them all back to their own space and time, he had needed to inform them of what lay ahead. Once she had passed through the portal, Demora Sulu must have checked the appropriate spatial coordinates and found the star. In the time since the *Enterprise* crew had escaped the Tzenkethi, Harriman had also confirmed its existence.

"Once we're on our way, somebody's going to need to address the crew," the admiral said. "Since there are no guarantees that this plan will actually work, they deserve to know what we're attempting." He and Demora had never discovered a means of controlling the transition from one universe to another. It had been—at least from their perspective—random, though based on their own experiences, they knew that it was at least possible for them to get back to their universe.

"I agree," Linojj said. "I can speak to the crew, but since you know more about this than I do, I think it should come from you."

"So do I," Harriman said. "I'll plan a shipwide statement for later today."

"Thank you, Admiral."

"All right," Harriman said. "Let's give this a try." Harriman moved to the navigation console, where he relieved Lieutenant Aldani, much to her surprise. As she withdrew to a secondary station on the outer ring of the bridge, the admiral sat down and worked the console. He located the star that he and Demora had named Odyssey, then plotted a course to it. Finally, because of the classified nature of the information, Harriman encrypted the course. He then recalled Aldani to the navigation console and relieved Ensign Syndergaard.

It's been a lot of years since I've done this, he thought as he sat down at the helm. *Probably back to my days on the* Hunley. He remembered his time serving under the late Captain Linneus fondly.

At the helm console, Harriman used his biometric information to call up and decrypt the course he'd just laid in. He locked it into the helm, then encoded it once more. When the admiral engaged the sublight drive at full impulse, the ship thundered to life around him. Amazingly, he recognized the sound of *Enterprise*, the rhythms and notes of its operation distinct.

Harriman followed *Enterprise*'s progress on his console as the great starship broke planetary orbit. When the vessel had reached a safe distance, he brought the ship to warp, settling it at factor eight. He didn't know where the journey would ultimately end up taking the thirteen hundred men and women aboard *Enterprise*, but they had started on their way.

2319-2320

Iliad

12

Sasine sat alone in a comfortable chair, in the cabin that Commander Linojj had assigned to her and John. Though not nearly as spacious or as nicely appointed as their quarters on Helaspont Station, the VIP guest accommodations would certainly suffice. Sasine had no notion of just how long she and John would need to remain aboard *Enterprise*, but from what he'd told her, they could be in for a considerable stay.

Peering down at the padd in her hands, Sasine continued reading Captain Hikaru Sulu's preliminary report of the incident that had sent his crew through the portal and destroyed *Excelsior*. He had appended his log entries, as well as those of his first officer, Ryan Leslie, which she found both fascinating and chilling. She could think of few traumas greater than having to abandon a failing starship.

After reading about the crew's encounter with a gruesome and deadly life-form, Sasine glanced over at the communications-and-computer interface set atop the desk in a corner of the living area. She saw that the time neared for her husband's shipwide address. A day earlier, after the recovery of the stranded Starfleet personnel, John had conferred with Linojj, explaining just what Demora Sulu had meant when she'd spoken of an "Odyssey solution," and telling the commander what he intended to do in order to attempt to return *Enterprise* and its crew and passengers to their own universe. Afterward, he finally shared the same information with Sasine.

Up until that point, John had kept the classified data about Odyssey to himself—refusing to disclose it even to his wife. Sasine took no offense, understanding both her husband's dedication to duty and his punctilious nature. He genuinely believed in the need for Starfleet Command—and Starfleet Intelligence, from whom he occasionally accepted missions—to keep certain information secret. Sasine trusted his judgment; he had never given her any reason not to do so.

Because of the uncertainty of Demora's proposed solution, John felt that everybody aboard ship should be told what would happen, despite the classified status of Odyssey. He hoped to avoid revealing precise details, such as the location of the star, speaking instead on a general level. Linojj had agreed that the crews of both *Enterprise* and *Excelsior* deserved to know what lay ahead for them. John offered the first officer and acting captain the opportunity to make the address to the two crews, but citing the admiral's specialized knowledge of the situation, she demurred.

Sasine looked back down at her padd, but she did not resume her reading. Instead, as she awaited John's statement to the crew, she thought about Demora Sulu. The outlook for the injured captain continued to improve, even though Doctors Morell and Chapel still kept her under sedation. Sasine considered paying a visit to sickbay to see her old friend, but thought that she should wait until Demora had regained consciousness. *Perhaps I should go find her father,* she thought. She had met Hikaru Sulu on a couple of—

The boatswain's whistle trilled. *"Attention, all personnel, this is Admiral John Harriman,"* announced her husband, his words calm and steady. She found it comforting just to hear his voice. *"As you all know, until yesterday, the crew of the* U.S.S. Excelsior *had been marooned on a desolate planet for eleven years, having traveled through an alien device into another universe. The* Enterprise *has now carried us through that same device, which was subsequently destroyed in order to prevent a superior Tzenkethi force from pursuing us, and also to ensure that the technology did not fall into the hands of the Coalition."* Sasine thought that John's last-minute plan to escape the Tzenkethi squadron, while at the same time preserving the possibility of rescuing the *Excelsior* crew, had been inspired.

"Commander Linojj had hoped that the Enterprise *crew could reverse the direction of the one-way portal, but that no longer remains an option. Prior to the injuries she sustained on the planet, though, Captain Demora Sulu imagined a*

different solution to get her stranded crew members back home—a solution she called upon me to help implement. I am aboard the Enterprise *for that purpose.*" Sasine knew that John wanted to provide justifiable hope for everybody aboard ship, but also to temper their expectations. According to him, he truly could not measure their prospects for a successful return home.

"*Some time ago, Captain Demora Sulu and I encountered an unusual and as-yet-unexplained astronomical phenomenon,*" John continued. "*Within a particular solar system in unexplored, unclaimed space, we passed through what is essentially a rift between universes. In some ways, it is like the portal that the* Enterprise *and* Excelsior *crews confronted, but where the alien device conveyed people and objects from one place to another, the rift moves them across many universes, without surcease.*" According to John, he could find no information about Odyssey and its effects other than what he and Demora had reported.

"*Even the existence of this phenomenon is classified, and it remains so,*" he went on. "*I am providing this information because it impacts every person aboard this ship. Before suffering her injuries, Captain Demora Sulu came to believe that the same phenomenon that she and I had encountered in our own universe also exists in the universe to which the portal connected. I believe it too. We are heading to that location now in the hopes of confirming that the rift also exists there. If it does, it my intention to take the* Enterprise *into it.*"

Sasine wondered what that would be like, constantly traversing from one universe to the next. *What will the stars look like?* In some ways, the prospect seemed like a thrilling adventure, though she understood that the reality would likely be something wholly different.

"*Even if we do find the rift, though, our success is not assured. As far as we know, there is no way to control the transition from one universe to the next, though we will of course seek such a process. Until we are able to develop one, we will employ sensor software to detect recognizable patterns of stars, so that if the* Enterprise *reenters our own universe, the ship will automatically be driven out of the rift.*" John paused, but Sasine knew that he hadn't yet finished.

"*If we can find the rift, it could take us a day to return home, or a month, or a year, or a decade,*" he finally continued. "*Or it might never happen. I do not expect any of us ever to surrender. As the former commanding officer of the* Enterprise, *I am proud of this crew—many of whom I have served with—for working so diligently to bring your missing personnel safely back to the ship. To Captain Hikaru Sulu and his* Excelsior *crew, you have provided a fine example of taking action in the face of adversity, of enduring in difficult circumstances with little or no chance of rescue. Let us bring that same level of determination to our new endeavor. Harriman out.*"

Sasine set her padd down on a small table beside her chair, stood up, and crossed the living area to the wide port above the sofa. She stared out at the stars as *Enterprise* soared past them, a sight far

different from the static spray of the distant suns—
and the nebula—visible from Helaspont Station.
She had served aboard starships—*Regulus, Enterprise,* and *New York*—but the bulk of her career
had been spent on outposts and space stations, so
she'd become acclimated to a stationary vista. *Better get used to moving stars,* she told herself. *It's a
brave new world we live in.*

As Sasine gazed out into space, she puzzled over
what role she would play on *Enterprise.* The ship
had more commanding officers than it needed—it
even had *two* Captains Sulu—not to mention an
admiral. She decided that she would wait for John
to return to their cabin and then discuss with him
what sort of contribution she could make.

Sasine thought about her own crew back on
Helaspont Station. She knew that Lieutenant
Commander Farish would do a fine job in the
short term, even through the trade summit. She
suspected, though, that Starfleet Command would
want somebody more experienced in that position
if Sasine failed to return to the station in a timely
manner. She'd sent a transmission to Admiral Mentir before departing Helaspont, explaining herself
in a way that she hoped would not see her court-
martialed for desertion when she got back.

*Court-martial might be the least of my wor-
ries,* Sasine thought, but then she dismissed the
idea entirely. She had no cause for concern, given
the difficult days ahead for both the *Enterprise*
and *Excelsior* crews. Although the situation had
improved dramatically for Hikaru Sulu's people
with their rescue, she worried about how anybody

aboard would react if the attempt to return home extended for a considerable length of time. *What if it doesn't take us days or weeks to get back to our own universe, but years?* She didn't know. Sasine certainly had no desire to lose all that she had accomplished in her career—she found tremendous satisfaction in commanding Helaspont Station and in leading her crew.

John knows that, and that's why he didn't ask me to go with him, she thought. *He didn't want to ask me to sacrifice those aspects of my life that he knows are so important to me.* She knew that he loved her and wanted to be with her, but it touched her that he hadn't wanted to force her to make such a choice, between losing the life she'd created for herself and possibly losing him.

But nothing in my life would mean as much as it does without John. Nothing means more to me than he does. She didn't know how many members of the *Enterprise* and *Excelsior* crews were involved romantically with one another, but she doubted any of them could claim a sixteen-year relationship. As much as she wanted to find a way back to their universe, as much as she wanted to resume her position as the commanding officer of Helaspont Station, she would still be happy even if those things never happened. She would miss Mère and Père, she would miss her siblings—her three sisters and her brother—and their families, not to mention her friends and crew, but she had John, and as much as she stood to lose, he balanced the scale.

Sasine had brought her home along with her.

◆ ◆ ◆

Hikaru Sulu stood at the far end of the intensive care ward and saw his daughter's eyelids flutter open. The sight made his heart soar. A week prior, he had watched those eyes close in what seemed might be a punishing twist of fate: having Demora come back into his life, only for him to immediately watch her die. But Doctor Chapel and her staff had gained ample experience in treating wounds inflicted by the arachnoid monsters populating the world that had become their home, including the formulation of an antivenin to counteract the creatures' venom. Although Demora had been impaled and some of her internal organs badly damaged, the *Excelsior* medical team had managed to keep her alive long enough to get her aboard *Enterprise* and onto an operating table.

Sulu's daughter lay on a diagnostic pallet, her body connected by various tubes to several pieces of equipment. While a complicated operation had stabilized her viscera, she would still require at least two more operations before she could fully recover. *Let it take as long as it needs to,* Sulu thought. After he had spent more than a decade on an inhospitable world, time had finally become an ally again.

Standing beside Demora's diagnostic pallet, Chapel gazed down at her patient, with *Enterprise*'s CMO, Uta Morell, also observing. After seeing to his crew's immediate needs after they'd all transported up from the planet, Sulu had spent most of the past forty-eight hours by his daughter's side. Just a few minutes before, a signal had brought both Chapel and Morell into intensive care, where they explained that Demora's readings indicated that she would shortly regain consciousness. Other than for a brief period after her operation, the doctors had chosen to keep her fully sedated, both to allow her body the best opportunity to heal and to spare her the pain and discomfort that they could not completely mask.

Chapel leaned in over her patient. "Captain Sulu," she said quietly, "how do you feel?"

Sulu's daughter opened her mouth as though to speak, but it took several seconds before her lips formed any words. "Like I've been run over by a Romulan bird-of-prey," she eventually said. "Twice." Her voice had a low, raspy quality to it.

"That's to be expected," Chapel told her. "Are you in any pain?" Sulu could see the diagnostic display above Demora's head, including the K3 gauge, the readout that measured pain. The indicator hovered at a high but not intolerable level.

"Yes, a fair amount," Demora said. She reached with one hand toward her midsection, but the movement caused her to wince and cry out.

"Easy, Captain," Chapel said, placing her hand on Demora's shoulder. "You *have* been run over by a bird-of-prey, and it's going to take some time for you to recuperate."

Demora nodded almost imperceptibly and closed her eyes. Although Sulu longed to speak with his daughter, he would gladly wait if her recovery required it. For the moment, it was enough for him just to see her, and just to know that she would be all right.

But then Demora's eyes sprang back open. "My father," she said. "I thought I saw my father."

Chapel bent in closer to Demora. "You need

to keep still, Captain, and you're going to need your rest," she said, "but yes, you did see your father." The doctor straightened and backed away from the diagnostic pallet. Sulu crossed the compartment to stand beside his daughter. Her eyes widened when she saw him and immediately filled with tears.

"Dad," she said, though almost no sound came out of her mouth. She started to reach for him, and he rushed to put his hands atop hers, wanting to keep her from causing herself any more pain.

"I'm here, honey," he said. He bent in close to her and kissed her cheek. "I'm here, and I'm so happy to see you."

"Dad," Demora said again, and then her eyes darted past him, toward Chapel. "Am I still unconscious? Am I hallucinating?" she asked the doctor.

"No, Captain," Chapel said. "You're awake and lucid."

Demora looked back at Sulu. "But . . . how . . . ?"

He felt Chapel's touch on his arm. "Captain," she said quietly, and he understood her meaning at once. At that moment, his daughter needed rest, not an account of what had happened to her father, nor details of what the *Enterprise* and *Excelsior* crews still faced.

"It's a long story," Sulu told Demora. "The important thing is that we found each other, and now we're both aboard the *Enterprise*."

"I . . . I can't believe it," Demora said. "I'm so . . . so . . ."

"I know," Sulu said. He heard the whisper of a teardrop on the bedclothes, and he realized that it had fallen not from his daughter's face, but from his own. "I love you."

"I love you, too, Dad." Demora closed her eyes, forcing tears to spill down her cheeks. Sulu began to turn away, but then he heard her voice once more. "Dad?" When he looked back, he saw an expression of concern on her face. "What about Ensign Kostas and Ensign Young?"

Again, Chapel tapped him on the arm, then gently squeezed his elbow. Once more, he knew what she wanted of him. "They're both back on board," he told Demora, not exactly lying—along with Ensign Young and the *Excelsior* crew, Kostas's body had been transported up to the ship—but willfully misleading his daughter. Knowing that she had lost a member of her crew would do her no good in the present circumstances. Later, when she did find out, Sulu told himself, at least he would be there to help her get through it.

"Good," Demora said. "Good." Her eyelids drifted slowly closed. Sulu waited to see if she would open them again, but her breathing quickly grew slower and deeper as she slipped off to sleep.

"Captain," Chapel said. "You really should get some rest yourself."

Sulu turned to the doctor. "Is that an order?" he asked of the only member of his crew who could issue him a command. Though he would have been content simply to stand there and watch his daughter sleep, he offered Chapel a smile to let her know he did not intend to object to her advice.

"It's an order only if it needs to be," Chapel said, returning his smile.

Sulu took one more glance at Demora, then started across the compartment, headed for the entryway. Before he got there, he stopped and looked back at the doctor. "Christine," he said, "thank you . . . for everything."

"It's my privilege, Hikaru."

Sulu exited intensive care and made his way through *Enterprise*'s sickbay to the corridor. When he reached the quarters he'd been assigned, he didn't even bother to remove his uniform—the clean, new uniform provided to him from ship's stores. He flopped onto the bed, exhausted but wondering how he would possibly be able to shut his mind off after his reunion with his daughter.

He fell asleep in minutes, and didn't rise for another twelve hours.

Tenger worked the tactical console, searching for something that had been only vaguely defined for him. More than a little frustrated, he peered over at the helm, to where Harriman sat. Tenger wanted to blame the admiral for the imprecise orders, but he recognized the unfairness of doing so. Despite being the highest-ranking officer on *Enterprise*, and despite having aboard two other active captains— Hikaru Sulu and Amina Sasine—Harriman had left Linojj in command. The first officer had remained in the center seat for four weeks while Captain Sulu underwent a total of three surgeries and a subsequent period of convalescence. When the *Enterprise*'s captain finally returned to the bridge, Linojj took her place in sickbay, where Doctor Morell had attached her new biosynthetic arm.

All of which means I should blame Captain Sulu, Tenger thought. The *Enterprise*'s commanding officer had been back on duty for ten days, and though she frequently consulted with Admiral Harriman about the mission they'd set themselves, she left no doubt that the final decision about the fate of her crew—and of everybody else aboard—fell to her. *But I don't want to blame the captain.* In addition to the great esteem he had for her, he also knew how much she had been through during the past couple of months, since the ship had first arrived at Rejarris II, up to the memorial service that the captain had held a few days prior for Galatea Kostas.

And our crisis still hasn't been resolved, Tenger thought. Aboard *Enterprise*, more than thirteen hundred Starfleet officers remained cut off from the Federation. Tenger knew that weighed heavily on Captain Sulu, and would until the day that their accidental exile ended. *If it ever does end.*

An indicator on Tenger's console flashed, and he checked his display. "We are approaching the Odyssey system," he announced. Admiral Harriman had encrypted the course he'd set for *Enterprise*, as well as the spatial coordinates of their destination, but it would have been far too risky to demand that the crew desist from monitoring sensors.

"Acknowledged," said Harriman from where he sat at the helm. "Bringing us out of warp." Knowing that *Enterprise* would reach Odyssey during alpha shift that day, Sulu had assigned the admiral to take over for Ensign Syndergaard.

The deep pulse of the warp nacelles eased, like

the heartbeat of a galloping Thoroughbred as the animal slowed to a trot. Tenger could feel the vibrations of the faster-than-light drive fading, replaced by the sturdy hum of the impulse engines. *Enterprise* halted its sprint across the galaxy in favor of a leisurely search through a solar system.

"We are crossing the termination shock," said the security chief.

"Are the navigational routines engaged?" Sulu asked from the command chair. The captain had taken the lead herself in writing a series of programs to process an image of the starscape surrounding *Enterprise*. Designed to recognize patterns of stars that had occurred in the Milky Way at any time during the previous year, or that would occur at any time during the next, the routines would, upon identifying such a configuration, automatically engage the impulse drive to move the ship directly away from the Odyssey star.

"The programs are operational and tied directly into navigation and the helm," replied Lieutenant Aldani.

Tenger had disagreed with the captain's decision to seek a return to the Federation at any point within the current two-year period. He felt that if the plan Sulu had chosen to pursue couldn't reasonably be counted upon to send them back home within a window of a month or two, then they should be seeking a course of action more likely to succeed. The uncertain nature of the so-called Odyssey solution had troubled the security chief from the moment he'd learned about it.

Minutes passed as *Enterprise* gradually made

its incursion into the system. Tenger regarded the main viewer, where Odyssey barely distinguished itself from the background field of stars. The yellow-white sun showed as a pinpoint of light at the center of the screen, marginally brighter than the other pinpoints surrounding it. It inspired neither hope nor confidence.

What were you expecting? Tenger chided himself. *A star emitting radio waves that translate as* THIS WAY TO THE FEDERATION?

He discovered, though, that he couldn't take his gaze away from the viewscreen. Nor, he realized, could anybody else. When he finally looked around the bridge, he saw every head turned toward the main viewer. *And why not?* Tenger thought. At that moment, as far as any of them knew, that one slightly brighter dot provided not just their best chance of going home, but perhaps their only chance.

"We are nearing the transition point," Harriman said. "Reducing speed in anticipation of a full stop."

"Commander Tenger," the captain said, "do sensors detect anything out of the ordinary?"

The security chief inspected the readings on his panel. "Negative," he said at last. "All measurements are showing well within expected limits: electromagnetic radiation, density, solar wind, gravity."

"Planets?" Sulu asked.

"None," Tenger reported.

The answers appeared to satisfy the captain. By degrees, the drone of the impulse engines faded, until at last the sounds of its motive force ceased entirely. Around the bridge, panels continued to issue feedback tones, noises that provided a lonely counterpoint to the silences of both the ship's engines and its crew.

At last, Harriman said, "We have reached the transition point. Thrusters at station-keeping."

Tenger scrutinized the sensor readings on his console. Nothing changed. When he looked up at the viewscreen, he saw only the same tableau of stars he had before, seemingly static points of light arrayed around the ordinary form of Odyssey.

The bridge crew seemed to hold its collective breath. The quiet of *Enterprise*'s drive systems spread as the silent crew operated fewer controls, the various consoles issuing fewer chirps. Everybody waited.

And still nothing happened.

The captain stood from the command chair. "Admiral?" she said.

Harriman worked the helm. "We're here," he said, frustration creeping into his voice. "We're here, but . . ." He did not finish his sentence. He didn't need to.

Sulu paced to the navigator's station, where she tapped Aldani on the shoulder. The lieutenant glanced up, surprise evident in her face, but she quickly recovered and surrendered her position. As the captain sat down at navigation, Aldani moved to a secondary console on the periphery of the bridge.

"Do you see?" Harriman asked Sulu as she operated her panel.

"Yes," she said. "This should be the location."

Tenger felt a mixture of relief, vindication, and anxiety. He did not disbelieve that both the captain and the admiral had in the past approached the star in the center of the viewscreen—or one like it—and found themselves thrown from one universe to another, but the notion that the same star existed in all realities seemed to the security chief like a tenuous assumption. At the very least, Tenger disliked plotting their entire strategy to get home around that unproven belief. Learning that Sulu and Harriman's Odyssey plan would not work, while removing one potential solution, would free the crew to pursue other ideas.

But what other ideas? Tenger asked himself. From his long experience, he knew that Starfleet officers had traveled to parallel universes and returned home by a number of different means. As far as he knew, though, such journeys had involved the same method of transportation, in the same place—essentially as though walking through a doorway from one universe to the next, and then returning through that same doorway. But with the apparent destruction of the portal, the door through which the *Enterprise* and *Excelsior* crews had traveled no longer existed.

At the helm, Harriman looked to the captain. "We need to institute a search plan," he said. The frustration that Tenger had heard in the admiral's voice remained, but it had been joined with doubt.

At the navigator's station, Sulu nodded and operated her controls. "A tight spiral," she said, "centered at the previous transition point, maintaining the same distance from Odyssey. One percent of overlap."

Harriman reached up and rubbed the bottom of his face. Tenger recognized the gesture, and he wondered if the admiral had at one time sported a beard and mustache. "At what speed?" Harriman asked. The two senior officers spoke only with each other, lending substance to the claim that they had together previously experienced a similar situation. The sight of a Starfleet admiral and captain working the helm and navigation stations seemed surreal to Tenger.

"One-eighth impulse to start," Sulu said. "As the radius of our search pattern increases, we can accelerate."

"Agreed."

The captain continued to work her panel. After a few moments, she told Harriman, "Course laid in."

"Engaging impulse engines," said the admiral.

The familiar beat of the sublight drive rose in the bridge. Tenger usually found the sound comforting, but at that moment, it felt like a lonely cry in the desert, an inconsequential drop in the ocean. He tried to determine how long it would take, traveling at impulse velocity, to exhaustively search every point a specified distance from a star. *Too long,* he concluded when the numbers began to ran incalculably high.

Enterprise traced its spiral through space, and the captain stayed at the navigation console. Twice, on the hour, Yeoman Plumley arrived on the bridge for the captain's signature on a status report. Other than the few brief words he exchanged with Sulu, nobody spoke.

As alpha shift progressed, Tenger's attention wandered. He would review his instruments, but then his mind would drift to the crew's predicament, to the solution that wasn't a solution, and to the improbability of *Enterprise* ever managing to find its way home. He was gazing forward at the viewscreen, mired in his own thoughts, when he saw the stars blink.

At first, it didn't register, but then Commander Linojj said, "Captain." The one word carried her excitement in it. Tenger studied the viewer, but the stars appeared as constant as ever.

At the helm, Harriman looked to the captain. "Where are we?"

"Not where we were," Sulu said, and though she kept her voice level, Tenger perceived a sense of anticipation in her. "The pattern of stars has changed. Reversing course." A moment later, the stars on the viewscreen jumped, one arrangement disappearing in favor of another. "All stop," the captain said.

"Engines answering all stop," Harriman said.

On the main screen, the collection of visible stars changed again, and again, and again.

Sulu exchanged a look with the admiral, and then she stood up and moved back to the command chair. Slowly, she gazed around the bridge at the crew. When she made eye contact with Tenger, all the doubts he had harbored about what they were attempting dwindled to nothing. He had followed Captain Sulu for eight years, and he knew his confidence in her was well-founded.

The captain finished looking around the bridge

by facing forward, toward the continuously changing array of stars on the viewscreen. "We've taken the first step on our way home," she said.

Ensign Hawkins Young reached up to the small panel beside the door, but then hesitated to tap the control surface. *Maybe I shouldn't do this*, he thought. By ship's time, the new year would arrive shortly, and he knew that many members of the crew intended to mark the occasion in some way. It had been four months since *Enterprise* had arrived at Odyssey and begun its journey through myriad universes, paradoxically by remaining in place, and the long, unsure path the ship traveled would doubtless temper much of the celebration. *Still, if Nurse Veracruz has plans for the evening—*

The single-paneled door glided open before him, revealing the pixieish form of Rosalinda Veracruz. She stood not much more than a meter and a half, with dark, wavy hair and dark eyes. "Oh," she said, clearly surprised by his presence in front of the door to her quarters.

"Sorry," Young said. "I didn't mean to startle you. I was just about to tap the door chime."

"Were you?" Veracruz asked. In the months Young had visited her for counseling sessions, she had almost never spoken to him in anything but questions.

"I was," he said. "But I also wasn't sure I wanted to bother you. I thought you might have plans tonight."

"Is there something you wanted to talk about, Ensign?" Veracruz asked.

Young shrugged, then scolded himself for the tentative gesture. The counseling sessions he'd had with the nurse after his rescue from the planet—the planet that wasn't Rejarris II—had helped him tremendously, both with the survivor's guilt he'd felt and his confidence in re-assimilating into the *Enterprise* crew. She had brought him around to see, and to truly believe, that he was not responsible for everything that had happened, for all the ills that had befallen his crewmates, for the horrible injury to Commander Linojj, for the death of Galatea Kostas, for the continuing separation of the crew from the Federation. Veracruz had allowed him to conclude on his own that if he hadn't chosen to climb atop the portal, where a tractor beam had then pulled him through the device, that a shuttlecraft sent down to the planet to investigate would likely have carried several members of the crew to the same fate. He had done nothing wrong, and he couldn't reasonably blame himself for the events that had followed his falling through the portal.

And if I did hold myself responsible for everything, he thought, *then I'd have to demand credit for rescuing the* Excelsior *crew.* None of it, he had eventually come to realize, bore up under scrutiny. He had discharged the duties of his rank and position, if not with distinction, then at least with competence. The captain and first officer had made the same point to him, but it had taken numerous sessions with Nurse Veracruz for him to believe it himself, and to internalize that belief in an organic, meaningful way.

After a month of intense counseling, Young's

daily talks with the nurse had become twice-weekly events, and after two months, she'd released him from any obligation to continue seeing her. He appreciated all that she'd done for him, and he'd told her so, but he had studiously avoided her after that. He knew that if he suffered guilt or doubts, he could and would make another appointment with her, but he also continued to be mindful of what he'd endured, and to deepen his understanding of all the emotions that had come with those experiences.

"Yes, there is something I wanted to talk about," he told her, forcing the words out in a rush.

"Are you uncertain, Ensign?"

"No," Young said, too quickly and without conviction. He decided to admit the truth. "Actually, yes, I'm not certain about this. But I don't want to keep you if you're going somewhere."

"I was headed to the mess for dinner," Veracruz said, "but I'm happy to make time for you, Ensign." She stepped aside so that Young could enter.

He didn't move. "Actually, Nurse . . . um, I mean . . . Rosalinda . . . I was wondering if you might want to have dinner with me."

For the second time, Veracruz appeared surprised. "I—" she started, but then she stopped. Young waited. He understood the concept of transference, the redirection of a patient's feelings onto a counselor. It had been for that reason that Young had stayed away from Veracruz for two months after his sessions with her had ended. He wanted both to confirm his genuine feelings for her, and to demonstrate to the nurse that she needn't worry about the true nature of his emotions.

When Veracruz didn't answer, Young offered her a smile and asked, "Are you uncertain, Nurse?"

"Actually, yes," she said. "I'm not certain about this at all." Young's heart sank, but then she smiled back at him. "But the new year is coming, Ensign, so why not try new things?"

"Please call me Hawk," Young said. He held out his arm to her, and she took it. They walked like that all the way to the mess hall.

13

All at once, a welcome sense of peace washed over her.

Captain Demora Sulu sat back in the command chair on the *Enterprise* bridge and regarded the dizzying tableaux of stars dancing on the main viewscreen. When she had first witnessed such a display seventeen years earlier, it had represented a forfeiture of virtually everything she held dear, an incalculable loss of all that she used to define herself: people and places, career and accomplishments, memories of the past and dreams of the future. She remembered being overwhelmed by the enormity of her deprivation only moments before her entire life—by some process she didn't understand, by a seemingly indifferent randomness—had been given back to her.

As Sulu watched one pattern of stars after another appear on the viewer, she wondered what had changed for her between then and now. She could see the simple answer. When she and Harriman had unexpectedly been whisked away from their universe by Odyssey and unceremoniously deposited in another—and then another, and another, potentially ad infinitum—she'd been sitting on a shuttlecraft with her commanding officer, rather than on the starship on which she'd lived for a decade, among a crew of hundreds, many of whom she counted as friends. She and John had also become friends by then, but they hadn't yet developed the closeness that they ultimately would. She had other, closer friends back on *Enterprise,* and in other places, too. Though she could not recall whom she'd been seeing at the time, she did remember that she'd been in a romantic relationship.

And, of course, there had been Dad.

The first time that Odyssey had robbed her of her place in the universe, it had taken away so much: the place she lived, most of the people she called her friends, a budding romance, and her family. It had taken away *everything.*

But this time . . .

Odyssey hadn't pulled Sulu from her universe; the portal at Rejarris II had. In the end, it had also brought *Enterprise* back to her, the place she'd called home for the past twenty-seven years, which amounted to more than half of her life. Almost all of her closest friends lived aboard the ship with her, and the portal had delivered to her one of them who didn't in John Harriman. She didn't have much of a love life at the moment, but she hadn't before everything that had happened in the previous eleven months.

And, of course, there was Dad.

Prior to encountering the portal, Sulu had lived with the grief and the never-ending sense of loss that had come with losing her father. Remarkably, he had been returned to her—or she to him. Either way, she once again had a parent, a man she admired and respected, a man whose company she enjoyed, a man she loved as she had loved no other.

And Odyssey represented only possibilities to her, and more than one. She and her crew—and the recovered crew of *Excelsior*—might one day find their way back to their own universe, but they might also find another in which they would settle. Perhaps they would find someplace spectacular.

That was the simple answer. The first time, Odyssey had taken everything from her. The second time, she had everything with her.

Sulu had never been a scientist, but she understood Occam's razor, the principle that, among competing theories, the simplest one is considered more likely to be true. But as she sat on the bridge of *Enterprise,* among not only her crewmates but some of her closest friends, with her father restored to her life, she didn't believe the simple answer. She didn't think that the pain she'd felt at Odyssey seventeen years prior, and the peace she felt at that moment, depended at all on what she had lost in the past and what she possessed in the present.

I think it's me.

Such a formulation sounded egocentric, perhaps even egotistical. Sulu didn't mean to discount her friends or her family; they meant more to her than she could put into words. She didn't mean to ignore the reality of having a home; she loved *Enterprise* and had no desire to leave it.

But if I didn't have these people, or this ship? Would I stop being me?

When Sulu had graduated from the Academy, she could have been assigned to any vessel in Starfleet. Her posting to *Enterprise* had been the result of her superior performance, but there had been other *Excelsior*-class ships out there, ships with distinguished records. If she had ended up on *Challenger* or *Constitution* or *Paris,* would she have had a substantially different life? Would she have been a substantially different person? She would have had a different home, and different friends, but she thought that she would still be Demora Sulu, a woman happy with her choices, contented with her life, and at peace with herself. She worked hard each day to be the best version of herself that she could be, open to learning new things, to exploring fresh perspectives, and to growing.

That didn't mean that she didn't understand loss. On the contrary, she had experienced it from an early age. But that first loss of her mother hadn't ended Demora's life; she had gone on. And when she thought her father had died, she'd hurt, but she'd also gone on then, too.

Life is what you make it, she thought. *Happiness is a choice.*

Actually, maybe Occam's razor did apply.

The sound on the bridge shifted. Sulu felt rather than heard the characteristic vibration of the impulse engines as they engaged, and then the familiar thrum permeated the air. "Ensign Syndergaard?" the captain said, even as she studied the main viewscreen.

"It's not me, sir," said the helm officer, excitement raising the level of his voice. He tapped at several control surfaces on his console. "It's the navigational routine."

On the viewer, the stars shined steadily. In the center of the screen a grouping of seven stars looked to Sulu like a backward question mark. She smiled, though she thought not so much for herself as for everybody else aboard.

Well, maybe for everybody but John and Amina, she thought, understanding that the husband and wife would have been happy wherever they'd ended up, as long as they'd ended up there together.

A boatswain's whistle sounded. *"Captain Sulu to the bridge,"* came her father's voice. Demora reached to activate the intercom on the arm of the command chair when she heard a second signal.

"Admiral Harriman to the bridge."

"Captain," Kanchumurthi said, "we're being contacted from all over the ship. Commander Buonarroti in engineering, Doctor Morell in sickbay, Lieutenant Ved in the transporter room."

Sulu stood up, a smile on her face. She appreciated everybody's excitement. "Sort them out, Ramesh," she said. "Tell everybody I'll be with them shortly."

"Captain, I can confirm from the observable stars that we have returned to our universe," Aldani said at navigation.

"Thank you, Gaia," Sulu said. "Lay in a course—"

"Captain," said Fenn, "something's wrong." Sulu turned toward the science officer, but she felt no panic, no disruption in the calm that had come upon her. "The locations of some stars aren't right."

"Why is that, Borona?" Sulu asked. "Have we not returned to our universe?"

"No, it's not that," Fenn said, obviously trying to make sense of her readings. "The collection of stars is right, the luminosities and spectral types are right, but—" Fenn's head suddenly snapped up from her panel. "It's not the right time."

"You mean it's not eleven months since we arrived at Rejarris Two?" Sulu asked. She knew that the program written to analyze the star patterns as Odyssey moved them from universe to universe contained a time component in it. She and John had determined seventeen years ago to do that when they'd been in the shuttlecraft, and she'd made sure of it that time, too.

"No, sir," Fenn said. "It's three weeks *before* we arrived at Rejarris Two."

Sulu laughed. "Well, then," she said, "I guess we haven't missed anything." She heard some of the bridge crew chuckle, but more out of relief than amusement, she thought. "Gaia, set a course for Starbase Twenty-Three, but keep us out of any shipping lanes or populated regions. I don't want to come into contact with any other ships. Torsten, I want low warp speed. Get us back to the Federation in a month, after Admiral Harriman and Captain Sasine have left Helaspont Station for Rejarris Two. We've done enough traveling from one universe to another. The last thing we need to do is alter the timeline."

As both Aldani and Syndergaard acknowledged their orders, Tenger spoke up. "Captain, what should we tell everybody contacting the bridge?"

Sulu turned to face her friend. "Tell them we're home."

Acknowledgments

One Constant Star would not exist without *two* of the stars in my writer's life: Margaret Clark and Ed Schlesinger. In the normal course of events, my editors provide me with a tremendous resource. Their creativity and professionalism always help me find my way from the beginning of the process—the dreaded outline stage—through the first draft, subsequent drafts, copy edits, first-, second-, and final-pass pages, and at last into print. For much of what's right with this novel, I have them to thank. With this particular project, both Margaret and Ed also demonstrated a personal level of understanding and compassion during a difficult time, and for that I am genuinely grateful to them.

That difficult time, I'm sorry to say, ended with the loss of a dear woman, Lillian Ragan. A kind and caring aunt, "Diamond Lil" welcomed me into her family with love and kindness. She lived a fascinating and unique life, and I have never met anybody quite like her. I hope that I can remember and savor the uncounted stories she related to me through the years. I miss her.

During the days, weeks, and months leading to and in the aftermath of Lillian's death, a number of people stepped forward to help and support her and others in the family. In particular, I want to single out Maria (Marianne) Olejnikova, a compassionate and loving woman who makes life easier for everybody around her. When the going got particularly tough, Marianne showed incredible strength and character, as did Colleen Ragan, Charlene Costello, and Audrey Nemes. To the sisters and to the significant others that stood with them, John Costello and Bob Nemes, I offer my heartfelt thanks. Likewise, I am grateful to Jesse Ragan and his wife, Krystle, who both gave so willingly of themselves over a long period.

I want to thank my friends Amy Sisson and Dr. Paul A. Abell, Ph.D., as well. When a cadre of us writers decided to get together for a long weekend somewhere, Amy, a fellow scribe, had the brilliant idea of congregating in Houston, where her husband, Paul, works as the Lead Scientist for Planetary Small Bodies at the National Aeronautic and Space Administration's Lyndon B. Johnson Space Center. Amy and Paul thought our group would enjoy touring the NASA site, but once they involved its Public Affairs Office in our visit, the experience grew into a truly once-in-a-lifetime event. Simply visiting JSC for the first time, even on a public tour, would have been fulfilling, but the outing that the PAO's Lynnette Madison and Linda Matthews-Schmidt put together exceeded anything for which I could have

hoped. Although I'm a writer, it is impossible for me to find appropriate words to describe our *ten*-plus hours at the Johnson Space Center. I count the d... as one of the highlights of my life. Many than... Lynnette and Linda, and to all the folks in t... who helped make the day happen, inclu... Anderson, Jeannie Aquino, Lisa C... Harris, Todd Hellner, Danial Ho... Knotts, Beth LeBlanc, Tammi... Kevin Moore, Robin Hart Pr... and Laura Rochon.

I am also very grat... neers, and technician... daily to turn the d... space into a realit... gave so much... the Space Ce... G. Love, p... Ret.; De... gratio... "Ca... S...

le... sta... the... case, quick... expert... I wo... in my life, included t... before, and... related to me... Ragan, Anita... Walenista mak... all for your end... Finally, I tha... George. Karen sh... me with her hum... and compassion, a... lect and her many ta... nights by her presenc... I love you, Karen, for...

gra... and K... Sample ... of Astromat...

Dr. Eileen Stansbery, Ph.D.; and Antarctic Meteorite Curator Kevin Righter. You are all inspirations.

It almost always seems to pass that, during the course of writing a *Star Trek* novel, I find myself having a very specific question that does not end itself to a simple research effort. In those instances, I oftentimes call upon the great minds of *Trek* universe to help me out. In this particular writers Greg Cox and Michael Jan Friedman y and happily gave me the benefit of their se. Thanks, Greg and Mike.

uld also like to thank the people closest to me people who are always there for me. I have em in my acknowledgments many times it's always for good reason. Whether by blood or not, Walter Ragan, Colleen Smith, Jennifer George, and Patricia e up my immediate family. Thank you uring love and support.

nk my constant star, Karen Ragan- nes on me with her love, brightens r, warms me with her kindness nd dazzles me with her intel- lents. She defines my days and e making life all that it can be. ow and ever.

About the Author

DAVID R. GEORGE III previously visited *Star Trek*'s *Lost Era* in the novel *Serpents Among the Ruins*, featuring Captain John Harriman and Commander Demora Sulu, and in the novella *Iron and Sacrifice*, which appeared in the *Tales From the Captain's Tale* anthology, and which featured Sulu after she had been promoted to *Enterprise* captain. *One Constant Star* marks David's fourteenth foray into *Trek* novels, a writing journey that ultimately began when he co-wrote the television story for a first-season *Voyager* episode, "Prime Factors."

David's work has appeared on both the *New York Times* and *USA Today* bestseller lists. *Sci-Fi Universe* nominated his *Voyager* episode in the category "Best Writing in a Genre Television Show or Telefilm." The International Association of Media Tie-in Writers nominated his *Trek* novel *Provenance of Shadows* for a Scribe Award.

You can contact David at facebook.com/DRGIII, and you can follow him on Twitter @DavidRGeorgeIII.